Praise for Irene Hannon

Trapped

"The queen of inspirational romantic suspense hits a home run with this compelling follow-up to *Vanished*."

—*Library Journal*

"The icy cold snowstorm won't be the only thing giving readers the shivers as RITA- and Carol Award–winning Hannon once again demonstrates her mastery at crafting spine-tingling romantic thrillers that, without graphic violence and language, utterly enthrall readers."

—*Booklist*

"Irene Hannon has written a tale of suspense that has all of the elements needed to become a bestseller. It comes as no surprise that she's a two-time RITA Award winner. She knows how to develop characters and stories that readers love to embrace. With just the right amount of suspense, danger, and deception, *Trapped* is engaging and satisfying. The prose is crisp and to the point, creating the scene effortlessly."

—*New York Journal of Books*

"You may have a case of white-knuckle-book-fever before the end, but the romance region of your heart won't be able to keep itself from rooting for Dev and Laura to save the day . . . and for them to finally be able to land in each other's arms."

—*USA Today's Happily Ever After* blog

Vanished

"Hannon's intricately developed characters struggle with complex moral issues, bringing into question whether the ends ever do justify the means. An engaging, satisfying tale that will no doubt leave readers anxiously anticipating the next installment."

—*Publishers Weekly*

"With the intense mixture of romance, mystery, darkness, and suspense, the author has done a great job introducing some truly interesting characters, including a 'bad guy' who will completely surprise readers."

—Suspense Magazine

"A wonderful mix of suspense and romance."

—RT Book Reviews

"A riveting storyline . . . one of those addictive books that once started, compels you to shut out the world till you reach the very last page."

—New York Journal of Books

"An excellent suggestion for readers who enjoy Mary Higgins Clark's subtly chilling brand of suspense."

—Booklist

DECEIVED

Books by Irene Hannon

DECEIVED

A NOVEL

IRENE HANNON

Revell

a division of Baker Publishing Group
Grand Rapids, Michigan

© 2014 by Irene Hannon

Published by Revell
a division of Baker Publishing Group
P.O. Box 6287, Grand Rapids, MI 49516-6287
www.revellbooks.com

Printed in the United States of America

Library of Congress Cataloging-in-Publication Data
Hannon, Irene.
    Deceived : a novel / Irene Hannon.
        pages cm. — (Private Justice ; #3)
    ISBN 978-0-8007-2125-1 (pbk.)
    1. Women journalists—Fiction. 2. Private investigators—Fiction. 3. Missing persons—Investigation—Fiction. 4. Mystery fiction. I. Title.
PS3558.A4793D45 2014
813'.54—dc23   2014014145

This book is a work of fiction. Names, characters, places, and incidents are the product of the author's imagination or are used fictitiously.

14 15 16 17 18 19 20   7 6 5 4 3 2 1

To Tom,
as we celebrate twenty-five years of marriage.
The anniversary may be silver,
but the memories are golden.

Thank you for the gift of your love . . .
and for being my hero.

Prologue

A stranger was coming up her driveway.

Decorative tube of icing poised over the cake, Kate Marshall froze as the crunch of gravel outside the open windows at the front of the house stopped by the porch.

Definitely not John. He would have headed straight to the detached garage in back, as usual. Besides, he and Kevin never cut their Wednesday fishing outings short. And none of their friends would make a social call at this hour of the morning.

A car door slammed, and she finished the last swirl of red icing on the y in *birthday*, frowning as a tingle of apprehension skittered through her. How silly was that? This was Hilton, New York, not New York City. A peaceful village of six thousand people. Just because she was a big-city girl who'd never quite acclimated to the solitude of their five-acre spread on the outskirts of town didn't mean it was unsafe.

Still, as the doorbell rang, she grabbed her cell out of her purse and slipped it in the pocket of her jeans—just in case.

But as she entered the living room and caught a glimpse of the dark-colored cruiser through the front window, her step faltered.

There would be no need for a 911 call.

The police were already here.

A sudden swirl of memories kaleidoscoped through her mind, catapulting her back sixteen years, to her eighteenth summer. A porch swing . . . a tall glass of tangy lemonade . . . a heart-melting romance novel. All the makings of a perfect June day.

Until a police car pulled up and a grim-faced officer emerged.

Two minutes later, as the man informed her and her mother that a faulty construction elevator at a job site had plunged her architect father three stories to his death, the perfect day had ended.

But history didn't repeat itself.

God wouldn't do that to her.

Would he?

Reining in her burgeoning panic, she breathed in, then out, and forced her feet to carry her across the living room.

Through the art-glass sidelight next to the front door, she had a distorted view of the uniformed man on the other side. He appeared to be young . . . and his expression was serious.

Her heart lurched.

Fingers fumbling the lock, she opened the door. "May I help you?" Her rote words seemed to come from a distance, leaving a hollow echo in her ears.

"Mrs. Marshall?"

"Yes."

The man clasped his hands behind his back and planted his feet shoulder-width apart, in military at-ease position.

But he didn't look at ease.

His posture was rigid, his features taut.

"I'm Trooper Peyton, New York State Police. Did your husband go fishing in Braddock Bay this morning?"

"Yes."

His Adam's apple bobbed. "I'm afraid there's been an accident."

No!

The denial screamed through her mind as she clutched the edge of the door, her slippery fingers leaving a smear of icing on the shiny white woodwork.

It looked like blood.

She tore her gaze away from the crimson smudge, forced her brain to process the man's statement . . . and came to the only possible conclusion.

John was hurt.

Badly.

Otherwise, he would have called her himself.

Cold fingers squeezed her heart as she choked out the question she didn't want to ask. "My son . . . is he . . . is Kevin hurt too?"

The uniformed man frowned. "Your son?"

She furrowed her own brow. "Yes. My husband and son were together. Kevin's f-four." Her voice hitched on the last word.

The officer reached for his radio. "Let me call that in. The last I heard, they were only looking for a man."

Looking for?

The room began to spin, and she grabbed the door frame with her free hand. Darkness licked at her soul, snuffing out the light like storm clouds advancing on the sun. "What do you mean, looking for?"

His features softened as his radio crackled to life. "I'm sorry, ma'am. All we have so far is an overturned boat and an adult life jacket."

Adult life jacket.

As the words reverberated in her mind, she shook her head, trying to clear the muddle from her brain.

No.

That couldn't be right.

"Wait." She plucked at the man's sleeve. "You shouldn't have found a loose life jacket. My husband and son always wore their vests."

He held up a finger and angled away to speak into the radio, conveying the news about Kevin in a crisp, official tone before he turned back to her.

"If you could give me a description of what your husband and son were wearing, ma'am, it would be very helpful to the search and rescue team."

He wasn't listening to her.

She stepped closer. In-your-face close. "Did you hear what I said? They always wore their life jackets. Always! John promised me they would, and he never broke his promises. There shouldn't be a loose life jacket. And where are they?" Her pitch rose as hysteria nipped at the edges of her voice.

"I don't know, ma'am, but we're doing everything we can to find them." The officer's reassuring tone did nothing to soothe her. "May I come in while I ask you a few more questions?"

She stared at him as an insulating numbness began to shroud her, weighing down her arms and legs, dulling her senses. "You expect me to just sit here while my husband and son are missing?"

"Professionals are handling the search, Mrs. Marshall. The most useful thing you can do is give us a description and answer some questions."

It wasn't enough.

But how else could she contribute? With her fear of the water, she'd hinder more than help if she showed up at the bay.

Closing her eyes, she sucked in a breath—and sent a silent, desperate plea to the Almighty.

The officer took her arm. Wondering, perhaps, if she was going to cave?

Not yet.

But soon.

Because even as he guided her toward the couch, even as she prepared to answer his questions, she knew with soul-searing certainty that nothing she told him was going to change the outcome on this day intended to celebrate the beginning of her husband's thirty-sixth year.

And she also knew there would be no more happy birthdays in this house.

THREE YEARS LATER

Kate sniffed the enticing aromas wafting her way from the food court, transferred her shopping bag from one hand to the other, and checked her watch. Nope. She was already behind schedule, and being late for her one-thirty client wasn't an option. No lunch today.

So what else was new?

On the plus side, maybe she could swing by Starbucks after dinner and apply those saved calories to the ultimate summer indulgence—a double chocolaty chip frappuccino . . . heavy on the whip.

A wry grin tugged at her lips as she lengthened her stride. Like that was going to happen. If this day followed her typical pattern, she'd be so exhausted by the time she got home she'd opt for a quick omelet or nuke a frozen dinner, then fall into bed—and the oblivion of sleep. But better catatonic slumber than nights spent watching the LED display on her bedside clock mark the slow-motion passing of middle-of-the-night minutes.

Cutting a path straight toward the escalator that led down to the first level of the mall, she averted her head as she passed the Mrs. Fields shop. Tempting, but not healthy.

When her stomach rumbled, however, her course somehow drifted to the right.

Maybe one cookie.

Two minutes later, cookie in hand, she took a large bite and closed her eyes as the warm chocolate chips melted on her tongue.

Nirvana.

And far tastier than the turkey sandwich in the fridge at work—the lunch she would have been eating if she hadn't volunteered last night to exchange her neighbor's defective heating pad during her lunch hour. But with the older woman's arthritis acting up . . . with the sweltering heat of a St. Louis July taking a toll on seniors who ventured out . . . with West County Center just ten minutes away from her office . . . how could she ignore the prodding of her conscience to do a good deed?

Besides, she might not be as old as her neighbor, but she knew what it was like to be hurting . . . and alone . . . and in desperate need of a respite from pain.

The chocolate lost some of its sweetness, but she finished the last bite of cookie anyway and picked up her pace toward the escalator. She was *not* going to let melancholy thoughts ruin this moment of pleasure. She'd done that far too often over the past few years—as her mother never hesitated to remind her during her occasional calls from the West Coast. Take what life hands you and get on with it, that was Angela Stewart's motto. And that philosophy had served her well as she'd forged her executive career. Unlike her daughter, she hadn't needed pills to get through her first year of widowhood.

Then again, she hadn't lost a child too.

Kate shoved the chocolate-smeared paper napkin in a trash can and straightened her shoulders. So she wasn't made of the same tough cloth as her mother. So she had a softer heart. But she'd survived the hard times and gotten her act together eventually, hadn't she? And that soft heart had turned out to be an asset in her counseling work.

A horde of Friday lunchtime shoppers jostled her as she approached the escalator, and she tightened her grip on the shopping bag. Good heavens, you'd think it was the day-after-Christmas sale.

Leading with her shoulder, she inserted herself in the middle of the surging throng, then maneuvered through the clusters of chattering women to claim a riser and begin her descent.

To think some people found shopping fun.

Her errand had gone smoothly, though. Assuming she got out of the parking garage without delay, she should be back at the office in time to grab a bottle of water, touch up her lipstick, and run a comb through her hair before—

". . . a poppysicle?"

As the eager, childish voice carried over the background hum of mall noise, the air whooshed out of her lungs, and she grabbed the railing.

Poppysicle?!

The only child she'd ever heard use that term was Kevin.

And that voice . . . it sounded like his.

How could that be?

Whipping toward the adjacent ascending escalator, she scanned the crowd. Several risers above her, moving farther away by the second, was a youngster about six or seven with hair the hue of ripening wheat.

The same color as hers.

The same color as her son's.

"Kevin?" Her incredulous whisper was lost in the cavernous echo of the mall.

She tried again, raising her voice. "Kevin!"

The boy angled her way. She caught a profile. Then a full

face. As they made eye contact, as he frowned and cocked his head, her heart stalled.

He looked just how she would have expected Kevin to look when he was seven.

As they stared at each other, the noise in the mall receded. Movement slowed. Everything faded from her peripheral vision. Only the little boy's face registered.

Dear God, is that . . . ?

No. Impossible.

Wasn't it?

All at once, a protective arm pulled the boy close, and the child turned away.

Kate jerked her gaze up. The T-shirted man attached to the arm averted his face, tugged the brim of his baseball cap down, and dipped his head as he spoke to the child.

Three seconds later, they stepped off the escalator and melted into the crowd.

No!

Heart pounding, Kate spun around and started to push back up the escalator, through the crowd stacked behind her, trying to keep the baseball cap in sight.

"Hey, what's going on?" The twentysomething behind her tucked her purse closer to her body.

"I need to get back to the top. Please. I have to . . . to catch someone." She craned her neck, but the duo had vanished.

"Just take the escalator back up." The woman motioned toward the first level below. "You're almost at the bottom."

Kate looked over her shoulder. Yes. That would be faster.

She swung around, more or less shoved the two middle-aged women in front of her off once they reached the bottom, and tuned out their muttered complaints as she bolted for the up escalator.

Once on board, she wove her way up, squeezing between

mall patrons, ignoring their dirty looks as she scrutinized the crowd milling about on the second floor, her gaze darting left, right, then back again.

Nothing.

At the top, she did a rapid 360 sweep.

Still nothing.

But that little boy was here somewhere. He and his companion couldn't have wandered far in the short time it had taken her to return to the second level.

Yet her frantic search of likely nearby places—food court, game store, kids clothing shop—yielded nothing. She sent the two-level JCPenney anchor store a dismayed glance. If they'd gone in there, it was a lost cause. The place was too large and spread out.

Besides . . . what was the point?

Legs suddenly unsteady, Kate stepped out of the flow of traffic and leaned a shoulder against the wall, forcing herself to take several slow, deep breaths. To think with her mind instead of her heart.

The little boy on the escalator couldn't have been her son. Just because the authorities had never located his body didn't mean he'd survived the accident. If he had, someone would have found him three years ago and called the police. Today was simply a regression. She was doing what she'd done in the early days after the tragedy, seeing Kevin in every blond little boy who bore the slightest resemblance to him. Letting herself fall back into the role of a wife and mother unwilling to accept the harsh reality of loss, whose inconsolable grief had led her to a desperate coping strategy that had taken months to shake.

No way was she going down that road again.

Ignoring the tremble in her fingers, Kate wiped her damp palms down her slacks. If she left this minute, she could still make it back to the office in time for her one-thirty appointment.

Never once, in her two years at the center, had she been late for a client meeting. Why break that record?

She started toward the escalator, deliberately placing one foot in front of the other, trying to ignore the picture of the little boy strobing across her mind.

Halfway there, her steps slowed.

Stopped.

No matter how hard she tried to wipe it from her brain, the image wouldn't go away. Nor could she tune out the echo of that poppysicle reference. And what about the momentary glint of what might have been recognition in his eyes when he'd spotted her?

Was it all just coincidence?

Squeezing her eyelids shut, she tightened her grip on the handle of the shopping bag.

Dear God, am I crazy? Is this just a manifestation of grief and loneliness and desperate hope? Please . . . tell me what to do. Should I walk away and forget this ever happened, or should I—

"Excuse me, ma'am . . . are you all right?"

She opened her eyes to find an older man with a concerned expression appraising her.

Somehow she managed a stiff smile. "I'm fine. Thank you."

"You sure? I'd be happy to get you a glass of water or help you over to a chair in the food court. You're kind of white—almost like you've seen a ghost."

Ghost.

Her heart skipped a beat, and she swallowed. "I-I don't believe in ghosts."

"Neither do I." He shoved his hands in the pockets of his baggy slacks and rocked forward on his toes. "Bunch of nonsense, if you ask me." A rumble of thunder shook the building, and he glanced up at the skylights. "Sounds like we might be in for some rain."

She tipped her head back. Dark clouds were scuttling across what had been a solid expanse of blue fifteen minutes ago. How could the weather change so quickly? "It was supposed to be sunny and dry today."

"That's God for you. He likes to throw us a few curves now and then, turn things upside down. At least he's giving us a sign of what's coming today, and I, for one, intend to heed it." He dug out his keys and jingled them. "You take care, now. Don't get caught in this storm those Doppler folks failed to predict." With a lift of his hand, he headed for the exit.

Kate watched him until he disappeared in the crowd, his warning echoing in her ears. Unfortunately, it had come too late. She was already caught in a storm, one far more unsettled than the St. Louis weather. But their brief conversation had served a purpose. All that talk about ghosts and signs and God turning things upside down had given her the guidance she'd sought.

She wasn't leaving without trying to locate that man and child.

Even if people thought she was nuts.

Taking a deep breath, she set her shopping bag on the floor, rummaged through her shoulder purse, and extracted her cell. Someone else would have to cover her one-thirty meeting. Because unless she saw that boy up close, talked to him, confirmed he wasn't Kevin, she'd be spending a lot of sleepless nights wondering if maybe, just maybe, this was one of those times God had thrown her a curve that could have changed her life.

"How can it be eighty-two degrees at eight o'clock in the morning?" James Devlin pushed through the back door of Phoenix Inc., then made a sharp left from the hall into the small kitchenette at the rear of the office suite. After dumping his jacket on the dinette table against the wall, he grabbed a paper towel from the dispenser and swiped at the beads of sweat on his forehead. "And how can you drink hot coffee in this weather?"

Connor Sullivan topped off his U2 mug and lifted it in salute. "Good morning to you too. And it's never too hot for coffee—unless you grew up in Minnesota and never learned to take the heat."

"There's heat, and then there's heat." Dev headed for the refrigerator. "You'd think after five and a half years here I'd be used to dealing with the atmospheric kind." He extracted a Coke and released the tab.

"Atmospheric. That's a big word for you on a Monday morning."

As a female voice joined the conversation, Connor turned toward the hall door and leaned back against the counter. A verbal sparring match between his partner and their office manager/receptionist would be an entertaining way to kick off the week.

"Don't start, Nikki." Dev took a swig of soda and strafed her a warning look.

"My, my. Did we get up on the wrong side of the bed this morning? Or maybe Laura came to her senses and gave back that ring you persuaded her to take on the Fourth of July."

"As a matter of fact, we spent yesterday planning our wedding."

"Yeah?" Nikki propped a shoulder against the door and crossed her arms. "So what were you complaining about, then?"

"The heat."

She tipped her head. "It's July in St. Louis. Get over it."

Dev flexed his soda can while he gave her a slow once-over, the aluminum pinging like the bell for round two. "I see you dressed for the weather. New color in the hair too."

Hiding the quirk of his lips behind the rim of his mug, Connor gave Nikki a more discreet perusal. Dangling gold ice cream cones were a nice seasonal touch in her triple-pierced ears, and her Caribbean-turquoise tank top matched the swath of neon color in her spiky platinum-blonde hair. The shimmering mother-of-pearl belt buckle on her tropical-print miniskirt was a little over the top—but it went with the shell necklace she'd brought back from her Hawaiian honeymoon a year or so ago. At least she'd worn heeled hemp sandals instead of flip-flops.

Still, Dev would have a field day with this outfit . . . and Nikki would match him barb for barb.

Connor settled in for the show and sipped his coffee.

"The color is called St. Bart's Blue. And if you think cool and act cool, you'll be cool." Nikki smoothed a hand down her abbreviated skirt.

"Thinking cool doesn't change the outside temperature. Neither does wearing beach attire to the office."

Nikki raised an eyebrow. "You have a problem with my clothes?"

"Problem?" Dev took another swig of soda. "Nah. They're very . . . colorful. And tropical. But you forgot the hat with fruit on top."

Connor covered his snicker with a cough.

Ignoring him, Nikki patted her hair. "You know, that's a thought. After all, Carmen Miranda was once the highest-paid female entertainer in Hollywood. Not a bad role model." She let a beat of dramatic silence pass, then delivered her zinger. "And I know just where to get the lemon for the hat."

Connor almost choked on his coffee.

A faint flush that had nothing to do with the outside temperature suffused Dev's face as he conceded the bout. "How come you never pick on Connor or Cal?"

"It's more fun to make your face match your hair." Nikki folded her arms and smirked at him.

"Ha-ha." Dev drained his soda and tossed the can in the

recycle bin. "Well, some of us may have time to stand around all day and gab, but I have work to do."

As he disappeared through the door, Connor refilled his mug. "It sure would be boring around here without you two."

"Hardly, considering some of the dicey cases you guys handle. But I'm happy to do my part to liven things up on the duller days—and Dev's easy to rile."

Only by her—and that was all show. If Dev didn't like their sassy receptionist, he wouldn't have offered to take in her teenage brother while she went off on a two-week honeymoon.

But Connor kept those thoughts to himself as he pushed off from the counter. "You know, if you're not careful, he might stop bringing you those lattes you like."

"Not if he wants me to tackle those mountains of files in his office, he won't."

"Good point. Did you want some coffee?" Connor inclined his head toward the pot.

As he expected, she wrinkled her nose. "I'm not as desperate for caffeine as you guys always are. I've got some herbal tea at my desk—and a new client waiting. Yours, by the way."

"Why don't you give this one to Dev or Cal? I'm beat after that weekend executive security gig."

"Sorry. No can do. Cal's meeting off-site with our favorite defense attorney to talk about some witnesses he wants tracked down, and Dev's going to be starting surveillance for a workman's comp case this morning—as soon as he finishes the two employee background checks buried somewhere in that mess on his desk."

So much for his hope of a quiet Monday morning. "Fine. What's the deal?"

"I don't know. She's not talking—to me. But she seems nervous." Nikki shook out Dev's jacket, picked off a piece of lint, and hung it on a hook by the door.

"How long has she been here?"

"She was waiting at the door when I went out front five minutes ago."

"Anxious."

"That would be a safe conclusion."

"Tell her I'll be out in a couple of minutes. I want to straighten up my desk first."

"It won't take you that long. There's not much to clean in your office . . . unlike our red-haired friend's work space."

"Maybe Laura will whip him into shape now that they're engaged."

Nikki snorted. "Fat chance. He's a lost cause, if you ask me. That pile of files in the corner of his office is higher than ever."

"More lattes for you."

With a nod, she started for the door. "I like the way you think."

Mug in hand, Connor followed her out of the kitchenette and crossed the hall to his office. A quick survey confirmed Nikki's assessment; there wasn't much to clean up. Pitch last Friday's *Wall Street Journal* and the empty bag of pistachios from that child custody case stakeout last week, put away the files on the skip trace and corporate fraud cases he'd planned to review this morning, slip on the jacket he kept handy for new-client meetings—he'd be set. Sixty seconds, tops.

And if fate was kind, perhaps this case would be straightforward, simple, and easy to solve so he could go home early and catch up on the shut-eye his two partners never thought he needed—no matter how many consecutive hours he worked.

||||||| **2** |||||||

This was a mistake.

Kate fidgeted in the upholstered seat and glanced around the Phoenix Inc. lobby. The place might be classy, with its nubby Berber carpet, glass-topped coffee table, comfortable chairs, and artsy still-life photos on the walls. The location, in the heart of one of St. Louis's nicer suburbs, might give the firm an added luster of legitimacy. The rectangular wooden plaque on the wall, emblazoned with the brass-lettered words *Justice First*—the same motto featured on the Phoenix website—might be admirable.

But no matter how professional these PIs were, she still had a sinking feeling they were going to discount her claim, just as mall security and the local police had after they'd listened to her story and done some research into the events of three years ago.

Why set herself up for another round of humiliation?

Because you've spent three sleepless nights revisiting your brief encounter with the little boy . . . over and over and over again. Because each replay grew more vivid . . . and more urgent. Because now there's a tiny flicker of hope burning in your heart.

All true. But surely she was fooling herself. Blowing the incident out of all proportion. Letting herself get carried away in search of a miracle that had no more chance of being granted now than it had been three years ago.

Wasn't she?

Kate rubbed her right temple, where a headache was beginning to throb. At this point, she had no idea. Somewhere along the way, she'd lost perspective on the whole thing—if she'd ever had it to begin with. Maybe she needed to give herself another twenty-four hours to reason this through before she made a fool of herself yet again. More time and space might restore her usual clear thinking. And if the urge to seek help was as strong a day or two down the road, she could always return.

Yes. Good plan.

Decision made, she rose—just as the beach-party-babe receptionist reentered the room through the door behind her desk, the unicorn tattoo on her forearm front and center as she pushed through. If the rest of this place hadn't been so tasteful, and if the police detective, undercover ATF, and Secret Service credentials of the PIs on the website hadn't been so impressive, she'd never have stepped foot inside when the twentysomething woman released the security locks on the front door promptly at eight o'clock.

"Did you need to use the ladies' room?" The platinum blonde indicated the door behind her. "Or I'll be happy to get you a beverage, if you've changed your mind."

"No. I . . . uh . . . think I'll just come back later." Kate made a pretense of consulting her watch as she edged toward the front door. "I have a meeting this morning and I still . . . I have a few things I need to pull together for it. This stop might delay me too much."

"Of course. Why don't I take your name and a phone number so I can pass it on to Connor Sullivan, the PI who was planning to speak with you?" The receptionist moved behind her desk and rummaged through a drawer.

As the woman made a project out of retrieving a pen and piece of paper, Kate bit her lip. She'd prefer to slip away anonymously, but what could it hurt to provide some basic contact information? All she had to do if the PI followed up was say she'd changed her mind.

After spending an inordinate amount of time shuffling through the drawer, the receptionist withdrew a pen, sat, and aimed an expectant look across her desk.

"The name's Kate Marshall." She edged closer to the exit. "My cell number is—"

The door to the back offices opened again. This time a raven-haired man in a tie and subtly patterned sport jacket stepped through, his assertive, take-charge air softened by a killer dimple.

"Sorry to keep you waiting." His gaze dropped to the keys she'd dug out of her purse, and he exchanged a glance with the receptionist.

"Ms. Marshall was concerned that meeting with you would make her late for a prior commitment. I was just taking her contact information." The woman inclined her head to the pad of paper in front of her.

He scanned it, then walked across the waiting area, hand extended. "Connor Sullivan. I don't want to delay you, but if you have even a few minutes to spare, a quick conversation now might save you a trip back later."

Cornered.

She eyed his lean, powerful-looking fingers as he paused in front of her. Short of being rude, she couldn't ignore his polite, professional overture.

So much for her fast escape.

Stifling a sigh, she transferred her keys to her left hand and placed her fingers in his. They were instantly swallowed in a warm, firm grip that somehow, with one squeeze, conveyed strength, competence, and integrity.

How had he done that?

She looked up—and up again—into his face. The Phoenix website hadn't identified which PI held which credential, but based on this guy's polished, clean-cut appearance—not to mention his authoritative bearing—she'd be willing to bet he was Secret Service.

As for her plan to bolt . . . she wavered as his eyes sucked her in. Dark as obsidian, they searched, discerned, and reassured, all in the space of a few heartbeats, prompting her to draw three rapid conclusions.

This was a man who would listen, evaluate, and come to sound conclusions.

This was a man who would treat her story with respect.

This was a man she could trust.

The silence lengthened, until the receptionist hidden from her view behind the PI's broad shoulders cleared her throat.

A fleeting frown marred the man's brow, then he released her hand, took a step back, and waited.

The ball was in her court.

Without overanalyzing her change of heart, she took a deep breath and tightened her fingers around the handle of her briefcase. "I can spare a few minutes."

Those dark eyes warmed like the volcanic origins of the black glass whose color they mirrored. "Good. Let me show you back."

Moving aside, he gestured for her to precede him.

As she prepared to pass the receptionist's desk, the woman looked up from her computer screen, toward the man behind her. A spark of . . . amusement? . . . glinted in her eyes.

Odd.

"Give me a sec to release the security lock." She angled into her desk, and a moment later Kate heard a distinctive click.

Connor stepped to her side, leaned around her, and reached for the handle, his solid chest mere inches away. He was close enough for her to get a whiff of his understated aftershave—which caused an uptick in her pulse.

Also odd.

"Second office on the left."

A tiny whisper of warmth tickled her cheek as he pulled the door back. Somehow it found its way to her heart.

What in the world was going on?

And why did she suddenly have the same off-balance feeling she'd experienced on Friday at the mall, when she'd spotted that little boy and the world seemed to shift beneath her feet?

No time now to figure it out, though. She had a story to tell, and despite her sense that the man following her down the short hall would respect her tale, it was possible she'd read him wrong. That he'd write her off as a wacko and escort her out before she even warmed a chair.

"Have a seat." Connor gestured to a small round table off to one side in his neat-as-a-pin office. "Would you like something to drink? We have plenty of cold beverages if tea or coffee don't appeal to you on this scorcher."

She inspected the half-full mug on this desk. Apparently this man didn't shy away from the heat.

And she wasn't going to, either.

"Coffee would be fine. Black."

"My preference too. Hang tight. I'll be back in a minute."

Once he disappeared into the hall, she eased back in the chair and expelled an unsteady breath.

Relax, Kate. What's the worst that can happen? If he thinks you're crazy and shows you the door, so what? You'll never see the man again.

While that possible outcome bothered her more than seemed warranted, her respiration did even out.

Better.

Setting her briefcase on the floor beside her, she wiggled her fingers to get the blood flowing again as she did a sweep of his office. The mahogany furniture was nice—much more upscale than the mismatched stuff in her own work space—but standard issue. The framed family pictures on the credenza behind his desk yielded far more clues about the PI's personality.

In the first shot, two preteen boys were flanked by a pleasant-looking man and woman, a panoramic view of the Grand Canyon behind them. Based on the clothing, it had been taken decades ago.

The closer-up picture beside it was more recent, though still at least fifteen years old. A grinning high-school-age Connor stood beside a slightly older version of himself, their arms slung around each other's shoulders while the older boy balanced a basketball on his finger.

Kate scanned the rest of the office. There were no recent photos anywhere; just these two from the past.

Interesting.

No evidence of a wife or children, either. And he wasn't wearing a wedding ring.

Also interesting.

The U2 mug on Connor's desk tipped her off to his taste in music—and reinforced the Irish heritage implied by his name—but she was more curious about the small, three-sided wooden object on the far corner. Its oblong shape suggested it was a nameplate, but the side facing the door was blank.

With a quick glance toward the hall, she rose and crossed to the desk, leaning sideways to see the slanted face. A star-shaped logo with a blue and red emblem in the center occupied the left side, the words United States Secret Service circling the emblem. So her conclusion about his credentials had been sound. To the right were five words: Worthy of Trust and Confidence. The Secret Service motto, perhaps?

Returning to her seat, she inspected the citations on the walls.

Lifesaving Award. Congressional Commendation. Valor Award. Impressive—and reassuring. A man who was worthy of trust and confidence in one life, whose exemplary service had earned him these kinds of honors, wouldn't leave his core values behind when he moved on to a new profession.

Connor Sullivan was the real deal.

The throbbing in her temple dissipated as her last reservations vanished. She'd see this through, for better or worse. Connor Sullivan would give her as fair and impartial a hearing as she was likely to get anywhere. If he punched holes in her story, if he told her it was impossible to track down the little boy and to give it up, she'd take his advice.

Because if this man couldn't help her, she had a feeling no one could.

Connor filled one of the sage-green guest mugs, set the coffeepot back on the warmer, and smiled. A great cup of coffee, an entertaining joust between Dev and Nikki, and now a beautiful blonde in his office.

Not a bad way to start a Monday.

She's married, Sullivan. You saw the ring.

Yeah, yeah. He didn't need a reminder from his conscience to know she was off-limits, married or not, given Phoenix's unofficial no-fraternizing-with-clients rule. But there was no law against appreciating beauty—and Kate Marshall had been blessed with more than her share. Tall and lithe—at least five-seven or five-eight—she had the build and classic features of a ballerina. Throw in shoulder-length wavy blonde hair parted to the side, jade-colored eyes, and the barest hint of a Southern accent . . . female beauty didn't come any finer.

But she was also in some kind of trouble or she wouldn't be here.

Connor tapped a finger against the mug balanced in his hands. Curious that she'd come alone—unless her husband was the cause of her distress. Yet he concurred with the word Nikki had written on the pad of paper at her desk. Kate Marshall seemed spooked, not angry or fearful. The absent husband likely wasn't the problem.

He pushed off from the counter and strolled toward the door. If she was half as sharp as he suspected, she'd used her three minutes alone to case his office. Hopefully the awards had served their purpose and reassured her he was competent and legit. Without her trust, they'd get nowhere.

As he retraced his steps down the hall and rejoined her, she gestured toward the walls. "Impressive."

Yep. One smart cookie.

Better yet, mission accomplished.

He lifted one shoulder and deposited her coffee on the table. "Just doing my job. Let me grab a notebook and pen." As he moved behind his desk and she took a sip of the brew, he cast her an apologetic look. "I hope that's not too strong for you."

She cradled the mug in her hands, her features softening. "No. My husband liked it this way, and he eventually converted me."

Liked. Past tense. But not a divorce, based on her tender expression. A widow, perhaps?

Connor took one of the two remaining chairs, uncapped his pen, and sent her an encouraging smile. "All right, Ms. Marshall. How can I help you?"

As she tucked her hair behind her ear, his gaze flicked to her hand. The tremble in her fingers didn't surprise him, given her obvious tension—but his sudden urge to give them a reassuring squeeze did.

Instead, he leaned back to offer her—and himself—a little breathing space.

"I had a very weird experience last Friday. It was . . ." She blew out a breath and shook her head. "There's no way to make this sound reasonable. You're going to think I'm crazy—just like mall security and the police did. This is probably a waste of time for both of us."

He processed that new information—mall security, police—as he studied her. So she'd already sought help and been dismissed, her story discounted. But she wasn't crazy. Her eyes might be guarded and troubled, but they were clear, alert, and focused. There was no guile or haziness in their depths, nor were her pupils dilated. She was tense but not hyper. Conclusion: she had, indeed, undergone some kind of traumatic experience, and she needed help making sense of it.

For whatever reason, he wanted to be the one to provide that help.

Based on the tight grip she had on her mug, however, and her ever-so-slight physical withdrawal, she was quickly getting cold feet. Again.

Time for damage control.

He set his pen on top of the lined tablet and folded his hands, pinning her with a direct look. "First of all, I see no evidence of mental instability in you—and I've done a fair amount of rapid personality assessment in my Secret Service work. Lives depended on my ability to scan crowds for potential threats, and I learned to read people fast, knowing one wrong judgment could lead to tragedy. I've also been responsible for investigating plenty of strange stories. I intend to approach yours the same way I approached those—with an assumption that it represents reality until proven otherwise. And if I can help you ferret out the truth, I will. Fair enough?"

Her fingers loosened, and there was an almost imperceptible softening in the rigid line of her shoulders. "Fair enough."

He picked up his pen. "If you have the time, rather than start with the incident that triggered this visit, why don't you give me some background on why your mall experience was so upsetting? That will help me put it in context."

She didn't even consult her watch before responding, confirming that being late for a prior engagement had simply been an excuse to flee.

"I have a few minutes to spare." She took a sip of her coffee, then carefully set the mug in front of her and focused on the dark depths. "Three years ago, on my husband's thirty-sixth birthday, he and our four-year-old son, Kevin, went fishing. They never came home. According to the authorities, the boat capsized and my husband drowned. They never found my son's body, but the assumption was he drowned too, since they did find his life jacket."

She paused to rub her temple, giving him a moment to absorb her story and do another quick assessment. Though pain flickered in the depths of her eyes, her face was composed. Whatever toll that tragic loss had taken, she'd dealt with it and moved on. That took guts. And strength. And perhaps faith, if the simple charm bracelet with a single cross attached was more than a piece of jewelry.

So if she'd survived all that, what could have sent her into such a tailspin at the mall?

More intrigued than ever, he waited, giving her the time and space she needed to compose her thoughts.

At last she traced the rim of her coffee cup with a manicured but unpolished nail and continued. "As you might imagine, it took me months to get myself back on track after that. But I finally did. Two years ago, I moved to St. Louis, took a job I love, and have been doing my best to get on with my life." She slanted him a look. "The crazy part is coming."

He acknowledged her warning with a nod.

Her eyes never wavered from his as she delivered her next line. "Last Friday, I think I saw Kevin at West County Center."

As her words resonated in the quiet office, Connor stared at her.

Kate thought she'd seen her dead son.

Whoa.

Struggling to maintain his neutral expression, stalling for time, he rolled his pen between his fingers. He'd heard some wild claims in his day, from the woman dressed like the Statue of Liberty who'd shown up at the White House gate, claiming she had a message for the president from God to the guy who'd believed he was a reincarnated former president and entitled to Secret Service protection, but this one was right up near the top.

No wonder the authorities she'd approached had dismissed her story.

Yet crazy as her claim sounded, he still picked up nothing in her demeanor to suggest she was unbalanced. There had to be some logical reason she'd come to this bewildering conclusion.

As he continued to search for an appropriate response, she leaned toward him, posture taut. "Look, I know it sounds off-the-wall. I understand why the authorities were skeptical on Friday. In their place, I would have been too. All the official documents say Kevin is dead. But there's no proof of that."

True. At least she wasn't claiming she'd seen a child whose body she'd mourned over and buried.

"Where did this accident take place?" He positioned his pen over the tablet, still stalling.

"Braddock Bay, off Lake Ontario in upstate New York."

Hundreds of miles from St Louis.

The credibility meter bottomed out again.

"I'm losing you, aren't I?" Resignation dulled her voice.

"No." Not yet, anyway. "But your story is on the . . . bizarre side. The odds of your path crossing in St. Louis with anyone—let alone a son who supposedly drowned—from upstate New

York are very, very small. And not all drowning victims are found, especially in large bodies of water."

"I know that." Impatience nipped at her words, telling him she'd heard that lecture already. "But here's a key point no one, in my opinion, ever paid enough attention to. When I was ten, I almost drowned in a boating accident, which left me deathly afraid of water. I wasn't crazy about these fishing expeditions, so John—my husband—promised me they would never set foot in the boat without putting on their life vests. And he never, ever broke his promises. Yet he wasn't wearing his life vest when they found him."

Interesting—but not all that compelling.

"I'm sure he valued his promise, Ms. Marshall." Connor chose his words with care. "But isn't it possible he might have removed the jacket briefly for some practical reason? Maybe he spilled coffee or soda on it. Or a fishhook tangled in the back and he couldn't reach it without taking the jacket off. Or he got hot and decided to remove a sweater he was wearing underneath."

Frustration tightened her features. "I can't argue with your logic. But this isn't about logic. It's about the heart. You didn't know John. Neither did the police who investigated the incident. Only he understood how important that promise was to me. He knew the only way I'd have any peace of mind about the fishing trips he and Kevin started taking that summer was if I had absolute confidence they would both be wearing their jackets at all times. He would never, ever have violated my trust. Not even for two minutes, no matter how inconvenient it was to him. That's what love's all about."

As her words rang with conviction in the quiet room, Connor shifted in his chair. He couldn't dispute her claim about the life jackets, not after that little speech. Nor could he disagree with her comment about the importance of trust—and keeping promises—in a relationship.

He'd learned the truth of the latter the hard way.

Pushing those memories aside, he refocused on the woman beside him. "What did the authorities say when you told them your concerns about the life-jacket issue?"

"They listened—then blew me off. Assuming, as you did, that there was some logical reason he'd taken it off. But even if he did remove it for a few minutes, why would he take off Kevin's jacket too? It never made any sense to me, and I told that to everyone who was investigating the case."

"What was their response?"

"They didn't have one."

Connor tapped his pen on the tablet. "How long did it take them to find your husband?"

She swallowed. "Three days. They used some type of sonar equipment to locate him. He had a gash on his head, so they assumed he'd stood for some reason in the boat, lost his balance, and fallen. The theory was he'd hit his head on the outboard motor and lost consciousness, tipped the boat as he fell over-board, and drowned."

The more he heard, the more questions he had about the investigation. But they could get to those later . . . if this went forward.

"Let's switch gears for a minute and talk about Friday. Three years is a long time in a young child's life. Your son could have changed dramatically. Why did this boy catch your attention?"

"It wasn't his appearance, although once I spotted him, he did look exactly the way I'd expect Kevin to look now. I noticed him because he used the word *poppysicle*—a term I've never heard any other child use." She leaned close again, her posture taut. "And this is even weirder. I spotted him on the up escalator as I was going down. When I called his name, he turned toward me—and there seemed to be a spark of recognition in his eyes."

Intriguing—though not enough to pull her story back from the fringe of plausibility.

She frowned, her knuckles whitening around the cooling mug of coffee. "Look . . . I know this is a huge stretch. Do I think the odds are great that boy was my son? No. Do I think there's a very remote chance he could be . . . maybe. That's why I forced myself to come here today and risk more ridicule. I needed to get a professional, unbiased opinion. Yours—or one of your partners." She watched him, skin pulled tight across her high cheekbones, eyes wary as she waited for his evaluation.

And what *was* his professional opinion?

He didn't have a clue.

Time for evasive maneuvers.

"I'll tell you what. Let me think about this, run it by my colleagues. Assuming we all concur it merits investigation, what would you like us to do?"

She didn't hesitate. "Find the boy from the mall. If you can identify him, prove to me he's not my son, I'll be able to let this go. Otherwise, I have a feeling it will haunt me for the rest of my life."

"Give me until tomorrow. Do you have a cell number where I can reach you?" He jotted down the digits as she recited them, then stood and crossed to his desk. "I'll give you one of our client forms to take with you. I don't want to delay you now, but if you could fill it out and fax it back later today, I'd appreciate it." He withdrew one from his desk, retraced his steps, and handed it over, along with one of his business cards.

She gave the form a quick scan, tucked both items in her briefcase, and stood. "I'll fit it in. Along with a few prayers."

So her bracelet was more than jewelry, after all.

"Let me walk you out."

Cal's office was dark as they passed, but in his peripheral

39

vision he caught a glimpse of Dev on the other side of the hall. His partner leaned around the pile of files on the corner of his desk to follow their progress.

No surprise there. Kate was a head turner.

As they entered the lobby, Nikki looked up from her computer screen, raised an eyebrow, and glanced at her watch.

He ignored her.

At the front door, Kate turned to him and extended her hand. "Thank you for not writing my story off as just a strange co-incidence."

The temptation to cocoon her hand between his and warm her cold fingers was strong. Too strong. Again. How bizarre was that? He didn't typically have problems keeping his emotional distance from clients.

Then again, not many of his clients looked like Kate.

"I learned in the Secret Service to take every story seriously until it was proven otherwise. As for coincidences—I like that old saying about them being small miracles in which God chooses to remain anonymous."

Her sudden full-watt smile almost short-circuited his brain. "I'll hold that thought. Talk to you tomorrow."

She tugged her hand free from his and slipped through the door. As she started down the sidewalk, he leaned sideways to keep her in sight as long as possible.

When he at last turned back to the lobby, Nikki was watching him with a smug expression. The kind she usually reserved for Dev when her uncanny intuitive abilities were fully engaged. He'd always been amused by it. Now that it was directed at him, however, he found it far less humorous.

"What?" A faint edge of irritation crept into his voice.

"You tell me."

"No. You tell me. I've had enough riddles for one day."

"Our new client brought you a riddle?"

"Let's just say she has an intriguing story. And she's not a client yet."

"She will be." Nikki swiveled back to her computer screen.

Connor thought about debating that conclusion. Decided against it. In all likelihood, Nikki would trump him, just as she routinely trumped Dev.

Besides, assuming Cal and Dev concurred, Kate Marshall might very well become their next client—at least for a preliminary investigation. The case interested him.

As did the woman.

A fact he did not intend to share with any of his colleagues.

3

Everything was going to be okay.

It had to be.

But how in the world had Kate Marshall ended up in St. Louis?

And it was her, no question about it. The white pages didn't lie. Neither did the *Post-Dispatch* article he'd found on the Net that mentioned her. Besides, the face he'd seen on the escalator last Friday had matched the one buried in the recesses of his memory.

Keeping his son in sight through the kitchen window, Greg Sanders took a swig from his daily predinner beer. He'd prefer something stronger tonight, but he wasn't going to let his drinking get out of hand again. Been there, done that, big mistake. Alcohol might numb the pain for a while, but the hollow ache always came back. Better to stay sober and deal with problems straight up as he'd done last time—*after* he'd dried himself out and gotten his act together.

Besides, this problem should be much easier to solve. It was really just a waiting game. In a week or two, the incident would fade from Todd's memory. Although the Marshall woman wasn't likely to forget it that fast, the odds of her trying to track them down—let alone finding them—were minuscule, and there was little chance their paths would ever cross again in a city the size of St. Louis. As for the insomnia once again plaguing him—that, too, would pass.

He watched as Todd and the boy from next door dashed from the swing set to the tree house he'd designed and built in the spring with the permission of his landlord, the two kids oblivious to the summer heat. That was youth for you. Too bad he couldn't tap into their endurance. It would come in handy on the scorching construction sites where he spent his days.

The microwave beeped, and Greg set his beer on the counter. Pot roast tonight, from Trader Joe's. One of Todd's favorites. The frozen oven fries he loved would be done in a minute too. And DQ sundaes were on the menu for dessert. Maybe a special meal like this would help distract him from asking any more questions about last Friday.

If it didn't . . . he'd just have to keep tap-dancing.

After setting the roast on the table, he moved toward the oven—but when his cell began to ring, he detoured to the charger on the built-in desk and scanned caller ID.

Diane.

Shoving his fingers through his hair, he expelled a breath.

This would require a whole different tap-dance routine.

The phone trilled again, and he rested his hand on it. He needed to keep his distance from Diane until Todd stopped asking questions—and remembering stuff he should have forgotten long ago—but he couldn't lose her. She was the best thing that had happened to him in years. Canceling the standing Saturday night pizza outing for the three of them had about killed him, though his upset-stomach excuse hadn't been a lie. He'd been queasy since Friday.

He picked up on the third ring and walked back to the window. "How's the prettiest woman in St. Louis?"

"Lonely."

The affection in her voice took the edge off her reproach. "Me too."

"I was thinking about making some of those chocolate chip pecan cookies you and Todd like. I could stop by and drop them off later."

"Boy, I'd love that." He put as much warmth into that statement as he could—because she wasn't going to like the rest of what he had to say. "But the heat zapped me today. By the time we finish dinner and I spend some time with Todd, I'll be ready to crash. Acclimating to the high temperatures and humidity that kicked in over Fourth of July has been a lot tougher than I expected."

"I imagine St. Louis is quite a shock after living in Montana." Her voice cooled a few degrees. "I won't keep you, then. Why don't you call me when you're up for a visitor?"

"Yeah, I will." The microwave sent out another piercing reminder that dinner was ready, and he jabbed the cancel button. "Listen, Diane, in case you're worried, I'm not seeing anyone else. But Todd . . . he's been having some bad dreams, and between that and this upset stomach thing I have going on, I haven't been getting a lot of sleep. The move was a big change for both of us, and we're still adjusting. I know life will get back to normal soon, if you can just hang in there a few more days. I promise I'll make it up to you. We'll try out that fancy new restaurant you were telling me about last week."

A few moments of silence ticked by before a soft sigh came over the line. "I'd like that. Sorry if I sounded put out or distrustful, but a philandering husband can do that to a girl."

The thread of tension in his shoulders eased. "I totally get that—and you don't have to worry about me on that score. I never once even thought about cheating on my wife. I'm a one-woman-at-a-time man. I'll call you tomorrow—and maybe by next weekend things will calm down around here so we can make up for the pizza we missed last Saturday."

"That would be great." The usual friendliness was back in her voice. "In the meantime, try to stay cool."

"Good advice." In more ways than one. "Talk to you later."

After dropping the phone back in the charger, he moved to the door and pulled it open. "Todd! Dinner's ready."

His son acknowledged the summons with a wave, then descended from the tree house by swinging down from a branch monkey-style rather than using the sturdy ladder. Greg started to call out a warning. Caught himself. Instead, he gripped the edge of the door, holding his breath until Todd was on the ground. One of these days he'd get past the urge to overreact whenever his son took risks typical for any kid his age. Todd was healthy and strong and resilient—the way an almost-seven-year-old should be. He didn't need to be coddled.

Todd called good-bye to his buddy and sprinted toward the house, legs pumping. He skidded to a stop on the stoop as Greg pushed the door wider, then squeezed under his arm.

"What's for dinner?"

"Nothing until you clean up. Hands, face, and—" Greg eyed the smudges of dirt on his T-shirt—"let's change this." He tweaked the sleeve.

"Aw, Dad."

"I'd hurry if I were you. Otherwise the fries will get cold."

Todd's eyes lit up. "You made fries? For real?"

"Yep. Pot roast too." Not homemade, like the meals Jen used to prepare—but a step up from frozen pizza.

"Whoa! Awesome! I'll be right back!"

To the background sound of water running and drawers slamming, Greg removed the plastic wrap from the pot roast, slid the oven fries onto a plate, and drained the water from the packaged corn on the cob.

Seconds later, as he removed a baking sheet from the oven, Todd zoomed back in.

"Wow! Rolls too!" His son slid into his chair. "This is almost as good as Thanksgiving. How come you cooked all this stuff?"

As Greg took his seat, guilt crashed over him. Had it been that long since they'd had a nice meal during the week?

Yeah, it had.

And the steady diet of fast food and macaroni and cheese they'd been relying on since he'd taken the construction job and moved them to St. Louis was getting old. He needed to do better, even if he was beat at the end of a full day in the unaccustomed heat.

"I just thought we deserved a treat." He cut the meat and put several slices on Todd's plate while the boy helped himself to a generous serving of fries. "And how does a DQ sundae sound for dessert?"

"Yeah! I love those almost as much as poppysicles."

Greg froze for a split second as he reached for an ear of corn, reliving again that stomach-dropping, this-is-impossible moment on the escalator at the mall.

Time for diversionary tactics, before his son remembered the incident too.

But as he picked up his corn and prepared to switch the topic to baseball, Todd spoke first. "Dad, you remember that lady I asked you about at the mall the other day?"

Too late.

"Yeah."

"Are you sure we don't know her?"

It was the same question he'd asked a dozen times in the past seventy-two hours. And Greg gave the same answer. "We're new in town, champ. We don't know that many people here yet."

"But we might have met her somewhere else, right?"

"The only other place we've been is Montana, and we didn't see all that many people there." He chewed a bite of meat, hoping it didn't stick in his craw when he tried to swallow. "Besides, I didn't get a very good look at her."

"I did. She had pretty hair, the same color as mine. And she looked right at me, like she knew who I was. I keep thinking I've seen her before." He screwed up his face and twirled a fry in the ketchup he'd squirted on his plate. "Maybe if I think real hard, I'll remember where."

Greg's stomach kinked. That was the last thing he wanted his son to do.

Still . . . how much could Todd possibly call up from memory? According to his research, kids didn't retain much from such a young age. But could an incident like the one on Friday trigger flashbacks of some sort?

Something to search out on the Net later tonight, after his son was asleep.

In the meantime, he needed to shift this conversation into more neutral territory.

"After we get our sundaes tonight, I thought we might watch the Cardinals game on TV."

"Yeah!" Todd chomped on the fry. "Who's pitching?"

They launched into a discussion about the team they'd adopted since moving to St. Louis, the incident on the escalator forgotten.

For now.

But Greg had a sinking feeling the respite would be short-lived.

"So . . ." Dev followed Cal into Connor's office, shamrock-bedecked mug in hand, and dropped into one of the two chairs across from the desk. "Since you avoided me yesterday until I had to cut out for that surveillance gig, you can tell us both about your hot new client at the same time."

Connor unlocked his desk drawer and pulled out a file, shooting his auburn-haired partner a disgruntled look as he tossed the keys onto the corner of his desk. "I haven't even had a chance to get my coffee yet. And what's with this hot stuff? You're engaged."

"But not blind." Eyes twinkling, Dev lifted his mug in a mock salute and took a sip.

"I'll get your coffee for you." Nikki paused in the hall as she passed by the doorway, mug in hand. "I need some more hot water. As for you . . ." She pointed at Dev. "That's what you'll be in if I tell Laura what you just said."

"It was a joke, okay?" Dev sent her a peeved look, then went on the offense. "And how come you're getting Connor's coffee? The one time I asked you to refill my mug, I got an earful about political correctness."

"He didn't ask. I offered. Big difference." Nikki swung toward Connor. "Back in a minute with your caffeine fix."

Cal glanced at his watch. "Not that I want to be a wet blanket, but I've got a nine o'clock meeting, so maybe we could move this along?"

"Right." Leave it to the Phoenix founding partner to rein in the staff and keep things on track. Cal was even more organized than he'd been in their college-buddy days. "My visitor yesterday isn't a client yet. I wanted to get your take before I pursue this. Her story is unusual, to say the least."

"Couldn't be any more unusual than Moira's vanishing person tale last year—and look what happened in that case. Not only did it turn out to be true, but you two got married." Dev nudged Cal with his elbow.

Connor folded his hands on the file. "It's at least as unusual as that."

"Now I'm intrigued too." Cal leaned back and crossed an ankle over a knee as he sipped his coffee.

"Here you go." Nikki sailed back in and set his mug on the desk—along with a plate of coffee cake and some paper napkins.

Dev's eyes lit up and he leaned closer. "Is that my all-time favorite caramel pecan stollen from McArthur's?"

Nikki pressed a finger against a stray crumb that had fallen on the desk and shrugged. "I stopped at Great Harvest for a whole-wheat bagel on my way in, and since I was passing by I decided to indulge all of you with this coronary-waiting-to-happen." She gave the three of them a dark look. "It's not like my eat-healthy campaign has had much impact on this group, anyway."

"You are my favorite person in the whole world. And it's not even my birthday." Dev helped himself to the largest slice.

She snorted. "Don't get used to it."

As she flounced out, Dev grinned after her and took a big bite. "So where were we?"

"Trying to focus on business." Cal raised an eyebrow at him as he picked up a smaller piece, then turned his attention to Connor.

Taking the cue, Connor jumped back in. "I'm going to give it to you the way Kate Marshall gave it to me. After I get your reactions, I'll fill you in on what I learned after she faxed me back the completed client questionnaire and Nikki and I did some additional research." He tapped the file in front of him and launched into her story.

By the time he finished, Cal was frowning and Dev was staring at him, his stollen lying forgotten on the napkin in his lap.

"That's a peculiar one, all right." Cal sipped his coffee, his comment measured, thoughtful, and nonjudgmental. Classic Cal.

"Is she a nut, or what?" Typical Dev.

"She's not a nut." His reply came out terse. Too terse, based on Dev's speculative expression. Buying himself a moment to regain control, he opened the file—even though he'd already committed the key facts to memory. "Kate Stewart was born and raised in Nashville. She attended college on an academic scholarship and went on to get a master's degree in psychology, emphasis in counseling. Following graduation, she worked as a high school counselor in Chicago until she married Dr. John Marshall and they moved to Hilton, New York. Her husband had a private pediatric practice specializing in neural disorders and conducted internationally recognized research at the University of Rochester."

"No slouches in that family." Dev picked up his stollen again.

"True. Kate got a counseling position at a women's shelter in Rochester, and she continued to work part-time once her son was born. She took a year off after the accident, then accepted a job here at New Start."

Cal tipped his head. "Isn't that some kind of job service organization for women?"

"How'd you know that?" Dev squinted at him.

"Moira mentioned it in that investigative series she did a while back about battered wives. I think it was one of the resources available to them."

"That's right." Connor consulted a sheet of paper in the file. "It's a vocational guidance center for women who are entering the workforce after an extended absence and who need help polishing their interviewing skills, making contacts, and gaining confidence. According to the background Nikki dug up on it, a lot of the clients are newly divorced or coming out of an abusive relationship. Kate started there two years ago as a counselor and was promoted to director of the center last year. She's also active in her church and delivers for their meals-on-wheels type program every Sunday."

Cal sipped his coffee. "Credible job, credible background, credible lifestyle."

"But incredible story." Dev took another bite of his coffee cake and spoke as he chewed. "So what's she want us to do?"

"Identify the boy she saw at the mall. Otherwise, she's not sure she'll be able to let this go." Connor closed the file.

"Seems like a reasonable request in light of all the facts—and her concerns about some of the aspects of the original investigation." Cal swiped a smear of caramel off the side of his mug with his thumb.

"Any idea what the security camera situation is at the mall?" Connor leaned back in his chair and steepled his fingers.

"I used to, when I worked at County. We investigated a few cases that took us there. But that was six years ago. However, one of my detective colleagues is the head of security there now. I could give him a call, get you an entrée. Since we have a time and location on the sighting, it shouldn't be difficult to isolate the relevant feeds. Reviewing them will eat up some hours, though. Does your client have a budget for that kind of thing?"

"She included a note with her questionnaire assuring us cost wasn't an issue. Apparently she received a large insurance settlement after her husband's death."

Dev finished off his stollen and licked his fingers. "Even if you spot this kid, the odds of figuring out who he is are minuscule. And despite the coincidences she mentioned, the chances are microscopic that he's her son. Seems to me the lady's wasting her money."

"She doesn't feel that way. The incident last Friday really got under her skin."

Dev wadded up his napkin. "Speaking of getting under the skin . . ."

As Connor's neck warmed, Cal stepped in. "I say go for it—in terms of viewing the surveillance video, that is. If you can't spot the boy, end of story. Let's defer any further discussion until after that."

51

"Fine by me." Dev grabbed the plate of coffee cake and stood.

"Hey!" Connor surged forward and snatched a piece. "This might be your favorite, but it's for all of us."

"I was just going to put it in the kitchen."

"After pilfering several more pieces to stockpile in your desk." Cal rose and followed Dev out. "I'll make the call to mall security and pass on the contact information once I get the green light. Keep us in the loop."

"I will."

As they disappeared down the hall, Connor opened the file, located Kate's cell number, and reached for his phone. She'd be happy to hear they were going to do some initial investigating, but he didn't want to build false expectations. Dev was right. There wasn't much chance he'd turn up anything useful. The little boy's identity would, in all likelihood, remain a mystery. But perhaps knowing everything possible had been done might give her some small measure of peace.

And considering all she'd been through in the past three years, that was the least he could do.

Thank you, God.

Cell phone pressed to her ear, Kate swiveled away from her desk, toward the window that gave her a view of the world through slanted privacy blinds. Connor Sullivan had come through for her—and her spirits were now as bright as the sunshine outside. "I have to admit, I was preparing myself for a letdown."

"That may yet be coming." She didn't miss the distinct note of caution in his baritone voice. "The mall's surveillance camera coverage may not be sufficient for our purposes. And even if we do spot the boy, identifying him is still going to be a challenge."

"I know—but at least you're willing to try. That means a

lot." The last couple of words rasped, and she swallowed past the sudden pressure in her throat.

If Connor picked up her momentary lapse in control, he let it pass. "Do you have a few minutes now? I'd like to get some specifics on time and location."

"Yes. My first appointment isn't until nine. I saw the boy about one-fifteen, on the escalator at the south end of the mall outside the Penney's store."

"What was he wearing?"

She closed her eyes and tried to visualize his clothing. Came up blank. "I'm sorry. All I remember is his face."

"What about the guy he was with? Can you give me a description of him?"

"I only saw him from the back. But he was wearing a T-shirt and a baseball cap."

"Did you notice the colors?"

She concentrated, trying to re-create the man's image in her mind. "The cap was red . . . but I can't remember the T-shirt."

"Any guesses on his age?"

"No, although he had broad shoulders and seemed muscular." She sighed. "That isn't much to go on, is it?"

"The red cap helps. So does the specific time and place. What about the boy? Hair color, build, any other identifying marks?"

"His hair was the same color as mine, and he was on the slight side. But he was too far away to see much detail." She turned her back on the window and rested her elbow on her desk, dropping her head into her hand as her mood took a nosedive. "I bet your colleagues think this is nuts, don't they?"

His momentary hesitation gave her the answer, though he couched it in more diplomatic terms.

"They're cautious. We try very hard to satisfy our clients, and the chances of doing that are lower in a case where the odds are stacked against us."

"Then you should know that you've already satisfied me by agreeing to look into my story—no matter the outcome."

"I'll keep that in mind. However, I'm still going to explore every avenue I find that might give us a clue to his identity—starting with a visit to the mall this afternoon. I'll be in touch as soon as I have anything to report."

"Thank you—for everything."

"My pleasure."

The line went dead, and Kate stared at her phone. Had there been a slight note of husky intimacy in his final comment? A suggestion that this case was more special to him than most? That *she* was more special than his typical client?

Shoving her hair behind her ear, Kate shook her head and answered her own questions. No, no, and no.

Connor Sullivan was a pro. Every job was important to him. She was no more special than any other client. End of story.

As for the little twinge of disappointment in the pit of her stomach when she reached that conclusion—she wasn't even going to try and figure it out.

Opening the file on her desk, she forced herself to focus on the background sheet for the new client who would soon arrive. No sense wasting any more time thinking about Connor Sullivan or his trip to the mall this afternoon. Either there were clues to find or there weren't.

But based on her brief meeting with him, and the aura of competence and determination he projected, she was certain about one thing.

If the clues were there, he'd uncover them.

4

Zoom in slowly on the entrance to the up escalator."

As the mall security officer adjusted the image on the screen, Connor leaned closer. None of the mall cameras were focused on the specific escalator he needed to see, but at least it was in the background on this feed. Better than nothing, though the image got fuzzier the closer the officer pulled it in.

He noted the time at the bottom of the screen: five after one. "Hold the zoom there. Let's run it from here."

The image came to life, and Connor focused on the monitor, searching for blond hair and a red baseball cap.

At one-ten, a red baseball cap moved into view. A man, based on the build. But as he swung onto the escalator, it was clear he was alone.

Three minutes later, another red-capped man appeared—with a blond-haired child in tow.

Connor's adrenaline surged. "Pull back so I can see the whole escalator."

"Spot your man?" The security officer adjusted the view again.

"I think so." He focused on the crowded down escalator, looking for Kate to verify the timing was right and this was the duo. A sudden movement near the bottom caught his attention, and then he spotted her vaulting off the escalator and pushing through the crowd to ride back up.

Noting the time and the camera number, he gestured toward the top of the escalator. "Zoom in on the exit."

The man complied. A few seconds later, the red-capped man and boy disembarked. The man seemed to be in a hurry as he hustled the boy through the crowd and moved out of camera range.

"Can you pick up the guy in the red cap on any other feed?"

"Maybe." The man punched some keys on the computer, and another view of the mall came up, cued to the same time. Twenty seconds later, Connor spotted the man in the crowd, closer up this time. For a few moments, the camera caught him and the child straight on. The man's head was bent, but the screen offered a reasonably clear image of the little boy. Then they disappeared from view.

"Any other feeds we can tap into?" Connor transferred his gaze to the man beside him.

"No. They just went into the garage. We lose them there."

Connor wasn't surprised. With rare exception, most malls focused their surveillance efforts indoors.

Too bad this couldn't have been one of those exceptions. A license plate would have made his job a whole lot easier.

"Can you play those two sections for me again? But this time I want to go in tight on the boy and the guy in the red cap and follow them to the top."

"Not a problem."

As the security officer reran the feed from the first camera, Connor scrutinized the screen, looking for something, anything, that might give him a clue about their identity.

Nada.

The guy wore jeans and a plain T-shirt, the fabric of the latter stretched taut over broad, muscular shoulders, as Kate had noted. Since the boy was on the other side of him, he caught only an occasional glimpse of the blond hair.

"Let's look at the other feed again. Go in tight on that one too."

The security officer pushed a few buttons, and the second feed came up. He zoomed in as the man and boy walked straight toward the overhead camera.

"Get ready to hold . . . now."

The officer froze the image on the screen, and Connor leaned forward. Mr. Red Cap's head was still bent and angled toward the boy as he hurried him along, his face in shadows. The only new piece of information he picked up was the St. Louis Cardinals logo on the baseball cap.

More telling, however, was the way the man had kept looking over his shoulder, back toward the escalator they'd just exited. As if he was afraid someone was following him.

Kate's bizarre suspicion inched up a fraction on the credibility scale.

He turned his attention to the boy. The youngster's head was tipped back as he looked up at the man beside him, and though the image was on the fuzzy side, there was enough detail to make a screen grab worthwhile.

"Can I get a printout of that?"

"Yeah. Matt said I could give you a couple of shots." The security officer hit a few more buttons, and a nearby printer whirred into action. "This isn't our usual protocol. You must have some pull."

"Not me. One of my partners."

The man rolled his chair over to the printer, extracted the sheet, and passed it over. "You want to see anything else?"

Connor slipped the printout into his briefcase. "I'd like to try and figure out where these two were before they got on the escalator. Any suggestions on other feeds we could look at to see if we can pick them up?"

The man scanned the monitors showing real-time activity in the mall, then scooted back to the console. "Yeah. We can try a few things, since the place is dead today. But it was a zoo here on Friday—so this will be needle-in-a-haystack stuff. You have some time?"

"All afternoon."

And that's how long he stayed—with little to show for his effort.

At five o'clock, Connor rotated the kinks out of his neck. The only significant sighting of the duo had been when they emerged from the Build-A-Bear store five minutes before they caught the escalator.

"Thanks a lot for your help." Connor stood.

"It passed the time on a slow day." The man took a swig of the soda he'd been nursing for the past twenty minutes. "But I'm not sure it was worth all the effort—or your client's money."

"Neither am I." Although the visit to the Build-A-Bear store might give him something to work with.

"Well, if you need anything else, let me know. Matt said to cooperate with you guys."

"Will do." He shook hands with the man and exited the office, into the mall.

As he passed the Build-A-Bear store on the way to his car, he paused. Neither the man nor boy had been holding a shopping bag in any of the security footage, so even though they'd come out of the store, it was unlikely they'd purchased anything—or left any sales information behind that might offer a clue to their identity.

Still, it was all he had.

Continuing toward the parking garage, he played with a couple of different pretexts that might ferret out some information— if there was any information to be had—opting for the one involving Nikki. She was adept at phone stuff, and she got a kick out of it.

But if that didn't pan out, the game was over. The little boy would forever remain nothing more than a blurry screen grab from a security camera.

And for the rest of her life, Kate Marshall would be left wondering whether a remarkable coincidence had been simply a fluke—or a miracle waiting to happen.

Six- to nine-year-olds can have verbally accessible memories from very early childhood. The ability to remember certain events from their early years doesn't begin to fade until double-digit age is attained, and very emotional incidents can be recalled earlier than nonemotional events, especially if a triggering incident occurs.

That was *not* what he'd wanted to discover.

Greg rested his elbows on the kitchen table and massaged his temples as he stared at his laptop, glad now that the baseball game had run late last night and he'd deferred this research for twenty-four hours. The delay had bought him one more day without this additional worry.

And it was a huge one.

Apparently the precautions he'd taken three years ago to buy them time so Todd's earlier life could fade from his memory had been useless. One glimpse of Kate Marshall was all it had taken for him to dredge up fragmentary recollections that Greg assumed had long ago disappeared into oblivion.

Every website he'd found on the subject concurred: it would take three or four more years for Todd's memories of that time to diminish enough to be harmless—especially now that they'd been triggered.

And what was he supposed to do in the meantime?

Rising, he began to pace.

Think. Stay rational. Don't overreact.

59

He repeated that mantra over and over until he felt more in control and his brain began clicking.

Okay. Maybe Todd had some vague images in his mind—but he hadn't made the connection. Might *never* make the connection. One quick glimpse in a mall, from a distance, that's all it had been. So he'd asked a few questions. So what? As long as they didn't talk too much about it, as long as he changed the subject whenever the topic came up, Todd would eventually lose interest.

Greg detoured from the path he was wearing in the kitchen floor and moved down the hall, stopping outside his son's bedroom. As always, Todd slept on his stomach, arms outstretched, legs sprawled. He was growing fast. So fast.

But not fast enough to banish the dangerous fragmentary memories.

Grasping the edge of the door frame to steady himself, Greg fought back a new surge of panic. He couldn't let anything jeopardize the life they had. The life he'd built for them. The life he'd salvaged from the ashes. He would do everything in his power to protect his son. Everything.

Failing a second time was not an option.

He watched the even rise and fall of Todd's back in the shaft of light from the hallway. Children were so trusting. So reliant on the adults in their lives to take care of them. To provide for them. To make sure they were safe and healthy and loved.

And he had no intention of betraying that trust.

He would guard and protect his son and preserve the life they had together.

No matter what it took.

"You were awfully quiet tonight. Didn't you have a chance to read the book?"

As Pauline Andrews dropped into the seat beside her while

the rest of the members of the Last-Tuesday-of-the-Month Book Club went in search of refreshments, Kate shifted sideways. "I read it. I just had a long day."

"Problems at work?"

"No."

When she didn't elaborate, Pauline tilted her head, reminding Kate of an inquisitive bird. The older woman might be on her second set of hips and have hair the color of fresh snow, but her eyes were as sharp and clear and insightful as someone half her age.

"Why don't we ditch this place and grab a cup of tea at Molly's? I don't need any of that high-fat dessert Susan made, and I surely don't want to look at that bulging envelope of photos tucked into the pocket of Lorraine's purse. I think it's fine and dandy she loves her grandkids to pieces, but those babies haven't changed that much in four weeks and I viewed the whole gallery last month."

"Me too."

"Then meet me at Molly's in fifteen minutes. I'll make our excuses to Susan."

"It's a date."

The woman winked. "You go ahead and get us a table. I'll be right behind you."

Glad to have a reason to escape the gab session that always followed the book club discussions, Kate grabbed her purse and slipped out the door. A chat with Pauline might be just what she needed. The older woman's wit and wisdom never failed to lift her spirits.

And they could use some lifting about now.

Because she hadn't heard one word from Connor Sullivan.

His lack of communication could mean one of two things. Either he'd struck out at the mall and simply hadn't had a chance yet to deliver the bad news, or he'd found something worth investigating and was waiting to call her until he had more definitive information.

The uncertainty was driving her crazy.

After strapping herself in behind the wheel, Kate started the engine and cranked up the air conditioner. It was odd how Pauline always seemed to sense when she needed a friendly ear. The woman's uncanny empathy and instincts had been a real blessing since she'd joined Kate's church. And thanks to Pauline's gentle pushing and prodding, her life now included more than work. She'd gotten involved in meal delivery for shut-ins. Joined the book club. Yoga class would be next, if Pauline got her way, though Kate was holding out on that one. She wasn't convinced her body could bend like that.

And since turnabout was fair play, she'd also convinced Pauline to volunteer one morning a week at New Start. That had been an unexpected blessing; the insightful older woman was wonderful with the clients.

The soothing strains of Vivaldi from her favorite CD filled the car as Kate drove, calming her thoughts, and by the time she arrived at Molly's she'd made the decision to share the events of the past few days with the older woman. Other than Connor, Pauline was the only other person she trusted to give her story a fair hearing.

She'd barely secured a table and placed their orders before the jingle of the bell over the door announced Pauline's arrival. The woman lifted a hand in greeting and bustled over.

"What would you like, my dear?"

"Already taken care of. I ordered your favorite jasmine tea and two of those shortbread cookies we like."

"You shouldn't have done that. I wanted this to be my treat." Pauline planted her hands on her wiry hips and gave her a reproving look.

"Next time."

"You said that last time."

"This time I mean it. Except after I tell you what's been happening in my life, you may write me off as a crazy woman and never want to associate with me again."

"Now you have me intrigued. Let me grab our order and then I'm all ears."

Two minutes later, their drinks and cookies on the table, Pauline took her seat, dunked her tea bag in the hot water, and gave Kate her full attention. "All set. Lay it on me."

Kate added some half-and-half to her decaf English breakfast tea, took a deep breath, and bared her soul.

When she finished, the other woman lifted her cup and rested her elbows on the table. "That's amazing."

"At least you didn't say ridiculous."

"Of course not. I've lived a long while, and the older I get, the more I've learned never to write off stories that sound implausible. In fact, I've lived a few of my own." She took a sip of her tea and set the cup back in the saucer. "Did I ever tell you about the time Charles and I went hiking in Donegal?"

"No." Kate broke off a bite of cookie and settled in. Pauline's stories might seem off-topic at first, but they always had a point.

"It was many years ago now, but I remember it clearly. We set out to see the second-highest sea cliffs in Ireland. But it was a misty day, and we had trouble finding the trailhead. After a lot of driving in circles, we came across a spot on the side of a barren, sheep-covered hillside that appeared to be it. There was one other car parked there, which convinced us to give it a try.

"Well, not ten minutes down the goat path that passed for a trail, we came upon another couple heading toward us out of the mist. We struck up a conversation, and you know what? Not only were they Americans, they lived ten minutes away from us. What on earth do you think the odds are that two American couples who were almost neighbors would run into each other in such a remote part of the world?"

"Infinitesimal."

"Exactly. So we agreed to exchange names and phone numbers and get in touch once we returned home—and that was the beginning of a beautiful friendship. Even though Charles is gone and they've moved to Florida, we stay in close touch. And it all started as a result of a strange coincidence that perhaps wasn't a coincidence at all. Thanks to experiences like that, I've learned never to discount possibilities because of the odds—because all things are possible with God."

Kate knitted her fingers together. Tight. "Does that mean . . . do you actually think that boy could . . ." She blew out a breath. "Other than the PI I hired, everyone who heard the story at mall security and in the police department thinks it's crazy."

"Do *you* think it's crazy?"

"Logically, yes. Kevin's been gone for three years, Pauline."

"What does your heart say?"

At the woman's gentle question, her fingers tightened on the cup. She whispered her response, almost afraid to voice the words. "It says maybe."

"And what does your PI—this Connor—say?"

"He's skeptical. He warned me not to get my hopes up, and that the odds of finding the boy weren't in our favor."

"But he took the case."

"I'm paying him."

"Does he strike you as the kind of man who would take money for a job he knew he had no chance of completing?"

Good question.

"No." Kate slowly shook her head, then spoke with more confidence. "No, I don't think so. I'm sure he believes there's a possibility he can identify the boy. But even if he does, it's a huge leap to think that boy could be Kevin."

"Why not take this one step at a time? Wait and see what he discovers at the mall. If it ends there, so be it. But I've always been pretty good at assessing people, even if I don't have a fancy degree like you do." Pauline winked and patted her hand. "You're a very level-headed young woman. Running into a boy who reminded you of Kevin, as upsetting as that might be, wouldn't send you into a tailspin. However, throw in the poppysicle reference, the fact that he turned when you called his name, the recognition you thought you saw on his face—I think you're doing the right thing by having this Connor try to find him. Do you think he's competent?"

"Very. He used to be a Secret Service agent. I have a feeling if he can't get to the bottom of this, no one can."

"Then there you go. No more reason to fret. Just put it in God's hands and trust things will work out."

Kate sighed and reached for a paper napkin to mop up the tea she'd managed to spill in the bottom of her saucer. "Easier said than done—and I speak from experience."

"I know you do. But despite everything that's happened, you've hung on to your faith. You keep hanging on and you'll be fine."

"Is that a promise?"

"Absolutely. You, my dear, are a survivor. Now"—Pauline picked up her cup—"let's drink this before it gets cold while I tell you about the show I saw at the Muny last night."

Somehow, Pauline managed to distract her while they finished their tea and snack. And by the time they walked out to their cars and parted in the parking lot with a hug—along with a cheery "See you Thursday morning" from Pauline—Kate's spirits were once again on the rise.

That could be short-lived, of course, depending on what Connor had to report. But until then, she was going to let the tiny ember of hope keep burning.

Even if, in the end, it flickered and died, leaving her heart colder than before.

5

Hey . . . just saw your email. What's this about a pretexting gig?" Nikki stuck her head in Connor's office, mug in hand.

He waved her into a chair. "You up for it?"

"Always." She sat. "Does this involve your new client?"

"Yep."

"You found something at the mall yesterday?"

"Not much. But before I let this go, I want to follow up on every possible lead." He brought her up to speed on the case. "Unfortunately, there was nothing in the security camera feeds to ID the boy or the man. However, I did spot them coming out of the Build-A-Bear store. No bag in hand, so I'm assuming they didn't make a purchase, but it's possible a clerk might remember them. If we can find someone who was there last Friday, and if you chat her up, maybe she'll pass on a piece of information that might be helpful."

Nikki crossed her legs. "That's a lot of it's possibles, ifs, maybes, and might bes."

Like he didn't know that.

"It's all I've got. If I come up blank here, the case is over."

"No pressure there." She took a sip of her tea. "What does the little boy look like?"

He pulled the screen grab out of the folder and handed it over.

"Cute kid."

"I never got a decent view of the father, but he was wearing a red Cardinals baseball cap, T-shirt, and jeans. Based on his build, my guess is he either works out or has a manual labor job."

She nodded and set the printout on the desk. "What kind of pretext did you have in mind?"

"How about this—your husband took your son to their store Friday, and somewhere in the mall your little boy managed to lose his backpack. You're hoping it's at Build-A-Bear."

"The mother act, huh? Might work. And not bad practice, either." She delivered the last line looking straight at him, her eyes twinkling.

It took a second for her meaning to register, and when it did, he grinned. "You're pregnant."

"Give the man a gold star."

"That's great, Nikki." If anyone deserved a happy domestic life, it was the woman across from him. Maybe this would help make up for her own abusive childhood and fractured family. "I'm happy for you."

"Thanks. Me too."

"Did you tell Cal and Dev yet?"

"I shared the news with Cal yesterday. I'll get to Dev sometime today. So back to the matter at hand . . . I'll give it a try. You do realize, though, that this is probably going to be an exercise in futility. There's a steady parade of kids in and out of a store like that. There's not much chance a busy clerk will remember one in particular."

"Yeah. But it's worth a call at least. Let me close the door, then I'll put the phone on speaker."

"I've got it." She rose and crossed toward the hall. "You dial."

Connor tapped in the number, worked his way through the

automated menu, pressed zero for a live person, and leaned back in his chair as Nikki took her own seat.

"West County Center Build-A-Bear. This is Carolyn. How may I help you?"

"Hi, Carolyn. I may be on a wild-goose chase, but I'm trying to track down a Spiderman backpack my son left somewhere at the mall on Friday." Nikki's tone was conversational, friendly, chatty. Perfect. "He and my husband were in your store around lunchtime, and I wondered if he might have forgotten it there."

"I didn't work Friday, but I'll be happy to check our lost and found."

"Thank you. I'd appreciate that."

As she sipped her tea, Connor throttled back the urge to offer advice about how to proceed when the woman came back with a negative report. Nikki's instincts and her ability to think on her feet were solid, and she'd never let him down on one of these playacting assignments. No reason to think she'd start now.

"Are you still there, ma'am?"

"Yes."

"I'm sorry . . . I'm not seeing any backpacks. Have you talked to the main lost and found for the mall?"

"Not yet. I thought it might be easier to begin with a place I knew they visited." She let out a protracted sigh that would be clearly audible on the other end of the line. "Is there, by chance, someone working today who was on duty Friday? I know it's a long shot, but if there is, maybe she noticed whether he had the backpack with him when he came into the store. It might help me get a better handle on when and where he lost it."

"Well . . . I think Rachel might have been here. Can you hold another minute?"

"Sure."

Connor gave Nikki a thumbs-up and mouthed "way to go."

Talking to someone who'd been on duty Friday had been the whole point, and she'd maneuvered herself there smoothly.

Thirty seconds later, another woman's voice spoke. "This is Rachel. May I help you?"

"Hi, Rachel." Nikki replayed her script. "So I'm wondering if you might remember seeing him, and perhaps noticing whether he had his backpack with him while he was in the store. I hate to bother you with this, but the backpack was brand-new and my husband is so not into noticing details like whether my son has all his stuff with him—or wears matching socks. I didn't even realize it was gone until today."

The other woman laughed. Masterful. Nikki could build rapport even faster than she came up with zingers to lob at Dev.

"I hear you. I don't know if I can help, but maybe if you describe your son, it might ring some bells."

Nikki picked up the printout. "He's almost seven. Blond. On the slight side. He was wearing a dark blue T-shirt. And my husband was wearing a Cardinals baseball cap."

"I'm sorry . . . that's not triggering anything. We were overrun with kids Friday—two birthday parties. Was he at one of those?"

Nikki darted him a quick glance. "Yes, he was."

"Was it the Garber party? That was around noon."

He grabbed his pen and jotted down the name.

"Yes."

"I helped at that one . . . and now that I think about it, there was a blond boy in the group. I noticed him because he was on the quiet side. You know, you might want to call the mother who hosted the party. If your son had his backpack with him when he arrived, one of the other kids could have picked it up by mistake."

"I'll do that. The last name was G-a-r-b-e-r, correct? I threw away the invitation and I don't know all the parents from daycare."

"Hold a sec." Silence on the line, followed by the clack of keys. "Yes. That's the correct spelling. Linda Garber."

Connor wrote down the first name.

"Perfect. Thanks so much for your help."

"No problem. I hope you find it."

Connor killed the connection. "Nice work."

She shook her head. "Don't get your hopes up. There's no guarantee she had the right kid in mind. Lots of little boys are blond. And didn't you say neither the man or boy was carrying a shopping bag?"

"That's right."

"Most of the time at those parties the kids build a bear and take it home with them."

That wasn't the best news he'd heard all day. Perhaps the duo had stopped in simply to window-shop after all.

He frowned and tapped his pen against the notepad. "There could be some reason the boy didn't have it in hand." Nikki's skeptical expression suggested the odds of that were slim, but already he was turning over next-step scenarios. "I'll give this a little more thought before I call Kate."

Nikki rose and moved to the door. Stopped. Angled toward him. "For what it's worth, your new client didn't strike me as the type who overreacts. It might not hurt to make a few phone calls. How many Garbers can there be in the phone book?"

"I was already thinking along those lines."

"I figured you were. You want me to peruse the phone listings while you and Cal are at the executive security meeting this morning? I could make a few preliminary calls, see if I can find the right Garber."

"Do you have time?"

"I'll have to push Dev's filing down on my to-do list, but that's no hardship."

"Then give it a shot."

"You got it."

As she exited, he leaned back in his chair, rolling his pen between his fingers. Maybe they'd hit pay dirt with one of the Garbers . . . but that was a big maybe.

Meaning much as he wanted to help Kate, if this didn't pan out, they were at the end of the road.

"Hey, Dad, I got my bear today! Lindsey's mom finally remembered to bring it."

At Todd's exuberant greeting, Greg took his son's hand and looked down at the Build-A-Bear shopping bag as they exited the daycare facility.

The thing turned his stomach.

Who could have fathomed a simple, innocent kid's birthday party would shake the foundation of his world?

"You want to see it?" Todd beamed up at him.

"Sure. But let's get in the truck first."

Sixty seconds later, as his son buckled himself into the car seat, Greg circled around, slid behind the wheel—and took a calming breath. Things could have turned out worse. If Linda Garber had been taking her daughter back to daycare after the party instead of heading home to pack for vacation, Todd wouldn't have needed to be picked up. Instead, he'd have been with Linda and Lindsey. What if Kate had spotted him then—and approached Linda?

He suppressed a shudder.

Using his brief lunch hour to rush to the mall to pick up Todd may not have been convenient—but in the end, it had averted disaster.

He hoped.

"Whaddaya think, Dad?"

Resting an elbow on the back of his seat, Greg angled sideways and studied the bear, which sported a Cardinals baseball uniform and cap. "That's pretty cool."

"Yeah." Todd tucked the bear next to him. "I wish I could have taken it with me the day of the party."

"But it was thoughtful of Mrs. Garber to offer to go back to the mall and pick it up after the lady at the shop found that ripped seam." Greg shifted around to face front, put the pickup in gear, and pulled away from the daycare center.

A few seconds of silence passed. "Do you think we might go back to that mall sometime too?"

A thrum of tension began to pulsate in his temples. "Why?"

"If we did, I might see that lady from the escalator again."

Five days, and still Todd wasn't letting the incident go.

"There's not much chance of that. It's a big place, and lots of people go there every day."

"Yeah." The car grew silent again, and Greg could almost hear the gears turning in his son's head. "Do you think I might have known her when I was a baby? Before I was adopted?"

His gut twisted. "You would have been too little to remember that far back, champ."

"I guess."

But he didn't sound convinced.

Not for the first time, Greg wondered if he'd made a mistake telling Todd he was adopted. After a lot of deliberation, though, it had seemed the safest choice on the off chance he ever ran into anyone from his old life who knew his history.

But he'd never expected to run into someone who knew *Todd's* history.

"I wish I had a mom."

At the forlorn comment, Greg tightened his grip on the wheel and merged onto the highway, heading toward the rental house they now called home—and regretting anew the day he'd decided it was finally safe to leave Montana.

"I wish you did too, champ." His throat tightened, and he forced himself to inhale. Even after five years, the pain of Jen's loss could overwhelm him.

"If you got married again, I'd have a mom, right?"

"Yeah. But we just moved here, and we need to settle in before we make any more big changes in our lives." Sweat beaded above his upper lip, and he tried to amp up the air conditioner. No go. It was already running at full blast.

But it sure didn't feel like it.

"I like Diane. She's nice."

At his son's hopeful tone, Greg pried his fingers off the wheel and flexed them to get the blood flowing again. It wasn't difficult to follow the youngster's train of thought. "Yes, she is."

"How come we didn't have pizza with her last Saturday, like we usually do?"

"I told you already. My stomach was upset."

"Is it better now?"

Hardly.

"It's getting there."

"So are we going to have pizza with her this Saturday?"

A police cruiser loomed ahead, watching from the shoulder for speeders. He eased back on the accelerator. The last thing he needed was a run-in with the cops.

"Dad? Are we?"

That had been the plan. Now he wasn't certain.

"I don't know yet."

"How come?"

"Look, let it go, Todd. I had a long day and I'm tired. We'll talk about it later." He hadn't planned to raise his voice. Or sound aggravated. But that's the way the comment came out.

Silence from the backseat.

He flicked a glance into the rearview mirror. Todd had picked up his Cardinals bear and was hugging him close, his face scrunched. Like he was going to cry.

Greg bit back an oath. All these years, he'd never once spoken to Todd in anger. He'd cherished him and nurtured him and had never, ever been unkind, even when administering necessary discipline. He treasured his son too much to ever hurt him.

But now, thanks to the stupid fluke in the mall that had put him on edge, he was taking out his fear on his child.

And that was plain wrong.

"Hey." He gentled his voice and waited for Todd to meet his gaze in the rearview mirror. "Sorry about that, champ. I guess I'm not used to this heat yet, and it can make me cranky. We'll get back to our pizza routine real soon, I promise. How does that sound?"

"Fine." At the tremulous response, Greg wished he could pull over and give his son a reassuring hug. Not going to happen during rush hour on I-270, though, so he did the next best thing. "I love you. You never forget that, okay?"

"Okay." Todd sniffled and wiped his nose on the sleeve of his T-shirt. Usually that drew a correction, but this time Greg let it pass. "I love you too."

The beautiful words were like balm on his soul, and the taut line of his shoulders relaxed.

Until Todd spoke again a few minutes later in a quiet, wistful tone that sent another wave of uneasiness crashing over him. "I bet that lady on the escalator is a good mom."

Greg didn't respond.

Instead, he once again squeezed the wheel and kept his eyes focused straight ahead. Wishing he could wipe out the past. Wishing he could pray for help.

But God wouldn't listen to the likes of him. Not anymore. He only welcomed back *repentant* sinners.

All he could do was hope Todd's obsession would diminish soon and that life would get back to normal.

Whatever that was these days.

As Connor tossed his suit jacket onto a chair in his office and went in search of a piece of the coffee cake Nikki had brought in yesterday, her voice wafted down the hall.

"Pregnant women aren't supposed to lift heavy stuff."

When that pronouncement was followed by a fit of coughing, his lips tipped up.

Dev had just gotten the big news.

Ignoring the growls in his stomach, he detoured toward his partner's office and propped a shoulder against the doorway. Dev had sprayed soda all over the files scattered on his desk and was still hacking as Nikki shoved a fistful of paper napkins at him.

"You need me to do the Heimlich maneuver?" Connor tried to rein in his grin.

Dev waved his question aside and focused on Nikki. "You're *pregnant*?"

"It happens."

"Did you know about this?" Dev looked his way and swiped at the soda-speckled folders on his desk with the wad of napkins.

"I found out this morning before Cal and I left for the meeting on that executive security gig—which ran very long, by the way. I hope you left some of that coffee cake in the kitchen. I'm starving."

Dev ignored that comment.

Not a positive sign.

After one final hack, his partner eyed Nikki. "So . . . are you doing okay? Everything's good?"

"Everything's great. And I was just kidding about lifting your files."

She bent to pick up a stack from the corner of his office, but before she touched them, Dev sprang out of his chair and raced around his desk. "Wait! I'll get them."

"I can do it." She grabbed the files and rose. "I'm pregnant, not incapacitated."

He tugged the files away from her. "Fine. But I'm here now. Where do you want these?"

She cocked her head. Shrugged. "On my desk. I need to go through them and identify the contents since you never bother to label the new stuff."

For once, Dev let the dig pass and exited in silence.

As he disappeared out the door to the reception area, Nikki winked at Connor and dropped her voice. "This could be fun."

He chuckled. "You're bad."

"Aren't I, though? But I'm good in other ways. Like digging for information." She handed him the slip of paper in her hand. "There were fifteen Garbers in the phone book. That's Linda's number. I was getting ready to put it on your desk."

A quick scan told him it was a Kirkwood-area exchange. Probably not far from their offices. "What was your pretext?"

"Build-A-Bear follow-up to verify she was satisfied with her birthday party. There were eight children at the event, three boys and five girls. The majority of them were daycare friends of her daughter, Lindsey, who's enrolled at STL Academy all day in the summer and for aftercare during the school year. She'll be in first grade this fall, and she dressed her bear in a pink tutu."

Connor stared at her. "How did you manage to get all that information?"

"Like I said, I'm good. Remember that when raise time comes around." She sent him a pointed look. "And don't get your hopes up about the coffee cake. Dev scarfed down the last piece about an hour ago."

As she started down the hall, the guilty party pushed through from the front—and held the door open for her.

Connor's eyebrows rose. That was a first. Meaning interesting—and entertaining—times should be ahead.

As for the latest information Nikki had unearthed—that, too, suggested interesting possibilities. If the blond boy the Build-A-Bear clerk had mentioned happened to be the same one Kate had seen, there was a better-than-average chance he attended STL. And if surveillance verified that, finding his last name would get a whole lot easier. It could be as simple as running the plate on the car that picked him up.

Beyond that . . . things could get trickier.

But for now, he had a positive development to share with Kate.

"Big news, huh?" Dev paused outside his office.

It took a second for Connor to realize he meant Nikki news, not case news. "Yeah."

"Hard to picture, though. Nikki with a baby . . ." Dev shook his head.

"She's had plenty of practice being a mother since she rescued her brother from that den of iniquity she grew up in and gave him a real home."

"True. But a baby . . . that's a whole different ball game."

"I have no doubt she's up to the challenge."

"Yeah. She does handle difficult situations—and people—well." One side of Dev's mouth hitched up. "Speaking of challenges . . . how goes the boy-returned-from-the-dead case?"

Connor waved the slip of paper. "I have a lead."

"No kidding? I assumed that was dead in the water . . . forgive the less-than-tasteful pun."

"I can forgive the pun. Eating the last of the coffee cake . . . not so much. That was going to be my lunch."

"At four o'clock?"

"The two-hour meeting ran five hours. The CEO's been getting death threats in the wake of recent union negotiations and wants to beef up in-house security for an upcoming trip to some of his facilities. Get ready to clear your calendar in mid-August. It's going to be a three-man job. As for my case—it isn't dead yet. I'll fill you in as soon as I know more. In the meantime, I need to update my client."

"Not exactly hardship duty . . . especially if you do it in person." Dev elbowed him as he brushed by into his office.

Connor let the jibe pass—because he agreed. Too bad this was business that could be handled over the phone. *Would* be handled over the phone with any other client. So to keep things professional, he'd deliver the update from his desk.

On the bright side, however, if things progressed on this case, there'd be plenty of opportunities to see Kate again.

And if they hit a dead end . . . maybe he'd find a reason to see her, anyway.

Kate closed the notebook on her lap, capped her pen, and smiled at the young woman seated across from her in the role-play corner of her office. "You did great, Sarah. Excellent eye contact, positive body language and facial expressions, and articulate answers. You've been practicing."

"Every day." Sarah Lange started to tuck her hair behind her ear, caught herself, and rested her elbows on the arms of her chair instead, keeping her posture relaxed and open. "I'm trying to pay attention to every detail. I want this job."

"I know." And not just for the money. After years of putting up with abuse from the husband she'd finally divorced, she could also use an infusion of self-esteem. "I think you have an excellent chance of getting it too. You've come a long way in the past eight weeks, and you have all the right qualifications."

"I'm not aiming too high, am I?" The words were laced with trepidation.

"Absolutely not." Kate kept her tone gentle but firm. "Art history might not be the most marketable college degree, but you've been a docent at the art museum for two years and you were the office manager for an art supply business."

"The art museum was a volunteer job, and the manager position was a long time ago." She lowered her voice and glanced at the four-year-old cherub playing with her doll in the opposite corner of the office. "Before . . . Steve."

At least she didn't flinch when she said his name anymore. Now, an undercurrent of anger colored the words. Better than fear, but she still had a ways to go. As did her too-silent daughter.

"Volunteer work counts, and you have outstanding references from both the art museum and your previous job, even though that was eight years ago. The gallery manager would be lucky to get you as his administrative assistant." Kate had said all those things before, but with Sarah's interview scheduled for nine tomorrow morning, it couldn't hurt to repeat them again as a confidence booster.

"I wouldn't have gotten this far without you. You not only coached me through all these practice interviews, you also polished up my résumé and found me this great lead. I just hope it works out."

"I have every confidence it will."

Sarah stood and reached for her purse. "Thanks again for squeezing me in for an emergency session today. I'm sorry I kept you so late."

"No worries. I'm often here far later than this." Kate rose, and while Sarah collected her belongings, she crossed to the little girl and dropped down beside her. "I like your dolly's dress today, Isabel. Yellow is such a happy color. It reminds me of sunshine."

The girl looked up at her with wide eyes that had seen too

much, her expression solemn. "I had a yellow dress once too. But it got torn, and my daddy threw it away."

Kate's throat constricted. Thank God Sarah had sought counseling for both of them.

"Come on, honey. It's time for dinner. Why don't we stop at Panera and you can get some of that macaroni and cheese you love? How does that sound?"

The girl's face brightened as she took Sarah's hand, but an undercurrent of apprehension colored her words. "Will you stay with me, Mommy?"

"Of course." Sarah sent Kate a worried look as she hugged her daughter.

Kate gave her client's arm a reassuring squeeze, a silent reminder that the clinginess would pass and counseling would help. But it would require patience. Damage to the psyche often took far longer to heal than damage to the body. She'd learned that in school, saw it demonstrated every day in the clients she served, and had experienced it firsthand. Loss, abuse, fear, anger, grief—they all took a heavy toll.

She followed the mother and daughter to the door. At six o'clock, the small suite was silent, the staff and volunteers gone, the individual offices dark. "Will you call me as soon as the interview is over?"

"The minute I walk out the door." Sarah held out her hand. "And no matter what happens with this job, thank you for making me feel competent, capable, and respected again."

"You're all those things . . . and more. Now you two have a nice dinner—and make time for some hugs tonight."

She watched them walk away hand in hand, then shut the door and wandered back to her office. It was late, but why hurry to leave? It wasn't as if she had anything exciting planned for the evening. Review some budget paperwork. Prep for another role-play tomorrow. Finish the presentation on New Start she'd be delivering on Friday at a women's club luncheon. There were no hugs on *her* agenda.

Fighting back a wave of melancholy, she straightened her shoulders, pulled her purse out of her desk drawer, retrieved her keys, and fished for her cell. She was through with pity parties. Once had been enough.

Cell in hand, she scrolled through voice mail. Only one new message, from four-ten. Not long after she'd started her session with Sarah.

She keyed in her access code and pressed the phone to her ear.

"Kate, Connor Sullivan. I have some news. Give me a call on my cell when you have a minute." He recited the number, and she grabbed a pen to jot it down.

The line clicked, and she took a steadying breath. Telling herself not to get her hopes up, she tapped in his number.

He answered on the first ring. "Sullivan."

Her respiration ticked up. "This is Kate Marshall. Sorry for the after-hours call, but I just got out of a meeting and found your message. It sounded promising."

"Promising might be a little too optimistic, but I do have a new lead."

As he filled her in on the latest developments, Kate's spirits rose—and even his final warning that they could still hit a dead end didn't deflate them.

"So what's next?"

"Surveillance. My plan is to watch the daycare center tomorrow during the morning drop-off period and hope I spot the boy from the mall security screen grab."

"I thought you said the image was fuzzy?"

"It is. Those kinds of shots usually are. But it's clear enough to get me in the ballpark, and I'll take photos of any boys who look similar. We can sort through them later and see if we have a match."

"Would it help if I went along? I might be able to rule some out immediately." Even as she made the offer, Kate's brow puckered. Where on earth had that come from?

Based on the silence on the other end of the line, Connor was trying to figure out the same thing.

Her cheeks warmed, and she lightened her tone in an attempt to smooth over the awkward moment. "Sorry. I'm sure the last thing you want is an amateur hanging around while you're trying to do your work."

"Actually, your offer has some merit." He spoke slowly, as if he was mulling over the idea. "As our office manager reminded me, a lot of young boys are blond. Having someone along who saw the child in person could make the process more efficient. But it would be an early start. The daycare opens for drop-off at six. I plan to be in a discreet position nearby no later than five-forty-five and hang around until nine."

"That's not a problem. I'm an early riser, and I can come to the office late tomorrow. My first meeting isn't until ten."

"Then why don't I pick you up at five-thirty in the parking lot at your office? When we're finished, I can drop you off back there."

"Sounds good."

"Two pieces of advice. First, dress casual and cool. I can't leave the engine and air conditioner running the whole time or the car will overheat. Second, don't drink much before you leave your house. Once we're in place, we'll be in the car for the duration. We could miss the boy if we have to make an emergency bathroom run."

"Got it."

"Turn in early, and I'll see you in the morning."

When the phone went dead, Kate dropped it in her purse and stood. Connor was right. Since she'd have to be up by quarter to five, she needed to head home, fix a quick dinner, and go to bed with the sun.

But as she exited the New Start offices, she had a feeling sleep was going to be elusive. Because while Connor had accomplished more than she'd even dared hope when she'd sat in his office on Monday and poured out her bizarre story, they were reaching the end of the line. If this lead didn't pan out, she'd be back where she'd been on Friday.

Wondering about the identity of the little blond boy who looked enough like Kevin to be her son.

6

This wasn't the smartest move he'd ever made.

As Connor maneuvered the Taurus under the Golden Arches in the lot next door to STL Academy, he slanted a quick glance at Kate. He'd told her to dress for the weather, but he hadn't expected a tank top that revealed such a wide expanse of creamy skin, a skirt that exposed a long length of shapely leg, and a ponytail that highlighted her classic profile.

If there'd been a collar on his T-shirt, he'd have been tempted to run his finger underneath to loosen it.

So much for staying cool on his end—and the sun hadn't even peeked above the dawn-tinted horizon yet.

Focus on the job instead of the client, Sullivan.

Right.

He chose a parking spot that would give them both a view of the front door of the daycare center, positioning the car so he could lower his dark-tinted window and take quick shots of potential subjects. After he used the automatic controls to open the two backseat windows, Kate's window, and the sunroof, he shut off the engine.

Despite the early hour, humid air flooded the car in seconds.

He sent her a rueful look. "Sorry. Doing surveillance in the heat—or cold—is one of the less glamorous aspects of being a PI."

"It's not too bad yet." She regarded his window. "You're leaving that closed?"

"To keep out prying eyes. I'll lower it partway to take pictures—after the camera's in front of my face."

"Seems very clandestine."

"Careful."

She conceded his point with a bob of her head, then motioned to the fast-food restaurant off to the side behind them. "At least this lot was conveniently located for our purposes."

"Yeah. I scoped the area out on my way home last night, and believe me, this is better than some of the places I've had to hole up." Far better. He reached back, grabbed two cases from the backseat, and handed her one. "Binoculars. Go ahead and adjust them to your eyes."

"There are a few cars pulling into the lot already." She gestured toward the daycare center as she opened the case.

"That's why I wanted to get here early." He removed his own binoculars from the case, set them on the console between their seats, and reached into the back again for his camera.

She fitted the binoculars to her eyes as he took the digital camera out of its case, twisted on the 100–300 mm zoom, and verified that the glare filter was in place. The last thing he wanted was a beam of sunlight bouncing off the glass in the lens. A careless sniper could lose his life that way—and a PI could lose the tactical advantage of covert surveillance. Once you were made, the job got a whole lot harder.

Not going to happen on his watch.

"These are really powerful." Kate lowered the binoculars and inspected the camera. "And that's an impressive piece of equipment."

"Let's hope we need it." He set it beside him. "Here's how

I'd like to work this. We'll both watch the arrivals with our binoculars. If either of us has any suspicion a particular child might be the boy you saw, I'll snap some shots. We can evaluate them later."

"Sounds reasonable."

"Then get set, because the rush is about to start." He motioned toward the parking lot in front of the center, where cars were beginning to disgorge adults toting babies, toddlers, and young children.

Kate leaned forward, planted her right elbow on the dash, and angled sideways to aim the binoculars at the entrance. That posture was going to get old fast, and she'd end up with a crick in her neck, but there wasn't much he could do about it. He needed his window positioned for photography.

As silence fell in the car, Connor put his own binoculars to use and settled in for the duration of the rush period.

Ten minutes passed.

"Blond boy at seven o'clock."

He felt Kate shift beside him as he spoke. "That's not him."

Several more minutes ticked by as the sun rose and the pink hue of the sky began to morph into blue.

"Another blond boy at eleven o'clock." Kate's tone was taut. "I'm waiting for him to move into a spot where I can see him better . . . he's the right height, and . . . no. It's not him." Disappointment etched her voice. "Wrong hair color. And he's heavier than the boy I saw."

For the next hour and a half, as the sun continued to climb and sweat beaded on his forehead, Connor counted ten boys who could have been the youngster in the video grab. He would have taken photos of them all, except Kate was certain eight of the ten weren't the boy she'd seen—and she was very skeptical about the other two.

As daycare traffic began to slow around seven-thirty, she set the binoculars in her lap, rotated her neck, and brushed back some strands of hair that were clinging to her forehead.

"How are you holding up?" He lowered his own binoculars and sized her up. The faint shadows under her eyes, hidden earlier in the dim morning light, told him she hadn't slept well last night. Or, more likely, hadn't slept well since she'd spotted the boy on Friday. Faint parallel lines scored her brow. The hair at her temples was damp, and the skin above the scooped neck of her top was glistening. His attention lingered there a moment too long before he snapped his gaze up. Thank goodness she was still focused on the daycare center.

"I'm fine. I just wish we had more to show for our efforts."

He fumbled for the lid of the cooler on the floor behind her seat, pulled out a bottle of water, and handed it to her. "He could be one of the later arrivals, depending on his parents' work schedules."

Bottle in hand, she gave the water a wary look. "I thought you said not to drink."

"I said not to drink too much. You need to stay hydrated. Just pace yourself. We only have another hour and a half." He pulled a bottle of water out for himself, twisted off the cap, and took a long chug.

After a brief hesitation, she did the same.

"Better?"

"Much." She recapped the lid and set the bottle in the cup holder between them. "Another arrival." Indicating the daycare center, she picked up her binoculars and went back to work.

By eight-thirty, the traffic had slowed to a trickle, and she once again sank back and took another long swig of water, the subtle slump of her shoulders communicating her dejection more eloquently than words.

Connor had never believed in creating false hope—but while her pessimism might be justified in a few days, he didn't want her to give up yet.

"You know, it's possible we have the right place but the wrong day."

Her head swiveled toward him. "What do you mean?"

"Maybe the blond boy you saw at the mall only attends three days a week. Or his parents might have kept him home today for some reason. I'll download the photos I took as soon as I get back to the office and send them to you, but even if neither boy is the one you saw, I don't think we should give this up after one try. Depending on your budget, I'd like to try again tomorrow and Monday."

"Money isn't an issue. As I said before, John had a large insurance policy, and my expenses are minimal." A tiny flicker of hope brightened her eyes, tempered by a hefty dose of caution. "After getting such a solid lead, I'd like to believe he'll still show up. But do you really think there's a chance he will . . . or are you just trying to let me down easy?"

He met her gaze straight on. "Letting people down easy is part of my job. Wasting clients' money isn't. If I thought this was over, I'd tell you. Our chances do diminish with every day that passes, but I'd prefer not to write this off yet."

She gave a slow nod. "I appreciate your candor . . . and your willingness to continue. But I've got early meetings both days."

"Not a problem. I'll just take a lot more pictures—and suffer through the heat alone."

"It is getting steamy, isn't it?" She plucked at the fabric of her tank top, which was now clinging to her trim midriff.

Steamy was a good word.

"Another car." She lifted her binoculars again.

Forcing himself to look away, he did the same.

"It's a little girl." Kate sank back on the seat. "And there's no one else in sight."

He kept the binoculars pressed to his face, buying himself a few more moments to regain control. Strange. He'd often dealt with beautiful women during his Secret Service career, and on occasion as a PI. Yet he'd never been tempted to cross the line between business and pleasure.

Until now.

The simple truth was, Kate Marshall intrigued him. She was a smart, determined, courageous woman with a generous heart. A survivor, with a gritty strength concealed beneath a deceptively fragile-looking exterior. From all indications, she'd also been a loving, loyal wife and a devoted mother who even now was fighting for her family despite enormous odds. She was the kind of woman who deserved to receive the same absolute commitment and priority she gave to the people and the responsibilities in her life.

And he could offer her those on the job.

He was also ready to offer them to the right woman on a personal level. Had been ready for quite a while, in fact—since Lisa had thrown him one of the biggest curves of his life and forced him to straighten out his own priorities.

Slowly he lowered the binoculars and turned to Kate.

She could be the right woman.

It was too soon to be thinking along those lines, though. He knew that. But one thing for sure—she was the first woman in five years who'd prompted him to even consider making the kind of commitment a serious relationship required.

When she looked over at him, he realized the silence between them had stretched too long.

"We'll stick it out until nine, but it seems like most of the action is over."

"Yeah." She scanned the daycare center again, smothering a yawn. "Sorry."

"Don't be. It was an early morning . . . and it sounds like you had a long day yesterday, if you were still at the office at six o'clock."

She lifted one shoulder. "That's par for the course for me. I expect you put in long hours too."

"Not as long as in my previous job."

She tilted her head. "May I ask how you happened to become a Secret Service agent? That's an unusual occupation."

"My older brother was a big influence."

"Is he in law enforcement?"

"No. The Secret Service was always his goal, but he—" Connor swallowed. "He died when he was twenty. Leukemia."

Sympathy flooded her eyes. "I'm so sorry."

He gave a stiff shrug. "It was a long time ago."

"But a hurt like that never goes away." Her voice was soft and tinged by a kindred sadness.

"No." Nor the repercussions.

Time to change the subject. Opening up to virtual strangers wasn't part of his DNA.

Yet the words that came out were still about Joe. "He would have been a great agent. As far back as I can remember, he was always rescuing hurt animals and protecting other kids—including me—from bullies. He was strong, but he had a gentle spirit and a passion for justice." The last word rasped, and he stopped.

After a few moments, Kate spoke again. "Did you have any other siblings?"

"No."

"That must have made the loss especially hard on you and your parents."

"Yeah." He could have left it at that. Didn't. "Too hard."

She loosened the cap on her water bottle. "What do you mean?"

Man, this was getting way too personal.

But still he continued.

"They couldn't handle the loss. They blamed each other for not noticing the symptoms soon enough, for making bad decisions about treatment, for choosing the wrong doctors. They ended up divorcing when I was sixteen, a year after Joe died. The whole thing was very bitter. I divided my time between the two of them until I went away to college, but things were never the same."

"And then you did what your brother had planned to do— you became a Secret Service agent." Her words were soft, her expression pensive.

He shook his head. "I wasn't living his dream, if that's what you're thinking. Once he planted the idea in my mind, it became my goal too."

"I didn't mean to imply it was vicarious. There's nothing wrong with being inspired by other people or sharing dreams." She lifted her hand, as if she intended to touch his arm, then drew it back and fiddled with the cap on the bottle instead. "So was being a Secret Service agent exciting?"

"More like high-stress and all-consuming. The glamor and excitement are vastly overrated."

"How long did you stay?"

"Nine years."

"I would guess that's a career job for most people." She studied him. "Did you enjoy it?"

Odd. No one had ever asked him that before. People always assumed he had. Who wouldn't enjoy such an elite, high-profile job? Yet Kate had picked up some nuance others had missed— proving once again she was sharp.

He transferred his gaze back to the daycare center as he formulated a response. "It had its moments."

"But not enough of them, or you'd still be there."

He glanced back at her. "Putting your master's in psychology to work?"

She arched an eyebrow. "You investigated my background?"

"Standard practice with new clients. We want to make sure

our services aren't being used for illegal purposes. You came out squeaky clean, by the way."

"Nice to know. But you didn't really answer my question."

He added tenacious to her list of attributes as he framed his reply, choosing his words with care. "I liked the job—a lot. The first six years, I worked in field offices on a variety of assignments, from global credit card fraud to busting counterfeiting rings in Colombia and Peru. The last three years, I was on the vice president's protective detail."

"Impressive."

"Also very demanding. The 24/7 schedule and constant, often spur-of-the-moment travel left no time for anything else." He surveyed the daycare center again. All quiet. "One day I had an epiphany of sorts and decided to make some changes in my life—and in my priorities. Cal and Dev were ready to add a third partner . . . and the rest is history. Now why don't you finish that water before you dehydrate?"

Picking up his own bottle, he hoped she'd get the hint and back off. He'd already told her more in five minutes than he told most people in five years.

Message received. After removing the cap, she tipped her head back and finished off the water, giving him a perfect view of the graceful line of her neck.

He gulped the rest of his, but the lukewarm liquid did nothing to cool him off.

This time he definitely intended to change the subject.

"So how come you worked late last night?"

Taking his cue, she gave him a recap of her late meeting, then answered his questions about New Start as their surveillance gig wound down and he drove her back to her office.

Once in the parking lot, he circled around to her car so she could retrieve her change of clothes.

"Thanks for letting me tag along." She picked up her purse from the floor and dug her keys out.

"It was very helpful. I would have taken a lot more pictures—and wasted both our time reviewing them—if you hadn't been there. Let me get the door for you." He started to open his own door, but an impatient honk from behind stopped him.

Kate looked over her shoulder. "I think we're blocking the way. I've got it."

She slid out, then opened the back door and retrieved her daypack. "Will you email me the shots you took of the two boys, just in case?"

"Yes. As soon as I get back to the office. But I'm going to swing by my apartment and shower first."

She sighed. "I wish I had time to do the same."

Kate.

Shower.

He tried to erase that image from his mind as she closed the door and hurried toward the entrance, perky little skirt swishing, daypack slung over her shoulder.

The guy behind him honked again.

Yeah, yeah, he was leaving.

He put the car in gear and headed for the exit, casting one more look in the rearview mirror as she disappeared through the door—but he hoped not from his life, no matter the outcome of this case. Because he wanted to see a lot more of her. Any woman who could get him to open up as much as he had today had potential.

As for the attraction that was beginning to sizzle—on his end, anyway—that had potential as well. Lots of potential.

And if, by chance, it led to a more serious connection . . . he'd learned his lesson.

This time, he wasn't going to blow it.

That was as good as it was going to get.

Expelling a frustrated breath, Kate gave her hair one final brush and stepped back from the mirror in the ladies' room. The car had been a lot hotter and stickier than she'd expected, considering the early hour. Too bad she couldn't have rescheduled her ten o'clock client meeting and run home for a shower, as Connor had.

Connor.

Shower.

Her heart skipped a beat.

Frowning, she shoved the brush back into her daypack and yanked the zipper closed. What was wrong with her these days? A new romance wasn't on her agenda—now, or perhaps ever. She still loved John. Would always love him.

Yet something strange had happened in Connor's car this morning. The air had practically sizzled—and not because of the hot weather. Maybe it was the intimacy of the confined space. Or the quiet dawn hours that seemed to foster the sharing of secrets.

Or it might have been the man himself.

She leaned against the counter, rubbed at the twin lines above her nose, and faced the truth.

It was curtain number three.

Connor Sullivan rocked.

The man had been impressive in his jacket, tie, and crisp shirt on Monday at the office, radiating competence, confidence, and professionalism—not to mention good looks. He'd been no less professional today, even if he'd exchanged the more formal attire for a black T-shirt that hugged his broad chest and a pair of worn jeans that sat low on his lean hips and hugged his long, muscular legs. But he'd also exuded an appealing masculinity

94

that had sent a tingle of adrenaline surging through her—and given her the courage to ask questions about his background that were none of her business. Questions that had taken him off guard. Questions he hadn't necessarily liked.

But he'd answered them . . . and Connor Sullivan didn't strike her as a man who did anything he didn't want to do.

So why had he responded?

Was it because he, too, had felt that sizzle of attraction?

Yes.

Even as the definitive answer echoed in her mind, her stomach fluttered.

Not good.

How could she feel attracted to another man if she still loved her husband?

When the answer proved elusive, she began to pace in the tiny ladies' room. Fortunately, the problem shouldn't be an immediate issue. From what she'd observed, Connor wasn't the type to let his emotions rule while working a case. He was too professional for that. This was a man who'd guarded the vice president. You didn't get handed that kind of responsibility without being disciplined, focused, and—in keeping with the Secret Service motto—worthy of trust and confidence. He'd toe the line while the case was active.

But if he'd felt the zip of electricity in the car this morning as strongly as she had, once their professional relationship was over, that same focused discipline might be redirected toward her.

Oh, man.

She stopped pacing and pressed her forehead against the cold tile above the light switch.

Unfortunately, it did nothing to cool her down.

A knock sounded inches from her ear, and she jerked back, heart hammering as she flipped the lock and pulled the door open.

Pauline stood on the other side, her expression quizzical. "Are you all right? You've been in here awhile."

"Yes." Her cheeks warmed as she held up the daypack. "Sorry for the delay. I had to clean up and change clothes."

"I know. I saw you dash in here fifteen minutes ago. Are you sure you feel all right? You have circles under your eyes and you're a little flushed."

"I'm fine." When another volunteer passed by and gave her a curious look too, she took Pauline's arm and guided her toward her office. This was why she kept her personal life to herself at work. If people knew too much, the staff gossiped and things got messy. At least Pauline was discreet.

Once inside, Kate shut the door. "My PI had a lead on the little boy, and I went with him to do some surveillance early this morning. I didn't sleep well, and I've been up since four-thirty. Plus, we were in a car without air-conditioning."

"Ah. That would explain why you seem a bit discombobulated. Any success?"

"No." She already knew neither of the youngsters Connor had photographed was the boy she'd seen at the mall. "But he's going to go back for a couple more days."

"Are you tagging along again?"

"Can't. I have meetings." She stowed her daypack in the credenza behind her desk. "He'll take photos of anyone who resembles the boy and run them by me."

Pauline perched on the edge of her desk. "So now that you've spent some extended time with this man, what do you think of him?"

She lifted one shoulder in what she hoped came across as nonchalance. "He's very nice. Empathetic, strong communication skills, an excellent listener. And he has a remarkable ability to instill trust and confidence. I suppose that could be a result of his training, but I have a feeling it's innate. He's one of those

96

people who makes a very strong impression and is hard to forget, if you know what I mean."

"Yes, I do." Pauline's eyes twinkled. "To be honest, I was looking more for a professional evaluation. But this was much more enlightening. I take it the man's not married?"

Once more, heat flooded Kate's cheeks. "No—but don't get any ideas, Pauline."

"Like what?"

Kate massaged the bridge of her nose. "Look, I know what you're thinking. And yes, Connor Sullivan is an attractive, appealing man. But my heart still belongs to John. He was the love of a lifetime—and a woman doesn't get that lucky twice."

"Don't be too sure. My sister married again several years after she was widowed, and both her husbands were wonderful men who claimed their own spot in her heart, neither taking anything away from the other. She never thought she'd find love a second time, either."

"But I'm not in the market for a second marriage."

"Neither was she. That's how it happens sometimes. We have one plan for our life, but God often has another."

"Not this time, Pauline. I still love John."

"And you always will. But the ache does ease in time. You can trust me on that." She crossed to the door and grasped the knob. "I don't know how the story that began last Friday in the mall will end, but even if the door closes on finding that boy, perhaps God's opened a window. Think about it."

As Pauline exited, Kate moved behind her desk and sank into her chair. She had only a few minutes before her client arrived, and she needed to prep, not ponder Pauline's comment.

But even with the file in front of her, she couldn't concentrate.

Was the older woman right? Could this whole sequence of events be leading her not to Kevin but to a new direction in her life?

Her stomach rumbled, and she pressed a hand against it. She'd had no appetite in the wee hours of the morning, and Connor hadn't suggested stopping for breakfast on the way back to the office. Maybe she could scrounge up some food in the break room, if their receptionist had brought in one of the home-baked treats she liked to share with the volunteers and staff.

She rose and headed down the hall. A quick bite would take the edge off her physical hunger.

But it wasn't going to do a thing to fill the empty spot in her heart that now ached with a different kind of hunger, thanks to a tall, handsome PI who'd stirred up a yearning that would be far more difficult to satisfy.

7

Diane tiptoed down the hall in Greg's house, cracked the bedroom door a bit wider, and peeked in.

Todd was still sleeping, covers thrown back, face flushed, hugging that cute bear he'd made at the birthday party last week. Poor kid. He'd been passed out most of the morning. The summer flu was no picnic, but hopefully the bug would pass in a day or two—for his sake.

From a selfish perspective, however, she wouldn't mind if he needed looking after for a few more days. It gave her something worthwhile to do—plus a chance to see Greg. The fact he'd called to ask for her help when Todd got sick last night had to mean he cared for her, didn't it?

Or maybe he'd just been desperate. Being new in town, he didn't have a whole lot of resources at his disposal to deal with a sick child—and she was handy.

Spirits plummeting, she closed Todd's door and wandered back down the hall toward the kitchen. What would she do if he dumped her? In the two short months they'd been dating, he'd banished the darkness from her life—though he had no idea how dark it had been. Sharing the story of her husband's philandering and abuse hadn't been easy, but admitting the extent of his ill-treatment had been impossible. The shame was too great. Only the women in her support group knew those stories in detail, and they understood the hold Rich had exerted on her. But Greg, with his kind heart and gentle ways, would think she was crazy for staying with a man who reveled in creating terror.

He might be right.

Except she wasn't crazy anymore. After one particularly nasty attack had put a support group friend in the hospital, her fear of staying with Rich had finally surpassed her fear of leaving.

And she was never going back.

Grabbing a can of soup from the cabinet, she tried to apply logic to the situation with Greg. It was possible she was over-reacting to his withdrawal this past week. He'd complained of stomach problems when he'd cancelled their standing pizza date last Saturday, so he could be fighting the same bug that had felled Todd.

On the other hand, if he was well enough to go to work every day, why couldn't he squeeze in a few minutes for her? She'd tried to make it convenient for him by offering to drop by with cookies. Accommodation was her middle name, thanks to the survival skills she'd developed during her years with Rich.

She jammed the chicken noodle soup can into the electric opener and watched the blade slice through the lid. At least her ex was out of her life now. Had been for six months. And while the adjustment had been challenging, her bruises had healed, her fear was receding, and her outlook was improving.

Thanks in large part to Greg.

After dumping the contents of the can into a bowl, she crossed to the microwave, set the soup inside, pressed the reheat button, and leaned against the counter.

It was strange how life worked. She'd been as low as a person could get the day Greg had offered to change her flat tire in the grocery store parking lot. If he hadn't had Todd in tow, she'd have refused, but the little boy was a charmer and they'd been in a public place. It didn't get much safer than that.

And Greg had been so polite. Almost shy. A widower, she'd learned, as he went about the task. And when he'd asked her if she'd like to meet him sometime for coffee—and promised to bring his son along—she'd taken the leap . . . and never looked back.

Until these past few days.

Her spirits drooped as uncertainty once again reared its ugly head. Was he pulling away because he'd found someone new, despite his claim to the contrary? He'd seemed sincere . . . but Rich had too, at the beginning. Had she done something to displease him? Made some mistake? Crossed some line she didn't even know existed? Brought this on herself by . . .

No!

Sudden anger coursing through her, she strode toward the cabinet, retrieved a glass, and slammed the door. Whatever Greg's problem, it wasn't about her. Just like it hadn't been about her with Rich. She hadn't done anything wrong, then or now. She wasn't going to play the victim again, wasn't going to . . .

A muffled summons from her cell phone sounded inside her purse, and she stalked across the room. She'd made too much progress to let any guy control how she felt about herself, no matter how much she liked him. With or without Greg Sanders, she'd be just fine. She had a whole new network of allies now apart from him.

And this was one of them, according to caller ID. Her support group friends might be new, but they were loyal.

She put the phone to her ear. "Hi, Sarah. What's up?"

"I got it!"

Diane frowned, trying to switch gears as her friend's almost palpable excitement came over the line. "Got what?"

"The job! At the art gallery, as administrative assistant to the manager. He offered me the position before I even left!"

Everything clicked. Sarah had shared the news about her upcoming interview at the support group last week, then called over the weekend to talk about it. Diane had been more than happy to offer encouragement. Bad as her own situation had been, Sarah's had been worse.

Diane set the glass down and leaned back against the counter. "I knew you would. You have the smarts, plus all the right qualifications."

"That's what Kate kept telling me. But I couldn't have done it without her. She's amazing. If you ever decide to get that job you keep talking about, you have to go to New Start. And they have a sliding fee scale, if money's an issue."

It wasn't. Rich was paying her enough to support the upscale lifestyle she'd become accustomed to as his wife—but she'd never shared how well off she was with the other members of the group. Some were financially secure, like her. Others were barely scraping by, Sarah among them. Proving that abuse knew no socioeconomic boundaries.

"Believe it or not, I've been giving that more thought in the past few weeks." Being a mother would be a fine full-time job, and she was growing very fond of Todd, but if things went south with Greg, she wasn't going to sit around the rest of her life waiting for some other guy to come along. She had a college degree; there was no reason she couldn't use it. "The idle life was fine while I decompressed, but I'm beginning to get bored."

"Then take the plunge. It worked for me! Let me know if you want Kate's number."

"I will. But today let's focus on you. When do you start?"

"Monday. It sounds as if the last assistant was seriously incompetent and left the office in complete disarray. No one can find a thing."

"In that case, we have to celebrate this weekend. Why don't I treat you and Isabel to dinner on Saturday night?" Since Greg hadn't said anything about getting together, and Todd was sick, why not make her own plans? Send a message that she didn't intend to hold her Saturday nights open for him just in case he decided he wanted to spend them with her.

"You don't have to do that, Diane."

"I want to—and I know the perfect place."

When she mentioned the high-end restaurant, Sarah gasped. "That's really expensive."

"Rich is paying for it."

The other woman gave a soft laugh. "In that case . . ."

"Be ready. Six o'clock. I'll pick you up."

"I will. And thank you."

"Not necessary. Besides, you can do the same for me if I decide to get a job."

"That's a promise."

The microwave began to beep, and Diane pushed off from the counter. "I've got to run. Congratulations again . . . and see you Saturday."

As they said their good-byes, a muffled cry filtered down the hall. She couldn't make out Todd's words, but he sounded scared.

Leaving the phone on the counter, she half jogged toward his room.

His cries grew louder as she approached, and when she paused at the threshold, she found him thrashing on the bed, the covers bunched in his fists.

"No! Come back!" Distress choked his voice as he muttered a string of unintelligible words, legs kicking, arms flailing.

This had to be one of those bad dreams Greg had mentioned.

As she crossed toward the bed, Diane wiped her palms down her slacks. Was there a correct way to wake a child from a nightmare? If there was, she'd never heard of it, and she had zip experience with kids.

Dropping down on the side of the bed, she reached out a

tentative hand and stroked Todd's arm. "It's okay, honey. Shh. I'm here."

He continued to thrash.

Now what?

·Music. Perhaps an old familiar lullaby would soothe him. Too bad she didn't know any except "Rock-a-bye Baby," a song for infants. But it would have to do.

Very softly, she began to hum the tune.

At first, Todd didn't respond. But slowly, as she continued to stroke his arm and croon the melody, he grew calmer. At last, with a shuddering sigh, he opened his eyes and peered up through the shadows created by the room-darkening shades. "Are you . . . the lady from the escalator?"

She stared at him. Where in the world had that question come from?

"It's Diane, sweetie. Your dad's friend." She placed a hand on his forehead. Still too warm.

His face sagged. "I thought you were her. She was here a minute ago."

"No, honey, no one's here but us. You were having a dream."

"Are you sure?" He raised up on one elbow, once more growing agitated as he scanned the room.

"Very sure." She pressed him back onto the pillow. "Sometimes our dreams seem real, but they're all make-believe."

"Not the lady! She's real. I saw her at the mall!"

Why not play along? Better to keep him calm and quiet. "Well, we can dream about real people too. Is she a friend of yours?"

He felt around for his Cardinals bear. "I don't think so. Dad says we don't know her, but she looked right at me, like she knew who I was." He hugged the bear close. "She was pretty and seemed nice. I was trying hard in my dream to run to her, but people got in my way and hands kept pulling me back. I wish I could see her again." His voice quavered.

"Maybe you will someday." Even as she reassured him, a tingle of unease ran through her. Wasn't it odd for a young child to be so fixated on a chance encounter with a stranger? She'd have to run this by Greg. He might have an explanation for it.

In the meantime, diversionary tactics were in order.

"I heated up some chicken noodle soup. Why don't you rest while I go get it?"

Instead of responding as she rose, he snuggled deeper under the covers with his bear.

Once back in the kitchen, she pulled the soup out of the microwave, filled the glass with water, and set both on a tray along with a few crackers and the bottle of children's aspirin.

Todd remained curled up under the covers when she returned, so she set the tray on the bedside stand and crossed to the window, raising the shade a few inches to let in some sunlight. She turned to find him watching her.

"Feeling better now that you're wide awake?" She circled the bed toward the nightstand.

He scrubbed at his eyes. "No. My legs and arms hurt."

"That's because you have the flu. Some soup might help."

He made a face. "I'm not hungry."

"Would you try a little if I sit here and keep you company?"

"I might throw up."

"I don't think you have to worry about that. If you had that kind of flu, you'd have thrown up already."

He gave her a wary look. "Are you sure? 'Cause I got the flu in Montana last year, and throwing up is yucky."

"You're right, it is. I'll tell you what. Why don't you try a few spoons, and if your stomach starts to feel sick, you can stop."

Before he could offer any further protests, she helped him scoot up and arranged two pillows behind him. Then she set a third one on his lap, placed the tray on top, and sat beside him.

He picked up the spoon and poked at a few of the noodles. "The lady on the escalator had hair the same color as mine."

So much for her diversionary tactics.

"A lot of people have blond hair. I do too." From a bottle, but that was true of most blondes.

He eyed her as he slurped up a spoonful of soup. "Yours is different than mine."

She couldn't argue with that. His was the color of burnished wheat, while hers had a brassy sheen. Chalk one up for his observation skills.

"That's true. There are a lot of different colors of blond."

He chased a noodle around the bowl. "Did you know I'm adopted?"

At the abrupt change of subject, she blinked. "Um, yes. Your father mentioned that to me once. But didn't you get a great dad?"

"Yeah." He stirred the soup. "Sometimes I wish I had a mom too, though."

As she tried to come up with an appropriate response, the landline rang.

Saved by the bell.

"You keep eating while I grab the phone—and drink some water too."

She dashed down the hall, snatching up the phone on the third ring when Greg's name appeared in caller ID. "Hi."

"You sound out of breath."

"I was in Todd's room, trying to persuade him to eat some soup."

"How is he? I've been worried sick all morning."

"He's been sleeping a lot, and he's still running a temperature, but when I left him just now to grab the phone, he was eating. That's a positive sign."

A sigh came over the line. "I don't know. Maybe I should call the doctor. I don't want to take any chances."

"If you want my opinion, you aren't. Not that I'm an expert on children, but he's got all the classic flu symptoms, and a friend of mine's daughter had a very similar virus last week. My guess is he'll be feeling much better in a day or so. And I can stay with him again on Monday if he isn't ready to go back to daycare. He's not a demanding patient."

"I hate to impose."

"You're not. Honestly . . . I don't mind doing a favor for friends. I like Todd—as well as his father." She held her breath, hoping he wouldn't reject her overture.

"I'm glad to hear that—because his father likes you too."

At the warmth in his tone, she exhaled. Unless the man was a great actor, he was being sincere. "Nice to hear."

"I told you, Diane . . . things will calm down soon, and we'll pick up where we left off. It's just been a rough week."

"Yeah, it has. By the way, Todd had one of those bad dreams you mentioned a few days ago too."

Silence.

When Greg finally spoke, his tone was cautious. "What kind of dream?"

"Nothing to be concerned about. It may even have been fever-induced. It was about some woman on an escalator. He was quite agitated at first, but he's fine now."

This time the silence on the line stretched so long she wondered if they'd been disconnected.

"Greg?"

"Yeah. I'm here."

Her fingers tightened on the phone. Those three words held an odd combination of emotions. Frustration. Anger. And . . . apprehension? She wasn't certain about that last one, but the first two were right on. After living with Rich all those years, she'd become an expert at discerning nuances. Her survival had depended on those precious few seconds of warning before he exploded, which gave her a chance to prepare for his blows.

"Has he had this dream before?" She did her best to keep her tone casual and conversational.

"A few times. I'm sure it will go away eventually. The sooner the better, though, as far as I'm concerned. It always upsets him. Did he say anything else about it?"

"Not much, except he seemed to think he knew her. Oh, and he mentioned she had hair the same color as his. Isn't it kind of odd he'd dream about some stranger?"

"Yeah, but who knows how kids' minds work?" She could tell he was trying to joke, but a subtle thread of tension sabotaged his effort.

Diane's heart went out to him. Here he was, a widower trying to raise his adopted son alone in a new town. A son he clearly cherished. He didn't have to pretend with her, or try to be macho. She understood his worry.

"Hey . . ." She gentled her voice. "It's normal to be scared when someone you love is sick or troubled. But Todd will get over the flu, and the bad dreams will pass. I think kids go through phases. And after living in the country in Montana for most of his life, St. Louis has to be a huge adjustment. Things will get better."

He sighed. "That's what I keep telling myself too. Listen . . . thanks for being there for us—and for the pep talk. I don't know what I would have done without you."

Her heart warmed again. "Anytime. You still planning to be home around four?"

"Yeah. Until the heat breaks we're sticking with the earlier starting time. Look, I know four is early for dinner, but I could grab a pizza if you'd like to stay for a while."

The snarl of tension in her shoulders relaxed. "I'd like that a lot. And I'll make some cookies to go with it."

"That sounds great. Gotta run, but I'll see you soon."

A sudden buzz in her ear told her he'd severed the connection, and she replaced the handset in the cradle. The phone link might be broken, but as she retraced her steps down the hall to Todd's room, she felt a whole lot more optimistic about a different kind of link.

Connor emailed the final batch of photos from the morning surveillance session to Kate, took a swig of soda, and set the printout of the little boy beside his computer. One by one, he compared each of today's images to the photocopy.

No matches as far as he could see—and he doubted Kate would find one, either.

Their great lead appeared to be tanking.

Not the best way to end the workweek.

"How goes it?"

At Dev's question, he swiveled around in his chair. The other man stood on the threshold of his office, holding a piece of what looked like caramel pecan coffee cake. "Is that what I think it is?"

Dev strolled into the room and set the generous portion on his desk. "Since I ate the last piece on Wednesday when you were starving, I thought I'd make it up to you."

"I hope you kept some for yourself."

"I'm already two pieces in." He dropped into the chair across from the desk and motioned to the printout. "How'd it go this morning?"

"Unless Kate spots a resemblance I'm missing, no match." He took a big bite of the cake. "I'm going back once more on Monday."

"Then what?"

He shrugged. "Send the bill and write it off."

"You going to write off the client too?"

Connor narrowed his eyes. "What's that supposed to mean?"

"Nikki thinks you two would make a cute couple." Dev smirked at him.

"Cute?"

"Her word, not mine."

Leaning back, Connor linked his hands over his stomach. "So was there a purpose for this visit—other than the peace offering and a dose of harassment?"

"As a matter of fact, yes." Dev's demeanor grew serious. "I took a call this morning from a potential client who has concerns about possible abuse at a nursing home. This might require some undercover work, and I wanted to get your take on strategy. I'll run this by Cal after he gets back too."

Dev's rapid-fire transformation from office cutup to cool, competent pro was, as always, amazing. He might like to joke around, but he knew when to be serious. Like Cal, he was as solid as they came—reminding Connor yet again how fortunate he'd been to team up with his two college buddies. He'd trust either of them with his life—and had done just that on more than one occasion.

"What do you have?"

As Dev briefed him on the new case, it was clear his partner had already thought through the options and developed a preliminary investigative plan.

"That all sounds logical to me. And Kate's case is the only hot one I have at the moment, so I can assist wherever needed."

His phone began to ring, and Connor glanced at the display. Smiled.

"Speaking of hot . . ." Dev's inflection went from serious to amused in a heartbeat. "Your smitten expression suggests that's her."

Connor flattened his lips. His partner had great instincts too. A valuable resource in dicey situations—not so good on the personal front, as he was discovering. In the past, he'd always been discreet about the women he dated . . . but it was hard to be discreet when a woman who interested you also happened to be your client.

"No need to answer. I'm out of here." Dev rose and strolled to the door. "And remember what Nikki said. Cute couple." With a wink, he disappeared.

He was going to have to have a long talk with their office manager.

Shaking his head, he picked up the phone. "Hi, Kate. You got the photos?"

"Yes. I've already reviewed them. No matches."

"I didn't think so, but I wanted you to take a look just in case."

"Are you still planning to try again on Monday?"

"Yes. Then we'll need to regroup."

The silence on the other end of the line told him she knew what that meant. If the boy didn't turn up, their options were limited.

But they did have a couple.

"We're not giving up yet, just to put your mind at ease. If nothing pans out at the daycare center, there are one or two other things we can try."

"Like what?"

"I could approach the birthday girl's mother and see if she'll give me the names of the party guests. It might be a challenge to come up with a credible pretext for the request, but we could consider it."

"What's a pretext?"

"A story."

"You mean . . . a lie?"

He'd had a feeling that question was coming. Although he'd worked out the moral rationale long ago, Kate struck him as the type who might view the technique as unethical.

He rested a finger on the Secret Service motto he always kept close at hand. "We try to keep lying to a minimum, but we do a fair amount of playacting in this job, very much like what undercover law enforcement operatives do. James Devlin, one of my partners, worked undercover for the ATF before joining Phoenix, and that allowed him to help put some very bad people behind bars. We use the same principle in PI work. No one gets hurt from our pretexts, and we only use the technique in the pursuit of justice."

"I've never bought the end-justifies-the-means argument . . . but in light of the way you presented it, it's hard to argue."

She didn't sound convinced.

"We do have another alternative. I could approach the woman, show her my credentials, and hope she simply tells us what we want to know. Unfortunately, there are a fair number of PIs with questionable principles, and they've given the profession a less-than-stellar reputation. As a result, it's often hard to get people to cooperate when we're up front. Plus, it can backfire. If the boy at the party is the one you saw, and if she knows the parents, she could alert them to our investigation. That makes it much more difficult to do surveillance, which is a key tool in a case like this. I'd suggest we use that only as a last resort."

"I agree." She expelled a breath. "I'm fine with the pretext idea."

"Good." He leaned back in his chair. "In the meantime, I'll be back at the daycare center on Monday."

"I hope the weather breaks by then. It was brutal in the car by the time we wrapped up yesterday."

And today had been worse . . . but he left that unsaid.

"By the way . . . are you missing a key? I found one on the passenger side floor of my car."

"So that's where it went. Yep, it's mine. My house key's been slipping off the ring lately. I keep meaning to get a new holder."

"Would you like me to run it by your office?"

"No, I keep an extra one hidden on my back deck. I can get the original next time I see you."

Hang up, Sullivan. She probably has a full schedule, and you have a pile of background checks to do.

But he didn't want to.

"Well . . . I should let you get back to work." She took the initiative, but she didn't sound any more eager than he was to break the connection.

He fought a sudden urge to suggest they meet after work for a frappuccino to discuss the case. But that excuse was lame— and she'd know it. It also broke Phoenix's unwritten rule about socializing with clients.

It was time to end the call.

"I'm sure you're busy too. I'll be in touch Monday, after I get back from surveillance. Have a nice weekend."

She returned the sentiment, and as he dropped the phone back into the cradle, he swiped a smear of caramel off the paper plate with his plastic fork and sucked it off the tines. It dissolved on his tongue, leaving a sweet flavor behind.

Kind of the same effect Kate had on him.

Grinning, he finished off the rest of the coffee cake in two large bites. Lucky thing the rest of the Phoenix crew wasn't privy to his thoughts or things could get as sticky as the caramel on his fingers.

But he'd better get used to their teasing.

Because once this case was over, he intended to put Nikki's cute couple theory to the test.

8

A company picnic was the last place he wanted to be on a Sunday afternoon.

Juggling a hot dog in one hand and a can of soda in the other, Greg nodded politely as his foreman droned on about his upcoming vacation, keeping one eye on Todd. Maybe he should have used his son's bout with the flu as a reason not to show, but the twenty-four-hour bug was gone and it wasn't smart to blow off an event hosted by the owner of the family-run company. Not when you were new and still trying to make a good impression.

". . . get used to it?"

At the raised inflection, suggesting his boss had asked a question, Greg refocused on the stocky man across from him in the cushy pavilion beside the private lake. "Sorry. I got distracted by the kids." He gestured to the group of youngsters whacking croquet balls.

"Yeah." The man shaded his eyes and looked toward them. "They seem like they're having a lot of fun. Me? I'll take a dog and a beer and a shady spot any day." He lifted his plastic cup in salute. "I was asking if you were starting to get used to this heat and humidity."

"Is that even possible?"

The man chuckled and took a bite of his relish-slathered hot dog. "Maybe—if you're a native. So what did you do out in Montana?"

Greg sipped his soda. This was why he avoided socializing. People asked too many questions. But he had his standard brief answers prepared. No one was going to learn any more about his past than he wanted them to—and that was very little.

"I was the caretaker for a guy's summer home."

"Yeah? Must've been one of those rich executive types."

"I imagine he had a few bucks."

"Big place?"

"About 250 acres."

"Nice. Were you there long?"

"Almost three years."

"So what brought you to St. Louis?"

An unkind twist of fate, in light of his encounter with Kate Marshall. But he left that unsaid.

"I wanted to be closer to better schools for Todd. One of my old construction buddies heard from his brother you were hiring, and I liked the idea of living in the Midwest. Good, solid values and all that." He shrugged. "So here I am."

"Does your buddy live here too?"

"No." Before the man could press for more information, he gestured toward Diane, who was fanning herself with a paper plate as she chatted with the woman beside her on the picnic table bench. "I need to go see if my friend wants another drink."

"Good idea. Always keep the ladies happy." He winked and wandered off, chomping on his hot dog.

A bead of sweat trickled down Greg's forehead as he walked toward Diane, and he lifted his arm to wipe it on the sleeve of his T-shirt. Would it be rude to leave the party after only an hour?

Probably.

Resigned, he gave her a small smile as she scooted over to make room for him, only half listening as she introduced the woman beside her.

"Don't let me interrupt. I'm going to concentrate on this hot dog for a few minutes." He held it up and proceeded to eat—not because he was hungry but because it gave him an excuse to distance himself from any more conversation.

The two women continued to chat, and he tuned them out to focus on the dock, where the company owner and his college-age son were uncovering two paddleboats. The youngsters crowded around them—all but Todd, who stayed at the fringes of the activity.

Greg stopped eating. There'd been no occasion in Montana to spend any time near the water, and that had been fine with him. Eventually he'd take Todd to a pool, see how he reacted, teach him how to swim. But he was in no rush—especially now that he was picking up a distinct wariness from his son. While the other children surged onto the dock, Todd hung back.

"All right, kids . . . who wants to go first?" The owner of the company turned to the cluster of children, laughing as they all waved their hands and shouted "Me, me!"

All except Todd.

The man surveyed the group. "I'll tell you what. I'm going to let the last be first. The four of you in the back . . . you get the first ride. You two girls"—he pointed them out—"and you two boys." He indicated Todd and the boy in front of him.

The boy grabbed Todd's arm and tugged him forward.

Choking down his bite of hot dog, Greg stood.

"Greg?" Diane touched his arm.

He didn't even look at her. "I'll be back in a minute." Without waiting for a response, he wove through the pavilion, hurried down the steps, and strode toward the dock.

By the time he arrived, the owner had strapped the two girls into child-sized orange life jackets, helped them scramble into the first paddleboat, and given them operating instructions.

"One lap, then we change places. Ready?" At their eager assent, he pushed them off and stood. "You're next, boys."

Greg scrutinized Todd. He was frowning as he inspected the water, his posture stiff.

"Bob." As the company owner looked his way, he gestured to his son. "Todd doesn't know how to swim."

"Not a problem. The lake's not deep, and I have my certified lifeguard standing by." He tipped his head toward his strapping son. "But I never put kids on the water without taking extra precautions." He crossed to the other side of the dock, leaned into a storage bin, and pulled out two more life jackets.

Greg's heart stuttered as he glanced at his son. The frown was still on his face, and he seemed to have gone a shade paler.

"Let's go!" The boy beside Todd grabbed his arm and pulled him forward again. "You don't have to be scared. I know how to swim too."

"Todd." As Greg moved beside him, his son looked up. "You can just watch if you'd rather."

It wasn't difficult to read the conflict in the boy's eyes. He didn't want to get in the boat—yet he didn't want to come across as a wimp in front of the other children, either.

But better a wimp than . . .

"No need to worry. Everything will be fine." Bob put his hand on Todd's shoulder. "Let's try this on for size."

His son gave a hesitant nod.

Greg considered refusing to let Todd participate, but that would call attention to them—and he'd spent the past three years doing the polar opposite. Staying as far under the radar as possible. They hadn't even gone into town very often.

But it had been a whole lot easier to lay low on the spread in Montana.

Perhaps he'd waded back into the mainstream too soon.

And running into Kate Marshall hadn't helped, either.

"Perfect fit." Bob straightened up, then helped the two boys into the boat.

Too late to intervene. He'd just have to hope this unexpected turn of events didn't shake loose any more vague memories.

He moved off the dock, to the edge of the water, watching as the boat circled the small lake, fists jammed in pockets, holding his breath.

The circuit seemed to take forever. But when at last they began to approach the dock, Greg started to breathe again.

Until all at once Todd and his boating partner collided with the other boat as it headed out with a new crew.

The boys' paddleboat, already low to the water, tipped. The girls in the second boat shrieked—but it was Todd's scream of terror that sent a chill down Greg's spine. As his son began to rise, making the boat rock more, Greg waded into the water, stumbling forward as fast as he could, his pulse pounding.

"Hold on, Todd. I'm coming. Sit still!"

If the boy heard him, he gave no indication. He just continued to scream.

As soon as Greg got to water deep enough to swim in, he struck out for the entangled boats. It took only a dozen powerful strokes to reach them, and within seconds he'd freed the girls' boat and pushed it aside. Then he moved beside Todd's seat.

All the color had leeched from his son's complexion, and though he'd stopped screaming, his breath was coming in short, shallow puffs as he clung to the side of the boat.

"Hey, champ. You're fine. I'm here." He kept his voice soft, reassuring, but his son merely stared at him with glazed eyes. If he didn't calm down soon, he was going to hyperventilate.

Greg looked at the other boy, who'd backed as far away from

Todd as possible and appeared ready to abandon ship if things got any creepier.

"I'm going to tow you guys back to the dock, okay?"

The kid bobbed his head.

Bob's son appeared in the water on the other side of the boat. "I'll guide it from this end."

Together, the two of them got the boat pointed in the right direction.

"You'll be back on the dock in a minute, champ. Hold on." Although Todd didn't respond, Greg continued to reassure him as they towed the boat through the water, staying as close to him as possible. His son was shaking so badly he could feel the vibration in the fiberglass beneath his fingers.

Once back at the dock, the other boy leaped off the boat and scrambled to solid land as fast as he could, disappearing into the crowd that had gathered.

Greg bit back a curse.

The last thing he'd wanted to do was create a scene.

Maneuvering the boat to position Todd's side closest to the dock, he climbed out of the water with an assist from Bob, then reached back for his son.

"Let go of the edge, Todd. I've got you. We're back at the dock."

His son looked up at him, the glassiness fading from his eyes as he lifted his arms, a sob catching in his throat.

Greg scooped him up and held him against his chest, stroking his back. "You're fine. I've got you."

His son's cheek pressed to his shoulder, he braced himself and turned to face the audience.

"I'm sorry about this." Bob laid a hand on his arm. "I shouldn't have pushed. I didn't realize he was scared of the water. Will he be all right?"

"Yeah, but I think we'd better call it a day."

"Of course."

With Bob's help, Greg worked the life vest off his clinging son. The silent crowd parted as he exited the dock, and Diane fell in beside him, her face mirroring the concern on the host's. To her credit, however, she didn't make a single comment or ask one question. She just walked with him to the car, her hand resting on Todd's arm.

The ride back to the city was equally subdued. Following his lead, she spoke little. Only when Todd fell asleep a few minutes from her house did she mention the incident, keeping her voice low.

"What happened back there? I was too far away to see, but I heard him cry out. The next thing I knew, you were in the water."

"The two boats ran into each other, and Todd's started to tip. He doesn't know how to swim."

"He had a vest on, though." Her expression was puzzled.

Play it down, Greg. Pass it off.

"But he hasn't been around water very much. It was too cold for swimming in Montana. And those paddleboats sit low in the water. I think he just got scared."

"I suppose so." Despite her verbal agreement, she didn't sound convinced. "Maybe you should teach him to swim."

"Yeah. It's on my agenda, but we haven't gotten around to it yet." In the rearview mirror, he checked on Todd. His son was passed out in the backseat, but his complexion had regained a touch of color. "Sorry to cut our day short."

"No problem. But you didn't get much food." She paused, and he knew what was coming. "I could make omelets and salad if you want to come in for a few minutes."

Much as he was tempted to accept, it wouldn't be wise. Until things settled down with Todd, he needed to keep his distance. Diane wasn't the pushy type, but she was smart. If things like the nightmare and today's incident kept happening, she might start to ask questions he wouldn't be able to answer. He couldn't take that chance—even if that meant he might risk losing her.

"Thanks, but I think I'd better get the little guy home. He's had a tough week, between this and the flu." He stopped the truck in her driveway and left it running as he came around to open her door.

She slid out, fidgeting with her shoulder bag. "Do you think he'll be well enough to go to daycare tomorrow? I'd be happy to watch him again if you want to give him another day to recover."

"Let me think about it, and I'll call you later tonight."

For a moment she hesitated, waiting for the quick kiss that had become part of their standard parting ritual.

But kissing was the last thing on his mind tonight.

A flicker of disappointment echoed in her eyes before she turned away in silence and walked toward her door.

For an instant he was tempted to call her back. To pull her close and pour out his worry. To share with someone else the burden he carried.

A futile wish if ever there was one.

Shoulders slumping, he closed her door, circled the pickup, and took his seat again behind the wheel. He was in this alone—and always would be. His was a secret that could never be revealed.

But he had Todd.

And in the end, that was all that really mattered.

Pay dirt.

Adrenaline surging, Connor watched through his binoculars as a blond-haired boy climbed out of a dark blue Dodge Dakota. The printout from the mall might be fuzzy, but that kid looked like a match.

Exchanging his binoculars for the camera, he lowered his

window, braced his forearm against the frame, and clicked shot after shot of both the boy and the muscular man accompanying him. A man dressed in T-shirt, jeans, and a baseball cap. Not red—but everything else fit.

Once they disappeared inside, he scanned the other arrivals who'd been waiting in the parking lot for the facility to open. No other blond boys in sight. He turned his attention to the Dakota, taking zoom shots of the license plate and the vehicle itself.

Three minutes later, the man reappeared minus the boy. Connor snapped more photos of him, though the brim of the baseball cap, pulled low over his forehead, kept his face in shadows. Nikki should be able to work some computer magic to brighten up the shots, however.

As he watched the Dakota pull away, he raised his window. Not that the man would pay much attention to a white utility van—his transportation for the new month in the musical chairs he and his partners played with company vehicles—but it always paid to be careful.

The temptation to follow the man was strong . . . but until Kate made a definite ID of the boy in the pictures he'd just taken, he needed to stick with the surveillance. This boy hadn't been at daycare on Thursday or Friday, and there might be others who hadn't been, either.

Keeping an eye on the steady stream of arrivals, he pulled out his phone and speed dialed Nikki's work number, bypassing her message as he punched through to her voice mail.

"Nikki, it's Connor. I need you to run a plate for me when you get in." He pulled up the image on his camera and recited the numbers and letters. "I'd do it myself, but I need both eyes for surveillance. Call me as soon as you have anything."

Message left, he focused on the center, trying to ignore the growing heat and the sweat soaking through his T-shirt.

Over the next two hours, a few other blond-haired boys

showed up, and he snapped photos of the ones he wasn't certain he'd seen during previous surveillance sessions. None, however, came as close to matching the mall image as the first boy.

At eight-ten, his cell began to vibrate. Nikki hadn't wasted any time.

Pressing the phone to his ear, he continued to watch the center even though the traffic had slowed to a trickle. "Morning."

"Back at you. I take it you found a trail to follow."

"Maybe."

"I've got your information. The truck's three years old and belongs to a Greg Sanders. Do you want his address?"

"Yes." He jotted the information down as she recited it. Somewhere in South County, based on the zip code. "What else do you have?"

"As far as I can tell from his driver's license data, he has a clean record. He's forty-six, five-ten, has blue eyes, weighs one-eighty-five. That sound like the guy you saw?"

"Close enough. Did you run his picture?"

"Yep. Want me to email it?"

"No. It can wait until I get to the office. Look for me about ten-thirty. When I wrap up here in forty-five minutes, I'm going to swing by his house, then head home for a shower before I come in."

"Thank you."

He grinned and picked up the bottle of water he'd opened twenty minutes ago. "You're welcome. And thanks for looking up the info so fast."

"Not a problem. It gave me a short reprieve from Dev's filing. See you soon." The line went dead.

After taking a long pull from the bottle of water, Connor scrolled down to Kate's work number and pressed autodial.

She answered on the second ring, sounding a little breathless—and anxious. "Connor? I didn't expect to hear from you this early."

123

Do you have good news?

Though she didn't ask that question, it hung in the air between them—and he didn't keep her waiting for the answer.

"I think I may have spotted the boy you saw at the mall."

She drew in a sharp breath.

"He was one of the first arrivals. I had Nikki run the plates on the truck. Does the name Greg Sanders ring any bells?"

"No."

The answer he'd expected. "I'm going to do a drive-by of his house after I'm finished here. Once I get to the office, I'll email you the photos and you can let me know what you think."

"All right." A moment of silence passed. "So if this boy is the one I saw, what happens next?"

"I think it would be valuable to have an artist do an age-progressed image of your son. See if the face she comes up with resembles the boy you saw. It's not a foolproof method, but I've worked with Elaine on a number of cases and her digital magic is amazingly accurate. Much better than any age-progression software I've seen. If we have a decent match, that's even more reason to continue to pursue this. Can you provide some photos from his younger years?"

"Yes. I . . . I have hundreds." Her quiet words were laced with pain.

Connor gritted his teeth. Of course she did. Any loving mother would be shutter-happy with her firstborn. The heat must be addling his brain—and melting his usual finesse.

"I'm sorry, Kate. I should have phrased that more diplomatically."

"No apology necessary. I just hope we need them." She sounded more normal now. Back in control. But he suspected that was an act for his benefit, to alleviate his guilt. "If the boy in the photos you send me matches the one I saw at the mall, I can run home at lunch and gather up some pictures. I have both prints and digital. The studio stuff is all prints. Would she want both?"

"Yes. A selection from all stages of development would be best. That will help her get a feel for how he was aging. But there's no need to make a special trip home. Take your time and look through them tonight. You can drop the JPEGs to a flash drive and put the prints in an envelope. I'll be happy to stop by your office tomorrow morning and pick them up after I tail our friend once he drops off the little boy. Assuming we have a match, I'd like to find out where the man works."

"That would be fine. My first appointment isn't until ten."

"I'll be there long before that. What time do you usually get in?"

"Seven-thirty."

"You put in long hours. You were there past six last Wednesday."

"Not all days run that late. And I'll be leaving on time tonight if we have a match. It will take me a while to go through the photos. I haven't pulled most of them out in years." Her voice caught on the last word.

It was on the tip of his tongue to ask if she wanted some company—and moral support—for the difficult task ahead, but he bit it back. It wasn't an offer he'd make to any other client, and he needed to keep things professional and impersonal . . . for now.

Even if he was suddenly tempted to ignore the house rules.

"I'm sorry to have to ask you to do this. I know it won't be easy, but I think the age-progression step could be helpful."

"I agree. I'll be fine."

He wasn't convinced of that, but he let it go. "Expect me around eight tomorrow, assuming our guy doesn't work somewhere in the far reaches of the county. If he does, I'll call and let you know I'll be delayed. But let's not get ahead of ourselves. I think the boy I saw this morning is a match, but you may not agree. Call me once you review the images and we'll go from there."

"Sounds good. Talk to you soon."

As Kate ended the call, Connor picked up his water again, watching the daycare center as he drained the bottle. Despite the lack of activity, he'd stick it out until nine—just in case. But he was pretty certain the boy he'd spotted in the early hours of the morning was the one they'd been trying to locate. All he needed was Kate's confirmation.

On the plus side, a positive ID by his client meant no more hot mornings under the Golden Arches.

But it also meant this investigation would move to a whole new level. One with a lot of potential risks.

Because if the boy did, in fact, match the age-progression image Elaine produced, and if Kate's suspicion that he might be her son became more than groundless speculation, someone had a dangerous secret to protect. Most likely the guy in the baseball cap. And if he discovered he'd been identified, things could turn nasty very fast. Anyone who threatened to expose him could be in peril.

Especially Kate.

*R*ing! Please ring!

Diane glanced at the phone an arm's reach away on the kitchen counter as she finished rinsing her dinner plate, but despite some powerful wishing and strong telepathic signals directed toward Greg's house, it remained silent.

Face it, Diane. He isn't going to call.

Sighing, she set the dish in the drying rack. So what if they'd spoken every day in the past month? It wasn't like he'd promised to call today when he'd phoned last night after getting Todd settled. But his tone, while friendly, had lost the touch of intimacy, of promise, she'd come to expect.

Things were changing between them—and she had no idea why.

She pulled the towel off the rack beneath the sink and dried her hands, eyeing the phone again. She could always call to ask how Todd was doing. That would be a considerate gesture, given the youngster's traumatic experience yesterday.

Or would referring to the disturbing incident make Greg pull back from her even more?

Wandering over to the phone, she chewed on her lower lip. Maybe things were calmer today. Maybe he'd be glad to hear from her. Besides, what was wrong with letting him know she was thinking about him, that she cared about both of them? At this point, with him pulling back anyway, what did she have to lose?

Before she could change her mind, she picked up the phone and pressed his speed dial number.

Todd answered less than a heartbeat into the first ring, sounding like his usual cheery self. At least things seemed to be back to normal in *his* world. Dare she hope the same was true for Greg?

"Hi, honey. It's Diane. Are you guys eating dinner?"

"Nope. We just finished. We had chocolate cake for dessert."

"Wow. That's my favorite."

"Me too. We have a whole lot left. Do you want to come over and . . ."

He stopped speaking, and she could hear a muted exchange in the background. Then Todd returned.

"Dad wants to talk to you. See you later."

As the phone on the other end exchanged hands, her palms started to sweat. The timing of Greg's interception wasn't random. He hadn't wanted Todd to ask her to come over. In fact, she had a feeling if Todd hadn't answered the phone so fast, Greg would have let it roll to the answering machine.

"Hi, Diane." Greg's voice was cordial, nothing more.

Calling had been a mistake. He didn't want to talk with her. Her lungs balked.

"Hi. I, uh, just wanted to see how Todd was doing." She did her best to mask her usual warmth and match his polite tone. "He sounds much better today."

"Yeah. He had a good day at STL and ate a big dinner."

"Great. How's everything with you?"

"Fine."

As the stilted exchange ended, she leaned her shoulder against the wall and closed her eyes. It was her turn to speak—and hard as it was, she forced herself to do what she had to do.

"Well, I have a few chores to take care of tonight. You two have a nice evening."

"Thanks. You too."

No inquiry about her day. No promise of a future call. No more reassurances that things would get back to normal soon.

Despite the tightness in her throat, she managed to inject her "talk to you later" sign-off with a lot more brightness than she felt.

But once she dropped the phone back into the cradle, the tightness turned into a sob.

What in the world was going on? One day she and Greg had been a cozy couple, then overnight he'd pulled back. It didn't make sense.

But what did she know? Her track record with men was dismal. Maybe there'd been signals she'd missed. Or maybe he thought she was too needy—and there might be some truth to that. While the support group was helping, she had a long way to go before she regained the confidence and self-esteem Rich had demolished.

And perhaps that should be her priority. Perhaps she needed to get her own house in order, find some meaning in her life apart from other people, before she tried to figure out someone else's problems.

One way to do that was to get a job, as Sarah had done.

Squaring her shoulders, Diane wiped away her tears, marched into the study, and booted up the computer. Once upon a time, she'd been a competent, fast-tracked accountant with a responsible position. That career had fallen by the wayside when Rich came along and convinced her to stay home so she could focus on starting a family. Not that she'd put up much resistance; what paycheck or promotion could compete with the joy of holding a child in her arms?

Too bad she hadn't realized Rich's true motivation sooner.

Her husband had had no interest in a family; he'd just felt threatened by her independence and success and wanted total control over her life.

But by the time the truth sank in, she'd felt trapped.

The user ID screen came up. Leaning forward, she entered her password and connected to the Net. Surfed until she found several examples of résumés. Began to type her own.

And come tomorrow, she was going to dig out the New Start phone number Sarah had pressed on her Saturday night and make an appointment with the woman her support group friend claimed could work miracles in building confidence and finding jobs.

Kate Marshall.

Connor flipped off the TV news, shoved the empty container from his nuked dinner aside, and drummed his fingers on the small island in his condo's kitchen. There were plenty of things he could do tonight. Work out at the gym. Run a few miles. Visit the range and log some target practice. All worthwhile, productive activities.

Except he wasn't in the mood for any of them.

He was in the mood to see Kate.

Expelling a frustrated breath, he rose, rinsed out the plastic dinner tray, and deposited it in the recycle bin. She'd put up a brave front at the end of their conversation earlier in the day, but now that she'd confirmed the boy in his photos was the same one she'd seen at the mall, she had a tough job tonight. One that might be easier to get through if she had some moral support close at hand.

Not an option if he played by company rules.

But why not call her? See how she was doing, ask if she had any questions? That would be a compassionate gesture, and a phone conversation didn't violate Phoenix's informal no-fraternizing policy.

Without giving himself a chance to second-guess those motives, he pulled out his phone and tapped in her number.

She didn't answer until the third ring, and when she did pick up, the unsteadiness in her greeting confirmed his suspicion—she was having a tough time with the chore he'd given her.

"Hi. It's Connor. I thought I'd touch base, see how you were doing with your photo search."

"I finished going through the digital stuff and dropped quite a few to a flash drive. Now I'm getting ready to dive into the prints." She stopped. Exhaled. "It took me a while to sort through the boxes in the storage closet, but I have the albums in front of me now. I was about to open the first one."

He walked over to the window and surveyed the dark clouds encroaching on the blue sky. The meteorologists had warned that a storm was approaching, and for once they seemed to be right.

"Look . . . if you want to spread this out over a couple of days, that's not a problem. I set up a meeting with Elaine for tomorrow afternoon, but I can switch it to Wednesday."

"No. There's no sense putting off the inevitable. It's probably time I dug these out. I just didn't realize it would be so . . ." As her voice choked, he tightened his grip on the phone. "Sorry. Looking at these brings everything back—good and bad."

Somewhere in the distance, a faint rumble of thunder heralded the looming squall, and the branches at the tops of the trees began to sway.

"Listen . . . would it make things easier if I came over?"

The offer was out before he could stop it—a blatant violation of company policy.

Unless he could come up with some sort of work-related rationale. Fast.

Grasping at the first thing that came to mind, he continued

without giving her a chance to respond. "I could sort through the photos with you, help you select the ones that might be most useful to Elaine."

Although the justification was weak, it held a modicum of truth—and it was the best he could come up with on the fly.

Kate's silence suggested she was as surprised by the offer as he was—yet she hadn't turned him down flat. At the same time, he could understand her reluctance to let a man she'd known all of one week hang around while she hovered on the brink of a meltdown. On the plus side, if she did decline, he wouldn't have to worry about crossing any lines.

But he hoped she wouldn't do that. If she did fall apart, he didn't want her to be alone.

"I'm sure you have better things to do with your evening, and you've already clocked a lot of hours on my case today." Her words were hesitant—but infused with a distinct touch of yearning.

She wanted him to come over.

Yet she was giving him an out. One he should take.

Instead of being smart, however, he not only leaped into the danger zone, he laid his cards on the table. "Nothing I was thinking about doing tonight is urgent. And I won't be charging you for these hours."

More silence on the line as she digested that. Perhaps, with the offer of gratis personal time on the table—and the underlying message—she'd back off.

But she didn't.

"If you're sure, I wouldn't mind the company. Going through the digital images was difficult, but I have a feeling handling the photo albums will be worse. Maybe I'll hold myself together better if someone else is around."

He wasn't certain her rationale was any more sound than his, but he wasn't going to dispute it.

"I live in Manchester, so it shouldn't take me more than fifteen minutes to get to your place. See you soon."

As he slipped the phone back on his belt and another rumble of thunder sounded in the distance, a twinge of guilt tugged at his conscience. Never once in the five years since he'd joined Phoenix had he been tempted to spend personal time with a client. His tenure with the Secret Service had taught him to toe the line and had honed his already well-developed sense of discipline.

So how could one lovely blonde-haired widow he'd known for less than a week undermine his self-control so quickly?

Shaking his head, he snagged his keys off the counter and detoured to the bathroom to dispatch his five o'clock shadow. Too bad he couldn't ask Cal and Dev how they'd avoided succumbing to the same temptation while working the cases for the women they'd fallen for. They must have struggled with the same dilemma he faced, and it would be helpful to know how they'd managed to keep their emotions under wraps until the cases were solved.

If he asked for their advice, however, he'd be publicly agreeing with Nikki's assessment that he and Kate made a cute couple.

No way was he going to open himself up to that kind of ribbing. Not when he'd always been the one who'd played his social life close to his vest. Who'd never once let a woman disrupt his professional demeanor. Who'd watched in tolerant amusement as both Cal and Dev struggled with the very dilemma he was grappling with.

He leaned close to the mirror, inspected his jaw, and shut off the electric razor. For now, he'd keep his predicament to himself—and hope Kate's mystery was solved ASAP so her role could change from client to . . . something else.

She should have told him not to come.

And she shouldn't have bothered changing from cutoff shorts and sport shoes to capris and sandals. Why should she care what he thought about how she looked? This wasn't a social visit.

Or was it?

Kate paced from one side of the small living room in her condo to the other as she pondered that question and came to the only possible answer.

Maybe.

Why else would he tell her she wouldn't be charged for these hours? Companies didn't offer their services for free.

On the other hand, Connor was a perceptive man. He'd caught her at a weepy moment, and she had no doubt he'd picked up on that. Perhaps comforting distraught clients was a complimentary service Phoenix offered on occasion. Given their steep fees, they might consider a little free hand-holding smart business.

She stopped, blew out a lungful of air, and combed her fingers through her hair. All of that might be true—but if she was honest with herself, Connor's motives weren't the main reason for her agitation.

Her own reaction was the culprit.

The fact was, she liked the man. Found him attractive. Hoped his visit tonight was prompted by more than Phoenix standard operating procedures.

All of which made her uncomfortable.

No matter what Pauline said, she wasn't ready to feel . . . tingly . . . about someone new. And until she was, she'd have to play this calm and cool.

Too bad she had no idea how to do that.

The sudden chime of the doorbell echoed in the quiet condo, and her heart stumbled—as if to prove her point.

Forcing herself to suck in a few deep breaths, she crossed to the foyer, peered through the peephole . . . and stared.

Dressed once again in snug jeans and a chest-hugging black T-shirt, Connor radiated magnetism even through the closed door. The sprinkling of black hair on his muscled forearms, his intense dark eyes, and that chiseled jaw didn't hurt, either.

Get a grip, Kate. Pretend this is purely a business meeting.

Right.

Grasping the knob, she exhaled, swallowed, and pulled the door open.

In greeting, Connor held up two cups bearing a familiar mermaid logo, each topped with whipped cream and capped with a plastic dome. "I come bearing gifts—which are melting as we speak."

Smiling, she moved aside and ushered him in. "The perfect antidote to a hot day."

"Since I didn't know your preference, I brought a strawberry and a chocolate chip. I'm fine with either, so take your pick."

After locking the door, she turned back to him. "I like both too."

"I guess we're easy to please." He handed her the drinks and fished a coin out of his pocket. "Heads or tails?"

"Tails."

He flipped the coin. "Tails gets chocolate."

They both bent to examine the penny as it came to rest, and as she caught a whiff of that subtle, masculine aftershave he favored, she actually felt dizzy.

This was ridiculous

Standing, she handed him the strawberry and took a swift step back. "I guess I get all the calories."

"Trust me, frappuccinos are equal opportunity when it comes to nutrition—or lack thereof." He fished two straws out of his back pocket and handed one over, pinning her with an assessing look. "You doing okay?"

Hardly. Not when his mere presence was setting off an

electrical storm inside her to match the one Mother Nature was brewing outside.

But he was talking about her chore for the evening, and on that score, at least, she could give him an honest answer.

"I'm hanging in." She brushed past him toward the dining room, leaving him to follow—and buying herself a few seconds to try and suppress the flush on her cheeks before she had to face him again. "But after you called, I decided to wait until you got here to start on the albums."

"Good. Reviewing the pictures together should make the job easier." He took a few moments to peruse the contemporary furnishings in her vaulted-ceilinged unit before joining her in the dining area. "Nice condo."

She set her drink on the table and tore the paper from her straw. "Thanks. But I have to admit it's never felt much like home. Probably because I sold most of the furnishings from my previous house before I moved, except for a few sentimental pieces. The therapist I went to for a while thought it would be healthier for me to start fresh."

He freed his own straw and refocused on her. "How long were you in therapy?"

"Not long enough, according to both the therapist and my mother." She poked her straw into the hole at the top of the plastic dome, giving her an excuse to look away from his probing eyes. "They both thought I was a mess—and they were right."

"You had reason to be."

At his quiet comment, she looked back up at him—and as the gentle compassion radiating from his eyes washed over her, she was blindsided by the sudden fierce pressure behind her own.

No!

She was not going to cry!

Crying didn't change a thing.

"Some people would have handled it better than I did." To her dismay, the words she tried to make casual and conversational came out shaky. Maybe he wouldn't notice.

His assessing expression dashed that hope. "Anyone in particular?"

Might as well be honest. This was a man who was used to delving for the truth.

She picked up her drink and played with the straw, creating swirls in the whipped cream. "My mother, for one. My dad was killed on a construction site when I was eighteen, and she didn't miss a beat. She did her grieving, reorganized her life, moved on, and never looked back. She didn't believe in lamenting about things that couldn't be changed."

Connor lifted his own drink as he studied her. "Some people feel more deeply than others. And I don't consider that a liability. In fact, those people tend to be even stronger. They have to be in order to survive."

Once again, pressure built behind her eyes. There was nothing he could have said to endear himself more to her than those few sentences.

Not trusting her voice, she took a sip of her drink before she responded. "I'd like to believe that—but I wasn't very strong in the beginning . . . and I made some bad decisions."

Dare she tell him about her biggest lapse in judgment? Would he revise his assessment of her if he knew just how weak she'd been?

"We all make bad decisions." A flicker of pain rippled across his face, come and gone so fast she wondered if she'd imagined it. "In your case, you had an excuse. Thinking processes can be compromised by trauma. And the fact you're standing here today, a fully functioning individual, tells me you've overcome whatever mistakes you think you made. Which I doubt were as bad as you seem to think they were."

The perfect opening to spill her secret—if she had the courage to take it.

She gestured to the table, stalling as she weighed the pros and cons of baring her soul to this man she'd known for mere days. "Please, have a seat."

In silence, he complied. Waiting. Giving her the time she needed to decide how much she was willing to share.

Sliding into her chair, she looked into his eyes, listened to her heart—and made her decision.

"You're wrong about the magnitude of my mistake. It was huge—and very foolish." Her words were steadier than she'd expected, rippled only by the barest of tremors.

He tipped his head but remained silent as he watched her.

She forced herself to maintain eye contact. "I used Valium. Too much of it. And I got hooked—big-time."

His expression didn't change. No disgust flattened his features. No disdain curled his lips. No condemnation crept into his eyes; just the opposite. If anything, they softened.

Or maybe she was seeing what she wanted to see.

Except his next words proved otherwise.

"I stand by what I said earlier. Breaking an addiction takes an enormous amount of strength."

She traced a bead of sweat down the side of her cup with her fingertip, not as willing to forgive herself as he was. "I shouldn't have gotten addicted in the first place."

"I'm sure that wasn't your intent."

"No." She took a sip of her drink, letting the sweetness dissolve on her tongue. But even the rich chocolate flavor couldn't overcome the sour taste stirred up by the memories of those awful months. "In the beginning, I only planned to take enough to help me sleep at night. But as I later learned, tolerance to Valium builds quickly, and before long I needed fifteen milligrams instead of five. That went on for six months, and by then, if I missed a dose, I'd feel ill and shaky. That's when I realized I was in trouble."

"Did you get help?"

She inspected her drink. The whipped cream had deflated—along with her spirits. "No. I should have, but I was too embarrassed. My parents had raised me to be strong, to stand on my own two feet, and instead I'd turned to drugs to help me get through a rough time. I didn't even tell my grief counselor. I just read everything I could find on Valium addiction and weaned myself off of it over the next few months."

Connor frowned. "That can't have been easy."

"It was hell." The words came out broken, and she took a few seconds to regain control. "From my research, I knew what to expect. Stomach cramps. Sweating. Tremors. Anxiety. Insomnia. Plus a lot of other bad things. But I was determined to overcome the dependence, and gradually, things did begin to improve—as did my outlook. I also made the decision to go back to work, and began looking for a job."

"How did you end up in St. Louis?" He finished his drink, set it aside, and linked his fingers on the table.

She shrugged. "My best friend in college grew up here. I came home with her on a couple of spring breaks and liked the city. It seemed as good a place as any to make a fresh start."

"Has it been?"

"Until the past two weeks." She rubbed the spot above the bridge of her nose where a faint headache was beginning to pound. "It's strange. I thought I was done with trauma. That I'd finally moved on, created a new normal. And then I have a chance encounter with a little boy that plunges me back into craziness. I'm trying hard to believe there's a purpose in this, but most of the time it feels like a cruel joke."

"Or an amazing opportunity."

She lowered her hand from her forehead and scrutinized him. "Are you suggesting that . . . I mean, have you changed your opinion about this being a wild-goose chase?"

"I never said that."

"I know. You were very discreet. But even I thought that at the beginning. You had to have had serious doubts too."

"I did—and still do—but I also have an open mind. Not all coincidences are random—and miracles do happen. Until we make a positive ID on that boy, I'm not writing off any possibility. So . . ." He gestured to the scrapbooks. "Where do we start?"

Feeling more upbeat than she had since the day he'd taken her case, Kate pulled Kevin's baby book toward her. The one she'd buried deepest in her closet. The one she'd been afraid to open for fear the glue on her carefully patched-together world would dissolve, leaving her as shattered as she'd been the day her son was declared dead.

But somehow she had a feeling Connor wouldn't let that happen. That he'd step in and hold her together if she started to fall apart.

And while she might be more resilient than she'd once thought, she had to admit the notion of being held in those strong, capable arms was very, very appealing—no matter the burden of guilt that admission dumped on her shoulders.

10

Excellent.

Greg Sanders and the little boy were back at the daycare center right on schedule Tuesday morning.

Adjusting his binoculars, Connor watched their body language as they walked from the car to the entrance.

Sanders was attentive to the boy. He took his hand as they crossed the busy parking lot, shortening his stride to match the youngster's. He looked down when the boy tipped his head up to speak, giving the child his full attention. Once on the sidewalk in front of the center, he tousled the boy's hair and put his arm around his shoulders, tugging him close as they walked.

The boy appeared happy too, as he trotted along beside Sanders. His expression was animated, he gestured freely, he laughed often. And when the man bent down to hug him, he returned the embrace.

The love between the two of them was almost palpable.

As they entered the daycare center, Connor lowered his binoculars, frowned, and tapped a finger against the steering wheel. Cases involving children were never easy. Even when the outcome was positive, someone always got hurt. Often the child suffered most . . . especially if he or she became the pawn in a custody battle.

That wasn't the case here—but if by some chance this boy did turn out to be Kate's son, his world was about to be disrupted. Again.

Sanders reappeared, and Connor watched him as he returned to his truck.

Interesting.

The man's demeanor had done a 180. The smile was gone, and his posture was more taut. As if he was worried.

Had there been a problem during the drop-off—or might his anxiety be related to his encounter with a blonde-haired woman on a mall escalator? The one he'd been keeping tabs on over his shoulder as he'd hurried the little boy toward the parking garage a week ago Friday? Or *appeared* to be keeping tabs on. The evidence to support that conclusion was circumstantial at best, but his behavior that day had been consistent with someone running from a perceived threat.

As Sanders climbed into his truck, Connor started the engine. Time to find out where the man worked.

Forty minutes later, after tailing him to St. Charles County, Connor stopped half a block away as Sanders pulled into a subdivision in the early stages of construction. While he watched through his binoculars, the man replaced his baseball cap with a hard hat and joined a crew gathered around a house. Within minutes, he was wielding an electric saw.

Mission accomplished.

Connor put the van in gear and headed east, back toward St. Louis. The man's profession fit the house he'd scoped out after Nikki gave him the address yesterday—a small ranch in a blue-collar area of South County.

He checked the clock on the dash. Not even seven yet. Too soon to stop by Elaine's and drop off the images of Kate's son that were resting on the seat beside him—a key to their investigation. Elaine had an amazing eye, combining science, digital savvy, and art to produce better age-progression photos than any he'd seen in his years with the Secret Service, despite all the resources available to the agency. If her picture wasn't a close match for the shots he'd taken of the little boy, he couldn't, in good conscience, recommend that Kate continue to spend money on this investigation.

And until he had Elaine's work in hand, it didn't make sense for *him* to continue to spend her money, either. Or even communicate with her. Aside from a courtesy call to confirm he'd dropped off the images, there was no professional reason to contact her again for several days.

Probably a plus, since he'd almost crossed the line last night.

He merged onto I-70 and turned up the air-conditioning, but the rising sun radiating through the front windshield wasn't the reason he suddenly felt too warm. The credit for that went to his client.

Flipping down his visor, he tried not to think about how much he'd relished the two hours he'd spent sitting beside her as she'd paged through her albums, sharing reminiscences about her son and a few about her husband, smiling one moment, close to tears the next. Giving him glimpses of a caring mother and a devoted wife with an infinite capacity to love. Of an admirable woman who'd lost and mourned and struggled, but who'd triumphed over her trials.

Mostly, though, he tried not to think about how appealing she'd looked as she'd said good-bye—and how tempted he'd been to respond to the subtle yearning in the depths of her eyes. She might not realize it yet—or perhaps she was fighting the realization—but the electric sparks between them had been as powerful as the flashes of lightning zigzaging across the sky outside the sliding doors off her dining room.

He'd come close—too close—to giving in, to leaning over to brush his lips across hers.

Even more reason to stay away for a few days.

So he'd call her this morning, tell her he'd be in touch once he heard back from Elaine—then get himself back under control and in 100 percent professional mode before they spoke again.

He hoped.

Greg's eyes flew open, and he stared into the darkness. What had awakened him at—he squinted at the digital clock on his nightstand—three in the morning?

He lay motionless, listening. The house was quiet save for the muted hum of the air conditioner. No suspicious noises intruded on the silence. Still . . . it wouldn't hurt to look in on Todd.

As he swung his legs to the floor, a muffled sound came from the direction of his son's room. A sound he recognized all too well. One he'd heard almost nightly in the early days.

The beginning of a nightmare.

He rose and flipped on the bedside lamp, waiting a moment while his eyes adjusted to the sudden brightness. He'd thought they were past this. That once the bad dreams had subsided, then disappeared, they'd never reappear. And they hadn't.

Until two weeks ago.

Now, thanks to a bizarre coincidence in a mall, Todd had regressed. The disturbing dreams were back—different in subject matter, but related—and fragments of memory were resurfacing. Nothing specific enough to raise concerns . . . yet. But who knew what else might get shaken loose?

Hurrying down the hall, he swiped a bead of sweat off his temple as the thrashing sounds and muttered cries grew louder.

As he reached the threshold of his son's room, one clear word emerged from the otherwise unintelligible mumblings.

Kevin.

No!

He fought for air, grabbing the door frame for support. Telling himself the name was just the product of a dream. That dreams fade quickly. That there was no danger. That Todd wouldn't remember what he'd said once he woke up.

So wake him up! Stop the dream!

Prodding himself into action, he lurched toward the bed and sank down on the edge.

"Todd." He grasped his son's shoulders and gave a gentle shake. "Todd . . . come on, wake up, buddy. You're just having a dream."

It took several tries, but finally Todd's eyelids flickered open. "Dad?"

"Yeah, I'm here."

Todd rubbed his eyes. "I had that dream again."

Not what he'd wanted to hear.

"What dream?"

"You know. The one I had when Diane was here the day I was sick, with the lady at the mall. I told you about it." He picked up his Cardinals bear and held it tight against his chest. "I kept trying to get to her, but people were pulling me back. And this time, there was water at the bottom of the escalator. Like a lake. Why would there be a lake in the mall? And how come I keep dreaming about that lady?"

He wished he knew.

"Hard to say, buddy." He kept his tone casual. Unconcerned. "Our brains can do strange things while we sleep. But I'm sure you'll stop having it soon." If fate was kind.

Not that it ever had been in the past.

Todd yawned and stretched, his eyelids already growing heavy again. "Do we know anyone named Kevin?"

Greg's breath hitched. So much for assuming he wouldn't remember what he'd said in the dream.

"I don't think so." Greg swallowed as a sharp pain pierced his midsection. "Why?"

"I don't know. That name's stuck in my mind."

Meaning he didn't connect it with the woman on the escalator—yet.

And Greg intended to keep it that way, if he could.

"You know, I think one of the guys who worked at the hardware store back in Montana was named Kevin."

Todd squeezed his eyes half shut, then shook his head. "I don't remember him."

"You were real little. But sometimes strange things stick in our brain, like you said."

"Yeah, I guess." He yawned again and snuggled into his pillow. "Dad, do you think we could go to church some Sunday?"

Where on earth had that come from?

"We can talk about that later. You need to go back to sleep now."

"Diane said we could go with her if we want to."

One mystery explained, at least. Diane had been after him for weeks to attend services with her after he'd mentioned he'd once been a churchgoing man.

Not going to happen—for him, anyway. Todd . . . maybe.

"You have books about the Bible and Jesus." It was the best he could do for now, even if it was less than Jen would have wanted. How could he do more when talking about God made him uncomfortable?

"It's not the same. She said they sing songs and have classes for kids and eat donuts afterward."

"We'll talk about it another time, champ." He tucked the sheet over his son and stood. "Right now we both need our sleep."

"Okay." Todd's eyelids drifted closed. "We're gonna have cupcakes at daycare tomorrow. I hope I get a chocolate one."

Greg watched him for a few moments, the steady rise and fall of his chest, the sturdy arms holding the Cardinals bear, the

placid features. This was all he'd ever wanted. His son, asleep
in his bed, looking forward to tomorrow.

With a sigh, he trekked back down the hall to his room, sat on
the edge of the mattress, and dropped his head into his hands.

What a night.

Kevin.

God.

Nightmares about blonde women and water.

Why couldn't all of his problems go away and leave him in
peace?

Even Diane had become a burden. The very woman who'd
given him hope that maybe, just maybe, he could start over. That
it didn't have to be him and Todd alone against the world. That
there might be room in their life for someone else to love. But
now that Kate Marshall had intruded, stirring up memories best
left forgotten, having Diane around was dangerous.

Having *anyone* around was dangerous.

Wearily, he lay back on the pillow. Once they got past this crisis . . . once Todd's memories ebbed back into the dark recesses
of his mind where they belonged . . . he might be able to try
again with Diane. But that could be way down the road, based
on the stuff he'd read on the Net about children's memories.
And most women weren't willing to hang around all that long.
Especially someone like Diane, whose trust in men was already
low, thanks to her jerk of a husband.

He bunched the sheet in his fingers. If only he could explain
things to her. Tell her he cared, and come up with a valid reason
for the temporary separation.

But creative thinking had never been his strong suit. He was
a practical, hands-on, analyze-the-problem-and-fix-it kind of
guy. Give him the right tools, he could work magic.

Except this problem couldn't be fixed with a hammer or
screwdriver.

Turning on his side, he reached over and flipped off the light. The room plunged into darkness—kind of like his life had of late.

His stomach gurgled . . . just like it used to. The burning in his chest had returned too, the piece of leftover pizza he'd eaten as a bedtime snack coming back to haunt him. He'd thought he was past all this too.

Yet the nightmare was starting again—the waking nightmare. The one where he battled against constant fear, wondering if this was the day he would lose his son. The one he'd finally wrestled into submission and overcome.

Still gripping the sheet, he tried to will the heartburn and indigestion away—but twenty minutes later he gave up and trudged to the bathroom. In the back of the medicine cabinet, he found the bottle of antacids. Almost full.

Good thing.

Because as he shook several into his palm, he had a feeling he was going to be using a lot of them.

"This was a very productive session, Grace." Kate knitted her fingers together on her desk and smiled at the fortysomething widow across from her. "I think you'll be ready to begin applying for jobs next week, and I'm lining some up for you to consider."

Grace closed her notebook and picked up her purse. "It's still hard for me to believe I have to get a job. I had no idea Sam had refinanced the house to fund those speculative investments, or that he'd let his life insurance lapse. He said if I handled the kids, he'd handle the money, and I trusted him, you know?"

"Yes. I know. And you're not alone. I hear that story a lot." They'd been over this many times, but sometimes the women she saw needed a sympathetic ear as much as they needed career counseling. Kate circled her desk and joined the woman by the door. "Let me walk you out."

"You've been very kind." Grace swiped at her eyes as they started down the hall. "I don't know what I'd have done if my friend hadn't recommended you."

"I'm glad I could help—but you're a survivor. You'll be fine." How many times had she repeated that mantra to clients? Too many to count. But repetition helped drive it home, and self-confidence was critical in job interviews. "Nancy will set you up with an appointment for . . ." Kate's voice trailed off as they reached the lobby and a tall man with dark eyes, dressed in a jacket and tie, rose.

"Mr. Sullivan has been waiting to see you, Kate." Nancy gestured to Connor from her seat behind the reception desk.

"I'm sorry. Did we run over our time?" Grace touched Kate's arm, drawing her attention.

"No. We're right on schedule. Nancy will get that appointment set up for you. I'll see you next week." She transferred her attention to her unexpected visitor. "Would you like to come back to my office?"

"Yes. Thanks."

"Nancy, would you get my calls for a few minutes?"

"Sure." The receptionist made no attempt to hide her appreciative perusal of Connor as he crossed the lobby.

"This way." Kate indicated the hall, and he fell in behind her as her spirits took a nosedive.

There could only be one reason for this visit.

He'd gotten the age-progressed photo back from Elaine, and it wasn't a close enough match to pursue.

Why else would he come in person, except to break the bad news? If there was a match, he'd simply have called and told her, and they would have discussed next steps.

Steeling herself, she gestured to the sitting area in her office.

"I heard from Elaine." He sat in the chair adjacent to hers and pulled a thin manila folder from his briefcase.

"That's what I figured." She twisted her hands in her lap. "It's not a match, is it?"

Instead of replying, he handed her the folder.

It felt flimsy in her unsteady hands. As flimsy as her whole story. As flimsy as the case this man had diligently worked on despite the long odds of success.

Her hopes crashing, she took a steadying breath and opened the folder.

The boy from the mall stared back at her, this time in a close-up head-and-shoulders shot.

Frowning, she looked behind the image. It was the only one in the file.

"I don't understand . . . where's Elaine's photo?"

"You're looking at it."

As his words registered, her heart stumbled, and the air whooshed out of her lungs. Dear heaven, could it be . . . ?

"I had the same reaction. That's why I came over. I could have emailed it, but I wanted to be here when you saw it." He pulled another file out of his briefcase and handed it to her as well. "That's the boy from the mall."

She flipped open the second folder. Both the grainy close-up shot from the mall and one of the high-quality images Connor had taken of the child at the daycare center were inside.

It was a remarkable match.

"Did Elaine . . . did she see your pictures before she did hers?"

"No. I'd never prejudice her in that way. This is her take on what your son looks like now based on the photos you supplied from his younger years."

"I can't believe it." The trembling in her fingers worsened, and as the images in her hands began to quiver, she lowered them to her lap. "I haven't let myself even think about what might come next. This seemed too much to hope for. So . . . what do we do now?"

He leaned forward and clasped his hands between his knees, his expression sober. "First of all, as remarkable as the similarity is, there's a very strong chance it's a fluke. Coincidences do happen, and people do have doubles. In this situation, I'd be inclined to think that was the case—except for a couple of other facts. The boy turned when you called your son's name, and he used a unique term from Kevin's childhood. Coupling those details with that photo"—he gestured to the file in her lap—"moves your story from the realm of improbable to possible. But it's still a long shot."

She nodded, doing her best to rein in her surging optimism. "I understand that."

"Then here's what I propose. We dig into Greg Sanders's background. Find out everything there is to know about him. I'll start with the Net, which is faster and less expensive than gumshoeing it. Depending on what I uncover, we might need to ramp this up and do some personal investigation, possibly travel to his former place of residence, if there is one. Maybe get my colleagues involved."

"What about DNA? Wouldn't it be simpler to try and get a sample from the boy, see if it matches?"

"Matches what? Do you have any of your son's baby teeth or a toothbrush, comb, or personal item of any kind?"

She exhaled. "No. All I have are a few pieces of clothing and his blankie, and all of those have been washed. I do have some hair from his first haircut, but don't you need the hair follicle to test the DNA?"

"For nuclear DNA, yes—and that's critical for paternity cases. But I'm not ruling out DNA. We only need the mitochondrial variety to determine whether two people share the same maternal line. For that, matching to cut hair samples works fine—yours, specifically. So if everything else we find continues to suggest a link, we'll try to get a sample of the boy's hair."

"How?"

"Follow them to a salon or, if Sanders cuts his son's hair, do some trash covers."

"What's that?"

He flashed her a smile. "A messy job. It means going through a person's trash."

"Is that legal?"

"Once trash is on the curb for pickup, it's considered abandoned property and fair game. I'd rather not go that route unless we have to, because if Sanders is cutting his son's hair, he's probably not doing it very often. We might have to run trash covers twice a week—depending on the pickup schedule in his subdivision—until we hit pay dirt, and someone could notice. That would be my last resort . . . but if it's the only way to establish a link, we'll use it."

She gripped the files in her lap. "And if we do establish a link?"

"We call in the heavy guns. In this case, the FBI. However, that's down the road a ways. We have a lot of work to do before we let ourselves get carried away." He closed his briefcase and stood. "I'm sure you have clients waiting, so I won't keep you."

She stood too. "Do you need these photos back?"

"No. I have copies."

Fingering the edge of the file, she exhaled. "I still can't believe the match. But if this boy is my son . . ."—she furrowed her brow as the implications of that scenario began to ping in her mind—"that raises a lot of disturbing questions."

"Yes, it does."

He hesitated, as if he wanted to say more, and Kate scrutinized his face. "Is there something you're not telling me?"

"No." His reply was immediate—and sincere. "You know everything I know at this point. But now that we're digging in,

I want to cover all the bases. Do you have a copy of the police report from the accident?"

"Yes. I could fax it to you when I get home."

"That would be fine. And now I'll let you get back to work."

She followed him out to the lobby, where he turned and extended his hand. Kate placed her fingers in his, but instead of a normal shake, he gave her a reassuring squeeze—and brushed his thumb over the back of her hand. For one brief moment, his intense gaze locked with hers. It was filled with . . . what? Some strong emotion she couldn't identify—but it sent a zing of adrenaline zipping through her.

Then he was gone.

For several more seconds, Kate stared at the closed door. Reminding herself to breathe. Relishing the lingering warmth on her hand from the stroke of his thumb. Wondering what it would be like to step into those strong arms and . . .

Enough.

She didn't have time for silly daydreams.

Turning, she found Nancy watching her.

"Hot guy." The receptionist arched an eyebrow.

Striving for a dismissive tone, she shrugged. "He's a business associate."

Nancy sighed. "Every guy I do business with is balding and has a paunch."

"Luck of the draw, I guess."

And there was some truth to that. She'd had no idea when she'd gone in search of a PI that the investigator who'd take her case would be movie-star handsome . . . not to mention smart, principled, and kind.

Yet as she walked back to her office, she couldn't help thinking that more than luck had been involved the day she'd walked into the Phoenix Inc. offices—and into Connor Sullivan's life. God's hand was in this.

But what, exactly, was his plan? Was he leading her to her son . . . to a new relationship . . . or possibly to both?

As Kate retook her seat behind her desk, a ray of late-morning sun peeked through the blinds, sending a ribbon of light across her desk. She swiveled around to look out her window, where blue skies had replaced the storms from earlier in the week.

Perhaps blue skies were returning to her world too.

Yet she couldn't stop the sudden shiver that ran through her despite the warming ray of sunlight splashing into her office.

Because if that little boy in the mall did turn out to be Kevin, someone had a secret to hide. A secret that involved a tragic father-son fishing outing three years ago during which her husband had died after apparently disregarding his promise that they'd wear their life vests—a promise she'd always been convinced he'd never break.

But if he hadn't broken it . . . if her son had disappeared, not died as the authorities had ruled . . . there was only one possible conclusion—which Connor was already considering, based on his request for a copy of the police report.

And it chilled her to the bone.

The so-called accident on Braddock Bay that fateful July day hadn't been an accident at all.

It had been kidnapping—and murder.

11

Sorry to delay the meeting." Connor directed his comment to Dev and Cal as he shrugged out of his jacket, tossed it on an empty chair in the Phoenix conference room, and took a seat.

"No problem. Sounds like you had a busy morning." Cal opened the file in front of him, clearly ready to get things moving.

"Yeah. Where were you going in such a rush an hour ago, anyway? You almost mowed me down in the hall—and got a shirtful of coffee as a souvenir." Dev lifted his mug.

"Unexpected meeting."

"Must have been urgent." Dev eyed him over the rim as he took a sip.

Connor uncapped his pen and shuffled through his notepad, searching for an empty page as he debated how to respond. His impromptu meeting with Kate hadn't been urgent; he could have emailed her Elaine's age-enhanced photo and they could have discussed next steps by phone. But after zero contact for three days, he'd wanted to see her—and delivering the photo in person had given him a quasi-legitimate excuse to do so.

A tidbit he had no intention of sharing with his partners.

He settled for a one-word reply. "Important."

"A new development in the little-boy case? You've been pretty closemouthed about it this week—and about your client." Dev waggled his eyebrows.

"As a matter of fact, there *has* been a development I want to discuss with both of you." Connor sent him a disgruntled look, then transferred his attention to Cal. "I don't want to take over your meeting, though."

Cal waved his concern aside and closed his file. "We can add an agenda item. My stuff will keep till the end. Besides, I'm interested in an update too."

Connor riffled through his briefcase and pulled out the folder containing his copies of the three photos he'd left with Kate, giving his colleagues a rapid-fire briefing on the progression of the case over the past few days. At the end, he opened the folder and spread out the fuzzy mall photo and the best of the shots he'd taken of the little boy at the daycare center. "And here's the age-progressed photo Elaine sent me this morning." He turned it over and placed it next to the other two.

Both of his partners leaned forward.

"Wow." That from Dev.

"I think you're on to something." Cal examined the photo for another few seconds, then leaned back. "I assume, based on this and the other suspicious circumstances your client mentioned, you're moving forward with a full investigation."

"That's the plan."

"This thing could get hairy." Dev continued to study the photos. "If this kid is your client's son, we're dealing with some serious crimes here. Kidnapping might be the least of them."

His partner didn't have to spell out his inference. They were all wired to draw the same conclusion: given Kate's insistence that her husband would never have removed his life vest—yet had been found without it—murder was becoming a very real possibility.

"I think we're all on the same wavelength." Connor tapped the pictures back into a stack and returned them to the folder.

"But until we have more than circumstantial evidence, we're not going to get any support from law enforcement."

"Might be illuminating to do a thorough background check on this Sanders guy." Dev doodled a series of concentric circles on the pad of paper in front of him.

"First item on my agenda. I'm going to put Nikki on it too."

Dev scowled. "There goes my filing. Down to the bottom of the priority list again."

"I could ask her to do that first."

"Nah." Dev waved the offer aside. "The pile in the corner isn't ready to topple yet. You can have her for a day or two."

"Thanks. If we get red flags on this guy—and my gut says we will—I may need you both to help me out with some pretexting or interviews or even some travel."

"Is your client on board with spending those kinds of bucks?" Dev added a bull's-eye to the center of the middle circle.

"Yes. She's been living with doubts for three years. She wants this thing fully investigated."

"Then we're all in." Cal folded his hands on the file in front of him. "The hottest assignment we have right now is the executive protection gig we're going to talk about in a minute. Other than that, I think the cases Dev and I are dealing with have some flexibility in terms of timing." He deferred to the other man, who nodded. "Anything else we need to talk about today on this?"

"No."

"Okay. Keep us in the loop. Now let me bring you up to speed on the logistics for the protection gig."

As Cal launched into the details about travel arrangements, agenda, and equipment for the upcoming three-man job, Connor did his best to switch gears. Considering that their Fortune 50 executive client was planning to travel to a world economic conference in New York despite receiving death threats, this was a high-risk job—one he should be spearheading, given his background. If Cal hadn't offered to do the heavy lifting, he wouldn't have been able to give Kate's case the focus it deserved.

This strategy session, however, required his full attention and detailed input. Time to put the compartmentalization skills he'd learned during his Secret Service years into action.

Unfortunately, they were proving elusive today, thanks to two big distractions: Kate—and his growing suspicion of murder.

Kate.

Murder.

Those two words in the same sentence didn't sit well.

So once this meeting was over, he'd start digging—deep—into Greg Sanders's background. And if he uncovered any credible evidence that the man had been involved in foul play, he was going straight to the FBI.

In the meantime, he intended to keep Sanders in his sights. Because from all indications on that surveillance tape, his subject had spotted Kate—and made a concerted effort to elude her. Meaning there was a strong possibility he knew who she was. And if he did, if he was culpable of serious crimes, he'd be nervous. On guard. Perhaps ready to flee.

But even if the man ran, he'd find him—whatever it took—and do everything in his power to restore to Kate the son she'd given up for dead.

"Would you like a soda or a cup of coffee or tea?" Kate spoke over her shoulder to the woman who was following her down the hall to her office, trying to psyche herself up for the last appointment of the day. Always a challenge when her energy was lagging, but more so on a Friday that had included an adrenaline-laced visit from Connor and a startling age-progressed photo.

"No, thank you."

"If you change your mind, just let me know." Kate entered

her office and gestured toward the casual seating area, bypassing her desk. Since her new client seemed on the nervous side, better to make things more sociable on this initial visit. They could get down to serious business next time.

The woman chose a comfortable upholstered chair. Kate took the one at a right angle to it and opened her notebook. Although she'd already reviewed the basic information sheet the woman had filled out after making the appointment, she scanned it again, giving her client a moment to get comfortable and relax. In view of the fact the referral had come from Sarah, this woman had probably also been a victim of domestic violence—and would spook easily.

"So, Diane, you've decided to reenter the job market?" Kate smiled at the blonde woman.

"Yes." She laced her hands into a tight knot on her lap.

"And you found me through Sarah."

"Yes. She said you did a great job for her."

Kate leaned back, keeping her posture open, friendly, approachable. "Nice to hear. And I'll do my best to help you find a position that's a good fit too. Why don't you give me a little background on your work experience and tell me some of the things you enjoyed most about your favorite job."

The going was slow at the beginning, with Diane offering abbreviated answers and shying away from any personal revelations. The woman gauged her words. Watched for reactions. Kept her arms crossed tight against her chest.

In other words, she had serious trust issues.

Not surprising, if she'd been a victim of abuse.

Still, this was the kind of challenging client Kate found most rewarding—once the barriers were down and they began working together. But it was going to take awhile to get there with Diane.

Half an hour into their conversation, however, the woman began to loosen up. She uncrossed her arms. The stiff line of her shoulders eased. She began to give more detailed answers. And she mentioned her previous difficult domestic situation.

The trust level was building.

Now they were getting somewhere.

Forty-five minutes in, after Diane hinted at the abuse—and the toll it had taken on her self-esteem—the woman teared up. "Sorry. I thought I was over crying about the bum."

"You've only been out of the relationship a few months. Hurts like that don't go away quickly." Kate handed her a box of tissues and touched her arm. "Are you sure I can't offer you a soda or a cup of tea?"

"You know . . . if it's not too much trouble, tea would be nice. Just the plain black kind. I never developed a liking for the fancy stuff, no matter how often Rich told me my tastes were too plebian."

"I'm a plain black tea person myself. In fact, I'll join you. Give me a couple of minutes and we'll finish up for today while we sip a cup."

Kate exited the office, closing the door behind her. It had been a productive session so far, and Diane Koenig showed a lot of promise. She was smart, articulate, and had a dormant sense of humor, based on a few of her comments. Hooking up with a loser like her ex-husband had derailed her, and she needed some help to get back on track, but she'd find the resources she needed to do that at New Start. Kate would see to it.

As she entered the small kitchenette and set about brewing the tea, she couldn't help but compare the men some of her clients had married with the PI who'd visited her this morning.

What a contrast.

But Diane would get through her ordeal. She'd taken constructive steps to turn her life around. And now that they were on their way to establishing a relationship of trust, Kate was certain Diane's experience at New Start would be a life-changing one.

Easing back in her chair, Diane rotated her neck to loosen the stiff muscles, took a deep breath, and let go of the last of her tension. This meeting hadn't been nearly as hard as she'd expected.

Thanks to Kate Marshall.

The New Start director was every bit as nice as Sarah had claimed. Sympathetic, attentive, thoughtful—and best of all, nonjudgmental. Of course, given the organization's mission and the many clients who came from difficult backgrounds, she'd probably heard every story in the book. One more woman who'd let herself be used by the man who'd professed to love her would be nothing new for the group's director.

Yet Kate had made her feel unique, special . . . and as if her future mattered to her not just as a counselor but as a person.

If her compassion was an act, it was Oscar caliber.

Somehow, though, Diane didn't think it was. Kate seemed genuine in her commitment to helping others improve their lives. Her passion about the organization's mission had come through loud and clear at several points in their conversation.

Feeling more relaxed by the minute, Diane rose and stretched. Thank goodness she'd followed through on Sarah's recommendation and contacted New Start. With Kate in her court, she had a feeling she'd be getting her life back on track sooner than she'd expected.

Flexing her shoulders, she strolled around the office. After forty-five minutes hunched in a chair, it was nice to get the blood flowing. A few circuits should help relax the kinks in her back too.

On her second lap, she stopped beside Kate's desk and leaned over to read the small plaque. The serenity prayer? That was a disconnect. Kate didn't strike her as the type who would easily accept that things couldn't be changed—not without first making a heroic effort to change things she thought needed changing. And that was an excellent lesson to take away from today's session. She, too, was done accepting the status quo. This meeting was her first step in a brand-new direction.

As she straightened up and started to turn back toward the seating area, her jacket caught the edge of a manila folder and sent it shooting toward the floor.

Heart tripping into double-time, she dived for it, praying Kate wouldn't return until she'd deposited it safely back on the desk. The last thing she needed was to have the counselor think she'd been snooping.

Although she managed to grab it before it hit the floor, a photograph of a child slid halfway out.

A child who looked a lot like Todd.

File in hand, Diane stared at the half image. Then, with a glance toward the door, she flipped the file open so she could see the whole thing.

Definitely Todd.

What in the world was Kate Marshall doing with a picture of Greg's little boy?

Voices spoke in the hall, close to the office door, and she pushed the photo back into the file, dropped it on the desk, and dashed back to her chair.

Five seconds later, Kate entered with two ceramic mugs. "Would you like sugar or cream?"

"No, thank you." She took the mug, wrapping her hands around it to warm her cold fingers as she tried to make sense of what she'd just seen.

Failed.

Nor could she ask about the boy without revealing that she'd been prowling around Kate's office.

Fifteen minutes later, when Kate stood to signal the end of

their meeting, she had no recollection of drinking her tea—
though the mug was empty—nor what the two of them had
talked about since the New Start director had returned.

"Diane . . . is everything okay? You got very quiet toward the
end." Kate took the mug from her fingers, concern softening
her features.

No. Things weren't okay. This puzzle was driving her crazy.

"Yes." She stood too. "I just . . . got distracted. I have a lot on
my mind." Like what the connection could possibly be between
Greg and Todd and Kate.

"All right. I'll walk you out, and Nancy can set up a convenient time for next week."

"No!" The vehement refusal was out before Diane could stop
it, and at Kate's startled reaction she softened her tone. "I'll get
back to you after I look at my schedule. And I can find my way
out. Thank you again for seeing me today."

Without giving Kate a chance to respond, she took off down
the hall.

At the entrance to the New Start suite, she paused long
enough to glance back. Kate was watching her from the doorway of her office, mug still in hand, her expression suggesting
she was puzzled—and troubled.

That made two of them.

And until she had a chance to decide what—if anything—
she was going to do about her disturbing discovery, she didn't
intend to come back.

"Are you working late?"

Connor angled away from his computer, toward Nikki. "Yeah.
You leaving?"

"Unless you need to me to stay and keep digging for info on
Greg Sanders."

"No. You sent me plenty of stuff to look through, and I've got a bunch of other leads to follow up on. Enjoy your weekend."

"I will. Don't stay too late. Remember, all work and no play . . ."

"Got it."

"As if you ever listen." She rolled her eyes. "There's more to life than work, you know."

With an effort, he kept his expression neutral. No one at Phoenix knew that was a sensitive subject for him—nor would they. His private business would stay private. "I'll keep that in mind."

"You do that. See you Monday."

Pushing aside the unpleasant memories Nikki had stirred up, he refocused on the task at hand—until Cal stuck his head in the office door twenty minutes later.

"Burning the midnight oil?"

What was this, a conspiracy?

Once more he swiveled toward the door. "It's only five-thirty. And who are you to talk? I don't see you rushing out, either."

Cal strolled in and sat in the chair across from his desk. "Moira's got a meeting with a source for an investigative piece she's developing. We'll be eating a late dinner. Very late." He did a slow survey of the littered mahogany expanse in front of him. "Given the disreputable state of your usually pristine desk, I'm guessing you had a busy afternoon. Find anything interesting on Mr. Sanders?"

"Interesting would be an appropriate word." He rolled his chair closer to the desk. "You want the skinny?"

"Or the fat. I'm in no hurry."

"Bear in mind, I'm just getting started. It took a while to piece together his social security number, but once we had that, we got all the basics through our favorite proprietary databases and information brokers." He tugged a sheet of paper from a folder. "Sanders was born in Cleveland and lived there his whole life—until three years ago."

Cal lifted an eyebrow. "Significant number."

"No kidding. He has a high school education and spent his career in the construction industry until five years ago, at which point there's a break in employment. Three years ago—the magic number again—he moved to Philipsburg, Montana."

"Doesn't sound like a bustling municipality."

"More like the middle of nowhere. Population is under a thousand—almost more elk than people, and that's not much of an exaggeration. And based on his Montana P.O. box address, my guess is he didn't even live in town."

"Perfect place to disappear."

"You have a suspicious mind."

"Inquiring. Your man have any run-ins with the law?"

"Nope. He's clean, as far as I can see."

"Married?"

"Was. His wife, Jennifer, died almost six years ago. Nikki dug up the notice in the local paper. No cause of death was noted, but donations to the American Cancer Society were requested in lieu of flowers. The write-up also mentioned she left a husband and a son named David."

Cal frowned. "How old is your client's son?"

"He'd be almost seven now."

"If Sanders's wife was battling cancer, it's not likely she had a child in the last year or two of her life. So assuming the kid your client saw is Sanders's actual son, he should be at least nine or ten."

"I thought the same thing. Except some kids look young for their age."

"Maybe." Cal crossed an ankle over his knee and laced his fingers over his stomach. "So when did Sanders show up in St. Louis?"

"March. He's back in construction again."

"What did he do in Montana?"

"An excellent question. It's on my list."

Cal stood and stretched. "Why do I think you're going to be putting in some long hours this weekend?"

"Because you know me too well?"

"Because you hate unsolved puzzles almost as much as I do. In your shoes, I'd be doing the same thing." He strolled over to the door. Turned. "If you need me to pitch in, call."

"Thanks, but you've put in plenty of hours this week already prepping for the security gig. Enjoy your time with Moira."

"Count on it." Without further delay, he disappeared down the hall. A few moments later, the back door opened, then clicked shut.

He was alone—as he would be for the rest of this Friday night and the empty weekend stretching ahead.

But perhaps his solitary status might change once he wrapped up this case and could think about elevating Kate's position in his life from client to date to . . . something more down the road.

Meaning he needed to focus on the case—and outline a course of action.

Connor picked up a pen and made a quick list of questions he needed answered. Some he could take care of through information brokers or public records. Others were going to require ear-to-the-phone and feet-on-the-pavement work—plus a fair amount of pretexting.

But it would have to be done carefully. Tipping off Sanders that PIs were on his trail could sabotage the investigation.

For tonight, he'd see what else he could turn up on the Net about Greg Sanders.

A discouraging half hour later, Kate's number flashed in the digital display on his phone.

A perfect way to end his day.

After returning his greeting, she got straight to business—and it was clear from the frustration in her voice that *she* wasn't smiling. "I wasn't sure I'd catch you before you left, but I wanted to let you know I've been trying to fax this police report ever since I got home twenty minutes ago. I know we couldn't live without our electronic gadgets, but thanks to days like this, for me it's a love-hate relationship. As long as you're still there, would you like me to drop it off? I'm not that far away."

He angled his wrist. Six-ten. Dinnertime, as the rumble in his stomach reminded him. "Have you eaten yet?"

"No. I started trying to fax this as soon as I got in the door."

"Why don't you go ahead and have dinner? I can swing by on my way home and pick it up. I'll be leaving soon, and a small detour your direction won't take that long." Besides, it would give him a chance to spend a few minutes in her company—an appealing fringe benefit.

"You probably haven't eaten yet, either."

"No."

"Well . . ." Pause. "There's a great Chinese takeout place down the street from my condo. It's my typical end-of-the-week dinner treat." Another pause. When she continued, her words came out in a rush. "If you'd like to share some Mongolian beef or sweet-and-sour chicken, I'd be happy to order extra as a thank-you for making a special trip tonight—and for all the effort you've put into this case so far."

She was inviting him to share her dinner?

Nice—even if he couldn't accept.

Could he?

While he wrestled with that dilemma, his mouth began spewing out words. "That would be great. Better than eating alone, especially considering the dire state of my fridge and freezer. But why don't you let me pick up the food on my way to your house?"

So much for his stoic, hands-off professionalism.

"No. I want this to be my treat. What time do you think you'll get here?"

As soon as possible?

Uh-uh. Better to sound a bit less anxious.

"How does six-forty-five sound?"

"Fine. I'll see you then."

They ended the call, and Connor leaned back, shaking his head. How did Kate consistently manage to short-circuit the left side of his brain? He should have refused her invitation. A handoff of the police report would have taken no more than thirty seconds and was far more prudent than spending an hour or two in her company.

Yet hard as he tried, he couldn't muster up one iota of regret.

This was going to be the best Friday night he'd spent in a very long while.

Swinging back to his computer, he tried to focus on one of the links Nikki had sent him as the numbers on the digital clock atop his credenza advanced with the speed of molasses. But he finally gave up and shut down. He was tired and hungry and preoccupied—thanks to a beautiful blonde with amazing green eyes—and he could miss some important piece of information if he continued. Tomorrow, he'd start fresh.

In the meantime, he'd enjoy tonight.

After retrieving his jacket, he flipped off the lights and headed toward the back door to set the security alarm, developing his strategy for the evening as he closed up shop for the night. He'd stick to business as much as possible, perhaps take a cursory look at the police report, ask a few questions. That would put a professional spin on the dinner. Other than that, he'd keep the conversation simple, light, and impersonal.

He'd also keep his distance.

And if he adhered to those rules, what could possibly go wrong?

12

Y ou must have eaten a big lunch."

At Connor's comment, Kate inventoried her plate. She'd put no more than a dent in the small portion of sweet-and-sour chicken she'd taken, and half of her Mongolian beef stared back at her.

Her lack of appetite had nothing to do with her lunch, however. The blame for that went to the man sitting an arm's length away in her dining room, eating a meal she should never have invited him to share. But somehow, her heart had bypassed her brain when he'd offered to swing by and pick up the police report. Pathetic, how she'd grabbed at the chance to avoid another long, lonely Friday night.

And definitely not wise. Neither of them needed any distractions in the middle of this case—and Connor Sullivan was one serious distraction. No wonder she'd spent the fifteen minutes since he'd arrived lamenting her lapse in judgment instead of eating.

"You know, I'm not bad at piecing together evidence like this"—he tapped the edge of her filled plate with a long, lean finger—"but I've never mastered mind reading. Was my hypothesis correct?"

Hypothesis? She tried to regroup. He'd commented on . . . her lunch. Right.

"No, not a big lunch." No lunch at all, in fact, since she hadn't found a spare minute to eat the chicken Caesar salad she'd toted home and stuck in her fridge. "I guess I'm just slower than you are—but the end result's the same." She forked a piece of beef, slid it between her teeth, and chewed, as if to prove her point.

The slight tapering of his eyes told her he wasn't buying her story—but to her relief, he dropped the subject.

"As long as you're still working through the first round, would you mind if I have second helpings? So you won't have to eat alone, of course." He gave her an engaging grin, displaying that appealing dimple.

The silence lengthened, and when she realized she was staring, she yanked her gaze away and gestured to the cardboard cartons on the table. "Help yourself. There's plenty."

He did so without further prompting, refilling his plate with two more full servings.

Despite her qualms about this cozy dinner, a smile snuck up on her. "Speaking of lunch . . . you must have eaten on the light side too."

"You might say that." He expertly scooped up some chicken and rice with the wooden chopsticks the restaurant had provided. The ones she always tossed because she'd never been able to get the hang of them.

"What?" Without losing a single grain of rice, he froze, food poised in midair.

"I'm admiring your deft handling of those." She gestured with her fork to the Chinese eating implements.

"On-the-job training from my Secret Service days. In some places I traveled, these were the only utensils provided. It was master them or starve." The chicken and rice disappeared. "I'll

170

let you in on a little secret: when my stomach's involved, I'm a fast learner."

Smile broadening, she dug into her own food.

"As for lunch . . . Nikki offered to grab a burger for me at noon, since I was too busy to go out, and I accepted. Big mistake."

"Why?"

He gave a long-suffering sigh. "She's been trying for months to get us all to eat healthier. I should have known she'd come back with some new-age bean curd/soy/wheat germ/tofu thing that looked like a hamburger, smelled like a hamburger—but most definitely did not taste like a hamburger. I think it even had garbanzo beans in it." Grimacing, he shook his head. "To add insult to injury, the side was zucchini fries . . . which weren't even fried." He scooped up more sweet-and-sour chicken. "Now this is real food."

Laughing, she tackled her own chicken. "Your receptionist seems to march—and eat and dress—to the beat of her own drummer."

"She does—but we couldn't live without her. She has a degree in computer forensics, and she can mine more stuff out of online databases than the three of us put together."

She stared at him. Were they talking about the same woman? The beach babe with the seashell necklace and the punk-rocker neon-blue streak in her hair?

"Your skepticism is showing." Connor sent her a teasing look. "But trust me, she's the real deal." As he secured a piece of beef with his chopsticks, his demeanor grew more serious. "You've heard the expression, if life hands you a lemon, make lemonade? Nikki's the lemonade queen."

Intrigued, Kate leaned closer. "How so?"

"She ran away from an abusive home at fifteen and lived on the street—a safer environment than being in the same house with her parents, which tells you a lot. Most kids like her wind up dead, addicted to drugs, or in prostitution rings. She was the exception."

"Why?"

"She crossed paths with a minister who not only helped her find her way to God but convinced her she could overcome her background. With his encouragement, she got her GED, then a full-time job, then applied for college. She worked all day, went to school at night, and kept waiting for the chance to rescue her kid brother from the family she'd escaped. In the end, she got her degree, got custody of Danny, and got the job at Phoenix. She married last year and just shared the news that she's expecting her first child."

"Wow." Kate finished the last bite of her chicken and set her fork down. "That's an amazing—and inspiring—story."

"Yeah. She's quite a woman. She and her husband coordinate the youth group at their church, and from what I hear, the teens love her. She speaks their language—filtered through faith—which makes her a perfect person to reach kids that age with important messages."

Kate rested her elbow on the table and propped her chin in her palm. "It just goes to show you should never judge by appearances."

"That happens a lot with my colleague Dev too. He tends to be a goof-off in the office and when he's not on duty, so few people who meet him casually would ever guess that when the pressure's on, he's a total pro—cool under fire, focused, deadly serious. Or that in his undercover ATF days, he went over to the dark side to infiltrate a ruthless Hispanic gang in the Southwest that dealt in drugs, gun trafficking, intimidation, and extortion."

"Double wow." Kate set her napkin on the table beside her empty plate—when had that happened?—and leaned back. "Is your other partner an intriguing mix too?"

172

Connor gathered up the last of his beef. "Nope. Cal is Cal. Steady. Calm. Reasoned. Serious. The kind of guy who does his homework and covers your back, no matter the risk to his."

"In other words, what you see is what you get."

"That about sums him up."

She picked up a stray grain of rice from the glass surface of her dinette table and scrubbed at the smear left behind. He'd been candid about his colleagues—would he be the same about himself?

Only one way to find out.

"So what about you?" She deposited the rice on her plate and took a sip of water. "Are you what you seem?"

For a fraction of a second, his hand hesitated as he scooped up more rice. If she hadn't been watching closely, she'd have missed the infinitesimal pause.

And it wasn't a positive sign.

Nor did the sudden undercurrent of tension vibrating in the room produce a warm and fuzzy feeling.

Bad move on her part.

As he chewed his last bite, taking far longer than necessary, she tried to figure out how to backtrack, to restore the easy camaraderie that had developed during their dinner.

But he responded before she could come up with a diplomatic way to change the subject. "Depends on what you see, I guess."

She toyed with her fork. Was he looking for honesty—or a lighthearted comeback? Hard to tell.

Yet how could he take offense at a compliment?

She gave him a steady look. "I see a conscientious, honorable man who knows his job and is willing to do whatever it takes to get that job done. Who has a clear understanding of duty and responsibility. Who's worthy of trust and confidence."

"You read the Secret Service motto on my desk."

"Guilty. And I have a feeling it's true both on the job—and off."

A muscle twitched in his cheek. "I appreciate the kind words, even if they're not 100 percent accurate." Before she had a chance to reply, he stood. "Could you point me to the bathroom? The soy sauce left me with sticky fingers."

"Sure. First door on the left." She gestured toward the hall, tucked under the steps that led to the two bedrooms on the second floor.

"I'll be back in a minute."

She watched him disappear. A few seconds later, a door clicked closed.

The symbolism wasn't lost on her. Nor the message.

Connor might be willing to talk about his colleagues, but his own life was off-limits. When he returned, he was going to change the subject, bring their impromptu dinner to a conclusion, and leave without clarifying his last comment.

And it needed clarifying.

Because based on the brief, sudden shaft of pain that had seared his eyes, his rebuttal of her praise hadn't been a standard-issue, modesty-prompted dismissal. She'd seen that look often in her counseling work. Unless her instincts were way off base, something had happened in Connor Sullivan's life that he wasn't proud of.

Sighing, Kate stacked their plates. It appeared she wasn't the only one involved in this case who was carrying around a lot of baggage. Even people like Connor, who presented a strong, in-control face to the world, had their scars—and their regrets.

But he didn't strike her as the type of man who shared them.

And she doubted he'd make an exception for her.

He should have realized where the conversation was heading and steered it in a different direction. Or responded with a witty comeback to Kate's are-you-what-you-seem-to-be question.

Instead, he'd given her an opening to pursue the subject. And pursue it she had.

Connor twisted the faucet and plunged his hands under the cold stream. Too bad her flattering assessment of him was flawed. He might have lived up to the Secret Service motto on the job, as she'd suggested—but in his personal life? Different story.

The very reason Lisa had walked away.

He shut off the water and dried his hands, the faint echo of a familiar heaviness settling in his chest. The ache of loss had dulled through the years, and he'd moved on, but the regrets—and shame—lingered.

Perhaps they always would.

Hand on the knob, he considered his strategy. He didn't want the evening to end on a strained note, not after he'd worked so hard to get Kate to relax once he'd realized he wasn't the only one having second thoughts about their dinner together.

On the other hand, it was possible he was overreacting to that awkward moment. His abrupt change of subject might barely have registered with his hostess. By the time he returned, she could be clearing the table and putting coffee on, the brief glitch in an otherwise pleasant evening forgotten. By her, at least.

Time to test that theory.

Leaving the guest bath behind, he retraced his steps down the hall to the dining area.

The table was empty, save for a couple of cellophane-wrapped fortune cookies and a folder. She was at the sink, rinsing off the plates. Coffee was brewing.

So far, so good.

He moved to the arched doorway that led into the kitchen. "You work fast."

She turned at his comment, an artificial smile pasted on her face, her shoulders taut.

Not so good.

She'd tuned in to his uneasiness after all. And why not? She was a counselor. A woman who dealt with problem-plagued people every day. Who was used to spotting issues and talking clients through them.

She was also a woman who'd dealt with plenty of her own trauma. Enough to recognize it in others, even without her training and professional experience.

"I put on some coffee if you're interested. And I left a copy of the police report on the table. I didn't know if you wanted to look through it here or just take it with you."

Take it with him and exit fast, if he was smart.

But his smarts seemed to have deserted him tonight.

Instead of doing the prudent thing, he walked over to the table and picked up the folder, weighing it in his hand. Not very thick for a report on two deaths. It wouldn't take long to read. But that was a job for later. He wanted total focus for that task—and he wasn't likely to achieve that with Kate a few feet away.

Yet he didn't want to leave.

Just do it, Sullivan. Get out of here.

Taking a deep breath, he turned back to her. She was leaning against the sink, arms folded, watching him.

"I'll give this a thorough review over the weekend. Thanks for dinner."

"You're welcome." She reached behind her and gripped the edge of the counter. "Look . . . before you go, I want to apologize. I have a feeling I stirred up some painful memories for you a few minutes ago, and I know how hard it is to be reminded of things you'd rather forget."

Connor's fingers tightened on the folder. She'd confronted the elephant in the room—and why not? This was the same woman who'd shared her story about Valium addiction, risked censure in the name of open, honest communication. The lady didn't back away from the hard stuff. She had guts.

176

More than he had.

Otherwise, he wouldn't have kept his less-than-honorable secret buried all these years, hiding it even from the partners who'd been his best friends since college days.

Truth be told, facing a bullet was easier than losing face or admitting his flaws.

So much for Kate's sterling assessment of him.

He loosened his tie, suddenly feeling too warm despite the hardworking air conditioner humming in the background. "There's no need to apologize."

"There's always a need to apologize when you cause pain. Even if it's unintentional."

Unintentional pain.

The perfect opening . . . if he was brave enough to take it.

But would she understand? Would she recognize that while he'd made mistakes, he'd learned his lesson and changed for the better? That now he truly was a man worthy of trust and confidence—both on and off the job?

And what if she didn't? What if she decided he wasn't worth the risk and backed off from the attraction flaring between them?

He looked down at the folder in his hands. Background on a tragedy she'd shared with him, just as she'd shared her darkest secret. And she deserved no less in return. Relationships needed to be based on full disclosure.

Might as well face the inevitable.

Summoning up every ounce of his courage, he gestured toward the table. "If you have a few minutes to spare, I'd like to tell you a story—even though it's not about my proudest moment."

Her eyes softened, and the taut line of her shoulders eased a fraction. "I have plenty of minutes to spare. My Friday nights tend to be quiet—and solitary. Would your story go down easier over coffee?"

Not likely. But at least a mug would give him something solid to hang on to.

"It might. Thanks."

Thirty seconds later she joined him, setting a steaming mug of black java in his place as she slipped back into her seat.

She'd remembered his coffee preference from their first meeting.

For some reason, that helped validate his decision to spill his guts.

He took a cautious sip of the undiluted brew, careful not to burn his tongue. "Do you remember the conversation we had about my Secret Service job, that morning we were watching the daycare center?"

"Yes. You said you liked your work, but that it dominated your life to the exclusion of everything else. You also mentioned an epiphany that led you to reorganize your priorities."

She'd been paying close attention then too.

"I can see why you're good at what you do. Those kinds of listening skills must serve you well with your clients."

Her gaze didn't waver. "I'm not wearing my counselor hat tonight."

Then what hat are you wearing?

The question hung between them, unasked—and unanswered.

Better that way . . . for now.

"Well, there was a specific incident that caused me to have that epiphany."

"There usually is."

He took another sip of coffee. For some reason, the straight-up taste he preferred was bitter on his tongue tonight. "This one involved a woman."

She remained silent, her placid, receptive expression unchanged, inviting confidences.

"Her name was Lisa. She worked in PR at the Kennedy Center.

Our paths crossed during a security detail I was in charge of for some visiting heads of state who wanted to attend a performance there. We began dating, and eventually I started thinking about marriage. Then, at the age of twenty-eight, she was diagnosed with breast cancer."

Sympathy flooded her eyes, and she reached out to touch his hand. "I'm so sorry."

He looked down at her slender fingers resting against his, wishing he deserved her compassion.

But he didn't.

He lifted the mug, disengaging from her—and missing the connection at once.

After swallowing the bitter coffee, he set it aside. "Before you jump to any wrong conclusions, she made a full recovery. Last I heard by way of a former colleague, she's been declared cancer-free."

Kate frowned. "I'm not sure I understand. If you had marriage on the mind, why aren't the two of you still together?"

"Because we were never together much to begin with—which was the crux of the problem. Being on the vice president's detail was a 24/7 job, much of it spent out of the country. Trips were often scheduled with very little notice. It was almost impossible to maintain any kind of personal life. I did manage to arrange some time off to be there for her first chemo treatment, but two days later I was called back to deal with an unexpected trip to the Middle East. Lisa wasn't feeling too rocky, so I didn't think it was a problem. But the rough stuff began a few hours after I left. To make matters worse, I wasn't there for the next two treatments, either."

The grooves on Kate's brow deepened.

Not a positive sign.

"Is that why you two broke up? Because you weren't there when she needed you?"

"Partly. But more than that, I think she assumed it was an omen of things to come. Lisa grew up with a workaholic father who had an international travel job, and she didn't want her children to have an absentee father. Nor did she want an absentee husband who put his job above all else."

Kate gave him a direct look. "I can understand that."

His own gaze remained steady. "I can too, in hindsight."

She gave a tiny nod, as if she approved of his answer. "So she decided it was better not to have a man in her life than to have a man who wasn't there anyway."

"That was part of it—but there's more to the story. During one of my trips, she became ill very suddenly. Her new neighbor intercepted her stumbling to her car and ended up driving her to the ER. They clicked. And despite the fact he was a senior-level international airline pilot, he managed to adjust his schedule to be on hand during the worst parts of her chemo treatments. He was the one who held her while she threw up. Who ran errands for her. Who picked up food to try to entice her to eat when her appetite disappeared. Long story short, they ended up getting married."

Compassion once more softened her eyes. "That must have been very difficult for you."

Again, more consideration than he deserved—and time for more true confessions.

He squeezed his mug, welcoming the sting of heat on his fingers. "Yes. I was blindsided by the breakup. But I shouldn't have been—and I wouldn't have been if I'd stayed close enough to know what was going on in her life. If you love someone, you should be there for them during the tough stretches, no matter the cost to yourself—or your job. Love's supposed to bear all things and endure all things. It's not supposed to fail."

Her eyebrows rose. "You know your Bible."

"I've renewed my acquaintance with it over the past few

years, after letting my relationship with God lapse for too long."

She studied him, her next words slow—and careful. "Since your love wasn't as strong as it should have been based on that guidance in Corinthians, could it be you didn't love Lisa as much as you thought you did?"

"Maybe." But it didn't absolve him from guilt. "She was fun to be with, and the relationship was convenient—for me, at any rate. But at the time, I thought it was true love. So I should have been there for her. Putting my job first, especially during a crisis in her life, was flat-out wrong."

Her silence told him she agreed, and his stomach coiled as he took another sip of his cooling coffee. Time to wrap this up—and try to deal with the fallout.

"After the breakup, I took a long, hard look at my life . . . and I didn't like the hotshot I'd become, whose job was always priority number one. As a result, I started going back to church, had a lot of heart-to-hearts with the minister, and decided if I ever got serious about a woman again, our relationship would get top billing. I also decided to make a new start. When the opportunity with Phoenix came up, I realized God was giving me the chance I'd prayed for. I walked away from the Secret Service and never looked back."

Silence fell in the kitchen as Kate studied him. "Since I didn't know you in your Secret Service days, I can't speak to the man you were then. But I stand by what I said earlier about the man you are now."

She wasn't holding his past mistakes against him.

Amazing.

He finished off his coffee before he attempted to speak, hoping his words didn't come out in a croak. "I appreciate that. And I want you to know one other thing. I've never told that story to anyone."

Surprise flickered in her eyes, along with a question. One she didn't voice.

He answered it anyway, since he'd already broken every rule he'd formulated for this evening and long ago crossed the line from professional to personal.

"You shared your story about your struggles with Valium; I thought it was only fair to reveal the skeletons in my own closet. I think honesty and transparency are important in any relationship, and I'm hoping once this case is resolved, we can get to know each other a lot better on a personal level—if you're interested."

She picked up one of the fortune cookies and played with the cellophane wrapper. When she spoke, he had to lean close to hear her soft words. "You know, after John died I wrote off romance. He was a wonderful husband, and I figured I'd had my chance at happiness. That he'd always be the center of my life, even if all I had left were memories. But much as I loved him, memories aren't enough to chase away the loneliness." She looked over at him. "That's a long-winded way of saying I'm interested."

Warmth filtered into the corner of his soul that had lain cold and dark and dormant for five long years. "Despite what I told you tonight?"

"In some ways, because of it. I'm honored you trusted me enough to share your story, and I'm impressed by the way you learned from your experience and changed for the better. That's all God asks of us; how could I expect more?"

Once again, his throat contracted. He wanted to tell her how much her words meant to him. Wanted to stand up, fold her into his arms, and press her close to his heart. To hold her—just hold her. That would be sufficient . . . for now.

But even that small display of affection was too much, too soon. No matter the confidences they'd exchanged, until this case was over, he needed to maintain some professional decorum. Or salvage what was left of it. He owed it to his colleagues to play by the Phoenix rules, as they had.

"Thank you for that." He picked up the police report. "I'm looking forward to the future, but for now I need to focus on this—and let you know there's an unwritten rule at our agency about fraternizing with clients."

"Not allowed?"

"No—though I obviously overstepped tonight. Going forward, I'll have to keep things as businesslike as possible. But once we solve this case and get the answers you need, I won't have to worry about that rule anymore." Leaning forward, he picked up the other fortune cookie and lifted it. "Shall we?"

The condo fell silent as they unwrapped their cookies, broke them in half, and extracted the thin slips of paper.

"I like mine. 'The project you are working on will be a great success.'" Connor set the paper on the table. "What does yours say?"

A soft flush crept over her cheeks. "Mine's kind of off-the-wall. Aren't these things supposed to be gender neutral?"

"Yes. They almost have to be. Why?"

In silence, she handed him her fortune.

Curiosity piqued by her enigmatic expression, he scanned it.

His heart was yours from the moment you met.

That *was* unusual. And uncanny.

Because even though they were just getting to know each other, he had a feeling it was true.

He folded the piece of paper in half and slipped it into his pocket.

She cocked her head. "Are you keeping that?"

"Yep."

"Why?"

"Evidence."

"Of what?"

"Your charm."

A smile tickled her lips. "Very smooth."

"Also very true." He winked, then rose. "Show me out?"

She followed him to the door, but he didn't linger. The temptation was too great to follow through on the impulse that had rocked him a few minutes ago and take her in his arms.

"I'll call you with any questions I have once I look this over." He lifted the police report.

"Okay." She folded her arms. As if she, too, was fighting the urge to reach out. "Have a good weekend."

"I'll try." *But it would be better if I shared it with you.*

He didn't speak the words, but her faint flush suggested she'd read his mind—and felt the same way. Did she have any clue how appealing she was with those big green eyes and those soft lips that were made for kiss—

Get out of here, Sullivan.

Right.

"I'll be in touch."

Without waiting for a reply, he plunged into the muggy August night—wishing it was a cold shower instead.

And praying the police report in his hand and the information he dug up on Sanders and the little boy from the mall would provide some answers—pronto—to the puzzle Kate had handed him the day she'd walked into his office . . . and into his life.

13

Diane stopped her car in front of Greg's house, turned off the engine, and squeezed the steering wheel.

This was dumb.

She should have dropped off Todd's birthday present yesterday, when no one was home, instead of waiting until today. If Greg and Todd were following their usual Saturday morning ritual, they were probably inside eating pancakes right now.

But was it so wrong to want to see Todd's reaction to the special gift she'd bought three weeks ago, before things between her and Greg had gone south? Maybe get a hug from the little boy who'd stolen her heart—just as his father had?

Besides, she wanted answers about the photograph she'd seen yesterday in Kate Marshall's office, and Greg was the only one who could provide them.

Unless he didn't know about the picture.

That would make the whole situation even more unnerving.

As the cool air in the car warmed, Diane picked up the colorfully wrapped box from the passenger seat and slid out. Might as well get this over with.

On the tiny front porch, she took a deep breath, pressed the bell, and waited.

Half a minute later, when Greg opened the door, shock rippled through her. Creases radiated from the corners of his eyes, and shadows hung underneath. The furrows embedded on his brow were new, as were the grooves beside his mouth.

He looked as if he hadn't slept since she'd last seen him a week ago.

Trying to keep her features neutral, she lifted the box. "I brought Todd a birthday present."

"Who is it, Dad?" The boy's voice floated in from the kitchen, followed by the sound of bare feet slapping against wood. A moment later, he poked his head under Greg's arm and gave her a gap-toothed grin, his face lighting up when he spotted the gift. "Wow! Is that for me?"

His unbridled enthusiasm and bubbly energy were a marked contrast to his father's taut, weary demeanor. "You're the birth-day boy, aren't you?"

"Yeah!"

"Let's see . . ." She pretended to consider. "Are you eleven or twelve today?"

He giggled. "I'm only seven."

"No! Are you sure? You look much older."

He puffed out his chest. "I guess I'm big for my age."

"I guess you are. And minus a tooth too."

"Yeah." He poked his tongue into the empty space. "It was loose, so I pulled it out last night."

"All by yourself? That was very brave."

"Well . . . Dad helped a little." He gave the present another eager perusal. "I love birthdays."

"Then this will help you get started with yours." She handed over the package.

He held it against his chest and looked up at Greg. "Can I open it now?"

"Sure."

As Todd began ripping off the paper, Diane swallowed back her disappointment.

Greg wasn't going to ask her in.

So how was she going to ask about the photo she'd seen in Kate's office?

"Whoa! An erector set, like the one you told me you had when you were a kid, Dad. This is awesome!" Todd extricated the carrying case from the shiny paper, his eyes glowing. "Thank you, Diane."

He launched himself at her, and she bent down, holding on tight as she savored the little boy smell and the brief taste of the maternal role she'd never played.

Maybe would never play.

"I wish you could stay and have cake with us." Todd's voice was muffled against her shoulder.

She swallowed past her melancholy. "It's kind of early for cake, honey."

He released her and stepped back. "You could stay for pancakes, except we ate those already."

Straightening up, she gripped her purse. "I had breakfast before I came."

"Would you like some coffee?"

She shifted her attention to Greg. His tone was no more than cordial, but the longing in his eyes told her he wanted her to stay.

Why would a man who'd always been vocal about how much he enjoyed her company suddenly clam up? Or perhaps she'd been reading him wrong, seeing what she wanted to see. Given her courtship track record with Rich, that was a distinct possibility.

She toyed with the idea of declining—but this was her opportunity to ask about the photo in Kate's office.

"Sure. I have a few minutes. But I'd prefer something cold."

"No problem." Greg moved aside and ushered her in.

"Can I open the box, Dad?" Todd glanced up from where he'd plopped on the throw rug in the living room.

"Yeah. Just keep everything together. Maybe later we'll build an excavator."

"Like the one on the construction site you took me to in the spring?"

"Close enough."

"Cool!"

As Todd refocused on his present, Greg followed Diane into the kitchen. "Would you like a soda or orange juice?"

"Juice would be fine."

He withdrew a glass from the cabinet and crossed to the refrigerator. "That was a very thoughtful gift. Too expensive, though."

She gave a dismissive flip of her hand as she claimed the kitchen chair that had become "hers" over the past couple of months. "I don't have the opportunity to buy birthday gifts for children very often. I enjoyed the giving as much as Todd enjoyed the getting."

"Well, you have my thanks too. That would have been out of my price range." He set the glass on the table in front of her but remained by the counter with his mug of coffee. Keeping his distance.

As his last comment registered, she frowned. Was *that* his problem? She'd always known money was tight for him, that his wife's battle with cancer had drained a lot of his reserves, but he'd never suggested her tonier lifestyle was an impediment to their relationship or that it intimidated him in the least. Greg didn't seem like the kind of guy who made class distinctions.

Could she have been wrong about that, though? Did he resent her ability to buy his son a gift that was beyond his means?

"Listen . . . I'm sorry if the cost of the gift is a problem."

His blank look spoke volumes—she hoped. "What do you mean?"

Lifting one shoulder, she sipped her juice. "You know . . . that it's more than you would have been able to afford."

"Why would I resent a gesture of kindness that benefited my son?"

So her reading had been correct. The difference in their financial situations wasn't the issue.

Then what was?

But figuring that out wasn't her mission today. She needed to focus on the photo of Todd.

The rattle of parts from the erector set was audible as Todd sorted through them in the nearby living room, so unless she whispered, he'd be able to tune in to their conversation. Not the best place for a candid discussion.

Rising, she gestured toward the back door. "Mind if I drink this out there? I'd like to get some fresh air."

Expression wary, he hesitated, then pushed off from the counter. "Sure. Let me tell Todd we'll be outside and I'll join you in a minute."

He opened the back door for her, closing it again once she exited onto the deck. Already the day was getting muggy, and she moved toward the small patch of deck shaded by a large oak tree.

Sticky weather she could handle for a few minutes.

The sticky situation with Greg . . . not as well. But she had to make an attempt to crack the puzzle that had kept sleep at bay last night.

And if Greg was as clueless as she about why Kate Marshall had a photo of Todd, she'd back off and let him solve the strange mystery.

Why had Diane relocated their conversation outside, where Todd would be unable to hear? Was she going to revisit the nightmare she'd witnessed the day he'd been sick, ask questions? Or was she going to press him for an explanation about his withdrawal? And if she did, what could he say to convince her he was still interested—just not right now?

Greg jammed his fingers through his hair as he walked toward the living room.

Why did life always have to be so complicated?

"Diane and I will be out on the deck, champ. You need anything?"

"Nope." Todd didn't even look up as he rummaged through the parts in the box, and Greg's heart warmed. It was the perfect gift for a little boy with an active mind who loved to make things—and a thoughtful gesture from Diane. No surprise there. She was a caring, thoughtful woman. One he didn't want to lose.

But as he studied her through the kitchen window overlooking the deck, her stiff posture told him he could be heading into a showdown . . . and that losing her might be a very real possibility.

Leaving behind the coffee he didn't want, he opened the door, stepped into the heat—and hoped the move wasn't symbolic.

Diane had claimed the only sliver of shade, so he stayed in the sun, leaned back against the railing, and started to sweat. "What's up?"

She took a sip of her orange juice. "I had an odd experience yesterday I wanted to share with you."

Not what he'd expected.

"Tell me about it."

"I decided to follow through on the idea of getting a job, so I went to the career counseling center one of my support-group friends recommended. Do you know a woman named Kate Marshall?"

The name was like a punch in the solar plexus.

Diane had run into Kate Marshall?!

His lungs deflated, and he grasped the railing behind him,

190

struggling to keep his face impassive, to breathe, as he tried to formulate a response.

Play it cool. Stay calm. This might mean nothing.

"Kate Marshall." He pretended to try and place the name, all the while willing his lungs to kick back in. "I don't think I've ever met anyone with that name. Why do you ask?" At least his voice wasn't quaking as much as his insides were.

"Because she has a picture of Todd."

The bottom dropped out of his stomach, and he jerked upright from the railing. "What?!"

"You don't know anything about this?"

"No." Greg's mind raced. Had the Marshall woman somehow identified him, found out where he lived, been stalking him? But that made no sense. If she'd found him, she wouldn't skulk around. She'd go to the authorities. Not that a move like that would do her much good. He was a law-abiding citizen, and there was nothing to link him to her—or her son. They'd have no grounds to investigate. But where in the world had she gotten a picture of Todd? "What kind of picture was it?"

Diane shrugged. "One of those studio head-and-shoulder shots with a plain blue background."

That couldn't be. Such a thing didn't exist. He'd taken very few photos of Todd through the years, and they'd never darkened the door of a photo studio.

What was going on?

He planted his fists on his hips. "You're right. This is bizarre."

"Since you don't know anything about it, do you think it's one of those look-alike things? They say everyone has a double."

If only it was that simple.

"That seems like a stretch." He shoved his fingers through his hair again and threw out a question to buy himself a few more moments to think. "Is this woman on the up-and-up?"

"As far as I know. She was very nice, and she's in charge of this organization. I doubt they'd hire someone with a shady background for a job like that. Why? What are you thinking?"

"I don't know." That was the truth. His mind was still trying to grapple with Diane's bombshell. He needed some time to process the news, plan his strategy. Not a task he could manage on the fly, nor while he was reeling. "But if that picture is really Todd, I'd sure like to know what's behind it."

"I thought you would. That's one of the reasons I dropped off his gift instead of leaving it outside the door."

"I appreciate that. Listen . . . can I call you later? I need to chew on this for a while."

"Yeah. I have to run a few errands this morning, but I'll be home later. Are you guys going for pizza tonight?"

"I'm letting the birthday boy pick a place for dinner. So far he hasn't made a decision, but I'll call you before we go."

She lifted the glass and drained her orange juice, a glimmer of disappointment in her eyes. It wasn't hard to figure out the cause. She'd hoped he'd ask her to join them.

And maybe he would. Since she already had an in with Kate Marshall, he might need her help.

But that wouldn't be the only reason he'd ask her. He wasn't a user. Never had been. He'd ask her because he owed her for this tip-off—and because he enjoyed her company and had missed her for the past week.

"Let me take that." He walked over to her and claimed the glass. "You made the better choice. It's too hot for coffee." Although the heat wasn't the main reason sweat was trickling down his back.

She searched his eyes, and he tried to infuse them with warmth and intimacy as he held her gaze. Willing her to understand he cared . . . even if he couldn't explain why he'd pulled back.

Yet in light of this new development, perhaps he should rethink his retreat. It might be safer to stay in closer touch and hope

Todd wouldn't remember anything else rather than keep her at arm's length while she was dealing with the Marshall woman.

Another thing to ponder once she left.

Behind him, the door slid open. He turned as Todd stuck his head out.

"The guy who owns the house is on the phone for you, Dad."

"Tell him I'll be right there." He shifted back toward Diane, grateful for the interruption. "I need to take this. The air conditioner's been struggling, and I want to get our landlord to send out a heating and cooling technician."

"I can see myself out." She started across the deck.

He followed her in silence, but as they reentered the house, he touched her arm. "I'll call you soon. Do you have any plans for tonight?"

A spark of hope ignited in her eyes. "No."

"I don't know what Todd's going to want to do. We could end up at the go-kart place. But as soon as I know, I'll be in touch. If you're still free . . . we can talk about it."

He expected her to jump at his vague offer, but to his surprise, her eyes cooled a few degrees.

"We'll see." With that, she called out a good-bye to Todd and strode toward the door.

She was miffed at all his hedging and ambiguity . . . and he didn't blame her.

Expelling a breath, he walked toward the phone. He wished he could be more definitive about their relationship instead of dodging and weaving around the issue.

But until he got his head around her news and put together a plan, this was the best he could do.

Connor flipped over the final page of the report Kate had given him last night, set the papers in a neat stack on his kitchen table, and frowned.

After poring over the medical examiner's findings, incident and collateral reports, and the crime lab's controlled substance analysis, he could understand why the official ruling in John Marshall's death had been accidental drowning. The external exam had revealed a sizable wound on the back of the man's head, so it was reasonable to hypothesize he'd stood, lost his balance, fallen backward into the outboard motor, and overturned the small boat as he pitched into the water. The internal exam findings were also consistent with drowning. Hyperinflated lungs heavy with water. Foam in the airways. Water and sediment in the stomach. Blotchy and irregular lividity on head, neck, and anterior chest, in keeping with the head-down position of a body suspended in water. Plus, all the toxicology tests had been negative. No drugs or alcohol involved.

On the surface, the conclusion appeared to be a no-brainer on a number of fronts. Drowning was the fourth leading cause of accidental death in the U.S. According to Kate's statement—the only one in the file other than a few sentences from the boat rental clerk—John Marshall had been a respected doctor, a pillar of his community, a churchgoer, a loving father and husband. He'd had no enemies. He'd been found with his wallet intact, ruling out robbery. There was no reason to suspect foul play.

But in hindsight, a lot of things didn't add up.

Why had Kate's husband taken off his life jacket—and his son's?

Why was there a boy in St. Louis who matched the age-progression photo of Kevin—and who used a term unique to Kate's son?

Why did Greg Sanders seem nervous in the mall video?

What had prompted Sanders to move from Ohio to the backwoods of Montana three years ago?

If the boy who resembled Kevin really was the man's son,

why did he appear to be younger than he should be, given the timing of Sanders's wife's death?

This thing was getting more and more complicated.

Connor rose, stretching. Barely past nine, and he'd already been up for three hours. Too bad his hour-long jog and half hour of weights hadn't burned off more of the restless energy generated by his visit with Kate last night and his fretful slumber. What little he'd managed to vanquish through exercise had returned in full as he reviewed the file.

He needed to talk through the case. Do some brainstorming. Get a fresh perspective.

And he knew just the person to call.

As he headed for the kitchen to scrounge up a frozen breakfast sandwich, he pulled his phone off his belt and tapped in a single speed dial digit. Two rings in, Dev answered.

Connor dispensed with a greeting. "You busy?"

"No. It's Laura's Saturday to work at the library. What's going on?"

"You up for some one-on-one?"

"Hmm. Let me guess. You're working on the little boy case and want to bounce some stuff off me. Pardon the pun."

"Good deduction."

"It's elementary, my dear Sullivan. You only call me on Saturdays if a case is driving you nuts."

"That's because I respect your personal time."

"Except when you have a hot case. But I could use the exercise. The usual place?"

"Yeah." As far as he could remember from the schedule he'd scanned last week after coaching the youth basketball team, the church gym should be wide open. "Forty-five minutes?"

"I'll be there. Prepare to be trounced."

As the line went dead, Connor slid the phone back onto his

belt. He didn't care how many jump shots Dev sank as long as he also jump-started some new ideas on the case.

Diane strolled through Macy's, fingering the new fall fashions that had arrived since her last visit two days ago. Like she needed more clothes. She had two closetfuls already, thanks to the buying binge she'd gone on after she and Rich split. Thankfully, those urges had waned once her life became more normal, and they'd disappeared altogether after she met Greg.

But she'd been here three times during the past week, even though her support group had taught her shopping sprees were a futile coping mechanism. While a dress or a new pair of shoes might give her spirits and her ego a temporary lift, the boost never lasted.

Besides, who was she trying to kid? She might have walked out of Greg's house with her head held high, might have played it cool and told him she'd think about whether she'd join them for dinner if he called, but she wouldn't hesitate to say yes if he did issue an invitation—despite the fact it would be a lot smarter to decline.

Grabbing a silk blouse off the rack, she stalked toward the dressing room. Why was she letting herself be manipulated by another man? She'd been down that road, and the scenery wasn't pretty. Greg might not be hitting her, but he was still trying to control her life, calling the shots, deciding when—and if—he'd communicate with her. If he had some kind of problem that didn't relate to her, as he'd implied, why couldn't he just be honest and tell her about it instead of jerking her around?

She marched into the dressing room and slammed the hanger onto a hook. She ought to swear off of men. For now, at least. Focus on getting a job, getting her life back under control, and learning how to feel positive about herself so she'd be less susceptible to others' opinions. That's the message the leader of her support group always hammered home, and she was right. If Greg wanted to cool things for a while, maybe that was a blessing in disguise. She could use the break to get her act together while he worked on his own issues.

As she started to unbutton her blouse, the ringtone from inside her purse announced an incoming call.

Greg?

Her heart skipped a beat, and she grabbed her shoulder bag, fumbling the clasp. Once she had the phone in hand, a quick glance at the display confirmed it was him.

Now what?

As the phone rang again, she jabbed the talk button.

"Hi. Did I catch you at a bad time?"

Vulnerable was a better word. Especially since his voice was warmer than it had been in days. She sank onto the chair in the small dressing room.

Be strong. Be cool. Be careful.

"No. What's up?" At least she didn't sound overeager.

"Todd made up his mind about his birthday plans. He talked to the kid next door, and they want to go to Chuck E. Cheese's later this afternoon. I know that's not the most appealing place for adults, but we'd both like it if you'd join us."

Diane leaned her head back against the wall, trying to tune out the mother-daughter skirt-length argument in the next dressing room. She ought to say no, just to show him she wasn't going to be at his beck and call or sit around waiting while he decided whether to summon her or not.

But she was tired of playing games. And she wanted to go. Even a noisy place that catered to kids was preferable to the quiet, lonely house that was far too big for one person.

As the silence lengthened, a weary sigh came over the line. "Look, Diane, I'm sorry things have been strained between us lately, but I've got some issues with Todd. I think he and I need more time alone together until we get past this rough patch. The move was hard for him, and adjusting to daycare has been a challenge after being with me 24/7 for years. Plus, I think he's worrying about starting first grade and meeting a bunch of new kids. I know we'll get back in the groove soon. I'm just asking for a little space for a while, not trying to break things off. That's the last thing I want. If it was up to me, I'd be seeing you every day."

He sounded sincere. And how could she object to a father putting his son above his own needs and wants?

If Todd was having adjustment issues, however, she hadn't seen much evidence of them aside from that one nightmare. The incident at the lake was a different matter altogether and not related to the nightmares as far as she could tell. Still, Greg would be a lot more tuned in to his son's problems. See things she might never notice.

The important thing was he'd talked to her. Tried to explain his actions. That counted for a lot.

The tension in her shoulders ebbed. "I'll meet you there." That would give her some control over their get-together and allow her to leave when she chose. "What time?"

"Four o'clock?"

"Fine."

"Todd will be glad to see you—assuming I can drag him away from the erector set. That was an inspired gift. One we both appreciate."

Once more, the warmth in his tone sent a thrill through her, and her own voice thawed a few degrees. "It was my pleasure. I'll see you there."

As she dropped the phone back into her purse and retrieved the blouse, preparing to return it to the rack without trying it on, the conversation from next door wafted her way again.

"Wearing a skirt that short sends the wrong message."

Dramatic sigh. "It's a fashion statement, Mom. Nothing more. All my friends are wearing skirts like this."

"Sorry. Your father would have a fit. I'm not dealing with that."

A hanger banged against the wall. "I hate how you let him run your life! He's such a control freak!"

The door in the adjacent dressing room slammed, rattling the walls, and the argument grew fainter as the occupants returned to the sales floor.

But the words *control freak* lingered in the air.

She knew all about those. Rich had run her life.

Was Greg made from the same mold?

Until a couple weeks ago, she'd have said no. But he'd been acting so peculiar lately. What if she was making a mistake? What if Greg turned out to be as bad as her ex, in a different way?

A chill rippled through her. No way was she walking back into a situation like that.

But she was committed for tonight, and she wasn't going to disappoint Todd on his birthday. If she got any negative vibes at all during their outing, though, she was leaving—for good. She had enough problems to deal with in her own life without trying to figure out what made a certain construction worker tick.

Fingering the blouse, she returned the hanger to the hook and set her purse back on the chair.

Might as well try it on as long as she was here.

D ev slam-dunked the ball, grabbed it after it bounced, and stuck it under his arm. "A little off our game today, aren't we? That's number three for me—but who's counting?"

"I have another game on my mind." Connor tipped his head and wiped his forehead on the sleeve of his T-shirt.

"No kidding." Dev propped a fist on his hip. "Think you can focus on this one for ten more minutes? I'm digesting the download you gave me when we got here, but since I came all this way, I'd like to get in a decent workout before we dive into business."

"Your place is only two miles from here."

"And two miles back." He tossed the ball over. "I'll let you lead off. Maybe you can redeem yourself."

Connor balanced the ball in his hands. Dev was right. They'd only been at this fifteen minutes, and his partner did some of his best thinking while he was in action, whether on the job or off.

So he'd give him action.

Crouching, he began to dribble the ball, keeping it low to the floor, left arm extended to ward off attack.

It didn't take Dev long to make his move. He sprang forward and swiped at the ball—just as Connor expected. Holding the ball at his hip, he did a reverse pivot, then continued dribbling down the court with the opposite hand, neatly sinking a jump shot.

Dev stopped and folded his arms. "Getting serious, I see."

"Isn't that what you wanted?"

"Yeah. Now that I know your head's in the game, we're gonna have some fun."

Connor bounced the ball. "Your competitive streak is showing."

"I like to win."

"So do I."

For the next fifteen minutes, Connor played hard as they pounded up and down the court. He faked a crossover when Dev came at him, disconcerting him long enough to go hard around his right side and score another jump shot. His jab step two minutes later threw Dev off balance, allowing him to drive to the hoop and do a layup.

Although Dev paced him step for step and did take the ball a couple of times, he only managed an air shot. Connor took possession of the ball on the rebound and landed a slam dunk.

Finally, breathing hard, Connor leaned over and rested his palms on his knees. "Had enough?"

Dev tossed him the ball, and Connor caught it with one hand as the other man wiped his face with the bottom of his T-shirt. "No. You're one up. But I'm ready for a time-out. Your coaching gig here has improved your game."

"I don't know about that, but it *has* reminded me of the importance of strategy. And speaking of strategy . . ."

"Yeah, yeah. We can talk about the case now, but first I need some water."

Ball under his arm, Connor led the way to the bleachers, pulled two large bottles out of his gym bag, and tossed one to Dev.

His partner caught it, twisted off the top, and chugged the whole thing.

Halfway through his own bottle, Connor recapped it and sat on the aluminum bench.

Dev joined him. "Here's my take. Based on what you told me earlier about the police report, plus all the recent developments, I think the cops came to too many conclusions too fast. They went with the theory that since it looked like a rose and smelled like a rose, it must be a rose."

"Like the burger Nikki brought me yesterday."

"Good analogy. I hope you made up for it at dinner."

"Yeah." But his impromptu meal with Kate wasn't on the agenda for today's discussion. "In light of everything we've learned, I'm liking the head injury—and the assumption Kate's husband broke his promise about wearing life jackets—less and less. It all strikes me as too convenient."

Dev fished another bottle of water from the gym bag. "So what's your theory?"

"I think the accidental death ruling is off base. With every piece of new information that turns up, this thing smells more like rotten garbage than a rose."

"If it wasn't an accident, there's only one other explanation." Dev twisted the cap off the bottle. "And to make that stick, you'd have to have a motive. Your client's husband sounds like a Boy Scout. Why would anyone target him? And if someone did have him in their sights, why kill—or take—his son?"

Excellent questions.

Expelling a breath, Connor stood and began to pace. "Let's think outside the box for a minute. The police assumed Kate's husband overturned the boat when he fell, and that her son's death was a tragic by-product. But suppose it wasn't an accident. Suppose someone did have a reason to want her husband dead. Why not find a way to kill him without involving an innocent child?" Connor stopped. Frowned. "Unless . . ."

"Unless the child was the impetus for the whole thing."

202

He swung toward his colleague. It was uncanny how their trains of thought often led them to the same destination. "Everything would fit."

"But if your hypothetical killer was after the boy, there are a lot easier—and less risky—ways to kidnap a kid. And why your client's son in particular?"

Shoving his fingers through his hair, Connor shook his head. "I don't know."

Dev took a swig of water. "Before you go too far down that road, it might be helpful to try and round up a picture of Sanders's son. If you can find one, and it's a close match to the kid in the mall, maybe it's a look-alike situation with your client's boy after all."

"Too many other things still don't fit, though." Connor picked up his water again and twisted off the cap. "I agree we need to find out more about Sanders's son. But let's say we locate a photo—a serious challenge, since Sanders isn't a social media kind of guy. I've already reviewed all the usual sites. And let's say the photo's obviously not a match. That would give our suspicions about the identity of the boy at the mall more credence, but it would also raise other questions."

"Like where's the real son?"

"Yeah. For starters."

Dev leaned over to tighten a loose shoelace. "If I were you, I'd dig deeper on the doctor too. A loving wife's opinion about her husband's sterling qualities could be more than a little biased. He might have had enemies he never mentioned to her."

"Or didn't know about."

"That too. But all that is a moot point if the boy at the mall ends up being Sanders's son. Which would suggest that getting a photo of the boy is a top priority. If it doesn't match the kid from the mall, you can follow up on your theory that someone took out the doctor. Dig deeper into his background.

Do the same with Sanders. Both their kids too. If there's a link between all of them, it's there, waiting for us to find it. It might require some extra hours, but hey—that's why they pay us the big bucks." Grinning, Dev stood. "Can I offer you any other nuggets of wisdom today, my son?"

Connor weighed the half-empty bottle of water in his hand. Their conversation hadn't been long, but it had helped him sort through the muddle of information and nail down some clear next steps. He'd have gotten there eventually on his own, but this was one of the beauties of having smart partners. They helped each other cut through the clutter and formulate the most efficient strategy.

"You've done more than enough for one day. I owe you."

"You can pay off the debt right now." Dev retrieved the ball from the bleachers. "Give me a chance to even up the score."

"You got it." Connor finished off his water, tossed the empty bottle in his gym bag, and rejoined Dev on the court. He'd pound the boards for another fifteen minutes.

But as soon as they finished, he was heading home to do some serious digging for a photo of David Sanders.

"Hey, Dad, can Kyle and me have some more tokens for the arcade?"

As Todd and the kid from next door trotted up to the table he'd claimed in Chuck E. Cheese's eating area, Greg dug into the stash of brass tokens he'd purchased. "Make them last awhile this time. I don't have an unlimited supply."

"When is Diane coming?"

"Soon." He doled out tokens to each kid. "After you use ten more, come back. We'll eat as soon as she gets here."

"Thanks, Dad."

The kids zoomed off again.

Greg jiggled his foot and looked toward the entrance of the entertainment facility, trying to tune out the raucous noise from the animatronic show in the background and the excited, high-pitched voices of the hundreds of frenzied kids darting about. At least it sounded like hundreds. And the noise level wasn't helping the dull pounding that had begun in his temples during Diane's visit this morning and intensified as the hours passed.

Why did Kate Marshall have a picture of Todd?

How had she gotten it?

What did she plan to do with it?

After rehashing those questions for hours, he was no closer to answers now than he'd been two minutes after hearing the startling news. But he needed to find them—and Diane was his only hope. She already had a connection with the Marshall woman. An in. The challenge was to convince her to help him.

And it was a formidable one, in light of her miffed reaction to his recent efforts to temporarily cool things down between them.

As he lifted his Coke and scanned the area again, he caught sight of her over the heads of a group of little girls. Rising, he waved until he caught her attention.

He watched as she wove through the clusters of chattering children and swiveled sideways, out of the path of a group of boys making a beeline for the arcade area. She looked trim and appealing in her jeans and silky blouse, every hair in place, her makeup perfect. Her ex-husband ought to be behind bars for the way he'd treated her. How could a man hurt a woman he said he loved? At least she'd dumped the bum. And despite her bad experience with men, she'd opened the door to a relationship with him.

Though judging by her taut posture, that door might be closing fast—and at the worst possible time.

He pulled out a chair as she approached. "Sorry about the setting, but it's better than go-karts."

"I'm sure the kids love it." Setting her purse on the table, she slid into her seat and plaited her fingers, her shoulders stiff.

Not good.

"You look very nice. New blouse?"

Her brow wrinkled. "Yes."

No smile. No thank you. Why would she take offense at a compliment?

Clueless, he changed the subject. "Thanks for coming. Todd and his friend are in the arcade, but he just stopped by to see if you were here yet. He was really excited about you joining us. In case you haven't noticed, he's one of your biggest fans."

Her forehead smoothed out. "The feeling's mutual. He's a great kid."

"Yeah, he is."

Silence fell between them, and suddenly he was grateful for the din. It covered the awkward gap in conversation.

Odd. In the past, they'd had no problem chatting. Their easy give-and-take was one of the things he liked most about being with Diane. If there was an occasional lull in their conversations, she always filled it with a humorous story about her day or a question about his.

At the moment, however, she was making zero effort to communicate.

Another negative sign.

He gripped the cup of soda, his stomach churning. Might as well get to the subject that was front and center in his mind. The noise in the place provided excellent cover for a confidential discussion, and the kids wouldn't be back for a few more minutes unless they ignored his warning and burned through their tokens.

Resting his forearms on the table, he leaned closer to her. "I've been thinking all day about that picture you saw in your job counselor's office."

She redirected her attention from a passing birthday party group to him. "Have you come up with any explanation?"

"No, but I'm more curious than ever. Where was it exactly?"

"In a file folder. She went out to get us some tea, and I decided to stretch my legs. As I passed her desk, my jacket caught the end of the folder and it flew off. The picture slid out as it fell."

He bit back a word he knew she wouldn't like. If the picture hadn't been visible and Kate didn't know Diane had seen it, how could she introduce it into conversation? Dig for information?

Greg sighed and took a long swallow of his drink. That probably hadn't been a realistic strategy, anyway. If the photo was of Todd, as he suspected, and there was some sort of investigation going on, Kate wouldn't talk about it with a client.

He set his drink back on the table.

"You're worried about this, aren't you?" Diane's gaze was fixed on his fingers, and he looked down at them. They were trembling.

Wrapping them around his drink, he nodded. No sense denying the obvious. "Yeah. I wish there was some way to find out the story behind it. Thinking about a stranger having a picture of my son freaks me out."

"I can understand that." She tapped a polished nail against the surface of the table. "You know . . . this might be a crazy idea, but since Todd is adopted, do you think there's any chance she could be his birth mother?"

His heart stuttered, and the breath jammed in his windpipe. "Why would you say that?"

"I don't know what your adoption arrangements were or who you went through, but I read once that some agencies require adoptive parents to send pictures and stuff so the birth mother can follow her child's progress. All without names, of course."

He pulled out the answer he always gave when questions about the adoption came up. "I've heard that too, and I never liked it. We used a lawyer who hooked people up with women who wanted to do private adoptions. Part of our agreement was that there would never be any contact and both parties would remain anonymous. I thought that would be less confusing for the child."

She shrugged. "So much for that theory."

"I appreciate you helping me think through this, though." Taking a chance, he reached over and covered her hand with his. She gave him a surprised look—but didn't pull away. "More than that, I appreciate having you in my life. You're the best thing that's happened to me in a long time. I'm also grateful for your patience while I work through this recent stuff with Todd."

Her gaze flicked down to their joined hands, and she drew an unsteady breath. "I don't like being left in the dark, Greg. Or being manipulated. That's how I've felt for the past couple of weeks with you."

"I'm sorry for that. The last thing in the world I want to do is hurt you or make you feel used. You've had enough of that kind of treatment to last the rest of your life."

Even before he finished saying the words, guilt rippled through him. He hadn't used her yet, but he was getting ready to—and there was no way around it. She was the only one who could get him the answers he needed.

On the other hand, he wasn't using her in a bad sense. He did care about her, and he'd tell her his story if he could. Since that wasn't possible, he'd have to solve this problem fast so he could get on with his life—a life he hoped would include Diane as part of a brand-new family unit. She wouldn't mind being used if she knew that was his goal, that he wanted them to be together.

Would she?

She searched his eyes, and he hoped she saw the caring, not the conflict.

Her demeanor softened, and he let out a breath he hadn't realized he was holding.

"If I have the opportunity to ask a few discreet questions at my next appointment with Kate, do you want me to see what I can find out? I won't mention you or Todd."

The very request he'd been planning to make.

"If you could, that would be great. And yeah, until we see what she has to say, I think it would be smart if you didn't say anything about Todd or me. When are you going back?"

"I left without setting up an appointment, but I don't think I'll have a problem getting in by Tuesday or Wednesday. From what I've heard, Kate finds time for clients who need to see her, even if she has to stay late."

"Hey, Diane! You came!" Todd skidded to a stop beside the table, Kyle beside him.

"I never miss a birthday party if I can help it."

"Can we eat now, Dad? We're getting hungry."

"Sure. How does pizza sound?"

"Awesome!"

"Sorry I can't offer you more gourmet fare." He smiled his apology at Diane.

Her return smile seemed genuine. "Pizza's fine."

Greg placed the order, and there was no more problem with awkward silences during the meal. The two boys chattered non-stop, and Diane joined in.

As they finished off the pizza and he dispensed the last of the tokens, she picked up her purse.

A wave of disappointment crashed over him. In her presence, the loneliness that plagued him always retreated. Once she left, it would come roaring back, despite the boisterous crowd. "Are you leaving?"

"Yes. I have a few errands to do." She rose.

He had no choice but to stand as well. "I'll walk you out. Boys, I'll be back in five minutes. Meet me here after you've used up all those tokens."

"Okay." Todd dashed off, his friend in tow.

He followed her toward the entrance, wishing he could convince her to stay a few minutes longer. Not that he blamed her for making a fast exit from noise city, but . . .

"Diane! Nice to see you."

A tall, gray-haired man with kindly eyes held out his hand, and Diane stopped to take it.

"Reverend Howard—what a surprise."

"I'm playing grandpa today." He gestured to the two young girls holding hands beside him. "These are Carol's daughter's children. They're in town for a few days." He leaned around Diane and offered his hand. "Bill Howard."

Greg returned the man's firm clasp and introduced himself.

"Sorry for my lack of manners." A faint pink stain crept over Diane's cheeks. "I was just taken aback to see you here. Greg is . . . a friend of mine."

At her slight hesitation, the minister's expression grew speculative, and Greg shifted under his scrutiny. Although the man's smile never wavered, his intent eyes suggested he could see things Greg had taken great pains to hide. His minister in Cleveland had been like that too. Another reason he'd stopped going to church.

"Well, in that case, let me issue a personal invitation to join us some Sunday for services. You'd be very welcome—and we serve great donuts."

"Thanks. I'll think about it."

The little girls tugged on the man's pants leg, and he gave Diane a sheepish shrug. "It appears my charges are growing impatient. Will I see you at church tomorrow?"

"Of course."

"Excellent. I'll be preaching on Ephesians 4:31–32. A great passage that offers excellent advice." The man's comment encompassed him, and Greg looked down and fiddled with the phone on his belt.

"I'll look forward to it. Your sermons are always wonderful."

"Thank you, my dear. Enjoy the rest of your day."

As the little girls pulled him farther into the cavernous facility, Diane continued in silence toward the exit. Greg followed.

At the front door, she paused. "I'm glad you got to meet my pastor. I think you'd enjoy his services—and as I've learned over the past few months, they mean even more when life is challenging. I know Todd would like the Sunday school, and attending might give you some comfort."

He doubted it. God wouldn't want the likes of him darkening the door of his house.

"Maybe someday, Diane." At the flicker of disappointment in her eyes, he threw in a caveat. "He seems like a nice man, though."

"Very." She glanced back in the direction he'd disappeared. "He's had a lot of his own problems to overcome, but things worked out. Getting to play grandfather is a blessing he never thought he'd enjoy."

"Why is that?"

"His first wife ran off many years ago and took their toddler daughter. Fell off the face of the earth, apparently. Reverend Howard searched everywhere—hired a PI too, from what I've been able to gather—but no one ever found a trace of either of them." Diane shook her head. "Can you imagine how devastated he must have been to lose not only his wife but the daughter he loved? Even if she wanted out of the marriage, why would a woman deprive a man of his child?"

Greg shoved his hands in the pockets of his jeans and fisted them. "Hard to say. So who are the kids with him today?"

"He remarried a few years ago, to a widow with two older children who've since supplied him with grandkids to love." She pulled out her keys. "I have to run. No need to walk me to my car. I found a space near the door." She gestured toward the lot, and he spotted her car a few spaces down the row directly in front. "I'll call you after my next appointment with Kate and let you know if I was able to find out anything helpful."

She started to turn away, and he touched her arm. "Thanks for doing this."

For a long moment, she searched his face. "No problem. Enjoy the rest of Todd's birthday."

He pushed the door open for her, and as she slipped out, the heat smacked him in the face. Taking a quick step back, he let the door shut. Within seconds, cool air enveloped him.

If only he could as easily escape the heat bearing down on him thanks to that photo in Kate Marshall's possession.

But he'd find a way to solve the problem. To remove any impediments to his security. He'd taken an enormous risk to build a new life with Todd, and nothing was going to jeopardize it.

Nothing.

He would protect what was his—no matter what the cost.

Because losing another son was not an option.

15

David Sanders was dead.

Connor stared at the death notice he'd stumbled across after two hours of fruitless searching the Net for a photo of the boy.

A photo he no longer needed.

He noted the date on the write-up from the *Cleveland Plain Dealer*—three and a half years ago—then read the short piece. David was identified as the beloved son of Greg and the late Jennifer Sanders. Services had been held at Community Christian Church. Burial had been private. No cause of death was provided.

But he now had confirmation that the boy in the mall wasn't Sanders's son.

Things were starting to get very interesting.

It was time to burrow into both Sanders's and John Marshall's background. To turn over every stone and delve into every crevice in search of the link Dev had referenced during their basketball game this morning. If the boy in the mall was Kate's son, the connection would be there—somewhere.

Positioning his fingers over the keys, he started with Marshall.

Two hours later, when his cell began to vibrate, he rotated the kinks out of his neck and pulled it off his belt. Dev.

"So did you find a picture of Sanders's son?"

Connor took a swig of warm soda that had lost its fizz while he'd been engrossed in his search. Grimacing, he set the can aside on his kitchen table. "You must be really bored if you're still thinking about my case."

"Nope. Looking for an excuse to take a break from vacuuming."

Connor's eyebrows rose. "You're cleaning your apartment? What's the occasion? A presidential visit?"

"Very funny."

"I'm not kidding. There has to be some compelling reason for your sudden interest in tidiness."

"You make it sound like I'm a slob."

"If the shoes fits . . ."

"Ha-ha. Okay, fine. Laura's coming over for dinner. I'm barbecuing. Satisfied?"

Connor grinned. "Yep."

"So did you come up with anything?"

"Not on the picture—but as it turns out, I don't need one. His son died three and a half years ago."

A beat ticked by. "What happened to him?"

"I haven't found out yet. But I've read a whole lot more about Kate's husband and his work."

"Say . . ." Dev's tone grew speculative. "Wasn't he some kind of pediatric specialist?"

Nice to know their minds were again tracking in the same direction.

"Yes. He treated and studied childhood neural disorders."

"I wonder if that's your link? Except Sanders lived in Cleveland and your client's husband practiced in Rochester."

"Top-tier specialists often consult with patients in other parts

214

of the country. And her husband was definitely big-league in his field, with a list of research papers and awards a mile long."

"Good point. Could Kate find out whether her husband ever saw Sanders's son?"

"I don't know." Connor leaned back and looked out the window at the pot of toasted geraniums on his porch railing. The gift from a grateful client had succumbed to the heat sometime over the past two weeks. Of course, it would have helped if he'd remembered to water it. Somehow that chore—along with a lot of others—had slipped his mind since Kate had slipped into his life. "HIPAA laws are tough . . . but I was getting ready to discuss it with her when you called."

"Then I won't keep you. Could be you're finally on to something."

Connor scrubbed a hand down his face and shifted his attention back to his computer screen. "Maybe. I'll be more certain of that once I get a cause of death for Sanders's son and can establish if he was a patient of Kate's husband."

"The latter might be tricky, but you lucked out on the first one, since Ohio has open access to birth and death records."

"There might be faster ways to get that info."

"Are you thinking pretext?"

"A strong possibility. But I'll initiate the query with Vital Statistics as a backup."

"Let me know if I can help."

"Considering how your apartment looked on my last visit, I think you'd better make cleaning your top priority unless you want Laura to back out of that engagement you talked her into."

"Yeah." A sigh came over the line. "The vacuum is giving me the evil eye as we speak. Talk to you later."

As the line went dead, Connor scrolled down to Kate's cell number and pressed autodial. She answered with a breathless hello.

"It's Connor. Sounds like I caught you on the run."

"I was heading out the door, but your timing is great. I'd forgotten my cell was in the charger and would have left without it. Do you have some news?"

"I'm working on trying to establish a link between Sanders and your husband."

"What kind of link?" Her tone was puzzled.

"To be determined. But if the boy in the mall is your son, and if your husband didn't willingly remove his life jacket, Sanders is in the hot seat. He was either involved in the so-called accident, or he has some serious explaining to do about how he came to have your son. I've been doing a lot of research today, and I'd like to talk to you more about your husband's background."

"Can we do that tomorrow? I'm supposed to be at church to help bake desserts for our meals-on-wheels program in twenty minutes."

"How long will you be there?"

"Until six or seven."

She'd be exhausted after a full afternoon of standing on her feet. Not the best time for the discussion he wanted to have.

"How's your schedule tomorrow?"

"Not much better. Services in the morning, then I'll be delivering meals until about two."

And he was coaching in the afternoon.

As the silence lengthened, she spoke again. "Could we do this by phone?"

Yeah, they could.

But he wanted to see her.

Besides, he preferred to deliver the news about Sanders's son in person.

"Face-to-face is always better." That was a stretch—although it was true in her case. "Why don't I tag along while you deliver your meals? We could talk during the ride."

"Are you sure? I only have three deliveries tomorrow, but they're kind of far-flung."

Extra legit time in her company.

Perfect.

"My morning and early afternoon are wide open."

"That would be great." She paused, and he heard her take a deep breath. "Look . . . as long as you're meeting me at my church, would you like to join me for the service? That way we could load up and leave as soon as it's over. You wouldn't have to stand around waiting for me if our minister gets long-winded." The invitation came out in a rush—as did the justification. Suggesting she wasn't at all certain the offer was wise.

Neither was he—but it was too tempting to pass up. "That works for me. My pastor won't miss me for one Sunday, and I like to try new churches on occasion. Shall I pick you up?"

"No. I'll meet you there." No hesitation now. "Why don't I wait for you in the foyer a few minutes before eleven?"

"That works. Give me the address." He jotted it down as she relayed it. "Got it. I'll see you tomorrow."

As they signed off, he rose and stretched. The energy from the sausage-and-cheese biscuit he'd nuked before the basketball game had been expended long ago, thanks to his early morning exercise binge. A turkey sandwich sounded appealing about now. Not as appealing as a lunch shared with Kate—but at least he'd see her tomorrow.

And if all went well, their little drive would give him the lead he needed to help establish a link between an esteemed doctor and an enigmatic construction worker.

Hands were holding him down.
The water was closing over him.
He was going to drown!

No!

Lungs aching, Greg fought against the pressure, thrashing as he stared up at the wavering image above the surface. Although the face of the person hovering over him, pressing him down, wasn't clear, he knew who it was. The blonde hair was a dead giveaway.

Kate Marshall.

But why was she here? The doctor's wife wasn't part of his plan for this day. He harbored no ill will against her. She bore no blame for her husband's guilt, even if she had to suffer because of it.

There could only be one explanation.

She'd discovered his plan and was trying to save her husband. To take Todd away from him.

But wait . . .

Her husband was already dead . . . wasn't he?

Greg's lungs screamed as the last wisps of air leaked out, as he fought against her, as he struggled to make sense of the tableau.

If he was still near the boats, he didn't have Todd yet . . . did he?

What was going on?

Summoning up every ounce of his strength, he kicked. Hard. Trying to free himself from the woman's hold. A hold far too powerful for someone who looked so fragile.

A sudden whimper told him he'd succeeded. That one of his punches or kicks had connected. That he'd broken free of the smothering water and could finally breathe.

He sucked in a lungful of air and—

"Dad?"

As the faint, frightened word infiltrated his subconscious, he stopped thrashing.

Was that David calling him?

No. David wasn't on the boat.

David was dead . . . wasn't he?

Opening his eyes, he wiped a hand down his face and tried to orient himself.

He was in bed, not in the water. The room was dark, but a small, cowering figure beside him was silhouetted in the dim light shining in from the hall.

"David?" He reached out a hand as he tried to shake the fogginess from his brain.

The figure shrank back. "It's me, Dad. Todd."

Todd.

Of course.

David was dead.

The past few minutes had just been a dream.

As the irony slammed into him, he wadded the sheet in his fingers. A few days ago, his son's nightmare had awakened *him*. Tonight his own demons had reversed that scenario.

Greg sucked in another breath, trying to calm the staccato beat of his heart. Then he pushed himself into a sitting position, leaned toward the nightstand, and turned on the light. Two-twenty-seven, according to the digital display on his clock.

Somehow he managed a smile. "Did I wake you up, champ?"

"Yeah." A shudder rippled through Todd, and when he spoke, his voice was tentative. Scared. "I heard you yelling. I thought someone had broken in or something."

"Nope. Just a bad dream. Want to sit by me?" He scooted over and patted the bed.

In silence, Todd climbed in beside him. As their arms brushed, his son recoiled. "How come you're wet?"

Was he? Greg pulled the damp fabric of the cotton T-shirt away from his body. Yeah. Almost as wet as if he *had* been underwater.

"The air conditioner must still be having problems." He swung his legs out of bed on the other side. Lame excuse. The repaired unit was working fine, judging by the shiver that rippled through him as the cool air hit his damp clothes. "Sit tight and I'll change my shirt."

As he exchanged the clammy shirt for a dry one, Todd spoke from behind him.

"Dad . . . who's Kate?"

Greg froze and squeezed his eyes shut, his pulse once again lurching into overdrive. He'd said the Marshall woman's name?

And here he'd been worried about *Todd's* nightmares triggering memories best left buried.

He yanked the shirt over his head and turned toward his son, stalling as he tried to figure out how to respond. "Why?"

Todd pulled up the blanket Greg had tossed aside earlier and huddled underneath. "You said that name. And you sounded mad."

He padded back to the bed and climbed in beside his son, thinking fast as he pulled the boy close. "Dreams are kind of weird. I might have had a fight once in high school with a girl named Kate. Who knows? When we dream, times and places and people can get all mixed up."

"Kind of like the one I had about the escalator with the water at the bottom?"

"Yeah. Usually they don't make any sense."

"But sometimes I kind of get a feeling they do. Have I ever known anybody named Kate?"

Keep breathing.

"There might have been a girl at daycare with that name."

"No."

"Well, you could have heard the name on a TV show."

"Maybe." He snuggled closer, sounding small and subdued when he continued. "How come you called me David?"

Jaw tight, Greg gave him a reassuring squeeze. At least Todd already knew he'd had another son. "I guess he was in my dream too. You never forget people you love, even if they go away."

Todd looked up at him, his expression earnest. "I'd never forget you."

His throat constricted, and he leaned down to plant a kiss on the boy's temple. "I'd never forget you, either. And now I think we both need to get some more sleep. Want me to walk you back to your room?"

He played with the edge of the blanket. "Do you want me to stay here instead? I could wake you up if you had any more bad dreams."

No way. The last thing he needed was for Todd to overhear any more of his subconscious thoughts.

Besides, he was done sleeping for the night.

"I think you'll get more rest in your own room." Greg swung his feet to the floor, circled the bed, and folded Todd's hand in his. "Would you like a drink of water after I tuck you in?"

"I s'pose."

Ten minutes later, after the drink, a quick story, and another kiss, Greg closed Todd's door halfway and leaned his shoulder against the wall in the hall.

What a night.

And he had three hours to kill before first light.

Shower first, to purge the thin film of sweat clinging to his skin—or coffee?

Coffee. He could use the caffeine for the long, empty hours ahead.

Padding toward the kitchen, he wiped a hand down his face. He could read for a while; that would help pass the time. With all the birthday excitement and the hours spent with Diane's erector set, he hadn't finished yesterday's paper. That should kill half an hour, minimum.

But forty minutes later, as he closed the final section of the paper and drained his third refill of coffee, he still had a couple of hours of darkness to fill.

Appealing as a shower was, it might be best to defer that. What if the pipes started banging, as they often did, and woke Todd again? Not worth the risk.

Was there anything else in the house to read?

Ephesians 4:31–32.

As the voice of Diane's minister echoed in his mind, he frowned. What was that all about? He hadn't opened his Bible in almost five years, nor touched it since he'd stuck it at the back of the shelf in the hall closet when they'd moved in here.

But the way that minister had looked at him . . . it was as if the man had thought he needed to read that passage.

So what was in it?

Might as well find out. He had nothing better to do at—he peered at his watch—three-fifteen on a Sunday morning.

After retrieving the volume, he walked back into the kitchen, flipped to the chapter and verse the minister had mentioned, and read the words.

"All bitterness, fury, anger, shouting, and reviling must be removed from you, along with all malice. Be kind to one another, compassionate, forgiving one another as God has forgiven you in Christ."

His heart skipped a beat, and beads of sweat popped out above his upper lip.

It was almost as if the minister had pulled back the veil from his soul and seen the darkness within.

But that was ridiculous. No one knew his secret. They couldn't know. Not after he'd been so careful.

He snapped the book closed and dropped it on the counter. Even if he wanted to follow the advice in the Good Book, it was too late to rewrite history. To rectify mistakes. The damage had been done, and he was in too deep.

222

Besides, the only way to atone for his sins would be to give up his son, and that wasn't an option at this point. Maybe two years ago he could have managed it, before they'd bonded. Before Todd had become the center of his world. Before love had trumped revenge as a guiding force in his life.

Now, there was no going back.

All he could do was move forward and deal with whatever obstacles popped up.

Like Kate Marshall.

He blew out a long breath and raked his fingers through his hair.

She was a risk. No question about it. But to get the authorities involved, she'd have to have some hard evidence, some credible testimony, to support any theory she might take to them. And she had neither. If she did, the police would already have paid him a visit.

On the off chance she did find some incriminating piece of information, however, he needed to prepare a backup plan that would ensure she couldn't touch him.

Sweat trickling down his temples, he paced as he grappled with the worst-case scenario—losing Todd.

But that wasn't going to happen. He wouldn't let it.

The question was, how far was he willing to go to protect their life together if the walls began to close in?

Easy.

To the ends of the earth.

Suddenly he came to a dead stop as a name from the past surfaced.

Emilio Perez.

Not his preferred solution, not by any stretch of the imagination, but it was a possibility. Hadn't Emilio once said that if he could ever return the favor, just pick up the phone?

Maybe, if things went south, he'd call in that chit. The address he had for Emilio was current, based on their last correspondence. The man had also sent along his new cell number.

And Greg knew exactly where it was.

In a few long strides, he crossed the room, tugged out the top drawer in the built-in desk in the kitchen, and removed the address book buried under this month's bills. The letter was inside the front cover, where he'd tucked it.

Greg ran a finger over the return address on the envelope as dampness once again seeped into his T-shirt.

He'd have to be desperate to go this route.

But he couldn't rule it out.

When it came to protecting his life with Todd, all options were on the table.

A drop of sweat seeped into the corner of one eye, and he blinked at the salty sting. A tear formed, and he shoved the address book back into the desk, swiping away the moisture as his mouth flattened into a grim line.

He was done with tears. Done with other people deciding his fate. Done with being passive. Playing by the rules hadn't worked in the past, and there was no reason to think it would work now.

On the other hand, he wasn't going to rush things. That could lead to mistakes. He'd wait until Diane met with Kate Marshall, see what she learned. Then, armed with that information, he'd make careful plans—just as he had the last time.

And he would succeed.

He would protect his life with Todd.

Whatever it took.

16

As Kate approached the tables in the church basement where volunteers were setting out the insulated carrying packs containing the meals to be delivered, Pauline gave Connor an appreciative perusal—just as every other woman in the congregation had.

Kate sighed.

What had she been thinking when she'd invited the man beside her to attend the service today?

So far, she'd been cornered into introducing him to the minister's wife, the widowed organist, the unattached-but-looking female youth group leader, and a woman whose name she couldn't remember from some committee she'd served on last year.

If Connor noticed all the attention, however, he gave no indication—even when Pauline beamed at him and pumped his hand with far more vigor than necessary.

"You must be the young man Kate told me about. Pauline Andrews. Very nice to meet you."

His response was gracious—as it had been with everyone he'd met. He treated Pauline to his killer dimple, exchanged pleasantries . . . and continued to draw interested looks from every female in the vicinity. No surprise there. Tall, dark, and handsome didn't come any finer than the Secret-Service-agent-turned-PI. In his crisp, open-necked shirt and a navy-blue blazer that emphasized his broad shoulders, he fairly radiated—

"Kate?"

At Pauline's prompt, she jerked her attention back to the older woman. "Sorry. I was . . . distracted for a moment."

"I can see why." The woman flicked a knowing look toward Connor. "I asked if you were clear on the directions for your three deliveries."

As warmth crept up her neck, Kate dropped her chin and rummaged for her car keys. "Yes. I've been to two of the places before, and I used MapQuest for the new one."

"Excellent. Then you can be on your way. How nice that you have some company for the drive today."

"Are these the meals?" Connor nodded to three insulated packs on the table in front of Pauline.

"Yes." The older woman watched as he hefted them into his arms. "I see you're a true gentleman."

"I try, anyway." He grinned at Pauline, then turned to her. "Ready to go?"

Kate nodded. "Yes." The sooner the better.

As she started to turn away, Pauline leaned across the table and touched her arm. "We must meet for tea again soon, my dear. I want to talk with you some more about that yoga class. I do think you'd enjoy it."

Yoga class, hah. The twinkle in Pauline's eye told Kate her friend was a lot more interested in discussing men than meditation. One man in particular.

"I'm still thinking about it."

"Don't overthink. You might lose a wonderful opportunity." The woman nodded toward Connor as he moved away from the table.

Oh brother.

Without responding, Kate wove through the gauntlet of church volunteers lined up to collect their meal deliveries, heading for the exit on the far side of the room. Connor followed in silence as she pushed through the door, easing past her as she held it open—and treating her to another whiff of his appealing aftershave.

Get a grip, Kate. You're as bad as the rest of the women in the congregation.

Huffing out a breath, she followed him to the car and opened the back door.

He bent down to slide the meals onto the backseat, then gestured to his jacket. "Mind if I ditch this?"

"Be my guest. Although in *my* car we'll have air-conditioning."

"It did get a little hot that morning at the daycare center."

"More than a little." And not just because of the air temperature.

Focus, Kate. This is a business meeting, not a date.

By the time he circled the car, tossed his jacket into the back, and joined her in the front seat, she'd started the car, cranked up the air, and done her best to switch gears.

"Thanks for inviting me today." He pulled the seat belt across his lap and clicked it into place. "The service was excellent, and you have a very welcoming congregation."

Especially the women—but she left that unsaid.

"I'm glad you enjoyed it. Now tell me the latest. I've been anxious to hear what you've discovered."

She put the car in reverse and prepared to back out, but he stopped her with a light touch on the arm. Surprised, she looked over at him.

"Before we leave, let me give you the biggest piece of news. Sanders's son died three and a half years ago."

Kate stared at him. Thank goodness he'd stopped her from

exiting the parking space. Otherwise, she might have clipped the bumper of the car beside her when he dropped that bombshell.

"Does this mean . . ." She took a deep breath and loosened her grip on the wheel. Better not to let her hopes soar until she got his take. "So what do you think all this means?"

"I think it means we have more reason than ever to keep digging. The so-called accident on Braddock Bay is smelling less and less like an accident every day."

She digested that as she cautiously exited the parking spot and drove across the lot. "You're thinking someone targeted my husband." Even as she voiced the words, she couldn't grasp that notion. The idea that anyone would want to hurt a kind, caring, generous man like John was surreal.

"I'd say that's a distinct possibility. And since the perpetrator could easily have chosen a different time and place to do that, I don't think your son's presence was a coincidence."

Pulling onto the road, she glanced over at him and frowned. "What do you mean?"

"Your son may be an integral part of this whole thing."

As she drove on autopilot toward her first delivery, she considered that theory. Dear, sweet Kevin in the midst of some kind of conspiracy?

That didn't compute, either.

She sent him a quick look. "If Sanders lived in Cleveland, how could there be any connection between him and my husband or son?"

"That's what I'm trying to establish—and it's why I need your help today. Now that we know David Sanders died young, I'm wondering if your husband's work might be the link between him and Sanders. We're going to try to establish a cause of death tomorrow, but did he ever treat patients from outside the Rochester area?"

"A few. He was gaining quite a reputation for his research on neurological disorders—Batten disease in particular. A lot of parents from around the country who had children with that disorder came to him for a consultation."

"Tell me about that disease."

"It's a terrible genetic illness that affects the central nervous system. In many cases it shows up when children are very young—sometimes by age two—and progresses rapidly. Long before victims reach adulthood, they become blind, bedridden . . . and die. There's no treatment and no cure."

She paused to make a right turn onto a residential street, a pang echoing in her heart as she recalled the tragic stories John had told her of suffering children and their desperate parents. "I don't know how John dealt with the heartbreak day after day. But he cared so much about his patients and their families—and they all loved him, even when he had to tell them the situation was hopeless."

Her voice choked as she pulled up beside the curb. Thank goodness this regular customer lived close to church. A couple of minutes' break would give her a chance to regain control of her emotions.

"First delivery." She motioned toward the small bungalow.

"Do you want me to carry the meal for you?"

Leaving the car running, she opened her door. "No, thanks. It will be simpler to make a fast escape if I say someone is in the car—though I don't expect that to be an issue today. Mr. Harrison will probably be glued to the Cardinals game, so it should be a quick handoff."

She slid out of the car, retrieved the dinner, and walked toward the front door, slowing her pace to give her emotions a chance to quiet down.

The older man answered on the second ring, the muffled sound of the baseball game wafting out as he took the meal. After a quick thank-you, he shut the door in her face.

At least some things were predictable.

Back in the car, she handed Connor a sheet of printed directions from MapQuest and pulled away from the curb. "Could you guide me to the next place while we talk?"

"Sure." He gave the directions a scan, set them in his lap, and focused on her. "You up for this? Because it's only going to get harder."

Great.

But what had she expected? She'd known that day in the mall how difficult this could get—and crumbling now wasn't an option. Not when the impossible hope that had seemed so misplaced a mere two weeks ago was slowly edging into the realm of possible.

Gripping the wheel, she nodded. "Yes. I'm fine."

"Then let's talk some more about your husband. Do you still have any contacts in his office? Someone with access to records who could find out if he ever saw Sanders's son?"

"I exchange cards and occasional emails with the office manager from the group practice." She caught her lower lip between her teeth. "But I don't want to get her in trouble, and the privacy laws are very strict now."

"I know—and I don't want to subvert the law, either. But I don't think it would be a problem for her to tell you if he *wasn't* a patient. If your husband did see him, she could reply with a no comment."

Meaning they would get the information either way.

Clever.

"That might work. I'll email her as soon as I get home."

"Good." He waited while she followed his direction for a turn, then made his next request. "What I'd like you to do is walk me through a typical day in your husband's life."

Her heart began to pound. Talking about the day John died was easy compared to this. After rehashing that account so often for the authorities, she'd learned to tell it with an almost clinical detachment. Their daily life as husband and wife—different story. Did Connor have any idea how hard that would be?

As if he'd read her mind, he reached out and stroked one long, lean finger across her whitened knuckles. "I'm sorry to have to ask you to do this, Kate. I know dredging up those memories will be painful, but it's possible some activity you mention, even one that seems ordinary to you, might suggest a line of investigation that will help me establish a connection to Sanders."

She looked over at him as she stopped at a red light. Caring, compassionate eyes met hers—and gave her the courage to venture into territory she'd vowed never to revisit. "I'll do my best."

So as they drove to the second house, Connor occasionally interrupting to feed her directions, she told him how she and John had always had breakfast together despite the early hours he kept. How he divided his workweek between seeing patients and doing research. How he often came home late but always made time to chat with her about their respective days. How, once Kevin came along, he cut back on his patient load to have more time for his son.

She also told him about the accolades and honors he'd received for his work. How he was loved by his patients—even the ones he couldn't help. How every child he lost to the terrible illnesses ate at his gut. And she talked about the weekly fishing outings during the last summer of his life, a father-son interlude both he and Kevin had cherished.

When she pulled up in front of the second house, her hands were trembling as she pried them off the wheel.

The quick glance he cut that direction told her he'd noticed.

Fighting against the sudden pressure behind her eyes, she fumbled with the door handle. "I'll be back in a minute. This is a new delivery, so I'll introduce myself and make a fast exit."

Without waiting for a response, she slid out of the car, grabbed the insulated container from the backseat, and walked toward the front door of the small house. She was *not* going to cry. Not now. Later, in the privacy of her condo, maybe. One last time.

For all that had been . . . and would never be again.

Two minutes later, after removing the meal from the container and handing it over to the woman recovering from hip surgery, she returned to the car to find Connor behind the wheel.

When she opened the back door to deposit the insulated case on the seat, he looked over his shoulder. "Why don't I take the last lap?"

She thought about arguing. How often had she driven while in much worse emotional shape? But in those instances, she'd had no choice. Today she did. Why not take advantage of a strong shoulder to lean on, if only for a few minutes?

Capitulating, she slid into the passenger seat. "Thank you."

"Not a problem." He pulled away from the curb. "If you're wondering about where we go from here, first thing tomorrow I plan to dig deeper into Sanders's background. We might also get some helpful information from the woman in your husband's office."

"But will it be enough to give law enforcement the evidence it needs to demand a DNA test?"

"Not likely. I'm just hoping we get a few more leads—because every lead brings us a step closer to solving the case. If we end up needing DNA, though, we'll find a way to get that hair sample I mentioned before." He wove through the traffic on the road, his hands on the wheel steady, confident and capable.

Kind of like the man himself.

"I'd be happy to help you go through Sanders's trash, if it comes down to that."

"I'll keep that in mind. Now why don't we switch gears for the last few minutes and talk about more pleasant things? Like that yoga reference Pauline Andrews made. Is there a lotus position in your future?"

Her PI didn't miss much—even offhand remarks.

"Not a chance. I prefer my lotuses in the form of flowers. Besides, I can't fit it in with the demands of my job."

"I already know you work long hours. So what's your typical day like?"

Prodded by his questions, she told him more about her job than she'd told anyone other than Pauline. The man had amazing listening skills, and based on his astute, insightful questions, he was attuned to things both said and left unspoken. He was also a master at reading between the lines—a skill that no doubt had served him well as a Secret Service agent and was just as valuable in his current profession.

When at last he pulled back into the church parking lot and stopped beside a white utility van, she was sorry to see her weekly food delivery gig come to an end.

"Where's your Taurus?"

He set the brake. "We play musical vehicles at Phoenix. The van is my wheels for this month." He shifted around to snag his jacket off the backseat. "I'd invite you to Starbucks for a quick drink if I didn't have to be at my own church in half an hour to coach our middle-school basketball team."

A guy who not only went to church but volunteered for a youth activity.

The man got better and better.

"I'll take a rain check."

"I'll remember that. Shall we brave the heat?"

"I guess so. I climbed over the gearshift once to get to the drivers' seat after someone parked too close to me at a shopping mall, but I was wearing sweats. I'm not dressed for those kinds of maneuvers today."

"I noticed." The appreciative perusal he gave her belted silk dress and open-toed high heels more than validated her decision to sacrifice comfort for fashion, despite the heat.

After a few charged seconds, he angled away and opened his door.

She did the same, though the muggy air did nothing to cool her down as she circled behind the car.

He was waiting beside the driver's door as she approached—jacket hooked over his shoulder, dark sunglasses now hiding his eyes. "Better get inside before you melt."

Excellent advice.

Yet as she looked up at him, the spark of electricity that jumped between them—more sizzling than the waves of heat radiating up from the pavement—held her in place.

Had he felt that high-voltage jolt too?

Hard to tell, with those sunglasses—until he lifted his hand, touched her cheek . . . and spoke in a voice that had gone a shade deeper. "I'll be in touch."

Innocuous words. Businesslike, even.

But as she slid behind the wheel, as he closed her door and strode toward his van, she suspected his air conditioner was about to be cranked up as high as hers.

No question about it; romance was in the air.

Yet until she had definitive answers about the little boy in the mall, her love life was low priority.

In the meantime, she would do everything she could to help find those answers—including sending a very important email.

ASAP.

‖‖‖‖‖ **17** ‖‖‖‖‖

Out of the corner of his eye, Connor saw Nikki come to an abrupt halt at his door on her way from the back entrance to the lobby.

"You're either picking up Dev's messy habits or you got a very early start on your Monday." She surveyed his littered desk. "Please tell me it's the latter."

"It's the latter."

"Whew. What a relief. One like Dev is enough."

"Enough for what?" Dev's question was followed by the bang of the back door.

Nikki sent him a withering look. "Where do you want me to start?"

"Good morning to you too." Dev stopped behind her and inspected Connor's desk over her shoulder. "Did you stop in over the weekend?"

"No, but I did work on the case a lot since Friday. I've been focusing on Sanders this morning. As soon as Cal gets here, I'd like to have a powwow. You too, Nikki."

Dev groaned. "That means he has a job for you. There goes my filing. Again."

"Quit complaining. I swung by on Saturday and got you

235

caught up." As Dev's expression grew sheepish, she narrowed her eyes. "Don't tell me. You came in over the weekend too, and pulled out a mound of stuff that now needs refiling."

"I wouldn't call it a mound."

Nikki glowered at him, and Connor reined in his grin as she turned his way. "I'll be ready for the meeting whenever you are." After directing another dark look toward her nemesis, she disappeared down the hall. A few seconds later, a muttered "Oh, good grief!" came from the vicinity of Dev's door.

Dev leaned back and called down the hall, "If you cut the dramatics, I'll bring you a latte tomorrow."

"That hardly makes up for ruining my Monday morning . . . but I'll take it." The door to the lobby banged shut behind her.

"Women." Grumbling under his breath, Dev propped a shoulder against the door. "You want to give your basketball buddy a preview of what you found?"

"Nope. I need to dig through some more material that just came in. Let's plan on nine."

"Fine. Make me wait." He looked down the hall after Nikki. "Maybe I'll get a present for the kid. That might put me back in her good graces."

"Until the next time you dump a bunch of filing on her first thing on a Monday morning."

"Yeah. Probably not the best timing."

"You know . . . you might want to work on that timing thing before you get married. How did the housecleaning go, by the way? Was Laura impressed?"

"I dazzled her with my barbecuing instead."

"Meaning you didn't finish the vacuuming?"

"Almost. See you at nine."

As Dev made a fast exit, Connor shook his head and shifted his attention to the stacks of material on his desk.

By the time the Phoenix team assembled fifty minutes later,

he'd organized his notes—and come up with an investigative plan that involved all of them.

He brought them up to speed on his weekend work, ending with the call he'd put in to the Ohio Vital Statistics office first thing this morning. Then he distributed a printout of the timeline he'd created, beginning with the death of Sanders's wife.

"As you can see, our guy had some serious back-to-back setbacks. His wife dies. Three months later, his employment ends for reasons unknown. A year and a half after that, his son dies. Weeks later, his house is foreclosed on—not long before the so-called accident in New York. He then drops off the radar for four months, resurfacing in Montana. There's no record of employment from the construction job in Cleveland to the one in St. Louis last March."

Cal took a sip of coffee as he reviewed the timeline. "No apparent income for five years. What was he living on?"

"Fumes." Connor pulled another sheet of paper out of the stack in front of him. "Since we're all ex–law enforcement types who try to abide by the rules as much as possible, I contacted our data broker in the UK in the early hours of the morning to see what kind of credit information he could dig up on Sanders."

When Cal squinted at him, Connor jumped back in before the senior partner could deliver the anticipated lecture. "You don't need to say it. I know that's pushing the boundaries of the Fair Credit Reporting Act."

"Pushing might be an understatement."

"I consider it a gray area—unlike Dev's blatant vandalism when he was working his fiancée's case."

"Hey." Dev straightened up in his seat. "Breaking a window isn't a federal offense. And it was life or death."

"Only verified after the fact. And my gut tells me this information may be life or death too. If Sanders killed my client's husband and kidnapped her child, I feel no compunction about

237

stretching the margins of the law to the max to gather data that will lead us to the proof we need."

Cal looked at him for a moment, then settled back in his chair. "Fine. Cut to the chase. What did our UK guy dig up?"

Consulting the paper in front of him, Connor exhaled. As straitlaced as Cal was about legalities, he could have taken him to task for jumping the gun. Their offshore information broker was always a last resort, and in truth he could have tried a few other avenues first. But he was anxious to move this case along for both personal and professional reasons—and he suspected Cal knew that.

Good thing they were friends as well as business partners.

"He found a lot. Prior to the move to Montana, Sanders was heavily in debt. His credit card was maxed out, it appears he refinanced his house a year or so before the bank foreclosed on it, and he'd fallen behind in his utility bills—although he's been steadily reducing that debt over the past three years."

"How, if he had no income?" Dev drew a dollar sign on the pad of paper in front of him.

"That question's on my list."

"The debt isn't hard to explain, though." Cal took a sip of coffee. "His family had a lot of medical issues. Those kinds of expenses can wipe people out."

"He should have had COBRA available for eighteen months after he lost his construction job. That would have covered most medical problems." Dev doodled a box on the tablet in front of him, frowning. "But there would have been a gap between the end of COBRA coverage and his son's death, so your point may be valid. What else did you find out?"

Connor scanned the sheet again. "I had the broker pull some detail from Sanders's credit card statement for the year before and after Kate's husband died. A couple of red flags showed up. The first, about nine months before the accident, was a significant airline charge—suggesting he bought a ticket—or two—to some far-flung destination. The other is that for four months around the time of the accident, there was no credit card use at all."

"He didn't want his activity—or location—traced for that period." Cal made a note on the tablet in front of him.

"That would be my take." Connor folded his hands on the table.

"So what can we do to help nail this guy?" Nikki leaned forward.

"I'm glad you asked. There are quite a few people I want to contact, and with a little help from my friends, I could wrap up that piece of the investigation pretty quickly."

"I'm in." Dev lifted his shamrock mug.

"Me too," Cal seconded. "I have a few calls to make this morning to iron out some details for our executive protection gig in New York, but I can clear my schedule after that."

"I'm up for anything that gets me out of filing." Nikki sent a pointed glance toward Dev.

"A temporary reprieve," Dev countered.

She made a face at him.

"Here's what I'm thinking." Connor distributed background sheets as he doled out tasks. "Dev, I'd like you to tackle Cleveland. See if you can track down Sanders's old boss or any former co-workers. Nikki, try connecting with someone on the staff of the church he attended there, which I assume is the one listed in the death notices for his wife and son. The high-school-buddy or old-neighbor-trying-to-reconnect pretext should work. Or use whatever seems appropriate. If phone contact doesn't turn up anything, a trip to Cleveland might be in my future."

Nikki picked up her pen. "What specific information are you hoping to get?"

"Cause of death of Sanders's son. Anything you can find

out about his expensive travel bill. Why he left his job. General information about the man's attitude and personality. Why he refinanced his house. Why he was in debt."

Dev finished scribbling and looked up. "You don't want much."

"I'll take anything—and everything—I can get. I'd rather end up with pieces that don't fit our puzzle than have gaps in the picture. Given his pattern, I think it's safe to assume he hasn't been in touch with anyone back in Cleveland, so we shouldn't have to worry about him being tipped off to our questions."

"What's my assignment?" Cal moved his coffee aside and picked up his own pen.

Connor extracted some clipped pages from his pile and passed them over. "That's a copy of the incident report and autopsy from the accident. With your police background, I thought it made sense for you to touch base with the local authorities and see if you can ferret out anything that wasn't in the report. Impressions, opinions, conjectures. I figured one of your old buddies at County might have a contact in New York who could smooth the way for you with an introduction."

"In other words, assure the cops up there I'm not one of the slimeball PIs."

"That was the general idea."

"Anything else?"

"If you can manage to track down any info on where Sanders was for the four months around the time of the boating accident when he dropped off the radar, that would be helpful."

Cal jotted some notes. "I'll give it a shot. I assume you're tackling Montana?"

"Yeah. I've already researched the town. There's a family-owned diner that sounds like a local hangout, from what I can gather on the Net. I doubt our guy was all that social, but chances are in three years he was in there at least a few times. And with a cute kid in tow, he'd likely be noticed. There's also a small neighborhood grocery store. I'm going to see if anyone remembers them, and dig for information on where he lived. If I can nail that, I'll talk to his landlord too. This one could also require a trip if the phone ploys tank."

"Sounds like a plan." Dev connected the two offset boxes he'd doodled, creating a 3-D image.

"Why don't we regroup around four with status reports?"

"Works for me." Nikki rose, notepad in hand, and his two partners stood as well.

"With all of us on this, we should be a lot closer to having some answers by the end of the day." Cal studied the documents in his hand as he walked toward the hall.

"I hope so." Connor followed them out, flipping off the light in the conference room as he exited.

And hoping a light would flip *on* during the next few hours that would throw some illumination on a case that was growing darker and more sinister with each day that passed.

As Kate added a packet of sugar to her coffee in the New Start break room, Nancy poked her head in the door.

"Your ten o'clock is here." She homed in on Kate's mug. "What's with the sugar?"

"I need an energy boost."

"Busy weekend?"

"Too busy. And not enough sleep." The latter thanks to a certain PI who'd invaded her thoughts—and to concerns about a little blond boy who, if he turned out to be Kevin, was in for another major trauma. Both had kept her tossing.

"I hear you. The boys both had softball games. Trust me, watching Little League is not a recommended activity for an

August afternoon in St. Louis. I was afraid I was going to melt like the wicked witch in the Wizard of Oz."

Kate offered a sympathetic chuckle. "At least I stayed cool most of the time."

"Well, I hate to tell you, but this day is heating up. I just had a call from Diane Koenig, that new client you saw last week. The one who wore the great Saks-Fifth-Avenue type outfit?"

Also the one who'd clammed up at the end of their session, then left in a hurry—without making an appointment.

"What did she want?"

"An appointment—today, if possible. I told her you were booked solid, but she insisted I ask if you could fit her in. You want me to slot her for tomorrow or Wednesday instead?"

Kate hesitated. She didn't have a spare minute today—but Diane had seemed so distressed when she'd left last week. Despite her designer clothes, she'd looked like a woman who needed a friend. A woman who was still fragile as she tried to carve out a new life and reclaim the confidence her abusive husband had destroyed. A woman who was now asking for help.

"See if five-thirty works for her."

Folding her arms, Nancy sent her a stern look. "You need to look after yourself too, you know. You're still going to take your four-day weekend, aren't you?"

Kate wrinkled her brow. "Is that this week?"

"Yes. You scheduled it in January. Don't tell me you're going to cancel this one like you cancelled the last two."

She lifted one shoulder and sipped her coffee. "Maybe. I don't have anything planned."

"Then plan something. Go to a movie. Read a romance novel. Eat out. Or just sleep in. But take the time. You're way overdue for some vacation."

Considering she hadn't taken off more than a handful of days in the past two years, the receptionist had a point.

"Fine. I'll let it stand." She edged past Nancy and started toward her office.

"Good. Are you ready for your next client?"

"Yes." Her cell began to ring as she approached the door, and she increased her pace. "Give me five minutes for this call."

"Will do."

Kate rounded her desk and dug her cell out of the purse on her credenza. The number was unfamiliar, but she recognized the Rochester exchange.

John's office manager, responding to her email.

Stomach knotting, she circled back to close her door and said hello.

"It's Barbara. Can you talk?"

"Yes. Are you on your cell?"

"I am—like you asked. I didn't look at my personal email until I got into the office this morning, and I had to wait for a break to duck out and call you. Your request to use my cell rather than the office phone was intriguing. What's up?"

Kate sat and gripped the arm of her chair. "I have a favor to ask."

"Name it."

"Not so fast. This might be a little dicey."

"Coming from you, I doubt that. You and John were the most aboveboard people I ever met."

"I hope you still feel that way after this request."

"Now you've really piqued my interest."

Kate took a deep breath and plunged in. "I can't tell you the details yet, but a strange situation connected to John's accident came up a couple of weeks ago and I'm trying to check out a few things. I know patient information is sensitive, but it's very important for me to find out whether a boy named David Sanders was ever seen by John. In all likelihood it would only have been a consultation or two, since the boy lived out of state. So

I was thinking that if he wasn't a patient, you could just tell me no, right? And if he was, a simple 'no comment' wouldn't break any rules, would it?"

As the silence stretched between them, Kate's fingers began to tremble. Heart thumping, she carefully set her coffee down before she spilled it all over the file on her desk.

This had been a bad idea.

"Look, I'm sorry, Barbara. I don't want to put you in an uncomfortable—"

"Hold on a minute. No apology necessary. I was thinking through your proposition. I know you wouldn't ask if this wasn't important, and handling it the way you suggested shouldn't be an issue." A few seconds of silence ticked by. "I'll tell you what. I'll do some digging on that name as soon as I get a chance and text your cell with a no or a no comment, like you suggested. How's that?"

Closing her eyes, she exhaled. "Perfect. I can't thank you enough for doing this."

"Not a problem. But down the road, I'd like to hear what's behind it."

"If things turn out the way I'm beginning to think they might, you'll be one of the first to know."

"Fair enough. Now it's back to work for me—and for you, I'm sure. Watch for my text."

"Count on it."

For a long moment after the line went dead, Kate held the phone in her hand. She needed a minute to psyche herself up for the intense hour to come. Her clients deserved her total focus.

But it wasn't going to be easy to concentrate today.

Finally, with a sigh, she dropped the cell into her purse. She'd have to do her best to put speculations out of her mind.

And try not to worry about where they went from here if Barbara's answer was no.

E lk Café. If you can shoot it, we can cook it. How can I help you?"

At the booming female greeting, Connor stifled a chuckle and eased the phone back from his ear. Already the Philipsburg eatery was living up to the down-home image on its website. That should increase the odds the woman would be receptive to his friendly Texan pretext and tell him what she knew about Sanders.

"Howdy, ma'am. I'm hoping you might be able to help me out with some information."

"I'll do my best, sweetie. Hang on a sec." When she spoke again, her voice was muffled, as if she'd covered the mouthpiece with her hand. "Wally! You workin' on JoJo's order? That tour bus is stoppin' by the mine this morning, and he's gettin' antsy." An even more muffled male voice spoke, the words indistinguishable, then the woman was back. "So what can I do for you?"

Connor leaned back in his chair, propped his ankle on his knee, and delivered the speech he'd prepared. "Well, I may be passin' real close to Philipsburg in a couple of weeks, and I was hoping to meet up with an old high school buddy of mine. Last I heard, he lived in your neck of the woods. I can't find a phone listing for him, so I googled the town and saw your place. It sounded real friendly, and I thought someone there might know how I could reach him."

"We do see most of the locals on a regular basis, since we're the best restaurant in town. A word to the wise—our sapphire omelet is to die for. People come from as far away as Butte and Missoula to order it, and we run it as a special on Sunday mornings with a side of hash browns and homemade sausage. You remember that if you get out our way. What's this guy's name?"

"Greg Sanders. He has a little boy who'd be about seven now. I heard he lost his wife a few years back."

"Hmm. Not a regular here, that's for sure, but the name does seem familiar. Hold again for a sec."

As she once more covered the mouthpiece and called out a question about Sanders, Connor frowned. Bad news if Sanders's name wasn't ringing any bells. The woman sounded as if she knew most of the residents.

Leaning forward, he reached for the slip of paper containing the number of the family-owned grocer. If this call went nowhere, the store was next on his list.

"Sweetie, did he work for Patrick Lodge?"

Connor grabbed his pen and jotted down the name, his adrenaline spiking. "I don't know who he worked for out there. He used to be in construction, but with the economy and all, he could have changed businesses. Unless this Patrick Lodge owns a construction company?"

"No. He's some big-shot executive with an aerospace company in Seattle. I think I know who you're talking about, though. Quiet guy, fortyish, kept to himself. He did have a little boy, and I'm pretty certain his first name was Greg, but I can't vouch for the last name. He never came in here that I recall, but I saw him around town a few times through the years."

"That could be him."

"If it is, I'm afraid you might be too late. Mr. Lodge and his family eat here whenever they're at their vacation house. They're partial to those omelets I told you about. Anyway, on their last visit he said he was looking for a new live-in caretaker for his place."

"How long ago would that have been?"

"Oh, three, four months ago, I'd say."

The timing fit.

"So much for meeting up with an old buddy—unless Mr. Lodge mentioned where Greg went?"

"Not that I recollect. But he did say he was sorry to lose him, so I expect he was a reliable worker. You might try calling him in Seattle, if he's in the phone book. He's real down-to-earth and a wonderful family man. His wife is the sweetest little thing, and his teenagers are as polite and well behaved as I've ever seen. I know he'd be happy to talk with you about your friend."

"I may give him a call."

"You do that, sweetie. It's always good to reconnect with friends from the past."

"Thanks for all the information. And if I get to Philipsburg, I'll stop by and try one of those omelets."

"You won't be disappointed, I can promise you that. I've been here fifteen years, and I've never heard a complaint. You ask for Belle if you come in and I'll see you get the VIP treatment." A male voice called her name in the background. "Gotta run, sweetie. Breakfast traffic is pickin' up. Good luck."

Once the line went dead, Connor swiveled toward his computer and typed Lodge's name in the browser, along with the words aerospace and Seattle.

Multiple hits showed up, and he worked his way through them—including interviews from the Missoula and Butte newspapers in which Lodge waxed poetic about the beauties of Montana and his two-hundred-plus-acre spread a few miles from Philipsburg. Lodge was, indeed, an aerospace executive, though not with one of the bigger players in the industry. He sounded more like a smaller subcontractor. That should make him more accessible.

First, however, a call to the grocery store was in order. Since the woman at the diner hadn't been able to verify the last name of Lodge's caretaker, better to nail the ID before contacting the executive.

Picking up the phone again, he tapped in *67, as he'd done with the diner call. Blocking caller ID might be overkill, but someone in Philipsburg could know that 314 wasn't a Texas exchange. No sense raising any red flags.

"Garrison's."

Another woman—but this one didn't sound as approachable as Belle.

After greeting her, Connor laid on the Texas charm again and launched into a repeat performance of his spiel, ending with a recap of his conversation with the woman at the diner. "She wasn't sure my friend was the one who worked for Mr. Lodge, so before I go bothering an important man like him, I was hopin' to verify that the Greg she thought she remembered was the one I'm trying to find. If he lived in the area, I figured he might have come to your store now and then."

"You say you're a high school buddy of his?"

Definitely more cautious than the woman at the diner.

"Greg was one of my best friends back in those days." Greg Martinelli, not Sanders, but no need to pass that on.

"Well . . . I don't usually give out information on my customers, but I can't see any harm in this. His last name was Sanders, and he did work for Mr. Lodge. I guess he was here about three years, give or take a few months. But you missed him. He moved away back in the spring. Came in and settled up his account—not that there was much to settle. I think he did most of his shopping in Butte or Missoula."

In other words, the man made himself scarce in the small town closest to his home, where people might ask questions. Behavior consistent with someone who wanted to stay under the radar.

He had everything he needed from the woman, but just to play the pretext to its logical end, he asked the obvious follow-up question. "I don't suppose he said where he was going."

"He didn't offer, I didn't ask. Patrick Lodge might have a forwarding address, if you want to track him down."

"I may do that. Thanks a lot for your help."

As the line went dead, Connor rocked back in his chair. Talking to Lodge carried some risk. If, by chance, the man had formed a friendship with Sanders and still kept in touch, he might mention the inquiry. Plus, as a savvy executive, he would likely be cautious about giving information to a stranger—unless that stranger had some credentials that merited trust.

Like a Secret Service background.

No pretext for this one, Connor decided, although he'd keep the details of the case vague—and ask the man for his discretion while the investigation was under way.

But he had some groundwork to lay before he placed that call.

Rolling toward his keyboard, he grabbed his phone en route and entered the name of the man's company in the browser. After tooling around the corporate website, he located the basic email format and the main corporate phone number.

Ten seconds later he had the operator on the line.

"I need to verify an email address for one of your employees. For some reason, I'm having problems getting it to go through." He rattled off his best guess.

"You forgot the dot, sir. It's Patrick dot Lodge."

"Ah. No wonder. Thanks for your help."

Setting the phone on his desk, he composed his email. Keeping the inquiry general, he referred the man to the Phoenix website, where he could verify the firm was legit, and asked him to respond ASAP with a convenient time to call.

Then he dug back into the data the information broker had sent after his 2:00 a.m. request, mining it for any nugget he might have missed.

Because more and more, he was beginning to believe that the strange story Kate had told him that first day in this very office was more true crime than fantasy.

***

No.

As Kate stared at the single word in the text from Barbara that must have come in during her last meeting, her heart sank.

John had never seen David Sanders as a patient.

So much for Connor's theory.

Now what?

Appetite fleeing, she shoved aside the tuna salad sandwich she'd retrieved from the fridge in the break room and pulled the folder with the age-enhanced photo of Kevin out of her desk drawer. Usually she suppressed the temptation to look at it until the end of the day. Only then did she allow her hope to surface. To let herself believe that maybe, just maybe, her future might be different than the one she'd resigned herself to when she'd moved to St. Louis. That a miracle could happen and she'd once again hold her cherished son in her arms.

Now that dream was crumbling.

If they couldn't find a connection between Sanders and her husband or son, there was no motive. And the most obvious connection had been the medical one Connor had suggested. What else could it be, given the distance between the two cities?

Her gaze traced the features of the little boy in the age-progressed photo, pressure building behind her eyes. She should never have let herself get carried away. From the beginning, the odds against this investigation leading to a reunion with her son had been astronomical. But while her mind had accepted that, her heart had stopped listening to logic. She'd even begun to imagine how it would feel to pull her son into a hug and hold him tight. To plan for the professional support he would surely need as he transitioned from the only life he could remember to a new one with his real parent. To look forward to the day when her world was placid and she could watch her son grow into—

A knock sounded on her door, and she swallowed. Took a deep breath. "Yes?"

Nancy stuck her head in, glancing at the sandwich as she spoke. "Your twelve-thirty is early. She hoped you might take her a few minutes sooner because she needs to run her daughter to the doctor. Why don't I give you five to eat that?" She gestured to the tuna-filled croissant.

Kate shook her head and rewrapped her lunch. "I'll finish it later."

"It doesn't look like you even got a start."

"My eleven o'clock ran long."

"You know . . . you need to use a timer, like those high-priced psychiatrists do. Want me to put that back in the fridge for you?"

"If you don't mind. Thanks." Kate handed over the sandwich.

As Nancy disappeared out the door, her phone pinged.

Another text from Barbara.

Odd.

She leaned closer to read the brief note.

Call me on my cell after work.

Her heart skipped a beat.

Had the receptionist found some connection after all?

No way to know for at least six hours, given her back-to-back appointments and the extra session she'd squeezed in after hours with Diane Koenig.

It was going to be a long afternoon.

When Patrick Lodge hadn't returned his call by three-thirty, Connor wrote him off. It was a common problem with people who were big shots—or thought they were. If he needed him, he'd find a way to make contact.

In the interim, it was time to regroup with his colleagues and compare notes.

Rising, he gathered up his files and started for the door—just as the phone began to ring.

He paused . . . then circled back.

The caller ID area code was Washington state.

Maybe Lodge had come through after all.

He picked up the phone and grabbed his pen. "Sullivan."

"Mr. Sullivan, Patrick Lodge. Sorry for my delay in responding. I'm not contacted by private investigators every day, so I wanted to do a bit of research on your firm. It's quite impressive—and highly reputable, according to the St. Louis County detective one of my local police friends called. The man he spoke with happened to be a former colleague of one of your partners. How can I help you?"

The executive had done his homework—exactly what he himself would have done in Lodge's position.

Nice to know he was talking to an astute, thorough professional.

"I'm working on a very sensitive case, and I believe you may be able to offer some helpful information and insights about the person I'm investigating. But I'll need to ask for your discretion in this matter. Until we have all of the data we need, we're playing this very close to our vest."

"Our conversation will remain between the two of us. Who is it you're investigating?"

"A man by the name of Greg Sanders. I understand he was employed as your caretaker for several years in Montana."

"Yes, he was." Lodge sounded surprised. "Is he in some kind of trouble?"

"That's what we're trying to find out. What can you tell me about him?"

"He was honest to a fault and absolutely dependable. When I hired him, I was planning to do an addition to our cabin, and I thought having a caretaker with a construction background would be helpful. That proved to be true. He kept a close eye on the work and offered several suggestions that improved the final product. From everything I observed, he was also a loving father who doted on his son—and the feeling seemed to be mutual. The two were always together."

Connor continued to scribble notes as he asked his next question. "How did you happen to hire him?"

"To be honest, I expected to employ a local. I put up flyers around Philipsburg and advertised in the Missoula and Butte newspapers. I was a bit taken aback by Greg's application, but he sounded perfect. And he came with stellar references from his pastor and his former boss."

"How did he hear about the job?"

"I asked that question in the interview. He said he'd always wanted to live out West, in the mountains, and after he was laid off from his construction job, he thought this was his opportunity. He said he'd been monitoring the newspaper ads in several western cities and saw mine. It was a great fit for both of us. I was sorry to lose him."

Connor flipped to the next sheet of paper in his notebook. "Why did he leave?"

"I think he missed the construction business, and of course the pay is much better for that kind of work, especially in a large city. So when a friend of his contacted him about a job in St. Louis, he decided to take it. I also got the impression he wanted to send his son to a bigger school too. The boy will be starting first grade in the fall."

"Are you aware of any financial problems he might have had, or any travel he might have done prior to working for you?"

"No. Greg never said much about his past. I know he lost both his wife and son a few years before he came west."

Connor stopped writing. "But he has a son."

"Yes. Todd's adopted. Apparently he and his wife were in the midst of the process, and after she died he carried on with it."

So that's how he was explaining the boy. Clever. Since adoption records were never publicly available and often sealed, no one could dispute his claim.

"You've been very helpful, Mr. Lodge. I appreciate you taking the time to talk with me. Is there anything else you can tell me about Greg that might give me some insights into his character or personality?"

"Not that I can think of. As I said, he was a quiet man and kept to himself, but I had absolute trust and confidence in him. He and his son lived in a small cabin on the property, and when we came for our periodic visits he stayed in the background unless we needed him. There was also a certain sadness about him, but I didn't find that unusual given the losses he'd suffered. If I think of anything else, I'll be happy to give you a call."

"I'd appreciate that."

Dev cracked the door, pointed at his watch, and raised his eyebrows.

Connor nodded and stood. "Thank you again for your help."

"You're welcome. I hope your investigation is successful—but I'd hate to hear that Greg was involved in anything questionable. He didn't have any other relatives, and I don't know where that would leave his little boy."

With his real parent—though Connor kept that to himself as they rang off.

"You ready?" Dev pointed at his watch again.

"Yeah." Connor grabbed his files and stood. "But it was worth the delay."

As he joined his partner in the hall, Dev smirked at him. "I walked by your door earlier and heard the phony Texas twang. Don't tell me anyone fell for it."

"Hook, line, and sinker. Belle even invited me to stop in for an omelet if I ever get out to Philipsburg."

"Belle, huh? You must have really laid it on thick."

"I was just my usual charming self."

"It's getting deep in here."

"Eat your heart out, buddy." He followed Dev into the conference room where Nikki and Cal were waiting. "Sorry for the delay. One of my sources returned my call as I was walking out the door to this meeting." He took the same seat he'd occupied earlier, opened his file, and launched into a recap of his phone conversations and his futile attempt to mine more relevant information from the data the information broker had sent.

"So we now know Sanders did have income during the three years before he came to St. Louis," Cal said. "That would explain the source of his funds for the debt payments he was making—but it still leaves a two-year gap in employment."

"Which I can explain." Dev flipped open his notebook. "I tracked down Sanders's boss at his former company in Cleveland. I used the high-school-buddy-trying-to-reconnect ploy."

"A popular pretext today." Connor released the tab on the can of soda Nikki had pushed toward him as he sat.

"I, however, didn't resort to a phony Texas accent." Dev consulted his notes again. "The man remembered Sanders very well. Said he'd worked for the firm for eight years and they were sorry to let him go. But after new construction projects in the city dried up, they cut their workforce in half. The people with less seniority were let go."

"Did you get answers to any of Connor's other questions?" Nikki asked. "Because I did."

"Fine. You can go next—but I'm not finished yet. His boss confirmed the wife died of cancer and that his son had been diagnosed with some sort of serious problem involving the brain."

Like Batten disease.

The pieces were all beginning to fall into place.

Now they just needed confirmation that the man had taken his son to see John Marshall. Perhaps the receptionist in Rochester would come through for them on that score.

"His boss said Sanders didn't talk a lot about his personal problems, but he knew money was tight from a few comments the man made. As far as his boss was concerned, Sanders was a hard worker who loved his family and tried his best to provide for them. Apparently he took his wife's death very, very hard."

After a moment of silence passed, Nikki spoke up. "Are you finished?"

"The floor is yours." Dev made a sweeping motion with his hand.

"I struck gold with the church secretary. After I got her name off the bulletin on the church's website, I skimmed through back issues to see how long she'd been employed there. Turns out she's a twenty-year veteran, so I knew she'd be a great source—if I could get her to talk."

"Why do I think that wasn't a problem?" Connor took a swig of soda.

"Because you've seen me in action. Most recently with the clerk at Build-A-Bear." She sent him a pert smile. "I told her I was a former neighbor and that I'd found some photos from a backyard barbecue I thought Greg might like to have, since his wife was in some of them. She didn't have any information on his current whereabouts, as I expected, but we had a nice long chat."

"I'll bet." Connor picked up his pen and prepared for the download.

"Can I help it if most people like me?" Nikki patted her hair and sent his red-haired partner a pointed look. "I won't repeat the stuff Dev said, since she agreed with all of it, but I did learn some new information. David Sanders died of Batten disease—the late infantile form, which the woman told me is very rare. He was diagnosed when he was four and got progressively worse."

"Why do we need the Bureau of Vital Statistics when we have Nikki?" Dev chugged his water.

"May I continue?" She arched an eyebrow at him.

"By all means."

"In the beginning, the Sanderses tried all the conventional treatments. Then Jennifer Sanders developed cancer, and the family had to juggle both diseases. After she died, David's condition continued to deteriorate—and Greg lost his job. Eventually his insurance ran out . . . along with most treatment options. The church held a fund-raiser for David, but it didn't begin to cover the expenses. Even though all competent medical authorities consider David's condition terminal, Greg apparently refused to believe the situation was hopeless."

A muscle ticked in Cal's jaw. "Our guy's had some tough breaks."

"That doesn't condone criminal activity," Connor shot back.

"I didn't say it did. I'm just saying trauma can push some people over the edge."

Though Cal's tone was mild, Connor knew there was a world of hurt buried under his comment. Losing a wife to murder was about as traumatic as you could get—and he had a feeling his college buddy had come close to the edge on occasion himself in his early days as a grieving, too-young widower.

"So what else did you discover?" Dev ripped open a bag of potato chips and directed his question to Nikki.

She skewered him with a disapproving look as he chomped on one.

"Hey . . . I'm hungry."

"There are more nutritious snacks."

"I like these better."

"They're your arteries." Shaking her head, she went back to her notes. "During the last six months of his son's life, he got desperate. He began to look into experimental treatments, hoping to have one approved by his insurance before it ran out. When that didn't happen, he remortgaged his house and took David to a clinic in China that used stem cell therapy to treat the disease. They were gone a month. Three weeks after they returned home, David developed encephalitis and pneumonia and died soon after."

"There's our explanation for the airline charges." Connor finished off his soda, rested his elbows on the table, and steepled his fingers. "Tickets to China cost a chunk of change. But my guess is that was a small expense compared to the treatment."

"It was. The woman at the church didn't give me any totals, but I got the impression the cost of the therapy and the living expenses in China were in the tens of thousands of dollars."

"And it didn't work, anyway." Connor's gaze moved to the vase of exotic flowers on the cabinet across the room. They appeared to be real, but on close inspection turned out to be fake.

Kind of like the hope Sanders had no doubt been offered by the clinic in China.

But desperate people took desperate chances for those they loved—no matter the risk.

And when things went south, they often searched for scapegoats.

As if reading his mind, Cal spoke. "Assuming your client's husband saw David Sanders, I wonder if revenge is our motive."

"That seems like a stretch." Dev drew a question mark on

the pad of paper in front of him. "Marshall's diagnosis would just have confirmed the medical community's position—that the disease couldn't be cured. Why go after him?"

"If Sanders saw Marshall . . . the most respected expert in the country on this disease . . . I'm guessing Kate's husband was his best—and last—legitimate option. Assuming he heard bad news, he may have cracked at that point. But I agree with your assessment. I think we're missing something." Connor frowned and tapped his index fingers together. "Revenge alone doesn't explain how Kate's son plays into this."

"While we ponder all that, want to hear my report?" Cal indicated the tablet in front of him.

"Go ahead." Connor picked up his pen again. "Unless you have anything else to add, Nikki."

"No. The woman at the church finished by saying that after his son died, Sanders stopped coming to services and eventually moved away. She had no idea where."

"I had an interesting conversation with the responding officer, who remembered the so-called drowning incident very well." Cal consulted the notepad in front of him. "As the report indicated, the overturned boat was spotted by a couple of fishermen, who called in the alert. The officer said the two guys are upstanding area businessmen, so they had no reason to suspect them of being anything more than responsible citizens."

Connor stopped writing. "Did the cop you talked with offer any off-the-record comments?"

"He didn't dispute the official findings, but he did admit that your client's concern about the life jackets bothered him. When I pressed, he went on the defensive and said they looked for other explanations, but there were no leads to follow and the situation did appear straightforward, other than the life jacket anomaly." Cal consulted his notes again. "I also talked to the owner of the tackle shop where Marshall rented his boat each week."

"What pretext did you use?" Dev crinkled his potato chip bag as he dug out the crumbs at the bottom, and Nikki rolled her eyes.

"I didn't—but I did give him my police detective background and referred him to our website, which he perused as we talked. He was happy to cooperate."

"Did he offer anything useful?" As his stomach rumbled, Connor eyed Dev's empty potato chip bag, wishing he'd eaten a bigger lunch—and that more than a frozen dinner was waiting for him at home.

"After I chatted with him for a few minutes, I asked him to review his records for the day of the accident and see how many people had rented boats. He came up with eight names."

Connor leaned foward. "Don't tell me—Sanders was one of them."

"I wish I *could* tell you that. But he wasn't. That would be too easy."

Some nuance in Cal's inflection caught Connor's attention. "You found something, though."

Cal flashed a smile. "I was a crack detective once, remember?"

"You still are." Nikki lifted her flavored water in a toast.

"Thank you." He acknowledged the compliment with a mock salute, then addressed the whole group. "I didn't expect Sanders to use his own name. Not if he was being careful about covering his tracks. So I asked Ed, the owner, if anyone on the list that day was a regular customer besides the doctor and his son. He said a Ralph Watson had become a regular in the weeks prior to the accident. When I asked him to check the days Marshall rented his boat, Watson's name appeared too."

Another spurt of adrenaline zipped through Connor. "Can you rent a boat without showing an ID like a driver's license?"

"You can if the boat's not motorized—or so Ed told me. Watson brought his own outboard motor and put a hefty sum down as a deposit . . . in cash. The doctor always rented one with a motor."

"I'm still struggling with the motive." Dev dug around for any lingering fragments of chips in the bottom of the bag.

"Before we get back to the motive issue"—Cal sent Dev a quick glance—"I also tackled the second question you gave me."

Connor leaned forward. "The one about where Sanders was for the four months he was off the radar?"

"Yeah. I can't help you with the last three months, but for the first month he was camped out at two state parks with convenient access to Braddock Bay. I called the closest ones and was able to persuade the clerk on duty to look up the records. Get this—he left the second one the day of the accident."

The room went silent for several charged beats.

"I think you need to get some hair for that DNA sample you mentioned to me a few days ago." The empty bag crinkled in Dev's hand, dumping salt onto the conference table.

"Especially if your client finds out her husband consulted on David Sanders's case." Nikki grabbed the chip bag from Dev and crumpled it in her hand as he gathered up the grains of salt.

"I agree." Connor was already thinking along the same lines. "We may need to put surveillance on him and hope he goes to a salon to get the boy's hair cut. Or, if he cuts it himself, we could resort to a trash cover."

Dev made a face. "Those stink. Pardon the pun. Too bad we don't have enough to turn this over to the cops or the FBI."

"Yeah, but everything we have right now is circumstantial. DNA would be irrefutable." Cal leaned back in his chair. "With surveillance in place, a haircut will be obvious to us as soon as it happens. If Sanders hasn't taken him to a salon, we'll know he did it at home and can target the night for the trash cover. Count me in."

"Thanks." Connor picked up his files and tapped them into a

neat pile. "I'll get with Kate tonight and put together a surveillance schedule. Since our guy works all day, I think we'd be safe
covering him from the time he picks up the boy at daycare until
bedtime and during the day on weekends. That would coincide
with salon hours."

"How often do kids get their hair cut?" Dev asked.

"Every four to six weeks, depending on how particular a
parent is." Nikki stood and tossed the empty chip bag in the
trash can. "I just had this conversation with a young mother
at church. Does the boy your client spotted need a haircut?"

Connor pulled the photo he'd taken at the daycare center from
his file. "It looks kind of shaggy to me." He flipped it toward
the group. "And with him starting school soon, my guess is our
guy will have it cut soon—or cut it himself."

"Then this shouldn't take too long." Cal collected the papers
in front of him. "Let us know what your client hears from her
husband's receptionist."

"I will." Connor rose and picked up his own material. "Thank
you all for your help today. I owe you a pizza lunch as soon as we
wrap this up. Veggie with whole wheat crust for you—I know, I
know." He waved Nikki off before she could chime in.

They filed out, and once back at his desk Connor picked up
the phone and punched in Kate's number. She'd have called him
if she'd heard back from the woman in her husband's office,
and at this hour she'd still be with a client. But he could leave a
message about the latest developments from his end.

And he hoped when they connected once her workday was
done, she'd have big news too. So far, all the pieces were fitting.
Verification that her husband had seen David Sanders was the
only missing link—other than a definite motive.

Unfortunately, that was a problem. Dev was right. Revenge
against a doctor who couldn't help your son was one thing. But
why add kidnapping to the list? If the doctor was dead, he'd

never know his son had disappeared. And what could Sanders have against Kate—the person who would suffer most if her son disappeared?

They were missing some important piece of information, some critical insight about what made Sanders tick. He could feel it in his gut. And until they got a handle on it, the man was a loose cannon.

Because even though everyone they'd spoken with had sung his praises, if he was guilty of murder and kidnapping, there was a cold, ruthless, dangerous side to the man.

And once the walls began to close in on him, it could surface again—putting anyone who threatened to expose him at deadly risk.

Sorry to keep you waiting. All my meetings seem to be running long today."

At Kate's greeting, Diane rose from the chair she'd claimed in the New Start reception area, fingers clamped around her purse. "Thanks for seeing me on such short notice."

Kate extended her hand. "No problem."

After prying her fingers free, Diane returned her firm shake in silence.

"Would you like a cup of tea, like last time?"

"No, thanks. I'm fine."

Forcing herself to take a few deep breaths, Diane followed the New Start director back to her office. What on earth had possessed her to agree to this sleuthing gig? She wasn't cut out for cloak-and-dagger stuff—and she didn't owe Greg a thing, especially after his recent standoffishness.

Just another sign she was still trying too hard to please. Still letting herself be manipulated.

"Have a seat." Kate gestured toward the comfortable sitting area as they entered her office, then moved to her desk to retrieve a notepad.

Diane's step faltered as her gaze fell on the file beside the notepad. Wasn't that the same one she'd knocked to the floor during her first session?

Yes. One corner was bent.

Suddenly shaky, she forced herself to keep walking toward the chair she'd occupied on her first visit.

A few seconds later, Kate took the seat across from her and set a glass of water on a small side table.

Once again, Diane found herself staring.

Why were Kate's fingers trembling?

She lifted her chin and scrutinized the woman's face. She seemed to be a few shades paler than last week too. And the shadows under her eyes and tautness in her features were also new.

The woman who'd been kind enough to squeeze her in after hours looked exhausted—and stressed.

It seemed her clients weren't the only ones dealing with pressure and worry and strain.

But was Kate's anxiety sourced from her professional or private life?

Diane glanced at the wedding band on her finger. Kate had never mentioned her husband, nor were there any family photos on display in the office. Did she, too, have problems at home?

And where did Todd fit into the picture?

That was the question she was here to investigate—but as the counselor smiled at her, she squirmed. She was so not cut out for this. Prying into the woman's personal affairs felt deceitful and underhanded . . . and dirty.

At the same time, the fact that Kate had Todd's picture meant she had some knowledge of *Greg's* personal affairs.

Her attention drifted back to the folder on the desk. She could understand Greg's worry. If some stranger had a photo of a child who belonged to her, she'd freak too.

Yet it was hard to believe Kate would be involved in anything nefarious.

"Diane?"

At the gentle prompt, she jerked her attention back to the woman across from her, a rush of warmth heating her cheeks. "Sorry. I'm a little distracted."

"No problem. I've had my share of distractions recently too. Now what would you like to talk about today?"

The reason you're distracted too. And why there's a picture of Todd on your desk.

Instead of voicing those questions, though, she focused on the original reason she'd visited the center—to get some career counseling and connect with a job. Perhaps in the course of that discussion, she could find an opportunity to ask some questions about the picture of the little boy.

Forty minutes in, however, she'd had no chance to broach the subject—and time was running out. Kate had kept the conversation on topic during the entire session.

Maybe she should venture a bit into her own sordid history. That might give her an opening to ferret out some personal information about Kate too.

Worth a try.

At the first lull in the conversation, she plunged in.

"You know . . . I had a very good job before I married Rich. I often wonder what my life would have been like if I'd kept working. But to be honest, all I ever really wanted to be in those days was a wife and mother."

Kate's expression remained pleasant, but there was a hint of sadness in the depths of her eyes. "There's nothing wrong with that. Both are noble roles."

"Not when you're married to an abuser like Rich." Her heart began to pound as she put the truth into words for the first time with someone outside her support group.

As if sensing the significance of the moment, Kate leaned over and touched her knotted hands. "I'm sorry you had to go through that—but you're taking proactive steps to fix the problems in your life and move forward, and that's a positive thing. It requires a lot of courage to start over."

Diane tipped her head, picking up some nuance in Kate's tone that suggested that comment was more than a professional platitude. Was this her opening? "You sound almost as if you've walked this path yourself."

"I have. Not the abuse part. My husband was amazing." She touched the ring on her finger, then straightened her shoulders and picked up her pen. "But I know about starting over."

She was preparing to redirect the conversation—but Diane wasn't ready to get back to business. Not yet.

"You referred to your husband in the past tense. Is he . . . ?"

Kate's throat contracted. "He was killed in a boating incident three years ago in New York."

At the quiet words, shock rippled through Diane. Not what she'd expected. "I'm so sorry."

"Thank you. I don't often digress into my personal history with clients." Kate studied her, as if debating how much more to say.

Diane leaned forward encouragingly. "You know, it helps to hear how others have overcome adversity. There have been days since I walked out on Rich when I think it's just me against the world. Sometimes I get really depressed and anxious and lonely. My support group is great, but I've come close a few times to resorting to alcohol to take the edge off, like I did on the worst days during my marriage."

"Don't do that." Eyes intent, Kate took her hand and gripped it. Hard. "Alcohol and drugs only offer a brief escape from problems. They don't solve them. That's not a healthy way to cope."

Diane studied her. Why such a fierce response?

As if she'd read her mind, Kate took a deep breath. Let it

out. "I speak from experience on that topic, Diane. I couldn't cope after the boating incident. I didn't just lose my husband; my four-year-old son was with him. They never found Kevin's body. I used Valium to help me get through the pain, but I got hooked. It took me months to wean myself off of it, to get my life back. Trust me—you don't want to go down that road."

Diane stared at Kate. The addiction revelation was surprising—but the news about her son sent a bolt of shock ripping through her.

One that kept building as parallels began to line up in her mind with almost military precision.

If Kate's son had been four when he disappeared, he'd be close to seven now—and Todd had just turned seven.

Todd had had a disturbing encounter with a woman on an escalator whose hair was the same color as his—and the same color as Kate's. A woman who'd lingered in his memory and appeared in his dreams.

At the picnic by the lake, he'd flipped out after the boat started to tip, exhibiting an abnormal fear of water—and Kate's son had been lost on the water.

The body of Kate's son had never been found.

Kate had a picture of Todd in a file on her desk.

Could all of that be more than coincidence? A *lot* more than coincidence?

No!

Greg couldn't possibly be connected to Kate . . . or involved in anything underhanded. He'd adopted Todd as a baby.

At least that's what he'd told her.

But . . . was it the truth?

Had he lied to her all along?

And if he had . . .

A shiver rippled through.

"Diane . . . I only told you that story to encourage you." Kate touched her hand again. "To illustrate that if I could survive all the stuff that was thrown at me, you'll be fine too. I didn't mean to upset you."

She nodded, struggling to untwist the knot in her stomach. "I appreciate that. I had no idea you'd dealt with such tragedy."

"Most clients don't. As I said, I don't share my story very often. But I want you to know I understand how difficult life can be, and that you have an ally if you need one."

She stood and walked over to her desk, where she scribbled on a business card. A moment later she returned and handed it over. "That's my cell number. I know you have your support group, but if you begin to feel overwhelmed and need a friendly ear, I'm available too. Call me anytime, day or night. You won't wake anyone up but me. I know all about loneliness too."

Diane fingered the cardboard rectangle, pressure building in her throat. When was the last time anyone outside of her support group had offered to be there for her 24/7? She couldn't remember. Certainly not Greg, though she'd hoped they might get to that point down the road.

But more and more, that road was beginning to seem like a dead end.

"Thank you." She rose and tucked the card in her purse.

"You're welcome. In the meantime, I'll start lining up some specific job opportunities for you. Why don't we set up another appointment for next week to discuss them and work on your résumé?"

"That would be great."

Kate walked her to the deserted lobby, booked the appointment for her since the receptionist had gone home for the day, then shook her hand again.

"Remember. Call me between now and next week if you need to talk. I'm here for you."

Tears choking her voice, Diane turned away and fumbled with the knob. "Thanks."

Pushing through the door, she escaped down the hall and into the August evening.

More confused than ever.

Kate seemed sincere. Honest. Caring. She didn't deserve whatever stress had caused the faint lines of tension beside her mouth and at the corners of her eyes that had developed over the past week.

Of course, she would have said the same thing about Greg's recent haggard appearance too—until recently.

Now she wasn't certain.

Maybe one of them *did* deserve the stress that had invaded their lives.

As to which one—she might have learned a lot about discerning nuances during her troubled marriage, but overall she had a better track record reading women than men . . . and she'd picked up no deceit in Kate.

As she approached her car, she popped the locks. Should she stick with her original plan and call Greg once she got home? Or sleep on it?

She didn't have a clue.

But one thing was certain.

She was getting seriously creepy vibes about this whole thing— like the ones she used to get before Rich went ballistic.

The outcome in those days had always been bad.

Would the same be true in this situation—or was she overreacting? Blowing the whole thing out of proportion?

She wanted to believe the answer to those two questions was yes. That there was a simple explanation for the unsettling coincidences, and that everything was going to turn out fine.

Yet as she slid into the car, another shiver rippled through her—because she couldn't shake the ominous sense of foreboding that once again her life was about to change.

And not for the better.

Why had she shared so much of her personal history with Diane?

Shaking her head, Kate strode back to her office. That kind of disclosure had been very out of character. She could count on the fingers of one hand the number of times she'd offered a client even a hint of the ordeal she'd endured over the past three years.

But Diane seemed so on edge, so in need of assurance that she was strong enough to make it past the turmoil she'd endured.

Unfortunately, since she'd seemed as on edge when she left as when she'd arrived, perhaps the soul-baring episode hadn't helped anyway.

Much as she always worried about her clients, however, she had other priorities tonight—the call to Barbara being top of the list.

Back in her office, she circled her desk and punched in the woman's cell number, praying for helpful news.

After two rings, she started tapping her foot. Three rings in, she accepted the inevitable. The call was going to roll to voice mail.

Resigned, she waited for the mechanical greeting to kick in—only to have Barbara answer.

"Sorry. I was maneuvering my way around a traffic accident." As Barbara spoke, Kate could hear sirens in the background.

"Do you want to call me back after you get past the congestion?"

"No, I can multitask unless this gets hairy. Listen, not long after I sent you the answer to your question, the medical director of an insurance company contacted one of our doctors. That prompted me to dig a little deeper. I don't know how much John told you about this, but on occasion the practice gets a call if an insurance company's medical director reviews a proposed treatment and doesn't feel qualified to make a determination. In those cases, they often consult an expert in the field."

Kate ran her finger along the edge of the file containing the age-progressed photo of Kevin. "I vaguely remember him mentioning that once or twice. As I recall, it wasn't a situation he dealt with very often."

"It's rare. Most of the time, determinations are cut-and-dried. And if it's an investigational/experimental treatment or procedure, an insurance company will automatically deny coverage. However, if there's enough push back from a patient and the proposed treatment is out of the realm of expertise of the medical director, a specialist might be consulted."

Kate was beginning to get a hint of where this was leading.

When Barbara continued, her tone was careful—and deliberate. "Without giving away any confidential information, I can tell you John did consult on a handful of such cases."

Including David Sanders?

She couldn't ask that. But why else would Barbara call back?

"I'm going to assume your comment has some connection to our earlier conversation." She voiced the thought cautiously, aware she was treading on sensitive ground.

"Assumptions are relatively safe if you have data to back them up." Barbara paused, then emphasized her final statement. "I deal with data every day."

Closing her eyes, Kate exhaled.

They had their link.

"Thank you, Barbara."

"No thanks necessary. I just gave you some background information on how insurance companies work and why medical directors sometimes call specialists. There's nothing confidential about those procedures." Another siren sounded in the background. "I think I better hang up. Looks like some accident gapers ahead of me are in the midst of a fender bender, and I don't want to join their party."

"I hear you—and I promise I'll be in touch after I have some answers."

"I'm counting on that. Talk to you soon."

As the line went dead, Kate put the receiver in the cradle, leaned forward, and opened the file containing Kevin's picture. Gently she traced the curve of his chin. Ran her fingers along the sprinkling of freckles across his nose. Brushed her thumb over the flyaway blond hair she'd been forever smoothing into place.

Would she have the opportunity to do that very thing again?

Was it really possible a chance encounter on an escalator was going to lead to a reunion with the son she'd given up for dead?

More and more, the answer appeared to be yes.

Sniffing, she fished in her purse for a tissue—and saw the blinking message light on her cell. A quick scroll through missed calls pulled up Connor's number, and she played the message back. It was short, just "call me when you have a minute," and she responded at once.

He answered on the first ring.

After greeting him, she apologized for her delayed response. "I had a late appointment, and this is the first chance I've had to check messages. But I have news."

"So do I. You go first."

She relayed the information she'd received from Barbara. "So even though John never saw Sanders's son as a patient, I think we can assume Sanders's insurance company contacted him about some sort of experimental treatment. Is that a good enough link?"

"Better than good enough, based on what we discovered today.

I put the whole crew to work, and we came up with a lot of new material. If you have a few minutes now, I can fill you in."

"I'm done for the day. My time is yours."

She listened to his briefing, her confidence they were on the right track building with each fact he ticked off. And it went off the scale when he mentioned Sanders's trip to China for stem cell therapy.

"That had to be what he was trying to get the insurance company to authorize."

"I think that's a reasonable conclusion. At this point, we have an excellent circumstantial case against him. But to get law enforcement to step back in, we need even more compelling proof. Namely, DNA."

"Which will require the hair sample we talked about earlier."

"Yes. That's become a top priority." He laid out the surveillance plan, ending with the final resort of a trash cover. "We're going to be racking up quite a few billable hours with late afternoon/evening surveillance plus a full day on the weekends. I wanted to make certain you were on board with that."

"A hundred percent." She gripped the arm of her chair with her free hand. "You know . . . I've been trying not to let myself get too optimistic, and I realize it's still possible the boy in the mall was Sanders's adopted son—but I'm beginning to believe there's a strong likelihood it was Kevin. What do you think?" She held her breath, knowing he'd give her a truthful assessment even if it wasn't what she wanted to hear.

There was no hesitation in his response.

"Until we have the DNA results, we can't know for sure. But based on the evidence we've uncovered, I don't think hope is misplaced."

She released her grip on the chair, opening and closing her fingers to get the blood flowing back to her white knuckles. "This is feeling very surreal."

"I agree. And frankly, I never expected this outcome. Thank God you followed your instincts that day in the mall and pursued this."

"Trust me, I've been thanking him every single day. Numerous times. If that coincidence on the escalator leads where I'm thinking it might, it's nothing short of a miracle."

"I think that's an appropriate description."

The silence between them lengthened, and she fiddled with a paper clip. She didn't want to end the call, but there was no reason to take up any more of his time.

Say good-bye, Kate.

"I guess I better let you get on with your evening. Any special plans?"

"I wouldn't call them special. I'm staked out down the street from Sanders's house, where I'll be until at least nine. Masquerading as McCarthy Heating and Cooling today, according to the magnetic sign on the side of the van."

Her eyebrows rose. "You started the surveillance already?"

"I figured you'd approve it, and the boy's hair is kind of shaggy. With school about to begin, he may get it cut any day. I don't want to miss the opportunity to follow them to a salon."

"If they go to one, how would you get a hair sample?"

"Most stylists would be happy to earn a quick fifty bucks for a few strands of hair."

And his charming smile would seal the deal. "Sounds like you've done this before."

"Not with hair."

She let that go, not certain she wanted to know details. "So once we have a sample, how long will it take to get the results from the lab?"

"A week if I push hard. Mitochondrial DNA testing takes longer. I'll need a sample from you too."

"Hair?"

"That or a cheek swab. I could collect either, but I'd rather send you to the lab so there are no chain of custody issues."

"Then what?"

"If we have a match, I turn it over to the FBI. Interstate kidnapping is their jurisdiction." A moment of silence ticked by, and when he continued, his crisp professional tone had been replaced with a warmth that seeped straight into her heart. "Hang in there, okay? We're down to the final lap."

"I will. And thanks for the pep talk."

"Part of the job." But his husky timbre said otherwise. "So what are you going to do tonight?"

She leaned back in her chair. "Write up some notes from the session I just finished, go home, eat dinner, and review some case files for tomorrow."

"Your evening sounds about as exciting as mine."

"At least it will be cooler."

"No arguments there." Once more, his tone grew serious. "Listen . . . in case you haven't already been thinking about this, you might want to consider how to smooth out the transition for your son if this plays out the way it appears to be heading."

"I've been mulling that over. No matter what I do, it's not going to be easy."

"For either of you."

"I know. From everything you've learned, it sounds like Sanders has been a loving father—and I'm no more than a stranger to Kevin now." As she gave voice to the concerns that had plagued her over the past few days, pressure built behind her eyes. "To be honest, I've even begun to wonder if I'm being selfish. I'll be uprooting Kevin from the only life and the only parent he remembers for a second time." She choked out the last few words.

"You're not being selfish." Connor's words rang with conviction, soothing her frayed nerves and alleviating her qualms. "Just the opposite. The mere fact you're wrestling with those

276

questions shows how unselfish you are, putting your child's welfare above your own. If this boy is your son, you have every right to reclaim him and step back into the role that was stolen from you. I have no doubt your love will win him over, and that with your support and guidance, he'll learn to deal with all that's happened. But if you need a helping hand through all that, you can count on me." His voice softened. "In fact, I hope you will."

Kate swallowed a sob. "Thanks for saying exactly the right thing."

"I've learned a few lessons myself over the years."

At his quiet comment, she thought back to the story he'd told her about his failed romance—and knew her assessment of him the day they'd shared Chinese food had been accurate. Whatever his shortcomings in the past, he was now, indeed, a man worthy of trust and confidence.

"May I say I'm glad I'm the beneficiary of those lessons?"

"You may. And for the record, I'm glad too. Now go home and eat some dinner. I'll call you with an update tomorrow."

In the silence that followed his call, the snarl of tension in her shoulders eased as she began gathering up the files she needed for the evening. Amazing how simply hearing Connor's resonant voice could reassure her. Make her believe everything would turn out fine.

John had been like that too. A simple phone call from him would restore the balance in her world on days when she had a problematic student, or Kevin was giving her fits during his terrible twos, or when she'd been in the doldrums with post-partum blues. His quiet strength, caring manner, and aura of competence had always smoothed the wrinkles from her world.

Based on what she'd seen so far, she had a feeling Connor would do the same.

And she was ready to find out. Much as she'd loved John, it was time to move on.

She paused to gaze down at the one-carat, flawless solitaire she'd worn since the night he proposed. Even on her wedding day, she'd pressed the tips of her fourth fingers together and transferred the engagement ring to her right hand before the ceremony so he could slip her wedding band in place without removing the solitaire.

Yet the intertwined set of rings was now part of a past that could never be recaptured, a reminder of what had been rather than what could be.

Squaring her shoulders, she tugged them over her knuckle. At first they resisted, but finally they slid off, leaving a bare ring finger.

No. Bad word choice.

Available ring finger.

And if things progressed with Connor the way she thought they might, if someday a different ring occupied that finger, she wasn't going to feel guilty about finding a new love.

She was going to feel twice blessed.

"I had a great birthday, Dad."

Greg tucked in the sheet that covered Todd. "I'm glad."

"I told everyone at daycare about it today. Chuck E. Cheese's was a lot more fun than the Build-A-Bear party—even though I like my bear." He tucked the baseball-themed stuffed animal into the crook of his arm. "I'm happy Diane came, aren't you?"

"Yeah." But he'd be happier after she reported on her return visit to Kate Marshall's office.

Unless she'd changed her mind about following through with the woman because she was still miffed at him.

"I miss our Saturday-night pizza dinners with her." Todd yawned. "Do you think we could do that again soon?"

"I hope so." He leaned down and kissed his son's forehead. "Better get to sleep now. We have to get up with the birds."

Todd hugged his bear tighter and smiled up at him. "I love you, Dad."

"Love you back." The words came out hoarse, and he reached over to flip off the light, struggling to hold on to his composure.

Once in the hall, he blew out a long breath.

Man, could he use another beer.

Too bad he'd already had his daily allotment.

Shoulders slumping, he wandered toward the kitchen. Diane should be home from her support group meeting by now. In the past, she'd always called him—but there was no guarantee of that tonight, given the mixed signals he'd been sending.

He wasn't going to get much sleep if he didn't find out whether she was going to help him, though. Might as well ask. At this point, what could it hurt?

He retrieved the portable phone, punched in her speed dial number, and waited while it rang. Once. Twice. Three times. Then it rolled to voice mail.

He throttled a curse. Unless she was acting way out of pattern, she'd gone straight home, exhausted as usual after her support group session. Meaning she'd seen his name on caller ID and was ignoring him.

When the beep sounded, he put as much warmth as possible into his greeting. "Hi, Diane. I thought I'd call and see how your session went tonight. Todd says hi too, and wanted you to know how happy he was you joined us for his birthday celebration on Saturday. I was too. Talk to you soon."

He hit the off button, slammed the phone back into the charger, and fisted his hands on his hips.

What was he going to do if she didn't come through for him? He had no other way to find out why Kate Marshall had Todd's picture.

But he had to assume the worst.

Shoving his fingers through his hair, he began to pace. If

things got dicey, he had two options. Run—or eliminate the threat.

Better be prepared for both.

He strode down the hall to his bedroom, flipped on the light, and locked the door. After removing the small key from the top drawer of his dresser, he crossed to the closet and retrieved the heavy fireproof storage box from the highest shelf. Once he'd set it on the bed, he inserted the key.

For several seconds he sat unmoving, his hand resting on the top. He hadn't opened this box in three years. Nor had he planned to so soon after moving to St. Louis.

But neither had he expected to face a threat like the one now looming over him.

Could this be God's way of punishing him for what he'd done?

As that unbidden thought singed his conscience, remorse cloaked him, as suffocating as the St. Louis humidity. Not for what he'd done that day on the bay but for making an innocent woman suffer.

An instant later, however, he flung off the shroud of regret. Why should he be the only one left to grieve? He'd lost a wife and son; she'd lost a husband and son. Fair was fair. If God didn't like it, tough. Since the Almighty had ignored his desperate pleas for help, he didn't owe him a thing. And he wasn't about to give up the life and the son he'd worked so hard to reclaim.

Clamping his teeth together, he opened the lid.

The birth certificate Emilio's contact had provided three years ago for Todd was on top, and he ran his finger over the raised state seal. The forger had done a great job on the document, as well as on the bogus adoption paperwork clipped behind it. Lucky thing he'd offered the head of the lawn crew that had cut his grass in better days a side job digging out some dead bushes. Luckier still that they'd shared a few too many beers after the man finished the job. Otherwise Emilio would never have spilled his guts during a moment of homesickness and admitted he was an illegal alien.

Greg set the paperwork on the bed. He'd never intended to rat the guy out; a man as ambitious as Emilio, supporting a host of relatives back home, deserved to make a few bucks under the radar. Still, after Greg promised to keep his secret, the man had been overwhelmed with gratitude and sworn he'd be forever in his debt.

That debt might soon be repaid in full if he called in all his chits.

Wiping his palms on the denim fabric of his jeans, he reached back into the box and withdrew the Colt .45 and the silencer. The weapon felt odd in his hand. Foreign. No surprise, since he'd only fired it on his one visit to the range as he prepared for that fateful day on the bay. It had been his insurance policy if things had gone wrong.

It was still his insurance policy.

He tightened his fingers around the grip. Pointed the stainless steel barrel toward the top of the dresser, at the baseball cap he'd worn that day on the escalator. Pulled the trigger.

The quiet click echoed in the room.

No bullets.

But he had those too.

From the bottom of the box, he withdrew an eight-round magazine. Positioned it under the handle. Pushed it up, into place.

The bullets added weight to the gun . . . and to his shoulders. He'd never wanted it to come down to this.

But if anyone tried to take Todd away from him, he wouldn't hesitate to aim this weapon straight at their heart—and pull the trigger.

ꞁꞁꞁꞁꞁ 20 ꞁꞁꞁꞁꞁ

Three-ten.

Kate glanced from her watch to her phone. Her four o'clock had just cancelled, and she had an unscheduled hour between three and four. There was plenty to do in her office to fill up the time—like finish the grant paperwork that had been staring at her for two weeks.

But she'd rather spend a few hours on this Tuesday afternoon hanging out with Connor. Might he be receptive to an offer of company during his surveillance at Sanders's house tonight? Or was that too pushy?

She drummed her fingers on her desk. He'd been clear about wanting to keep things professional between them, but the case was winding down—and this wouldn't be like a date or anything.

To ask or not to ask?

When no clear answer emerged, she bypassed the mental gymnastics, picked up the phone, and tapped in his cell number. Worst case, he'd say no thanks.

"Sullivan."

The distracted greeting wasn't what she'd hoped for.

"Hi. It's Kate. You sound busy."

"Not too busy for you." His voice warmed. "Sorry if I was

282

Irene Hannon

a little curt. It's been a bear of a day, and I grabbed the phone without checking caller ID. A messy case came in this morning, and we're all scrambling to gather intel. What's up?"

The man doesn't have time for frivolous suggestions, Kate. Say you just wanted an update and let him get back to work.

But different words came out. "I was wondering if you'd like some company during your surveillance at Sanders's house tonight."

Silence.

She cringed and closed her eyes as dead air hung between them. Time to backtrack.

"Listen, I . . ."

"If you . . ."

When their words overlapped, they both stopped—but he jumped back in first.

"If you don't think you'll be bored, that would be great. Conversation instead of music would be a nice change of pace. Best of all, Dev's covering for me until six-thirty while I finish up here and run home to change and grab some food, so it won't be a long gig. Lights-out at the Sanderses' house is always around ten. Why don't I pick you up at six?"

"Are you sure? I don't want to get in your way."

"Do I sound uncertain?"

Not in the least.

"Okay."

"Dress cool."

"And don't drink a lot of water. I remember the drill."

"Watch for the carpet cleaning van."

"How many signs do you guys have?"

"You name the business, we probably have the sign. See you soon."

As the line went dead, she smiled.

An evening with Connor.

A vast improvement over her usual Tuesday night.

Slinging her purse over her shoulder, she gathered up her things and flipped off the light in her office.

When she entered the lobby, Nancy's eyebrows rose. "What's up?"

"I'm cutting out early."

"I can see that. Are you sick?"

"No. But I'm done with my appointments for the day, and . . . an unexpected opportunity came up for this evening."

The woman considered her. "This wouldn't have anything to do with that hot guy who stopped by the office a few days ago, would it?"

Kate felt a flush creep over her cheeks.

"Never mind." Nancy sent her a smug grin. "I'd play hooky for a guy like that too."

"I didn't say he was the reason I'm leaving early."

"You didn't have to." Nancy waved a hand. "Just have fun."

She didn't respond.

Fun was pushing it.

But she did intend to enjoy her evening in the company of a certain handsome PI.

Diane pulled the car close to the curb in front of Greg's house, set the brake . . . and hesitated.

Was she making a mistake, paying him an unexpected visit? Would it have been better to call?

No. She needed to see his reaction when she told him about her visit with Kate. That was the only way she'd have any chance of discovering the truth—and she had to get to the bottom of this mystery. It was driving her nuts. She'd replayed her meeting with the counselor multiple times over the past twenty-four hours, and there was no doubt in her mind the woman was legit.

The trauma she'd suffered was real, and her offer of a round-the-clock friendly ear had been sincere.

Meaning there had to be a logical reason why there was a picture of Todd on her desk—one she hoped Greg would shed some light on after she gave him a report on her visit.

As she approached the front door, the muffled sound of the TV in the living room seeped through the walls. Good. They were finished eating, since Greg reserved mealtimes for conversation, not cartoons. Those were an after-dinner treat. Her timing was perfect, just as she'd hoped.

Heart tripping into fast-forward, she pressed the bell.

Through the door, she could hear the sound of running feet. Five seconds later the knob twisted and she was face-to-face with a beaming Todd.

"Hi, Diane!"

At his enthusiastic greeting, her spirits rose a notch. At least one member of the family was happy to see her.

"Hey, Todd." Over his shoulder she caught a glimpse of pieces of the erector set strewn across the living room floor. "Looks like you're enjoying your birthday present."

"Yeah. It's awesome! You want to come in and see the crane Dad and me made?"

As he issued the invitation, Greg rounded the corner from the kitchen, wiping his hands on a dish towel. He came to an abrupt halt when he spotted her, and his eyebrows rose in surprise. The smile he finally managed, accompanied by a hi, was more a stretch of the lips than a genuine welcome.

Her stomach bottomed out.

"Can I show her what we built, Dad?"

"Sure."

Todd grabbed her hand and led her toward the living room, chattering nonstop. Greg remained in the background while she did her best to enthuse over the crane, but he stepped in when Todd asked her if she wanted to help him build a skyscraper.

"Maybe later, champ. Diane and I are going to visit while you finish watching the cartoons."

Heaving a sigh, he plopped back on his stomach in front of the TV set.

As they entered the kitchen, Greg continued toward the counter and tuned the radio to a music station, then ramped up the volume. "What can I get you to drink?"

He was setting the stage for a private discussion. Masking their conversation.

Not a bad idea. Todd didn't need to hear about the woman who kept his picture on her desk.

"Just water, thanks."

She looked around while he filled a glass. An empty cardboard box that had contained frozen chicken nuggets lay on the counter, along with a burnt-around-the-edges French fry and a bottle of ketchup. No vegetables in sight, other than the charred fry. Not the healthiest meal for a growing boy or a hardworking man. If this was her family, they'd be eating nutritious homemade fare every night.

But it wasn't her family—and according to her support group, it was far too soon to be even thinking about committing to someone new. She needed to take care of herself and get her act together before she assumed responsibility for anyone else's welfare.

That was sound advice.

But why was it so much easier to agree with when she was surrounded by her support group rather than sitting in a homey kitchen with a man who'd seemed like a dream come true until a couple of weeks ago?

"Are you sure that's all you want?" Greg set her water on the table and sat at a right angle to her.

"Yes." She eyed the bottle of beer in his hand. "Did you skip your predinner drink?"

He twisted off the cap. His complexion, already ruddy from all the hours he spent in the sun, went a shade darker. "No. It was just a hot one today."

As he took a long pull, she sipped her water. One beer a day, that was his rule—or so he'd told her not long after they'd met. He hadn't given her a reason for it, but she'd gotten the feeling he'd overindulged at one time and now kept himself on a tight leash.

His lapse tonight was yet one more sign things were out of whack.

Setting her water back on the table, she folded her hands. Might as well get right to the point. "I went to see Kate Marshall yesterday."

He leaned closer and lowered his voice, his eyes intent. "Did she tell you anything about the picture?"

"No. But I found out a lot of other interesting stuff."

Instead of taking another swig of the beer, he put the bottle on the table and sent her a guarded look. "Like what?"

She told him everything Kate had shared with her—ending with the information about her son.

Diane watched him as she spoke, trying to gauge his reaction—but it was impossible. His expression remained neutral. No flicker of emotion betrayed his thoughts, nor did he speak. If he saw the parallels between Todd and Kate's son, he gave no indication of it.

She'd have to broach the subject herself.

Wrapping her hands around the sweaty glass, she put the question on the table. "Don't you think it's odd that her son would be about Todd's age?"

"It is kind of strange." He finished off his beer in several long swallows.

"Here's another weird thing. Kate's hair is the same color as Todd's—which is also the same color hair the woman on the escalator had in his dream. Remember? I told you about it the day I came to stay with him when he was sick."

Instead of responding, he stood and started to pace.

Now she was getting a reaction.

"Maybe this woman saw him the day we went to the mall for the Build-A-Bear party." He spoke slowly as he prowled around the kitchen, as if he was trying to work through the bizarre coincidences himself. "That's all I can think of. Where else would she have seen him? Todd and I never lived in New York."

Diane tipped her head. "How did you know she was from New York?"

He stopped, and his face went blank. "You must have mentioned it while you were telling me her story."

Had she?

Not that she recalled.

But she'd been so focused on watching his reaction, perhaps it had slipped out and she'd forgotten. How else would he know where Kate had lived?

Greg stopped behind his chair and gripped the back, his demeanor grim. "It sounds to me like she spotted Todd, saw the resemblance, and now thinks he's her son. Maybe she's been stalking him. Maybe she snapped a picture and doctored it up to look like a studio shot. If she was in bad enough shape to get hooked on Valium, she could still be having delusions of some kind."

"I don't think so. That was three years ago." Diane pulled a paper napkin from the holder and sopped up the ring of moisture from her glass. "She seems totally normal."

"So did you, when you were married to Rich. No one suspected you were abused. In public, you kept up a good front. But he did a number on you . . . and obviously the drowning did a

288

number on this woman if she had to resort to drugs. For all we know, she might still need them to sleep at night."

"No." Diane shook her head. "She said she'd beaten the addiction, and I believe her."

"People can slip back into old habits. It happens."

She slanted a glance at the empty beer bottle on the table. "Not Kate. I have a feeling the main thing she battles now is loneliness. I gather she's pretty much all alone in the world."

"Then how do you explain what's going on here?"

His intense gaze bored into her, and she suppressed a shiver. "I don't know."

He continued to stare at her for a moment. At last he resumed pacing, agitation seeping from his pores. "I don't like any of this. Plus, we don't know for sure how she got that picture of Todd."

There were a *lot* of things they didn't know. Like why Todd had freaked on the lake that day.

She kept that thought to herself, however. She had a feeling he'd pass it off, continue to disavow any connection between the two boys.

But more and more, she had a feeling there was a link—and Greg had to be doing the same math she'd done yesterday. He was a smart man. He had to know things weren't adding up.

Conclusion? He was either in denial—or he was hiding something.

She weighed both possibilities in silence as he continued to pace but came up with no answers. Or none she was willing to consider.

When he sat again at the table, his neutral expression was back—but there was a look in his eyes she'd never seen before. It was equal parts distress, panic, steely determination . . . and some other emotion she couldn't identify.

Whatever it was, though, it scared her. As did the soul-deep detachment in their depths.

A wave of panic swept over her, so startling in its intensity she vaulted to her feet.

She needed to escape from this place.

Now.

"I have to get going."

As she unhooked her purse from the back of the chair, Greg stood too. "I appreciate your efforts to find out more about the photo."

She slung the purse over her shoulder and edged toward the door. "I was there anyway."

"Are you going back?"

"Yes. Next week."

I Ie followed her. "It might be better if you keep this conversation between the two of us until I figure out what's going on."

"I guess it might." She moved into the hall, toward the door. "Bye, Todd."

The little boy looked up from his position in front of the TV, disappointment etching his features. "Aren't you going to stay and build a skyscraper?"

"Not this time, sweetie. Maybe on my next visit." When—or if—that ever happened.

And that was a big if.

Because despite what Greg had said, she intended to be honest with Kate—ASAP. She would tell her she'd seen the picture and ask her who it was and how she'd gotten it.

Greg wasn't going to like that . . . but she had a feeling talking to the counselor was the only way she was ever going to make sense of this whole thing.

"Please, Diane? Just for a few minutes? I hardly ever see you anymore."

As Todd stood and trotted over to her, she hesitated. Strange. When Greg had begun to pull back, she'd thought she'd miss him the most if their relationship fell apart. Now she wasn't as certain. Todd was sweet and loving and guileless—and she had a feeling he'd stolen her heart even more than his father had.

So why not indulge him tonight? If things continued to go south with Greg, she'd lose Todd too. Why not tuck away one more brief memory to savor during all the lonely nights to come in her empty house that had never rung with the laughter of children?

She set her purse on the floor by the door and took his hand. "Five minutes."

"Yeah!" He tugged her toward the living room, leaving Greg standing in the hall.

And though Diane knew he remained behind her, watching them, she didn't look back.

Not once.

Connor parked the van several doors down from Sanders's house and plucked the cell from the storage compartment that separated him and Kate.

"Where's your partner?" She peered through the dark-tinted windows, resting her left hand on the dash as she leaned forward.

He homed in on the empty fourth finger of her hand.

She'd removed her wedding and engagement rings.

That had to be a positive sign for the two of them, didn't it? Why else would she—

"Connor?"

"What?" He jerked his gaze to her face and tried to regroup.

"Where's your partner?"

"Around the corner up ahead. By that pink bush." He gestured toward the cross street a few doors beyond Sanders's house.

She looked toward the SUV. "Can he actually see the house from there?"

"Trust me. Dev is a master at finding unobtrusive surveillance spots with great lines of sight."

Before Connor could key in Dev's speed dial number, his cell began to vibrate. He held it up so Kate could read his partner's name on the digital display. "See what I mean?" He grinned and put the phone against his ear. "I take it you saw us arrive."

"Us?"

Connor winced. Oops. Too late to backtrack. "Yeah. I have company."

"Let me guess . . . it wouldn't be your client, would it?"

"I'm following your example from a certain teen disappearance case."

"That wasn't surveillance. It was investigation."

"You're splitting hairs." He turned off the ignition, mouthing a silent "sorry" to Kate as the fan on the air-conditioning died.

"We'll talk about it tomorrow."

"I don't think so. Any action?"

"Not on my end. How about on yours?"

"You can leave now."

"That's my plan. At least I got a free sauna out of this gig. By the way, you might want to run the license on the car in front of Sanders's house."

Connor sized up the Mercedes. "I thought you said there was no action?"

"There hasn't been. Just a visitor—of the female persuasion. About ten minutes ago. I was going to run the plate, but I got a call from Cal that lasted longer than I expected."

"I'll take care of it."

"Then I'm out of here. I'd tell you to stay cool, but that's probably not possible with a hot chick in the front seat."

"Good night, Dev."

To the sound of his partner's laughter, he punched the end button, then logged on to the Regional Justice Information Service. How did PIs in the old days manage without instant cell access to databases like REJIS?

"What's going on?" Kate cracked her window.

"You can open it more than that. Otherwise we'll bake despite our shady spot." He lowered his own window a couple of inches too. "I'm running the plate on the car in front of Sanders's house. My partner says a female went in a few minutes ago."

Silence descended in the van while he entered his security codes and the plate number.

As the owner's name flashed onto the screen, Kate let out a gasp.

"Diane Koenig!"

"You know . . . ?" Connor's question trailed off as he shifted his focus to her. She wasn't reading his cell screen, as he'd expected—she was looking at the woman who'd stepped out of Sanders's house.

"And there's the boy from the mall!" Kate leaned forward and gripped the edge of the dash.

"Kate." He touched her arm, but her attention remained riveted on the little boy. Sanders was beside him, his hand resting on the child's shoulder. "Do you know that woman?"

"Yes. She's one of my new clients. I just saw her yesterday."

Connor grabbed his binoculars and zeroed in on the threesome at the front door. They exchanged a few words, then the woman gave the little boy a lingering hug. But when Sanders reached out to her, she pulled back, her posture stiff.

Telling.

After backing up a few steps, she turned away and walked quickly to her car. She waved once more before sliding behind the wheel, and as she drove off, the man and boy retreated into the house.

As the door closed, Kate sank back into her seat, her face a mask of confusion. "What in the world was Diane doing here?"

"I'd like an answer to that too. Tell me what you know about her."

She angled toward him and caught her lower lip between her teeth. "A lot of what I discuss with my clients is confidential."

"I understand the protocol for counseling work, but if she's a plant by Sanders, you don't owe her any professional consideration."

"She's not a plant."

"How can you be sure?"

"She came to New Start on the recommendation of a friend."

"Her high-end Mercedes would suggest she doesn't need a job."

"I don't think she does for financial reasons. But she's . . . fragile, and she needs the self-esteem."

Connor set the binoculars down and thought back to the intel he'd uncovered on New Start after Kate's first visit to Phoenix. The organization wasn't just a vocational guidance center—it had a reputation for catering to women who were newly divorced or coming out of abusive relationships. If that was Diane Koenig's background, and she had the kind of money her car suggested, it made sense she'd seek career counseling from the best resource available if she was going to reenter the workforce.

Namely, the woman sitting beside him.

So maybe she wasn't a plant. Her parting from Sanders would suggest things weren't all that rosy between them.

Angling in his seat, he rested one arm on the wheel. "We can dig up a lot about her, Kate, but you'll save us time if you tell me some basics."

Kate shifted toward him. "I can tell you we had kind of a . . . different . . . conversation during our session yesterday."

Connor's antenna went up. "Define different."

"She called early in the day and asked if I could squeeze her in. Since it sounded urgent, I did. When she arrived, she seemed distracted—and a bit uncomfortable. But as the session progressed, she began to open up and tell me about her background. I could see she was down, that the pressures of the changes in her life were starting to make her consider some inappropriate coping mechanisms."

"Such as?"

"That's not important for our purposes. But because she shared that, I did something I rarely do. I told her a little about what I've been through and my Valium addiction. In all my years of counseling, I've only revealed personal information a handful of times."

"Was she surprised by your story?"

"More than surprised. Shocked might be a better word. I'd hoped it would encourage her, but she wasn't any less stressed when she left." Kate rubbed at the indentations above her nose. "I know the timing of her visit is odd, but I can't believe she's doing anything underhanded. She's not the devious type."

"That could be why she seemed uncomfortable. Do you think she's stable?"

Kate lifted one shoulder. "As stable as anyone with her background would be. If you're asking whether she's vulnerable enough to get involved with another manipulator—it's possible. We've never really talked about—"

A faint ringing sound came from the floor, and she groped for her purse. "I might need to take this. One of my clients had an interview late this afternoon, and she promised to call after it was over and give me a report."

"Do you ever have any downtime?"

She arched an eyebrow. "Let's see . . . it's six-forty-five and you're still on the job. What's that old saying about a pot and a kettle?"

"Not every day is like this for me."

"Me neither. In fact, I'm taking a four-day weekend this week." She pulled out her phone and gave him a sheepish look.

"In the interest of full disclosure, though, I had to be coerced by . . ." She froze as she scanned caller ID.

"What is it?"

In silence, she turned the screen toward him so he could read the name.

D. Koenig.

His adrenaline spiked. "Go ahead and answer it. Tell her you need to put it on speaker because you're in the car." He dug a small notepad and pen out of his pocket.

She pressed the button and put the phone to her ear. "Hi, Diane. I saw your name pop up in the display. Can I put you on speaker? I'm in the car." Silence. "Hang on a sec." Kate pressed the speaker button and set the phone on the console between them. "I'm set. What can I do for you?"

"I need to talk with you about—a personal matter." The woman sounded tense, agitated. "It's very important. I don't want to impose, but is there any way we could get together even for a few minutes tonight? It has to do with . . . a child."

As Kate glanced at him, Connor debated their options. He'd prefer to run some background on the woman first, but based on her tense parting from Sanders, she was no longer in the enemy camp—if she ever had been. Plus, if they waited overnight, she could change her mind about whatever she wanted to discuss.

"Kate?" There was a frantic edge to Diane's voice.

"Yes, I'm here." Kate's tone was calm and soothing as she bought him a few more seconds to think through strategy. "I'm just surprised, since we saw each other yesterday. I'm in the middle of running an errand, but I'd like to accommodate you."

He jotted "9:30—your place" on the pad of paper and turned it for her to read.

"I wouldn't ask if this wasn't important." Diane sounded on the verge of tears now.

"I know that. I'll tell you what. I'll be home by nine-thirty. If that's not too late, you're welcome to stop by my condo."

"Nine-thirty is fine."

"Let me give you directions."

As Kate talked her through the route, Connor pulled up Diane's driver's license on his phone and gave it a quick scan. Everything looked clean. With her date of birth in hand, he moved on to a quick search of one of his favorite proprietary databases. Too bad he didn't have her social security number; that would speed things up. But as far as he could see based on the information he had, Diane Koenig had no black marks against her. It also appeared she'd lived in St. Louis for years, suggesting there wasn't much chance she'd known Sanders before the man moved here.

"I'll see you later this evening. Call if you get lost." As Kate rang off, puzzlement scored her features. "What do you make of this?"

He slipped his own phone back into its holster. "I'd be concerned Sanders put her up to this, except they didn't seem to part on the friendliest terms. You want my gut reaction? She trusts you, and she's seen or suspects something that concerns her. She either wants clarification—or she wants to pass on a warning."

Kate blinked. "A warning about what?"

The temptation to reach for her hand was strong—but he gripped the wheel instead. He'd told Cal he'd keep this professional, and he needed to honor that promise as best he could.

"Sanders may appear to be a loving father. He may even *be* a loving father. But if the boy in that house is your son, violence occurred. Deadly crimes were committed. And he's been smart enough to elude detection for a long time. He also appears to have bonded with the boy he claims he adopted. Plus, he has a new job and, given Diane's presence, perhaps a new girlfriend.

My guess is he doesn't want to give any of that up. In light of the extremes he's gone to in the past to accomplish his goals, I doubt he'd have any qualms about using lethal force in the future. Bottom line, we're dealing with a very dangerous man."

Some of the color drained from Kate's face. He didn't want to scare her, but the more they learned about Sanders—and the closer they got to nailing him—the more perilous the situation became. Though he appeared to be living a normal life now, the man had apparently cracked once; there was no reason to think he wouldn't do so again, given sufficient pressure . . . or an imminent threat.

"I guess I assumed we were safe as long as he didn't know we were investigating him." Kate looked toward Sanders's house again.

"I doubt we've been totally safe since the day on the escalator. He knows you saw the boy, and he has to wonder if you're trying to find some answers. But my guess is he doesn't expect you to get anywhere—nor hire a crack PI firm." He threw the last in, hoping to coax a smile from her. While the situation was beginning to get sticky, he didn't want her freaking out.

It worked—barely. "Phoenix *is* a crack firm—one PI in particular. As for delving into what I saw that day . . . when it comes to the people I love, I have the tenacity of a pit bull."

"I figured that out. And I have a feeling he may have too. That's why I don't want to put off the meeting with Diane." He pulled his phone off his belt again.

"How do you want me to handle the meeting?"

He punched in Dev's speed dial number. "First of all, I don't want you to handle it alone. I plan to be . . . Dev?" He held up a finger to her. "I have a big favor to ask."

"I'm not going to deliver takeout to your van."

"Nothing that simple. I need you to come back and relieve me."

"Ha-ha."

"I'm not kidding."

"No. There's been a development Kate and I need to pursue."

"What kind of development?"

"It involves the woman you saw. I'll fill you in tomorrow."

"I'm not even home yet."

"I'll make it up to you."

"You better." A theatrical sigh came over the line. "Can I at least pay a quick visit to the Golden Arches and grab a burger?"

"No problem. We have a few minutes to spare."

"Gee, thanks. What did *you* have for dinner?"

"Same thing you're having."

"That makes me feel a little better. See you in twenty."

Connor broke the connection and turned to Kate. "Here's what I have in mind. I want to swing by the office and get some equipment, then stop by my place so I can take a quick shower and change into more professional attire before I run you home."

"Why?"

This was the part he had a feeling she wasn't going to like.

"I'd like to be in on your conversation with Diane, but my presence could spook her. Until we know what she wants to talk to you about, I need to stay close but out of sight. My preference is to have you wear a wire. That way, I can listen in from the street."

She stared at him. "You want to eavesdrop on us?"

Why did the van suddenly feel ten degrees hotter?

"I don't like deception any more than you do, but if she's aligned with Sanders, she's deceiving *you*. I have no qualms about using a wire in that case. If she's on our side, and you get a clear indication of that as you talk with her, tell her who I am and that I'd like to sit in on the rest of the conversation. If she agrees, I'll come in. She never has to know I was listening the whole time."

Kate shifted in her seat and swiped at the moisture above her lip. "Is this legal?"

"Yes. Missouri has a one-party rule for electronic listening or recording. As long as one of the people involved gives consent, it's legal."

"But not necessarily moral."

"Neither is kidnapping—or murder."

She flinched . . . but he needed her to remember that bad guys had no scruples.

"True. But if I think she's with us, I'd like to bring you in as quickly as possible."

"That's fine. I trust your judgment." He pulled a bottle of water from the cooler behind the front seat and handed it to her. "However, don't rush that determination. Tipping our hand to the wrong person could short-circuit the whole investigation."

Her fingers closed over the bottle. Brushed his. He held tight, and she sent him a questioning look.

"Home stretch, remember?"

Eyes troubled, she nodded.

But as he released the bottle and she took a long swallow, exposing a long, graceful curve of throat, he wished this race was over. Because lots of things could go wrong in the home stretch.

And victory didn't always go to the most deserving.

21

As the TV continued to blare in the living room, Greg slammed the dishwasher closed and punched the start button.

He'd blown it with Diane tonight.

Big-time.

But how could he have known the Marshall woman would plant seeds of doubt in her mind by revealing so much personal history? Since when were professional counselors that open with clients?

All he'd wanted Diane to find out was how Kate happened to be in possession of a photo of Todd, not learn enough to begin making connections.

Worst of all, the most vital question remained unanswered.

Why did Kate have the picture?

He blew out a breath.

The whole reconnaissance mission had turned into a bust.

Panic clawing at his throat, he stalked to the refrigerator and yanked open the door. His stash of beer stared back at him from the bottom shelf, and his fingers itched to grab another bottle. But he'd already had two—double his daily limit. Didn't matter. He wanted more. Needed more. Just this once. Tomorrow he'd go back to his usual routine.

Leaning forward, he reached for the closest brew, twisted off the cap, and began to pace again.

He had to think. Had to be logical. Had to control his panic. Lifting the bottle, he took a long drink.

Diane—the sweet, caring friend he'd thought might be part of his future—was pulling back from him as he'd pulled back from her. Her stiff posture, wary expression, and chilly good-bye tonight had been like a punch in the stomach after her previous warmth and caring. In a short two months, she'd offered him the kind of companionship he'd never expected to find again, given him hope he might be able to re-create the family unit that had once been the center of his world.

Now that hope was shriveling.

A bead of sweat rolled down the neck of the bottle. It dripped onto his finger . . . reminding him of a tear.

He could relate.

Fingers gripping the brew, he took another swig.

All might not be lost with Diane, though. Surely she still cared about him. Everything they'd built over the past two months couldn't disintegrate in a mere couple of weeks. And if she did care, she wouldn't make waves. Not if he repaired the relationship, restored her trust.

But how could he do that?

Pausing by the back window, he surveyed the withered grass that had succumbed to the relentless heat. Maybe he'd send her flowers tomorrow to thank her for visiting Kate. She'd like that. And why not ask her to join them for a midweek pizza too? If he reversed course, spent more time with her, he'd be in a position not only to do damage control but perhaps even convince her to find some other career counseling service. Kate Marshall and New Start weren't the only game in town.

As Greg finished off his beer, the *Looney Tunes* song filtered in from the living room, accompanied by Todd's giggle. Fingers tightening on the neck of the bottle, he closed his eyes. This was all he wanted. All he'd ever wanted. A joyful home shared with the people he loved.

But both the home and the people had been stolen from him. God hadn't listened to his prayer for either Jen or David, nor had the high and mighty John Marshall deigned to authorize the one treatment that had any hope of extending his son's life.

And now the man's wife was threatening to disrupt his world yet again.

He crossed to the recycle bin by the back door and flung the empty bottle inside. It shattered . . . reminding him how he'd felt inside the day the nurse had quietly turned off all the machines that had been keeping David alive.

And in the silence of that lonely hospital room, holding on to the cooling hand of his dead son, he'd vowed to get even.

Months later, after a numbing detour into alcoholic stupor, he'd succeeded.

Failure hadn't been an option back then.

Nor was it an option now.

Clenching his fists, he forced himself to take a deep breath. To think with his mind, not his heart, as he resumed his pacing.

Okay. So he didn't know how Kate had gotten that photo of Todd. But if she had any proof to substantiate her suspicions, the authorities would be snooping around, asking questions. Since they weren't, she must not have any credible evidence. Nor would she easily get it. He'd covered his tracks well.

With the right people doing the tracking, however, there was a small possibility she could begin to make troublesome connections. And in light of that picture she had of Todd, there was a chance she had those kinds of people on the job.

Yet Todd had never had a studio portrait taken.

Unless . . .

He stopped pacing. Maybe it wasn't a photo of Todd at all.

Maybe it was one of those age-progression images they talked about on the TV detective shows. That would explain the studio look. In fact, it might be the *only* way to explain the plain blue background Diane had described.

But just because an age-progressed photo of her son resembled Todd didn't prove anything. Lots of people had doubles.

Still . . . he didn't have a good feeling about any of this. And if Kate Marshall was on his trail, leaving town wouldn't protect him. On the contrary. Taking a drastic step like that would only heighten suspicion.

He dropped into a chair and raked his fingers through his hair. Would it be better to sit tight and hope she eventually gave up trying to prove her case, or was there something he could do to stop her from pursuing her quest?

Like what?

What did he know about her that might help him eliminate any threat?

She was addicted to Valium.

As Diane's words echoed in his mind, Greg propped his elbows on the table. Could he use that knowledge to his advantage?

Thirty seconds ticked by while he toyed with that question. No plan came to mind—but his gut told him the information had potential . . . and that he needed to be prepared to capitalize on it.

At least he had Valium on hand. He'd only used a few of the pills his doctor prescribed after David died, since alcohol had done a much better job relieving his anxiety. Were they still potent after three years? A quick search on the Net later would give him that answer.

But suppose the walls began to close in on him? Suppose the Marshall woman found some piece of evidence provocative enough to interest law enforcement before he had a chance to eliminate the threat?

In that case, his options would be reduced to one.

He'd have to disappear. Start over. Assume a new identity, like government-protected witnesses did in the WitSec program.

To do that, though, he and Todd would need new documents. Birth certificates. Social security numbers. A driver's license for him. It was important to have those on hand ASAP—just in case.

Time to contact Emilio.

Greg stood and grabbed his keys off the counter. On the off chance his phones were being monitored, calling the man from home or on his cell wouldn't be smart. Better to use a pay phone—like the one in the hall near the DQ restrooms.

He moved to the door into the living room, where his son remained focused on the cartoon mayhem splashed on the screen.

"Hey, champ, want to go to DQ for a sundae?" He jiggled the keys.

Todd twisted his neck to look back at him. "For real?"

"Yep."

"Awesome!" He aimed the remote at the TV. A second later the screen went blank, and he began tugging on his shoes. "I wish Diane had stayed longer. She could have gone with us."

"Yeah. But I'm thinking about asking her to go out for pizza with us tomorrow night."

Todd stopped tying his shoes. "In the middle of the week?"

"You have a problem with that?" He conjured up a grin.

"No way! That'd be cool!" He finished tying the laces and jumped to his feet, face beaming. "I sure like it when we do stuff together, Dad."

"Me too." And he planned to keep doing father/son things for a long time to come. "Why don't you wash your hands and change that shirt, then we'll head out?"

"Awesome." Todd zoomed toward the hall, and a moment later the sound of running water filtered into the living room.

Greg returned to the kitchen, grabbed some change out of the bowl on the counter, and retrieved Emilio's letter from the address book in the desk. The man would come through for him, of that he had no doubt. And after this, he'd consider their debt fully paid. Because if he had to disappear, he'd never again contact anyone from his former life. It would be too risky.

But that was fine. He'd have Todd, and in the end, that's all that mattered. Giving up Diane would be hard—but maybe someday, down the road, he'd find someone else to love. There had to be more Dianes out there.

"I'm ready, Dad." Todd dashed into the kitchen.

Greg's jaw compressed into a firm line. "So am I."

As her doorbell rang at nine-thirty, Kate adjusted the belt on the capris she'd donned after her quick shower and tried to ignore the small mic taped to her skin, under her blouse. This still felt deceitful—but Connor was right. If she'd read Diane wrong and the woman was trying to get information for Sanders, Connor needed to hear what was being said.

On the other hand, if Diane was here to help, that should be obvious very early in the conversation and she could bring Connor in, keeping everything aboveboard.

A quick peek through the peephole confirmed the identity of her visitor. After unlocking the deadbolt, she took a calming breath and pulled open the door.

"Hi, Diane. Sorry this had to be so late."

"I'm just glad you were willing to see me." The woman entered, Coach purse gripped in her fingers, eyes troubled. John had always said money didn't buy happiness, and her visitor was living proof of that.

"Let's sit in the living room." She gestured to her left and ushered the woman in. "Can I offer you a soda or some tea?"

"No, thanks." Diane chose one of the upholstered chairs beside the fireplace.

Kate sat on the couch, a few feet away. Connor had told her the mic was powerful and she didn't need to worry about staying too close, but why take chances?

"You have a nice place." The woman looked around.

"Thanks. It feels a bit big sometimes for one person, but I do like the layout."

Silence fell between them, and Kate crossed her legs while Diane fidgeted with her purse, her body language spelling tension in capital letters—shoulders hunched, face taut, respiration shallow. She was in far worse shape than she'd been during their session yesterday in the office.

Her first instinct as a counselor was to spend a few minutes trying to put the woman at ease. But this was Diane's show. So she waited her out.

"I need to tell you something. Then I have a question." Diane's knuckles whitened around her bag. "The first time I visited your office . . . while you were making us some tea . . . I got up to stretch my legs. I walked past your desk, and I accidentally knocked a file off your desk. A picture of a little boy slid out."

A surge of adrenaline zipped through Kate. Given Diane's visit to Sanders's house tonight, she had to have seen the resemblance to his son—and had likely told the man about the picture, putting him on alert.

Not good.

Who knew what he might do if he thought they were closing in?

Trying to rein in her panic, Kate leaned forward, reminding herself she wasn't supposed to know about the connection between her new client and Sanders. "Why are you telling me this?"

"After we talked yesterday . . . after you told me about your son . . . a lot of things started to add up."

Her adrenaline spiked again. "What do you mean?"

Diane twisted her hands in her lap. "That boy in the picture in your office . . . he looks just like the son of a friend of mine. This friend . . . he said Todd was adopted, but . . ." She combed trembling fingers through her hair, distress darkening her eyes. "I'm not sure I believe that anymore. He asked me to visit you again, to see if I could find out anything about the picture. But when I went over to Greg's tonight—that's my friend—and told him what you said yesterday, I got really bad vibes. I also got the feeling he knew more than he was telling me. This thing is driving me crazy, and I hoped you might be able to clear up the mystery about how you're connected to Greg's son."

Unless the woman was an Academy-Award-quality actress, her distress—and doubts—were real. She was on their side, Kate was certain of it.

But before she tipped their hand, she needed to make certain Connor concurred.

Standing, she spoke their agreed-upon affirmative code phrase as she moved to the front window. "I'm glad you came. Let me shut the drapes so we have more privacy."

She reached for the pull, looking across the street to where Connor had parked. A lighter flicked on. Burned for a moment. Went out.

One light.

He agreed they should both talk to the woman.

Kate closed the drapes, retook her seat, and leaned toward Diane.

"The photo you saw in my office is an age-progressed image of my son, showing how he would look today. You're obviously friends with Greg Sanders. I saw him and the boy in the mall three weeks ago, and was so shaken by the encounter I hired a private investigator. After a lot of digging, he was able to identify your friend. We suspect the boy he calls his son may be my Kevin. I talked to the PI about your call tonight, and he's outside now, in his car. I'd like to bring him in so he can hear what you have to say."

All the color had drained from Diane's cheeks. "I don't want to get Greg in trouble."

"If he's in trouble, you're not the cause." Kate touched her hand. "I want my son back, Diane. I've already lost three precious years with him. Years that can never be made up. I've mourned for him, night after night. Even now, I sometimes wake up and think I hear his voice calling me, like he used to. Wanting a drink of water or his blankie or . . ." Her words choked, and the room blurred as moisture clouded her vision.

Compassion flooded Diane's face, and she touched her hand. "I'll talk to your PI."

"Thank you." Fighting to regain her composure, Kate dug her cell out of the pocket of her capris and tapped in Connor's number. He picked it up instantly.

"She says you can come in."

"I'm already on my way."

Kate set the phone on the coffee table. "He'll be right here."

As she started to rise, Diane restrained her with a touch, her features strained. "If Todd is your son, how do you think . . ." She swallowed. "Do you know how Greg got him?"

"No." She'd leave it to Connor to get into theories if he thought that was wise.

"So it's possible he's just an innocent party in all this? I mean, except for the past few weeks when he hasn't been all that attentive, he's been a nice guy."

The desperate hope in the woman's eyes tugged at Kate's heart. Innocent, however, wasn't a word she'd use to describe Sanders—no matter how this played out. Not after the furtive look he'd cast her direction in the mall and the way he'd hustled the boy out of sight.

"I don't know." It was the best she could offer, but from the droop of Diane's shoulders, it wasn't sufficient.

The doorbell rang, and she turned away to answer it, leaving the other woman slumped in her chair. Though Diane had been concerned enough to seek answers late on this Tuesday night, it was also obvious she still cared about Sanders. And disillusioned or not, if her heart was involved, she could shift her loyalty back to him unless they convinced her the man might be guilty of far worse crimes than neglecting a girlfriend.

She could only hope her instincts about the woman were sound, and that Diane would realize it was in her own best interest to play it cool with Sanders until this thing was resolved.

If she didn't, if she told Sanders he was being investigated, the man might take off before they could get their DNA sample.

But Connor wouldn't let that happen. He was a pro. A man used to assessing risks, protecting people, keeping the enemy in his sights. Sanders wouldn't be able to elude him. Everything would be fine.

It had to be.

Because she'd already set her heart on welcoming a seven-year-old boy who liked poppysicles into her home—and her arms.

Connor read the concern on Kate's face the instant she opened the door—and it wasn't misplaced.

They were taking a risk trusting Diane Koenig.

But his client had excellent instincts, and from what he'd heard, he was comfortable she'd made the right call. Diane didn't sound as if she was solidly in Sanders's camp, and after they finished speaking with her, he hoped any lingering loyalty she felt for the man would evaporate.

"Everything's going to be fine." He kept his voice low as he gave her arm a reassuring squeeze.

With a nod, she stepped back to usher him in, then led the way to the living room, where she made the introductions.

"It's nice to meet you, Diane." He smiled and held out his hand to the blonde.

Eyes guarded, she stood to return his greeting. Her fingers were ice cold, and a pulse thumped in the hollow of her neck, but as she gave him a once-over, the taut line of her shoulders relaxed slightly. Stopping at home to change clothes had paid dividends, as he'd expected. A woman who wore designer labels and drove an expensive car was apt to be a lot more impressed by the Armani sport jacket, Ralph Lauren dress shirt, and Gucci tie he kept in reserve for meetings with well-heeled clients than the jeans and T-shirt he'd been wearing when they'd spotted her leaving Sanders's house.

"Diane, Connor is a former Secret Service agent. His partners at the PI firm are an ex-ATF agent and a former St. Louis County police detective."

As Kate added that bit of information, the wariness in the woman's eyes diminished.

"Why don't we sit?" Connor gestured toward the chairs and sofa.

Kate took a seat across from Diane, leaving him the sofa—the closest spot to the woman.

"Diane said when she saw Greg Sanders earlier tonight, she got some bad vibes. I already filled her in on the basics of the case." Kate gave him an abbreviated recap of the conversation he'd already heard.

After she finished, he took over. "Why don't you tell me more about these bad vibes, Diane?"

Her throat worked. "It's just that some . . . weird . . . things have been happening, and Greg didn't address any of them."

"What kind of weird things?"

As she told her story, including Todd's escalator nightmare

311

and the incident at the lake, he glanced at Kate—and read her thoughts in her eyes.

With or without DNA, I know that boy is my son.

He agreed.

But they needed the DNA before law enforcement would step back in.

"Even though Greg's been acting kind of odd lately, I can't believe he would be involved in anything . . . illegal." Diane rubbed at the frown lines embedded in her forehead as she finished.

"What do you mean by odd?"

She shrugged. "We had a good thing going for the past couple of months, then all of a sudden he pulled back. I was afraid maybe he'd met someone else, but he says he hasn't. He claims Todd is having some adjustment problems and they need more one-on-one time together . . . but now I'm thinking his withdrawal may be related to all of this."

"That would be my guess." Connor leaned forward and clasped his hands between his knees. "How much do you know about Sanders?"

"I know he lived in Montana for a while, after his wife passed away. He moved there from Cleveland. And he told me Todd was adopted."

"Did you know that a year and a half after his wife died, he also lost his young son to a fatal neurological disease?"

Diane's eyes widened. "No."

"We also have reason to believe Kate's husband, who was a physician and an expert on that disease, didn't endorse an experimental treatment in China for Sanders's son when he was contacted by your friend's insurance company."

Her mouth slackened, and he gave her a few moments to digest that new information.

"Are you suggesting that . . . do you think Greg was involved in . . ." She looked at Kate. Back toward him. Swallowed. "You don't think the drowning was an accident, do you?"

"Not anymore. We have evidence Sanders was in the vicinity of Braddock Bay when Kate's husband died."

The woman's face lost its last vestige of color. "Then why aren't you going to the police?"

"Everything we have is circumstantial. Once we have definitive proof, we'll hand it over to the FBI."

A tear leaked out of Diane's eye. "Boy, I know how to pick winners, don't I? First an abuser, now a . . . criminal. What's that old saying—fool me once . . . ?"

"Don't blame yourself for this one." Connor touched her hand. "From everything we've been able to learn about Sanders, he loved his family deeply and has taken excellent care of the boy he calls his son. He isn't a career criminal."

"Then why would he . . . how could he do what you think he did?" Confusion clouded her eyes.

"Even normal, well-adjusted, caring people can crack if they're forced to endure enough stress or loss or grief. We all have our limits."

At Kate's quiet response, Connor turned toward her. She was thinking about her own battle with Valium—but that was in a whole different league than Sanders's fall from grace. She needed to understand that.

"That's true. We all occasionally cope by doing things that aren't in our own best interest. But venting rage or expressing anger through violence crosses a very big line . . . and I don't have a whole lot of sympathy for that, no matter the cause."

"I don't either." Diane's heated statement pulled his attention back to her. The confusion in her eyes had been replaced with disgust—at herself or Sanders, he wasn't sure—until she continued. "I'm sick to death of being a victim—and I'm tired of being manipulated. If Greg did the things you suspect . . . and if he stole your son"—she looked at Kate and straightened her shoulders—"he deserves to rot in prison. I might never get my ex behind bars, but I'm not going to slink away from *this* fight. Is there anything I can do to help you get the proof you need?"

He slanted a glance at Kate. She seemed as surprised as he was by the offer—and by Diane's sudden infusion of gumption.

"Let me think about that." He pulled a card out of his pocket, flipped it over, and jotted his cell number on the back. "I'll be in touch if I come up with any ideas. In the meantime, if you think of anything else that could be useful, call me day or night."

She tucked the card in her purse, then stood and faced Kate. "I'm so sorry for everything you've been through—and everything you're still going through."

"Thank you. And thank you for coming forward tonight. That means more to me than I can say." She rose and gave her client a hug.

"We women have to stick together, you know." Diane hugged her back, her voice laced with tears. "Guys can be jerks."

Kate smiled at him over Diane's shoulder. "There are some good guys out there too, though."

As Diane stepped back, she looked his way. "Yeah. I guess there are."

His neck warmed, but he covered the awkward moment by leading the way toward the foyer.

After the flurry of good-byes, he closed the door behind Diane and turned to Kate. "That was enlightening."

"I'll say. I think she's totally in our camp. What's your take?"

"I agree. You made a good call."

"After some of the stories she told us about Sanders's so-called son, I feel more certain than ever he's Kevin."

"So do I. And now that we know Sanders is aware of the age-progressed photo, we need to be prepared for him to take drastic action."

"Like what?"

"Skip town, for one thing. I know this is going to cost some bucks, but I'd like to crank up the surveillance to 24/7 until we have our DNA, beginning first thing tomorrow morning."

Panic flared in her eyes, and her posture stiffened. "Should we wait that long?"

"Based on the Braddock Bay incident, I doubt the man will bolt without having solid plans in place—and a chance encounter on an escalator, much as that might have spooked him, probably isn't sufficient to vault him into crisis mode."

"But the photo in my office might." She fisted her hands at her sides, shimmers of tension radiating off her.

Connor touched her arm. It was cold as ice. "He only found out about that on Saturday, and three days isn't much time to put together an escape plan."

"Are you certain?" She searched his face, her features taut.

Close enough to be comfortable waiting a few hours to begin surveillance—but if it relieved Kate's mind to have someone sit in front of the man's house all night, he wasn't about to turn her down.

"I'll tell you what—I'll head back over there and hang around, just to be sure."

She bit her lip and began to pace. "Am I overreacting?"

"No. You're behaving exactly as any mother would who doesn't want to let the chance of a reunion with her long-lost son slip through her fingers."

"Meaning I'm not being logical." She lifted a hand and massaged her temple. "But . . . but what if Sanders loses it and h-hurts Kevin?" A touch of hysteria raised her pitch.

"Everything we've discovered and observed indicates he loves your son, Kate. I don't think Kevin is in immediate danger—and we're going to do everything we can to resolve this before that becomes a credible possiblity."

She exhaled. Dipped her head. "Okay. I trust your judgment. Go home and get some sleep. Tomorrow's soon enough."

He appraised her. "Are *you* going to be able to sleep if I do that?"

She swallowed and locked gazes with him. "I might be able to if you promise me I don't have to worry."

No pressure there.

He hesitated—but only for a second. He trusted his instincts, and they told him it would be safe to wait until tomorrow to punch up the surveillance. "You don't have to worry."

She nodded, rubbing her arms up and down. "Give me a minute while I take off the mic."

As she disappeared down the hall, he moved back into the living room and pulled out his cell to respond to messages—but only made it through two before she returned.

"Here you go." She dropped the mic into his hand. It was still warm from her body.

Sliding it into the pocket of his slacks, he walked toward the door and reminded himself to keep breathing. "I'll call you tomorrow with an update on the surveillance plan and any other developments."

"Okay."

She sounded so forlorn—and close to losing it—that he turned back to her.

Big mistake.

She'd followed him to the door and stood a mere arm's length away. Close enough for him to get lost in her jade green eyes. Close enough to hear the shallow, anxious cadence of her breathing. Close enough to smell a subtle, sweet fragrance that made him think of lazy summer days and starlit skies and a world where everything that mattered was wrapped in his arms, close to his heart.

He needed to get out of here.

Now.

But as he reached for the doorknob, she touched his arm. "Thank you for offering to sit up all night just so I could sleep. That means more to me than I can say." Her voice was tremulous, tear-laced—and as warm as a cozy fire on a frosty night.

He steeled himself before he shifted toward her. "Goes with the territory."

"Right." She withdrew her hand and took a step back. "I appreciate it anyway."

Her warmth had chilled a few degrees . . . and he wanted it back.

Get out of here, Sullivan.

Instead, he moved closer to her. "If it . . ." His voice hoarsened, and he cleared his throat. "If it puts your mind at ease, I'd do it even if I wasn't being paid."

A sheen appeared in her eyes. "Thank you."

Silence hung between them. And something more. Something powerful enough to compel him to take another step toward her, erasing the distance between them.

She tipped her head back to look up at him, and at the need in her eyes, his resolve crumbled.

One kiss. That was all he wanted. Just one simple kiss that would send a message about his intentions once he was free to pursue her. A quick brush of the lips that would barely qualify as a breach of Phoenix rules. A gesture as much about comfort as romance.

Ignoring the little voice in his brain that said he was rationalizing, Connor lifted his hand, touched her cheek—and stopped breathing.

Cliché or not, her skin was like satin against his fingertips.

With a soft sigh, she swayed into his hand as her eyes drifted closed.

He was cooked.

Maybe some superhero type with an iron will would be able to resist that invitation, but he was a healthy, normal, human male.

Nerve endings tingling, he leaned down, keeping a slight distance between them—for safety's sake. Then he gently pressed his lips to hers . . . and the rest of the world melted away.

By the time the kiss ended, his hands were framing her face, and the safe distance he'd left between them had disappeared.

So much for a simple little kiss.

Breaking contact at last, he kept a firm grip on her arms as he backed off.

She gazed up at him, her eyes slightly dazed.

"I-I thought this kind of . . . stuff . . . was off-limits for now."

"It is. I broke a rule tonight. Consider it a preview of what to expect once this case is over." He released her, stepped back and reached for the door. "You sure you're going to be able to get some rest tonight if I don't sit outside Sanders's house?"

Worry and fear flickered to life again in her eyes. "I'll do my best."

Translation? Not likely. There wasn't much chance she'd have another restful slumber until her son was back in her arms.

And it was his job to make that happen.

"I'll talk to you tomorrow."

"Thanks again—for everything."

He strode down her walk, pausing beside the van to look back. She stood framed in the doorway, the light from behind illuminating her slender form. Calling him back.

This time he resisted.

Instead, he slid behind the wheel and started the engine. It was getting late, but after that charged clinch he wasn't tired. Why not run by Sanders's house, just to verify everything was quiet? Maybe the detour would give his pulse a chance to drop back into the vicinity of the normal range.

And if it didn't, there was always a cold shower.

22

Greg stared at the arc of blood shooting from his left forearm.
Of all the stupid . . .

"Hey! You're bleeding, man! Bad!" From the adjacent saw-
horse, Sal gestured toward the spray of red with his circular saw.

Like he couldn't see that.

Setting his own saw on the ground, Greg looked around for
something to stanch the flow of blood from the cut. He'd never,
ever slipped up like this on the job before. His injury-free record
had always been a source of pride for him.

One more thing in his life that had gone down the tubes.

Seeing nothing appropriate nearby, he yanked off his T-shirt
and wrapped it around his arm. If he'd been concentrating on
the job instead of thinking about Diane and formulating escape
plans and wondering about the progress Emilio's friend was
making on his documents, the saw would never have slipped
and . . .

"What happened?" The foreman hustled over as a small crowd
gathered around him.

Great. Now he was the center of attention.

"Just nicked my arm. I'll be fine."

"I don't think so." The foreman planted his fists on his hips,

319

his gaze on the makeshift dressing. "It's already bleeding through the shirt."

Greg examined it. The man was right. Slapping a bandage on this cut wasn't going to fix it.

"Let me take a look." Some hard-hat-wearing guy he didn't know elbowed through the group. "I used to be a medic's assistant in Iraq. Are there latex gloves in the first-aid kit?"

"Should be. Somebody go get it from the office." The foreman gestured toward the construction trailer.

Two of his co-workers took off at a sprint.

"Why don't you sit down?" The guy with the hard hat put a hand on his shoulder and guided him toward a sixty-pound plastic bucket of drywall joint compound.

He didn't want to sit. He wanted everyone to disappear and leave him alone.

But when his legs suddenly grew shaky, he sat.

His co-workers returned with the first-aid kit, and the medic's assistant snapped on a pair of latex gloves with practiced ease. If the guy was a pro, maybe he could stop the bleeding and they could all get on with their day.

But as he carefully unwrapped the T-shirt and examined the gash, he shook his head. "I can't do anything for this except apply a compression bandage. It needs stitches. Possibly even surgery, if you nicked an artery—but I'm not seeing a lot of evidence of that. You need to get to an ER or an urgent care center ASAP." As he spoke, he quickly slapped on a thick sterile dressing and began to wrap a stretchy bandage around it.

"There's one a few miles down the road. I'll take you." The foreman motioned over his shoulder to someone Greg couldn't see. "Keep an eye on the place while I'm gone."

This whole thing was getting out of control.

"Look . . . I'm sure this will stop bleeding on its own."

"Don't count on it." The ex-soldier rose and held out a hand.

"Keep your arm elevated as much as possible until you get this treated. That will help reduce the bleeding."

With the hand extended and everyone watching him, he didn't have much choice except to take it. After accepting the assistance, he tapped his watch. "Listen . . . this isn't going to work. I have to pick up my son from daycare in an hour."

"Is there someone you can call?" The foreman took his un-injured arm and started tugging him toward the area where the workers parked.

No, there wasn't. That was why he'd listed his neighbor as a contact on the daycare application—unbeknownst to her—since the school required a secondary contact. But he'd been on the verge of asking Diane if he could put her name there instead.

Would she pick up Todd?

"Greg? You with me?" The foreman tightened his grip.

"Yeah." Unfortunately, she'd ignored the message he'd left last night about going out for pizza this evening. His flowers should have arrived by now, though. They may have softened her up. And she cared for Todd. She'd do it for his son even if she wouldn't do it for him. "I can call the friend I brought to Bob's picnic."

His boss gave a low whistle. "Now there's a looker. You sure know how to pick 'em."

He ignored that comment as they approached the man's car, using the dead airspace to retrieve his cell, praying she'd answer.

She didn't.

Mind racing, he considered his options as he waited for her voice mail to kick in. Worst case, he could call STL, tell them he was delayed, and shell out the extra bucks for overtime. They were there until six, and hopefully he'd be past this crisis by then—but in case he wasn't, it would be better to connect with Diane.

The answering machine beeped.

"Diane, it's Greg. Listen . . . I had a little accident at the job site. Looks like I'm going to need some stitches. I'm on my way to an urgent care center now, and I was hoping you might be able to pick Todd up at daycare for me at three-thirty. I'll wait about fifteen minutes, and if I don't hear back from you, I'll try something else. Thanks."

"No answer, huh?" The foreman helped him with his seat belt, then put the car in gear.

"I'll give her a few minutes."

"If she's like my wife, you're hosed. Martha never turns her cell phone on. Says it's just for emergencies—on *her* end, mind you, not mine. But I can't complain too much. At least she's not one of those women who talk your ear off, if you know what I mean."

"Yeah." He bent his left arm, supporting his elbow with his right hand to keep the gash elevated.

The man glanced at the spreading crimson stain on the bandage and pressed harder on the accelerator. "I bet that hurts. We'll be there in less than ten minutes. Hang on."

Like he had a choice—about anything these days.

He turned his head and watched the passing scenery, fighting back a wave of despair. This wasn't how he'd expected his move to St. Louis to play out. It was supposed to be a new start, a second chance.

Instead, another Marshall was wreaking havoc in his life.

Resentment curdled in his belly, and as rage began to simmer in his heart, he made a vow.

Kate Marshall wasn't going to win this game she was playing.

Yes, she might come up with enough evidence to get the attention of law enforcement. Maybe even enough to have the case officially reopened. It would be difficult, considering how careful he'd been about covering his tracks—though not outside the realm of possibility.

But if it came to that, he'd find a way to make her pay before he disappeared with his son.

Just as he'd made her husband pay.

"So who do you have on tap for the night shift?"

Connor looked up as Cal, soda in hand, stopped in his doorway. "Dale. His wife is out of town visiting her sister this week, so the night schedule suits him."

"Suits me too. I'd rather spend my nights with Moira."

"I figured as much. And Dale's reliable. I trust him not to fall asleep."

"So do I. He was a force to be reckoned with when he and I worked cases together for County. They lost a good man when he took early retirement a few years ago."

"They've lost a couple of good men in the past few years."

Cal shrugged, uncomfortable as usual with compliments. "So Dev's on for now, and you're picking up the afternoon/evening shift?"

"Right. You're on tomorrow."

"Got it. Have you . . ."

As his cell began to vibrate, Connor held up a hand and pulled it off his belt. When Diane Koenig's name appeared in the LED display, his eyebrows rose.

"I need to take this." He punched the talk button.

With a lift of his hand, Cal disappeared down the hall.

"Hi, Diane. Connor here. What's up?"

"I've had two calls from Greg."

"Since we talked last night?"

"Yes. There was a message on my answering machine when I got home, inviting me to join him and Todd for pizza tonight. I never returned it. Then, about noon, a bouquet of flowers arrived. A peace offering, I take it. And he just called again, on my cell. There's been an accident on the construction site, and he asked me to pick up Todd from daycare while he goes to urgent care. Being new in town, he doesn't have many friends, and I hate to leave Todd stranded. Do you see any problem with me doing this?"

Connor frowned and turned his pen end to end on the desk, evaluating the unexpected opportunity and toying with an idea. If Diane could pull it off, it would expedite their case.

"Does your offer to help us still stand?"

"Yes." There was no hesitation in her response—a positive sign. "Why?"

"We need a DNA sample from Todd. That's the best way to establish a credible connection between him and Kate. Once we have that link, law enforcement will step in. We've been waiting for an opportunity to get one, but if you could take care of it for us, that would speed things up."

"What kind of sample?" Wariness crept into her tone.

"A few strands of hair. A dozen, max, and as long as possible. But they'd have to be gathered without arousing the boy's suspicion to lessen the likelihood he'll tell Sanders."

"That could be a challenge. How were you going to manage it?"

"Follow them to a salon or go through the trash if he cuts the boy's hair at home."

"But how could *I* get one without being obvious?"

Connor swiveled in his chair, toward the picture of him and Joe as teens. The two of them had gotten into several scrapes involving loss of hair during their growing-up years. Like the time Joe had run into the tree with his sled, a stunt that had left him with several stitches and a shaved patch on his scalp. Or their initiation into the neighborhood tree house club that had required them to contribute a lock of hair to the club's collection. Not to mention the day their mother had intervened moments after ten-year-old Joe began giving him a Mohawk

324

haircut. Then there'd been the day his giant bubble of gum had broken on the back of Joe's head. His mother had had a bear of a time getting it out of Joe's hair and had finally resorted to scissors for the gummiest strands.

That could work.

He swung back to his desk. "Does Todd like bubble gum?"

"Bubble gum?" Diane sounded puzzled.

"Yes." He relayed the story about his own childhood escapade.

"Hmm." Her voice grew thoughtful. "I can't say I've ever seen him chew any—but what kid doesn't like bubble gum? And I was a world-class bubble-blower in my younger days. I think I can pull this off without arousing suspicion. What should I do with the hair?"

"Seal it into a ziplock bag. You can call me as soon as you leave the house, and I'll meet you around the corner so you can hand it over. The key is to make this all seem natural. We don't want to give Todd any reason to bring it up to Sanders."

"I understand. I'll do my best."

For a few seconds, Connor hesitated, debating the downsides of the plan. Worst case, Todd would mention the incident to Sanders. The man would either pass it off as inconsequential and innocent, or his suspicions could be further aroused. But by then they'd have the sample, and within a week the lab would have the analysis. In the meantime, they'd be keeping the man under surveillance. He wasn't going anywhere without a tail. If they passed up this opportunity, they might have to wait another two or three weeks just to get the sample.

When the silence lengthened, Diane spoke again. "In case you're worried, as the wife of an abuser I became very adept at deception in my former life. You learn to say and do whatever you have to in order to keep yourself safe and deflect suspicion—in that case, misplaced. I can do this job for you, now that we have a plan."

Her confident tone sealed the deal.

"I'm sure you can. Call me on my cell as soon as you have the sample."

"I will. Talk to you soon."

As he weighed the phone in his hand, he debated whether to tell Kate about this latest development. No. Better to wait until he had the sample in hand.

But once he did, this thing would shift into high gear.

And by the middle of next week, if everything went as he expected, a long-separated mother and son would be in the midst of an extraordinary reunion.

"So is Dad hurt bad?"

As Diane showed her ID to the woman behind the desk at STL Academy and signed out for Todd, she gave his shoulder a reassuring squeeze. "No. He cut his arm on a saw and had to get some stitches, but the doctor's fixing him up right now. As soon as we get to my car, I'll call his cell and let you talk to him. How does that sound?"

Todd clutched his daypack and stared up at her, eyes wide as he gave a silent nod.

The poor kid was scared out of his mind.

But if everything that PI and Kate had told her was true, the little guy was in for a lot more upheaval.

Life stunk sometimes—even for innocent kids.

The woman behind the counter pulled out a booster seat and handed it over. "You or Mr. Sanders can return this tomorrow or the next day."

"Thanks."

Juggling the seat, Diane took Todd's hand as they walked toward the parking lot. "Everything's going to be fine, you'll see. Why don't we stop on the way to your house and get a soda? Would you like that?"

"Dad never lets me have soda before dinner."

"I think we can make an exception this once." She opened the back door, secured the booster seat, and helped Todd buckle up. Then she circled the car, slid behind the wheel, and pulled her cell out of her purse.

Greg answered on the second ring. "Did the daycare place give you any trouble?"

"No. Your call to them smoothed the way. How's it going with you?"

"The urgent care center is a zoo. This must be the day for accidents. I'm estimating another hour at least, maybe more. Sorry to inconvenience you."

"No problem. Todd would like to talk to you."

"I want to talk to him too. Sorry again to put you out. I'll be home as fast as I can."

"Don't rush on my account. Todd and I will keep each other entertained." She handed the phone over the seat. "Here you go."

As she backed out of the parking space and headed toward Greg's house, she listened in on the one-sided conversation.

"Are you hurt real bad, Dad?"

Pause.

"No. She was waiting for me. They even let us borrow a car seat."

More silence.

"Yeah! That will be twice this week! And Diane said we might stop for a soda on the way home too. Can I have soda and a sundae on the same night?"

Another pause.

"I love you too, Dad. Bye."

Diane's throat tightened. Their mutual affection was so endearing . . . yet she had only to recall Kate's tearful comments yesterday about hearing her absent son call to her in the night to know she was doing the right thing. And she'd see it through. This was one thing in her life she wasn't going to mess up.

Spotting a 7-Eleven, she spoke over her shoulder. "What kind of soda would you like?"

"Can I have a Mountain Dew?"

"Sure." She swung into the lot and found a spot near the door, eyeing the counter and the soda dispenser beyond it. She could see the car from the store; no need to take Todd in with her. "I'm going to run in real fast. Can you wait here for me?"

"Yeah. I'll look at the book about dinosaurs I borrowed from the library at daycare."

"Great idea."

Exiting the car, she locked the doors and hurried inside. No one was in line, and in less than three minutes she was back with two sodas, a pack of bubble gum tucked in her purse.

"Here you go." She stuck a straw in Todd's cup and handed it over the seat, then put her own Diet Coke in the holder beside her. "So tell me all the fun things that happened today—and the stuff you've learned about dinosaurs."

He was off and running as she drove to Greg's house, chattering away as she fed him questions. By the time she pulled up in front of the bungalow, the sodas were gone and Todd's worry about Greg seemed to have been assuaged.

"Your dad said you know about a key that's hidden behind the bush next to the front door?"

"Yeah." Todd released his seat belt and pushed the curbside door open as she set the brake. "I'll get it."

Daypack thumping against his back, he dashed toward the bush and dived underneath as she pulled the borrowed booster seat out of the car.

"Here it is!" He held aloft a small ziplock bag, waving it triumphantly—and reminding her of the real motivation behind her good Samaritan deed.

Once in the house, Diane disposed of the soda cups, set her

purse on the table, and pulled out the pack of gum. "Would you like a piece?"

Todd gave it a covetous look. "Dad doesn't let me chew gum very much."

"I have a feeling he wouldn't mind today." She unwrapped a piece and held out another for him.

"I guess I could have one piece."

As he undid the wrapping, she sat at the kitchen table, working the gum with her teeth. "Do you know how to blow bubbles?"

"Not very well."

"I used to be able to do this. Let's see how much I remember."

As he watched, she positioned the gum with her tongue and managed to blow a midsized bubble.

"Wow. That was real good." Todd's expression was tinged with awe.

"You try."

His inaugural effort produced a small bubble.

"Not bad." She coached him through a few more attempts. "You're doing great. I'll tell you what . . . why don't we have a contest for the biggest bubble?"

"I'll lose."

"You never know." She stood and took his hand, leading him toward the mirror in the guest bath. "When my friend and I had contests, one of us had to stand on a chair, but since I'm taller, this will work." She positioned him in front of her and bent down until she was just above his head. "Now we can watch ourselves and each other and judge who has the biggest bubble. Ready . . . set . . . go!"

Her bubble came out fast and large, as she'd hoped . . . and she lowered her chin as it popped, one scant edge collapsing on his hair.

"Whoops!" She straightened up as Todd kept blowing, making an impressive-sized bubble.

A moment later, his burst too.

"I think you won." She smiled at him in the mirror.

"I don't know. Yours was bigger . . . but it broke faster. I guess it was a tie."

"Excellent call. Now let's see if I can separate my gum from your hair. Why don't you go get your comb for me?"

As he took off down the hall, she returned to the kitchen, feeling in the pocket of her skirt to verify the small pair of scissors and ziplock bag she'd slipped inside. Still there.

"Here it is." Todd waved the comb as he skidded to a stop beside her.

"Turn around and let's have a look."

As he complied, she surveyed the damage. Not bad. Her aim had been spot on. Combing through the fine strands, she was able to remove the evidence of their contest. But she pretended to work on a nonexistent tangle.

"There's just one spot here . . ." She gave it a slight tug. "Gum and hair don't mix very well." Fingering the hair with one hand, she reached into her pocket and withdrew the scissors. "I might have to snip this out." She cut off a tiny clump close to his scalp and slid her hand back into her pocket, aiming for the bag.

Done.

Taking a deep breath, she fiddled around with his hair for another fifteen seconds before handing over the comb. "Good as new. While you put this away, I'll see what's in your fridge and get dinner started. After that, why don't we build that skyscraper with your erector set?"

"Awesome!"

As he disappeared through the door, she sealed the ziplock bag and stowed it and the scissors in her purse.

Then she did a long, slow scan of the kitchen where she'd enjoyed such happy times with Greg and Todd. Where she'd hoped to enjoy many more.

But if the hair sample she passed on to Connor proved Todd belonged with Kate—and that Greg had never been the man she'd thought he was—the future she'd allowed herself to dream of would end up being nothing more than a sham and an illusion.

Just as her marriage to Rich had been.

Except this time she was going to be the victor, not the victim.

Straightening her shoulders, she crossed to the refrigerator. No matter how this ended, she was going to be okay—even if the worst happened, and the loving father and considerate suitor she'd come to know and care about turned out to be a cold-blooded killer and kidnapper.

A shiver rippled through her that had nothing to do with the blast of cold air emitted by the freezer.

It was hard to believe Greg could be capable of those heinous things—yet all the evidence added up. And she should count her blessings she'd learned of his dark side sooner rather than later, leaving her free to walk out of his world in an hour or two and never look back.

Kate, however, wasn't so fortunate. She couldn't walk away, not with her son's future hanging in the balance. And now that Greg knew about the photo, he had to suspect Kate was trying to track him down. Could that put the woman who'd befriended her in danger?

As another shudder swept through her, she grabbed a pack of ground beef and slammed the door shut. She didn't need to add worries about Kate's safety to all her other problems. If there was any threat, Kate had that smart, handsome PI watching her back. A guy who'd protected world leaders—maybe even the president himself—wasn't going to let anything happen to her. She'd be fine.

Wouldn't she?

From the depths of her purse, Kate's cell rang as she maneuvered through the door of her condo with an armload of shopping bags.

After dumping everything on the kitchen table, she fished it out and greeted her favorite PI.

"Hi yourself." The warmth in Connor's response sent a little tingle through her. "How'd you sleep?"

"I've had more restful nights." She pulled the box of cherry popsicles from the grocery bag and slid them into the freezer. "How about you?"

"I'll plead the fifth. What did you do on your day off?"

She surveyed the results of her whirlwind shopping expedition. "Let's just say I've been busy."

"That's not what days off are supposed to be all about."

"Busy is better than pacing around my condo battling the urge to knock down Sanders's door and snatch my son. Besides, I had a lot of errands to run. The lab was first on my list."

"I know. They called to tell me both tests were already in process. I wanted to let you know I've alerted an acquaintance at the local FBI office to expect a case in the next few days."

She sank into a chair, fingering the package of baseball-

332

themed sheets she'd purchased for the twin bed that would soon occupy her unfurnished spare bedroom. "How much did you tell him?"

"Everything."

"What did he say?"

"That he'd bone up on the official background and put everything in place for a fast response once they have proof in hand."

"He doesn't think we're crazy?"

"Far from it. Nick's handled an odd case or two in his day—including one that involved a Raggedy Ann doll and the woman who's now his wife. That's why I called him specifically. He'll be ready to move the instant I bring him the results of the DNA test."

"What do we do in the meantime?"

"Wait—and watch."

She blew out a breath. "That is a really, really hard assignment."

"I know. Just keep hanging in. We're in the final inning."

She clenched the baseball-themed sheet. "Did Sanders go to work today?"

"No, but he did take Todd to daycare."

"So what's he up to?"

"According to Cal, who's tailing him at the moment, not much. He stopped at Home Depot, gassed up his car, paid a quick visit to his bank. Nothing out of the ordinary."

"Do you think he knows we've identified him?"

"Hard to say. But he has to be worried about it."

"What if he runs?" The last word hitched.

So much for her attempt to sound composed.

"We've got it covered, Kate. Try not to worry. We're on his tail 24/7. And if he heads for an airport, Nick's prepared to muster FBI resources to keep him in sight at his destination until we can get there. That's why I wanted him in the loop ASAP. Agents don't come any sharper than Nick Bradley."

In the background, another male voice spoke, the words indistinguishable. Connor responded with an "I'll be right there," then returned to their conversation. "I need to run. We've got a conference call on a hot job that's coming up. I'll be in touch at least once a day with updates, but feel free to call if you need anything in between."

"Thanks—for everything."

"My pleasure. Take care."

The phone went dead, and Kate tucked it back into her purse as she scanned the pile of bags on the table, most of which contained decorating items that would turn her empty bedroom into a welcoming, baseball-themed haven for her son.

But did he like baseball as much as he had three years ago, when the two men in her life had spent many a Sunday afternoon on the sofa, rooting for their team? Three years was an eternity in a little child's life. What did she know of the boy he'd become? Of his favorite color and favorite food, the books he liked, the hobbies and sports he enjoyed?

He was a stranger to her in so many ways—and she to him.

Fighting back a sudden wave of panic, she ascended the stairs and wandered down the hall to the empty room she'd originally planned to make an office. Strange how she'd ended up gravitating to the kitchen table for work instead. Almost as if she'd known this space was destined for some other purpose.

She stopped on the threshold, imagining how all the things she'd purchased would look once they were in place. The Cardinals-themed bedspread and matching curtains. A baseball-shaped lamp. Three throw pillows in bright red. The team's most recent World Series poster.

Perhaps she'd been foolish, buying things she didn't even know if Kevin would like. But if he didn't, she'd return them and redo the room to suit the tastes of the little boy he'd become.

Leaning a shoulder against the wall, she folded her arms tightly against her chest, drew an unsteady breath—and imagined.

Kevin, back in her home.

Kevin, back in her arms.

Kevin, alive not just in her heart but in the flesh.

All thanks to a chance encounter on an escalator.

Coincidence is a small miracle in which God chooses to remain anonymous.

Connor's words echoed in her mind, ringing with truth.

Except if Kevin was restored to her, the miracle wasn't small. It was huge—and God's hand was all over it. He'd graced her with compassion the day she'd agreed to run an errand for her neighbor in the mall, despite her busy schedule. He'd timed her exit so she'd caught a glimpse of the son she'd thought long dead. And he'd led her to the perfect man to help her sort out the mystery—a competent, professional PI with a boatload of integrity . . . and charm.

A man who also appeared to be destined to play more than a professional role in her future.

God was, indeed, good.

But much as he'd done for her up to this point, she needed him now more than ever for the daunting challenge ahead—earning back the love of the son who'd stolen her heart in the maternity ward when he'd locked those big blue eyes on hers and grasped her index finger with a grip so strong even the nurse couldn't pry it loose.

Closing her eyes, Kate took a shaky breath and sent a silent prayer heavenward for strength, courage, and wisdom to deal with the challenges she and Kevin would face once they were together again.

Assuming, of course, there were no glitches on the way to their reunion. Connor seemed confident a positive end was near, however. That it was just a matter of waiting for the test results and keeping Sanders in their sights. She was the one who was antsy. Anxious. Impatient. Worried.

But she needed to do her best to chill. To put her trust in the PI who'd earned it—and in God.

Besides, after coming this far and getting this close, what could possibly go wrong?

"Haircut time, champ. We can't have you starting school looking like a shaggy dog." Greg waved the scissors at his son from the kitchen doorway.

"Aw, Dad, do I have to?" Todd sent him a pained look from the living room floor, where he was engrossed in building an airplane with Diane's erector set.

"I know it's not your favorite Sunday afternoon activity, but you're overdue."

"You never cut my hair this often in Montana."

"That's because we lived in the mountains and didn't see a lot of other people."

Todd rose slowly, dragging his feet as he walked toward the kitchen. "Sometimes I wish we'd stayed there."

That made two of them.

"Well, we're here now. And it will be good for you to make a whole bunch of new friends in first grade." That was still the plan—unless Kate Marshall botched it up for them.

He tightened his grip on the scissors and gritted his teeth. After all these years, who could have guessed danger would be lurking on an escalator in a new town from a woman he'd never expected to see again?

The whole thing was surreal.

Unfortunately, it was also very real.

"I wish you could just teach me stuff, like you used to in

Montana." Todd climbed onto the two phone books piled on the kitchen chair and sighed.

"I have a job away from the house now." Forcing thoughts of Kate from his mind, he draped a towel around Todd's shoulders and began trimming the fine hair that reminded him of David's. Sometimes, the tactile sensation was so similar he could almost pretend his first son was still with him.

"Didn't you like taking care of Mr. Lodge's ranch?"

"Yeah. I liked it a lot. It was a beautiful place. But I like construction too—and I wanted you to go to a bigger school. Learn from teachers who know a whole lot more than me." As he snipped, a few matted strands near Todd's ear caught his attention. He tried without success to comb through them, then looked closer. "You've got some snarled-up hair back here. Did you get glue in it at school?"

"That must be from the bubble gum. Diane gave me a piece the day she picked me up from school, when you hurt your arm."

He poked at the tangled hair. "But how did it get on the back of your head?"

"We had a bubble-blowing contest. Hers was a really big one, but it broke and some of it got in my hair. She had to cut a little out in the back. Can you tell?"

Frowning, Greg leaned closer to scrutinize his son's scalp. In the end, he located the small section where the hair was cut close to the scalp more by the bristly feel than by sight. "Yeah, I found it." But he wouldn't have if Todd hadn't mentioned it.

Why hadn't Diane brought it up?

Then again, there hadn't been much opportunity. After telling him burgers were in the broiler and offering him an indifferent thank-you for the flowers he'd sent, she'd hotfooted it out of the house as fast as she could, stopping only long enough to give Todd a fierce hug.

The kind of hug you'd give someone you didn't expect to see again for a long time, now that he thought about it.

All at once, fear congealed in his belly, and a wave of nausea rolled through him.

Something was up.

"Dad?"

"Yeah."

"Are you done cutting my hair?"

He refocused. "Almost." He lifted the scissors, the slight tremble in his fingers mirroring the quiver in his stomach.

It was possible the gum incident was innocent . . . but his instincts said otherwise. Diane liked Kate Marshall. Kate was searching for her son—most likely with professional help—and Diane knew the picture the woman had was a dead ringer for Todd. Miffed as she'd been with him, might she have told them about Todd, offered to assist them in establishing a concrete connection? With all the testing labs could do today, a hair sample would be devastating.

"Todd . . . what did Diane do with the hair she cut off?" He moved in front of his son to trim his bangs, doing his best to keep his tone casual.

The boy shrugged. "I dunno. I guess she threw it away."

Easy to confirm. He'd taken a bag of trash out to the can in the carport Wednesday night. If there was a matted clump of hair and gum in there, it should be near the top.

He finished up the bangs and pulled the towel from around Todd's shoulders. "All done."

"Finally. Can I go finish building my plane now?"

"Sure."

The boy scampered off.

After sweeping up the hair on the kitchen floor and depositing it in the trash can beside the cabinet, Greg went out to the carport. Only one small plastic bag was in the metal trash can, and he pulled it out—along with some newspapers from the recycle bin.

Once back inside, he crossed to the door on the side of the kitchen. "I'll be in the basement for a few minutes, Todd."

"Okay." The boy's distracted voice floated back to him.

Ten minutes later, after a painstaking search through the trash he'd spread out on the newspapers, beads of sweat popped out on his forehead.

No blond hair.

Diane hadn't thrown it away.

He muttered a curse and began to pace.

There was a small chance—very small—she'd disposed of it some other way. But based on the sinking feeling in the pit of his stomach, the explanation wasn't that simple.

And if she'd given Kate Marshall and her cohorts a sample, he had just one option.

Run.

Fast.

Meaning he needed those documents from Emilio's contact. Now.

The man had promised to have them in his hands by Tuesday—but would that be soon enough?

Still . . . what choice did he have? Without ID, he'd get nowhere. He'd have to wait.

At least he could make optimal use of the time, firm up the plan he'd begun formulating in case things went south. It was a solid plan, simple and straightforward. And it would work.

Favoring the arm sporting a dozen stitches, he began gathering up the garbage he'd strewn about the floor as he mentally walked through the steps he'd take.

First, rent a car, using his real ID. Tell the clerk he needed it for two weeks, to buy him some breathing space to disappear before the rental people missed it.

Second, pack up the camping gear he'd used after he'd driven away from Braddock Bay with Todd asleep in the backseat. Camping had been an inspired idea; by the time they'd spent three months at a variety of state parks before continuing on to Montana, his son had stopped crying for his mother at night and begun to respond to the care he'd lavished on him. They wouldn't need nearly that long now, however. Ten days, max, to let Todd get comfortable with his new identity. Michigan would be a perfect spot for that. There were plenty of places to camp there.

Third, after they were done camping he'd ditch the car near the Greyhound terminal in Detroit and take the bus to Chicago, using their new identities.

And finally, in that metropolis, they'd disappear among the throngs of people who called the Windy City home and start over yet again.

Greg folded up the newspapers and stuffed them into a plastic bag, averting his head when the foul odor of the garbage invaded his nostrils.

The plan was sound—but there was one complication. He had to assume Diane had told Kate and her people who he was. So unlike the last time, there was a high probability he was being watched.

He'd lucked out with the location of this house, though. While he hadn't liked backing up to a strip mall initially, the lower rent had persuaded him he could live with the noise.

Now his frugality was going to pay dividends he'd never expected.

Garbage bag in hand, he climbed the stairs back to the kitchen, detouring to the carport to dispose of it. Fists on hips, he inspected the privacy hedge at the back of the property. It would be an easy matter for him and Todd to slip through and walk a couple of miles to a rental car office. He'd driven past the Enterprise location on Lindbergh and the Hertz place at the Holiday Inn near South County Center dozens of times.

When he returned, he could park the rental car in the strip mall, cut through the hedge, and enter through the back door—while his own car stayed in the carport, giving no clue he'd left the property.

It was brilliant.

Tonight, after Todd went to bed, he'd sort through his camping equipment, setting aside only the bare essentials. He'd pack a few necessities for both of them. And if the documents arrived Tuesday as promised, in seventy-two hours he and Todd would be long gone.

But before he slipped away, he had one last piece of business to take care of. A final debt to settle.

A wasp buzzed near his ear, stinger poised, and he ducked, swatting the insect away with his hand. Getting stung—by bees or people—wasn't in his plans.

Entering the house, he detoured to the fridge for a beer. He had to dot all the i's, cross all the t's. There could be no slipups. He had to pull off the plan for retribution that had formed and jelled in his mind in the dark hours of the night as perfectly as he'd carried out the Braddock Bay mission.

He grabbed a beer and twisted off the cap, jaw tightening. He hadn't felt one iota of remorse as he'd watched John Marshall sink into the murky depths of the bay. The man who'd played God, who'd made the decision to cut his son's life short, had deserved his watery end.

Nor would he have any regrets about meting out punishment to the man's wife. If Kate Marshall succeeded in her quest, she'd kill something as dear to his heart as David had been—the life he'd created with Todd.

He couldn't let that happen.

Guzzling the beer, he walked down the hall to his bedroom.

Opened the top drawer of his dresser. Pulled out the bottle of Valium and weighed it in his hand. Once again, that prescription was going to come in handy for a whole lot more than his doctor had intended.

He took another drink, and despite the anger churning in his gut, his lips lifted in a grim smile. There was a certain beauty to the end he had planned for Kate Marshall. A sense of continuity. Of irony, even.

And this little bottle was the key that would set everything in motion in just over forty-eight hours.

The countdown had begun.

don't know why you bothered to take off last Thursday and Friday if you were going to work late yesterday and today." Nancy hoisted her shoulder purse into position and jingled her keys from the doorway of Kate's office. "It's past quitting time. Five-twenty to be exact. Can't whatever you're working on wait until tomorrow?"

"Yes, it can." Kate rotated her neck to loosen the kinks. "I'm planning to shut down soon."

"That's what you said when I left last night, but scuttlebutt has it your Monday didn't end until after eight."

Kate finished off the last of her lukewarm soda, eyeing the New Start receptionist. "Who's your source?"

She arched an eyebrow, folded her arms—and remained silent.

Must be one of the cleaning people. Or the security patrol who cruised through the parking lot. Or . . . who knew? Nancy always seemed to have the inside information on everything. "I'm not staying that late tonight."

"Glad to hear it. Why don't you call up that to-die-for guy who stopped by a couple of weeks ago and go to dinner or get an ice cream or something? You never did tell me who he was, by the way."

"I know." Nor did she intend to. It would only raise questions she wasn't ready to answer. And despite their receptionist's inside sources, she doubted Nancy was well-connected enough to dig up any info on her favorite PI.

"Maybe someday?" Nancy gave her a hopeful look.

"Maybe."

She huffed out a breath. "I think you carry this confidentiality stuff too far—but I'll get it out of you eventually. In the meantime, don't work too hard." With an impudent grin and a lift of her hand, she disappeared down the hall.

When the faint click of the office-suite door sounded a few moments later, Kate leaned back in her chair and reached around to rub the sore muscle in her shoulder—a souvenir of her redecorating spree and mega furniture juggling over the weekend. The twin bed and mattress weighed a ton. But the results were worth it. The room was ready and waiting to welcome her son—perhaps as soon as tomorrow, if the lab delivered the DNA results on schedule.

A shaft of panic darted through her, just as it did whenever she allowed herself to think about their approaching reunion—the very reason she'd loaded up her schedule for the past two days. Staying busy helped keep anxiety—and impatience—at bay.

Besides, it wasn't as if there was anything else she could do to prepare. She'd already stocked the kitchen with food she hoped Kevin would like. Created a warm and welcoming haven for him. Lined up a top-notch child psychologist to help him work through the transition. And she'd prayed. A lot.

The only thing left to do was wait—a herculean task, when every instinct in her body screamed at her to *do* something. Now!

At the sudden jangle of her desk phone in the silent office, she jerked, hand flying to her chest. Her nerves weren't just frayed—they were in shreds.

Willing her heart rate to slow, she glanced at caller ID, plan-

344

ning to let the after-hours call roll to voice mail—but when she saw Connor's name, she grabbed the handset. Her daily dose of his calm, everything's-under-control voice was the only thing keeping her sane.

On the other hand, if he'd heard from the lab, this might be the big call.

Her pulse thundered into fast-forward as she gave him a shaky hello.

As if reading her mind, he addressed her concern as soon as he greeted her. "Nothing on the DNA yet, but I talked with the president of the firm twenty minutes ago. We go way back, and he promised to call me with the results the instant they come in—first thing tomorrow, he hopes. How are you holding up?"

"Okay." *Liar, liar.*

"I used to have a habit of working longer hours when I wanted to distract myself too."

He must have caught the quiver in her lame response.

She fingered the edge of the file containing the age-progressed photo of Kevin. "Are you sure you're not the one with the counseling degree?"

"Nope. I got my people skills in the school of hard knocks. So do you want to let me in? I'm parked out front, but I assumed your offices would be locked up tight and I didn't want to alarm you by banging on the door."

She sat up straighter, a rush of gratitude calming her jitters a few notches. "What are you doing here? I thought you were on afternoon/evening surveillance today."

"I am. But I conned Dev into covering for me for an hour. I come bearing Panera chicken Cobb salads and chocolate cookies."

How like him to tune in to her nervousness. It was almost as if he knew she'd spent most of last night tossing and done nothing more than nibble at a sandwich today.

"Sold. I'll open the door."

"Look for me in three minutes."

By the time she ran a comb through her hair and touched up her makeup, he was waiting.

When she pulled open the door and ushered him in, he gave her a quick scrutiny. With that sharp eye of his, there wasn't much chance he'd miss the shadows under her lower lashes or the pallor that blush couldn't disguise.

"You look tired." His words were soft, as was the touch of his thumb as it grazed her cheek.

Her breath hitched, and the urge to move into his arms and claim part of the space occupied by the large bag he was carrying was strong. Very strong.

Wrestling it into submission, she retreated a step on the pretense of surveying his cutoffs and T-shirt. "And you look hot."

"A vast understatement."

She waved him toward the hall. "The conference room is the first door on the left. Grab a soda—or two—from the fridge."

"Don't mind if I do."

He was pulling the food out of the bag and already gulping down a Coke when she joined him after relocking the door.

"So to what do I owe this visit?" She sat and opened her container of salad.

"I wanted to fill you in on the finale." When she stopped eating, he gestured to her food while he wolfed down his own. "Continue while I talk. I hate to eat alone."

Doing her best to comply despite the butterflies that had taken wing in her stomach, she gave him her full attention.

"I've alerted Nick that I expect this thing to break within twenty-four hours. He's up to speed on the official records, and the FBI is set to move as soon as I turn over the DNA results. He's also done a background check on you and connected with Child Services so there shouldn't be any hassles with you taking immediate custody." He fixed her with one of his intent looks. "Now let's talk about you. Are you ready to have a seven-year-old boy invade your condo?"

She finished chewing a crispy piece of lettuce. "I think so." She set down her fork and told him all she'd done to prepare, including the discussion she'd had a few days ago with the New Start chairman of the board about her likely need to take a sudden, temporary leave to deal with family issues.

When she concluded, his eyes softened, and his warm fingers enfolded hers. "Despite all the bad stuff that's happened in his life, Kevin is one lucky little boy to have you."

"I have a feeling he isn't going to think so." She clung to his hand as a fresh surge of doubts assailed her.

"Maybe not in the beginning. But after he gets to know you again, after he realizes how much you love him, he'll love you back. Guaranteed. It would be impossible not to." He gave her fingers a squeeze and went back to eating.

She had a feeling he was talking more about himself than Kevin—and that was comforting. There were two male hearts she was set on winning, and it was nice to know she'd laid a solid foundation with one of them.

"Thanks for the encouragement. But he's still going to miss Sanders."

"The psychologist you have lined up will help him deal with that—and you will too. Are you going to be in your office tomorrow?" He finished off his salad and pulled a cookie from the sack.

"Yes, but I kept my schedule focused on paperwork rather than appointments. I knew you might need me to come at a moment's notice."

"Perfect." The cookie was gone in a few large bites, and he washed it down with the last of his second soda. "I hate to eat and run, but Dev and his fiancée are supposed to pick out china tonight, and I promised I'd be back in an hour. I didn't expect an accident on I-270 or a long line at Panera to eat into our time together."

"I appreciate the effort you made."

"It was no effort." He skimmed his fingers over her cheek. "And Dev won't mind if I'm late. I'm certain he'd rather swelter in the heat—or eat slugs—than look at dishes. However, I do want to stay in Laura's good graces." He stuffed his napkin into his empty salad container and closed the lid. "Where do you want this?"

"I'll take care of it." She closed the lid of her own container, hiding the remaining half of her dinner.

"You're going to finish that, right?" Connor stood.

"At home."

"Promise?"

She nodded and rose as well. "Let me show you out."

He followed her to the door, waiting while she twisted the locks and pulled it open. "Are you leaving soon?"

"Ten minutes."

He touched her arm. "One more promise."

Curious, she tipped her head. "What?"

"If you have any trouble sleeping tonight, call me."

Gratitude tightened her throat. "No sense both of us being awake."

"I'll be on duty until midnight—and I doubt I'll sleep much after that, either. Promise?"

No way did she intend to disrupt Connor's night—so she left herself some wiggle room. "If I'm awake and need to hear a friendly voice, I'll call. How's that?"

"A hedge. But the offer's there, and I hope you'll take it if you need it."

"Just knowing I have that option will help me sleep better."

"I'll call the second I hear from the lab."

"I'll be ready."

As she watched him stride toward the main entrance, then disappear around a corner, her parting words echoed in her mind.

And as she slowly closed the door and prepared to call it a night, she hoped they were true.

Greg pulled into the parking lot of the mall behind his house, aimed the rental car toward the far end, and let out a long, slow breath.

Everything was falling into place.

Emilio's friend had come through for him, and their new identities had been waiting for him in today's mail.

He'd withdrawn his entire checking and savings account balance on his way home from work, a sizable enough sum to last for a while since he'd spent little during their years in Montana except to pay down debt.

In a few minutes, he and Todd would be back in their house, their getaway car safely stowed where he could load it up in a trip or two under the cover of night.

And in five hours, they'd be on their way out of town . . . after he paid a visit to Kate Marshall and tied up that one loose end. Piece of cake, since she lived alone. That nugget of info from Diane had proven very helpful.

So far, so good.

"I still don't get why we can't take our truck."

He sighed. His son was proving to be more of a glitch than he'd expected.

"Like I told you before, it's getting older. I don't want to have a breakdown while we're on vacation and get stuck somewhere. Do you?"

"I guess not . . . but why can't we park this car in our driveway?"

Greg glanced in the rearview mirror. Todd's brow was

furrowed, and he was hugging the Cardinals bear tight against his chest. Obviously he hadn't bought the explanation that advertising their camping trip to neighbors would alert everyone the house was empty and create a security risk. Plus, Todd was picking up on his elevated adrenaline, attuned as usual to the subtle vibes around him.

That didn't bode well for the rationale he'd concocted about why they had to change names—but he'd have ten days to work on that. They just had to get past the next few hours.

"Sometimes robbers watch neighborhoods to see when people are on vacation." He kept his voice even and calm as he pulled into the parking space and shut off the engine, one eye on the lot in the rearview mirror. This end wasn't too populated, but he wanted to make sure no one was around to notice him and Todd slipping through the hedge. "If newspapers pile up, or houses stay dark, or they see people loading luggage in their car, they figure it's safe to come back in a day or two and break in. We wouldn't want that to happen, would we?"

"No. But what would they take from us? We don't have anything that costs a lot of money, do we?"

Good point. Other than a bulky TV that would be difficult to transport, they had nothing worth stealing.

"No, but a thief wouldn't know that until after he broke in." Greg took one more quick scan of the lot. All clear. He motioned toward the hedge. "Want to race me to the basement door?"

Todd's face lit up, and he grabbed the door handle. "Yeah!"

"You remember where we came through the hedge?"

"Yeah. Right over there." Todd pointed to a slight gap in the greenery.

"That's it. On your mark. Get set. Go!"

Todd was out the door in a flash. Greg followed more slowly, taking time to lock the car, but was close on Todd's heels as the boy dived through the hedge.

Less than a minute later, letting Todd keep the lead, he reached the door that provided access to the walk-out basement.

"You won." Greg fitted the key in the lock and pushed the door open. "You get faster every day."

Beaming, Todd trotted in ahead of him. "So are we going to eat dinner now? I'm hungry."

"Next on my list." Greg followed him past the bare-bones camping gear, neatly piled by the door, and the two small bags of clothing and toiletries he'd packed. They could pick up everything else they needed once they were on the road.

Todd stopped to examine one of the sleeping bags. "Our camping trip is going to be awesome. How come you didn't tell me about it until tonight?"

"It wouldn't have been a surprise if I'd told you sooner, would it?" He ruffled Todd's hair.

"I guess not. Can I watch cartoons while you fix dinner?"

"Sure. I have a couple of things to do first, anyway."

Once upstairs, Greg dropped the keys to the rental car on the kitchen counter while Todd continued toward the living room. A moment later, cartoon sounds filled the house.

After casting a glance at the little boy sitting cross-legged in front of the TV, Greg moved down the hall to his bedroom and closed the door. From the top drawer of his dresser, he withdrew the bottle of Valium pills, frowning at the tremble in his fingers. Last time he'd used these, he'd been steady. Confident. In control.

Then again, he'd had months, not days, to plan. Plus, he'd been dealing with a four-year-old, not an inquisitive seven-year-old.

But Todd loved him. Trusted him. He'd believe the fabricated story about needing to get a new name like the people on the TV show they'd watched recently who'd entered the witness security program. The important thing was to make it convincing—and scary enough to seal his son's lips. The story he'd concocted might lead to another bout of nightmares, but they'd get past those. Once entrenched in a new life and a new city with new identities, the nightmares would fade away.

And they'd be safe at last.

Greg opened the bottle. Shook two of the yellow pills into his palm. Ironic that they had a heart-shaped cutout in the center, considering how they'd helped him secure a new son to love—and how they would ensure that love went unchallenged.

He examined the 5 mg tablets. He'd only used half a pill on that August day in New York—two-and-a-half times the normal dose for a four-year-old, according to the Net—and it had knocked Todd out. But he was older now, and it was important that he stay fast asleep.

Two pills ought to do it.

That would leave him plenty for the doctor's wife, plus a few to drop on the floor.

Shoving the bottle into the pocket of his jeans, he closed his fist over the two pills and headed back toward the kitchen.

It was time to assemble the ingredients he'd purchased for strawberry smoothies.

A perfect bedtime treat.

Dad was acting really weird.

Todd watched as his father pulled the blender and the recipe for smoothies Diane had given them from the cabinet under the sink. Smoothies were good. At least, the ones Diane made were. But whenever he and Dad wanted a treat, they went to DQ. Why was he making smoothies instead?

And how come they'd watched a movie on a weeknight? Dad never let him stay up this late.

He squirmed in his seat at the kitchen table, giving his teddy bear a squeeze. He didn't need the bear anymore, not since he'd turned seven. Teddy bears were for little kids. Still . . . it was kind of nice to hold on to.

Especially when everything suddenly felt creepy—like that day he'd seen the lady with the blonde hair on the escalator.

As his dad pulled stuff out of the refrigerator, he stood and moved close beside him—the place where he always felt safe. "Dad?"

"Yes?" He sounded kind of far away, like he wasn't paying a whole lot of attention.

"How come you decided to make these?"

"Seemed like a nice way to celebrate our camping trip." He crossed to the freezer and pulled out a box of ice cream.

"But you never made them before. And it's a lot of trouble."

His father kept working. "It's no trouble. You know I'd do anything for you, David."

Todd's stomach started to feel funny, like it had when his dad called him David after that scary nightmare he'd watched from the bedroom door. How come he was starting to do that?

"Why don't you go wash your hands and face while I finish up?" His dad turned on the blender, and he cringed at the loud whirring sound. It seemed a lot noisier than when Diane made smoothies.

Edging toward the door, he chewed on his lip. It was nice of Dad to make their favorite drink, but he felt kind of like he had when he got the flu last year, right before he threw up. And thinking about drinking a whole smoothie made it worse.

He dawdled in the bathroom, playing with the soap dispenser until his dad called him.

"Todd? The drinks are ready."

At least he'd used the right name this time.

After drying his hands, he trudged back toward the kitchen. Dad was sitting at the table.

"There you go, champ." Dad slid the smoothie with the straw stuck in the top in his place. "So tell me what you did today."

Todd crossed to the table and slid into his chair. Dad seemed okay now, even if the air felt kind of buzzy and crackly, like before a lightning storm. But Mrs. Stein at daycare was always saying he had an overbusy imagination . . . or some word like that. So maybe everything was fine. Maybe Dad's arm was just hurting or he had a headache from working in the sun all day.

He took a tentative sip of his drink and told him a little about the animal posters they were making in art class. When Dad asked a bunch of questions and paid a lot of attention like he usually did, the drink started to taste better and his stomach stopped wobbling. So he told him about his favorite dinosaur book too, and the airplane pilot who had come to talk to their class, in uniform and everything.

As his dad finished off his drink, he slurped up the dregs of his own.

"That was real good, Dad."

"I'm glad you liked it." He stood and took their glasses to the sink. "We'll make them again sometime."

A yawn snuck up on him.

"Someone must be getting sleepy." His dad had that teasing look that always made him feel happy.

"Yeah. I guess."

"Why don't you go brush your teeth and I'll come in to say good night?"

He tried to think of some excuse to stay up later, but Dad wouldn't listen. Not when he was already up way past his bedtime.

Besides, he was getting really tired. And as he headed for his room, his legs felt the same as they had the day he'd wandered into that patch of mud in Montana that kept sucking his feet down.

Yawning again, he bypassed the bathroom and sat on his bed. Dad wouldn't care if he lay down for a minute before he brushed his teeth.

He pulled off his shoes and cuddled up with his bear, glad the night had turned out happy after all. They'd laughed and talked like they always did. And tomorrow they were going camping.

Burrowing into his pillow, he let his eyes drift closed. He sure was lucky to have such a great dad.

The only thing that could make his life even better was if he had a mom too.

Maybe someday.

25

Why in the world was her doorbell ringing at eleven-forty at night?

Moving from Kevin's room to the second-floor landing, Kate paused above the dark foyer. It couldn't be Connor. He was on surveillance duty until midnight—but who else would have any reason to come to her door at this hour?

Hand on the banister, she hesitated. It was possible those two girls who shared a unit on the other side of the cul-de-sac might be having a repeat performance of last weekend's wild party, when a drunk twentysomething guy had knocked on her door at two in the morning after losing his bearings.

Except they'd never had a rowdy gathering in the middle of the week before.

The bell rang again.

Hmm.

Better investigate. She had sturdy locks; no one would get in unless she invited them.

She descended the steps, detoured to grab her cell phone out of the charger on the kitchen counter, then pressed her eye against the peephole.

Nothing but shadows.

Why was it so dark out there? Had her dusk-to-dawn porch light burned out? One more chore to add to her to-do list for tomorrow.

She squinted as she surveyed the porch. The corners might be murky, but it was clear no one was standing on the other side of her door. The bell ringer must have been some prankster.

But as she did one final scan and prepared to turn away, a small mound on the floor of the porch, near the steps, caught her eye.

She zeroed in on it.

Froze.

A little blond-haired boy who looked just like Kevin was lying against the railing.

And he wasn't moving.

No!

Tossing the phone onto the hall table, she fumbled with the locks on her door, her shaking fingers refusing to cooperate. Had Sanders grown tired of playing father to a boy who wasn't his own and dumped him on her doorstep now that the heat was on?

Or had he flipped out, and in a fit of rage taken more drastic measures to rid himself of his problem?

No!

Denial screamed through her brain as the floor rippled beneath her while she struggled to flip the locks.

Hurry, hurry!

If Kevin was hurt, every second could count.

At last the door swung open and she charged toward the prone figure, kneeling beside him in the dim illumination from the streetlights at the curb.

"Kevin?" She touched his cheek. It was warm.

Yes!

She leaned closer, putting her face near his nose. His breath tickled her cheek.

"He's alive. For now."

At the cold, emotionless male voice, she whirled around—and found herself inches from the barrel of a pistol with some sort of apparatus on the end.

A silencer?

No matter.

It was pointed straight at her head.

Her heart lurched.

"Take the boy inside."

She scrutinized the shadowed man towering over her. His features were too dark to make out, but his athletic build and the baseball cap pulled low on his forehead were familiar.

Sanders.

He hadn't waited for them to come to him. He'd come to her—and found the perfect way to lure her out of her secure condo.

This wasn't how the finale was supposed to play out.

Besides . . . how had the man left his house without alerting Connor?

"I said, take the boy inside." The man's voice, though still low, was sharper now—and scored with irritation. "And keep your mouth shut."

Kate didn't know much about guns, but she doubted it was wise to try the patience of a man who was holding one.

Bending over her son, she worked her arms under his shoulders and knees and struggled to stand. Four-year-old Kevin, at thirty-seven pounds, had been an armful. But he had to weigh fifteen pounds more now. His head flopped against her chest as she staggered to her feet.

"Move inside." Sanders gestured with the gun.

Kate shifted Kevin in her arms and glanced at the street. The cul-de-sac was deserted, and air conditioners cranked up to full blast would insulate sleeping residents from a cry for help.

Too bad those noisy neighbors weren't having a party tonight after all.

"I said move!"

At the sharp command, Kate tottered forward under her heavy load, pushing the front door open with her shoulder while shielding Kevin's head with her arm.

As she entered the foyer, she heard the door close behind her.

"Put him in the living room. Then go into the kitchen."

Keeping a tight grip on Kevin, she crossed to the couch and gently lowered his limp form onto the plush seat. When he remained unresponsive despite all the jostling, panic clawed at her throat, and she turned to Sanders. "What did you do to him?"

"Not as much as I'm *going* to do if you make this difficult. Get into the kitchen."

In the dim room, she still couldn't read his eyes—but his tone frightened her as much as the gun. This was the man everyone had called a loving father? There was no evidence of that tonight. But would he actually harm the boy he'd treated as a son for three years?

Maybe.

A man capable of murder was capable of anything.

Hate bubbled up in her heart, intense and visceral, as every instinct in her body screamed at her to dive for his legs and take her chances.

But if she failed, she wasn't the only one who could die.

With one more look at her son, she forced her shaky legs to carry her into the kitchen.

"Stand over in the corner." Sanders gestured with the gun to the inside wall.

Once she complied, he circled the room, verifying that all the mini-blinds were tightly closed. Then he flipped on the light over the table and faced her.

"Fill a glass with water and sit at the table."

Keeping one eye on him, she followed his instructions.

As she perched on a chair, he withdrew a small square of

aluminum foil from the pocket of his jeans and tossed it to her. "Take those. Now."

Tearing her gaze from his latex-gloved hands, she worked the crimped foil loose and folded it back.

Six 5 mg Valium pills stared back at her.

What in the world . . . ?

She shot him a questioning look.

"I said take them."

Six pills at once? It wasn't enough for an overdose, but she'd be knocked out cold.

Like Kevin.

She sucked in a breath. "Did you drug my son too?"

A muscle flexed in his jaw, and his eyes narrowed to slits as he pointed to the pills. "Now."

Her mind raced. What was his game? If he'd come to kill her, six Valium wouldn't accomplish that. If he was trying to put her out of commission while he fled so she couldn't raise an alarm, why not just tie her up?

He stepped closer, and the barrel of the gun glinted in the light.

Fingers shaking, Kate picked up one of the yellow pills. If she took all six pills, she'd have less than thirty minutes of lucidity, tops. Tonguing a couple into her gum would reduce the effect somewhat, since they didn't dissolve very fast. And maybe, if she faked a faster zone out, he'd relax a bit, give her a window of opportunity to knock the gun from his hand and lunge for one of the knives in the rack on the counter.

As far as she could see, that was her only chance—slim as it was.

Putting the yellow tablet on her tongue, she picked up the glass of water and took a drink.

She took the pills one by one under Sanders's watchful gaze, managing to secrete two of them in her gums.

After she swallowed the last one, he stepped closer. "Open your mouth."

Heart thumping, she did so, praying the pills she'd hidden wouldn't be visible.

The taut line of his shoulders eased slightly.

Thank you, God!

Now if she could get him talking, distract him from the task at hand long enough to lower his guard—and perhaps lower the gun—there might be an opportunity to lunge for the knives two steps away.

"So what's going on?" She folded her hands to hide the tremors in her fingers, keeping her tone as conversational and non-confrontational as possible.

He studied her in silence.

One eternal second after another ticked by.

Just when she'd concluded he was going to ignore her question, he lifted one shoulder. "With all the stress you've been under, no one would be surprised if you took a few Valium from the secret stash you've kept on hand for the past three years in case things got too bad."

Diane had told him about her addiction.

She hadn't mentioned that in their tête-à-tête.

Then again, who could have known Sanders would find that piece of information useful?

But the man obviously hadn't done his homework if he thought six pills constituted an overdose. That was a plus.

His next words, however, chilled her.

"Accidents happen when people do drugs."

Her lungs stalled.

What kind of accident did he have in mind?

And how could she thwart it?

"I never wanted to hurt you, you know. If you'd left well enough alone, none of this would be happening. Your husband was the one who deserved to suffer."

An icy clot formed in her stomach. "So you admit you . . . you killed him?"

"I punished him for killing my son."

A wave of anger surged through her. "John never killed anyone. Everyone knew he was a kind, caring doctor who did his best for every single patient."

The man's features hardened. "I know all about his reputation. I did my homework before I had my insurance company contact him. And I did my homework on the treatment in China I wanted for David. But based on your wonderful husband's input, my insurance denied it."

Kate swallowed and spoke softly. "Batten disease isn't curable."

His eyes glittered. "I know that. But I wanted as much time as possible with my son, and that treatment could have extended his life. The clinic had the statistics to prove it. Statistics your husband dismissed. So I had to raise funds for the trip and the treatment myself. That delayed us for weeks—precious weeks David didn't have. By the time we went, it was too late." His words rasped, and he stopped. When he continued, his tone was grim and unyielding. "Your husband had to die—and he owed me a son."

She stared at him as the pieces suddenly fell into place. "You took my son to replace yours."

"I only took what was mine."

As she processed what he'd just told her, a wave of nausea swept over her. "Are you saying you let my son watch while you killed his father?"

Sanders moved closer, the gun never wavering. "He saw nothing."

She frowned, trying to make sense of that. "He was in the boat."

"Asleep."

362

"He slept through what happened?"

"With a little help."

She cast a glance toward the living room, where her son remained in a drug-induced slumber. "But . . . how did you . . . ?" Her voice trailed off.

Sanders smiled, but the taut stretch of his lips communicated malice rather than humor. "I told you. I did my homework. After following your husband for weeks, I knew all about those Wednesday fishing expeditions. So I rented a boat and happened to run into your husband in the off-the-beaten-path marsh area he favored. He came to my assistance when I had engine trouble. We chatted. I offered your son homemade lemonade or hot chocolate. He picked the hot chocolate. Said it was his favorite. Still is, by the way."

He leaned a shoulder against the wall, but the gun stayed level. "The next week I ran into them again—armed with a special batch of hot chocolate. I stayed nearby while your son drank it, and once he started to nod off, I headed back to retrieve my mug. The good doctor was quite concerned about your son's sudden sleepiness, and when he bent over to see what was wrong, I had my hammer ready. It was all over in a couple of minutes. He was too groggy to fight me much while I took off his life vest, dumped him over the side, and held him under the water until the bubbles stopped."

Bile rose in Kate's throat, and she gagged.

Sanders was beside her in an instant, the silencer pressed hard against her temple. "Throwing up isn't going to save you. I have plenty more pills, not even counting the ones I'm going to leave in plain view."

Struggling to contain her nausea, Kate forced herself to block out the images Sanders's story had called to mind. She needed to focus on the future, not the past. Because if she didn't think of some way out of this, she might not *have* a future.

"Stand up." Sanders backed off a few paces and motioned with a flick of the gun.

A faint fuzziness was beginning to infiltrate her brain, and as Kate pushed to her feet, the room tilted. Gripping the edge of the table, she drew in a deep breath.

The four pills she'd swallowed were working too fast.

A surge of panic-induced adrenaline temporarily chased away the dizziness—but she needed to pretend it hadn't. She had to lull Sanders into thinking she was growing too disoriented to present a threat.

"Let's take a walk upstairs. I don't want to have to carry you later. We'll wait up there. Bring the glass with you."

"Wait . . . for what?"

Instead of responding to her halting question, he motioned her toward the front of the house—away from the knives on the counter.

Her only weapon.

Not good.

As she balked, he gave her a shove.

"Move!"

Stumbling forward, weaving slightly, she aimed for the living room. She could hear him following behind her, but she veered toward the couch rather than the steps.

"I said upstairs."

"I want to check on Kevin."

She started toward her son, who hadn't moved a muscle as far as she could tell—only to have her arm taken in a firm grip.

"He's fine. And if you want him to stay that way, you'll follow my instructions."

She angled toward him, searching his face for some sign of compassion, some sign of the devoted father who'd nurtured her son for the past three years. If it was there, she couldn't detect it. "I thought you loved him."

No response.

"I don't believe you'd do anything to hurt him." She delivered that statement with far more confidence than she felt.

"Do you really want to test that theory?"

He'd called her bluff. There was no doubt in her mind, based on what they'd learned over the past weeks, that the man who'd invaded her house *had* loved Kevin. But if he thought they were closing in on him and had snapped, he might not be that man anymore.

He might be the man who'd murdered John in cold blood.

Who'd watched the life bubble out of him.

Another wave of nausea swept over.

"I'll g-go upstairs." Hard as she tried to sound calm and in control, her words came out shaky.

"Now you're being smart." He released her and gestured toward the stairs.

As she started up, clinging to the railing for support, she could feel him following close behind her. At least with her back to him, she was able to extract the mushy pills she'd concealed in her gums. And by faking a stumble, she managed to drop them off the edge of the open staircase.

"Keep moving." Sanders prodded her in the side, and she rose from her knees to continue toward the second floor.

To whatever fate he had planned for her.

Not that she was giving up. She would use every lucid minute she had left trying to think of some way to thwart him without putting Kevin in danger.

But as a bone-deep lethargy began to overtake her, she knew she'd have to think—and act—fast.

Because time was running out.

‖‖‖‖‖ **26** ‖‖‖‖‖

As his cell began vibrating against his hip, Connor twisted his wrist. Eleven-fifty-nine. His replacement was right on time, as usual.

"Hi, Dale." Phone pressed to his ear, Connor scanned Sanders's street. The retired detective had obviously approached with lights off and slipped into a surveillance position unnoticed. Good man.

"Hi. How are things on your end?" In the background, classical music played.

Connor flipped off his U2 CD. "Quiet. Lights went out about ten, as usual. Car's in the carport. I expect you'll have an uneventful night."

"No complaints about that. Still expecting this to wrap up tomorrow?"

"If all goes well. I'll give you a call by four if we need you for another midnight shift."

"Got it. Drive safe and get some sleep."

"That's my plan."

Slipping the phone back on his belt, he did one more quick canvass of the blue-collar neighborhood. Most house lights were off. There'd been minimal street activity for the past hour.

Everyone—including Sanders—seemed to have turned in for the night.

The next item on his own agenda.

He cranked up his CD again, tossed back another handful of pistachios, and started the engine. As the air conditioner kicked in, he guided the van down the street.

But instead of pointing it toward home, he detoured toward Kate's condo. Professional protocol might have required him to keep his distance for the past week, but there was no rule against drive-bys. And he'd been doing one every night before heading to his own place. Official reason? Security check. Unofficial reason? He liked being close to her. Besides, her place was practically on his way home.

Shaking his head, he hung a right onto the entrance ramp of I-270 and accelerated north. Talk about having it bad.

But according to Cal and Dev, this was what happened when you met the right woman. You knew almost from the get-go she was different. That there was serious potential. Given that both his partners had recently been down this path, who was he to argue with their assessment?

He hummed along with a few tunes as he drove but sat out "I Still Haven't Found What I'm Looking For"—since he was pretty certain he *had* found what he was looking for—and in less than twenty minutes he was turning into Kate's condo complex.

After weaving through the tree-lined streets to her cul-de-sac, he slowed as he approached her unit, frowning at the light burning on the second floor. Sleep had eluded her after all—yet she hadn't taken him up on his offer and called.

He pulled into an empty parking space and drummed his fingers on the wheel. Should he call her? But if he did, he'd have to admit he was lurking outside. That he'd been driving by every night for the past week. It sounded kind of like . . . stalking.

Would she freak—or be touched?

Hard to say . . . but he was about to find out. Because no way could he drive off and leave her alone to pace the night away worrying about a reunion with the long-absent son who was likely to drop back into her life tomorrow.

Make that today.

He shut off the engine, retrieved his cell, and tapped in her home number.

Her phone was ringing.

As Kate struggled to remain alert, Sanders stopped pacing in the small hall upstairs where she sat propped against the wall. Waiting for what, she still didn't know. Worse, she was beginning not to care. That's what Valium could do to a person. But she had to care. Had to fight this. Couldn't let the man who'd killed her husband and stolen her child win.

The phone rang a second time.

Gun in hand, Sanders loomed over her. "Who would call you this late?"

"I don't know." Her reply came out slurred.

"Don't lie to me!" He leaned down and jabbed the gun into the side of her neck.

She flinched and pulled herself into a protective tuck. "I'm not. No one ever calls me at this hour."

The echo of the third ring faded, and the condo fell silent again.

Sanders straightened up.

Started to pace again.

Stopped abruptly as a different ringtone broke the stillness. "What's that?"

"My cell. It's in . . . the charger . . . in my bedroom."

Three rings in, the phone went silent again.

Grabbing her arm, Sanders hauled her to her feet, dragged

her down the hall, and dumped her on the bed next to the nightstand. "Play back your voice mail. And put it on speaker."

Fingers fumbling, she pushed the appropriate buttons.

"You have one new message. Wednesday, August seventeenth, twelve-twenty-five a.m."

"Kate, it's Connor. I tried your home number first. I'll give it ten minutes and try again. If you get this before then, give me a call on my cell." The message ended with the hum of a disconnected line.

Her spirits soared. Connor was checking on her! And when she didn't respond to his call, he'd investigate.

"Who's Connor?" Sanders prodded her with the gun again, his finger twitching on the trigger.

She tried to coax her sluggish brain into action. If Sanders didn't know who Connor was, he wouldn't know the man was a PI, either. That should work to her advantage.

"A friend."

"Why would he call you in the middle of the night?"

"He knows I . . . haven't been sleeping. He might think . . . I'm still awake."

Sanders didn't move for several heartbeats.

At last he grabbed her arm and propelled her into the hall, pausing for a moment outside the door of the bedroom she'd decorated for Kevin. His nostrils flared as he glared into the shadows, as they had when he'd first noticed it. Then he towed her the rest of the way down the hall, into the bathroom.

"You're going to get some rest tonight, Kate. The eternal kind. But we're done waiting for the Valium to knock you out. I'd give you more, but I want this to look accidental." He lowered her beside the tub. "Put in the stopper and turn on the water."

She blinked up at him. "Why?"

"Just do it."

Moving even more slowly than her drugged state dictated, she dragged out the task as long as possible. As water at last began to fill the tub, he waited in silence.

She wasn't as far gone as he thought, but she was slipping. Badly. Her vision was going in and out of focus, her balance was evaporating, and the weakness in her limbs was bordering on debilitating.

From her spot beside the tub, she watched Sanders spread a few Valium tablets on the vanity next to the water glass he'd told her to bring up, trying to figure out what was going on. And praying Connor would realize there was a problem sooner rather than later.

Once the water in the tub reached the halfway point, he backed into the doorway and looked at her. "Take off your clothes."

Her jaw dropped. "What?"

"It's bath time, Kate. As soon as the water gets deep enough."

And then she knew.

He was going to drown her, just as he'd drowned John, and make it seem like another accident. A poor, grieving woman who'd leaned on the crutch of drugs again and slipped under the water when she'd fallen into a stupor after taking one too many pills.

Kate stared at the rising water—her nemesis since childhood. Even after all these years, she could recall with heart-thudding intensity the feeling of slipping beneath the waves as the sailboat her father had rented on a family vacation capsized, of sucking in a lungful of salty sea, of blackness and suffocation and choking.

No!

She wouldn't die that way. He'd have to shoot her first.

And as she looked into his hate-filled eyes, she had a feeling that was a distinct possibility.

370

She still wasn't answering.

Connor punched the end button on his cell, his attention focused on the illuminated window on the second floor.

Something was wrong.

Very wrong.

He could feel it in his gut.

Time to arrange for backup—and take action.

After tapping in Dev's speed dial number, he pulled out his compact Sig and moved toward the back of Kate's condo, staying in the shadows of the trees and bushes that bordered the front yard.

"This better be important. You're interrupting my beauty sleep."

At Dev's mumbled greeting, he cupped a hand around his phone. "I need you on standby."

Three seconds passed—and when Dev spoke again, no vestige of sleep remained in his voice. The man's ability to go from cutup to über professional in the blink of an eye never failed to impress. "What's up?"

He gave his partner a rapid-fire debrief. "She told me once she kept an extra key on her deck. I'm heading that direction now. If you don't hear back from me in fifteen, get 911 here."

"You want them now?"

"No. If something is going on in there, I'd rather take them by surprise." He stopped next to the small deck and gave it a quick inspection. There were several potential hiding places for a key.

"You think this involves Sanders?"

"I don't know how it could. His car is still at his house."

"Okay. I'm on standby, and the clock is ticking."

Tucking the phone back into its holster, Connor searched the most likely places for a hidden key.

He hit pay dirt with the water-filled plastic dog bowl beside the back door, stenciled with the name Rocky. The key was taped underneath Kate's frugal security system. Probably effective, though. How many thieves would want to risk tangling with a canine named after a famous boxer?

Except he had a feeling it hadn't worked tonight.

Sig at the ready, he fitted the key in the back door. Turned it. Twisted the handle.

Nothing.

There must be a dead bolt.

The key probably worked only on the front door.

Uttering a word he seldom used, Connor circled back to the front at a trot and tried again.

This time the door opened.

No lights were lit on the first floor—but faint illumination shone on the steps leading to the upstairs bedrooms.

He moved toward them, his rubber-soled sport shoes silent on the hardwood floor.

"No!"

At Kate's sudden, panicked cry, a surge of adrenaline catapulted him up the stairs two at a time.

On the top step, however, he stopped, pressed himself against the wall, and looked around the corner, down the hall.

Light spilled from two rooms—and the sounds of a scuffle emerged from one of them, along with darting shadows.

"You want your son to live? Do it!"

The bottom dropped out of Connor's stomach. That had to be Sanders. But how had he gotten away from the house undetected—on *his* watch?

A sob tore through the silence—and through Connor's heart. "How do I know you won't kill him too? That you won't use your gun on him after you're finished with me?"

Sanders had a gun.

Bad news.

And Kate's words were slurred, as if she was barely conscious. More bad news.

Crouching, Connor hugged the wall in the hall and crept closer.

"You'll just have to trust me."

More sounds of struggle. Fabric ripping. And then Kate burst through the door, her ripped blouse flapping about her, Sanders on her heels.

They both saw him at the same time.

But Kate was directly in front of Sanders, giving the other man a human shield.

He took advantage of it.

Throwing one arm around Kate's neck, he pulled her back against his chest and aimed a Colt .45 at her head.

"Drop your gun." Sanders's voice was curt, but his hand was shaking. Whatever his plan had been, it was disintegrating—and he knew it.

But that didn't help their situation. Desperate people were inclined to do desperate things.

Slowly Connor lowered his weapon to the floor.

"Move back."

He retreated a few steps.

Sanders closed the gap between them, pushing Kate ahead of him until he was beside the gun. Then he kicked it behind him.

Connor did a quick assessment of Kate. Her pupils were dilated, and she seemed to be having trouble focusing and standing.

What had Sanders done to her?

"Go downstairs." Sanders motioned for him to precede them down the steps.

Turning his back on a gun-toting maniac wasn't his first choice, but when the man tightened his grip on Kate and she gasped, he didn't have much choice.

No reason to tarry, however. He went down as fast as he'd come up and swung back toward Sanders, who was having difficulty maneuvering his human shield down the staircase.

While he was off balance and paying attention to his footing would be the best opportunity to take him down. The gun jiggled every time they descended a step, and a well-timed lunge for his arm to shove it toward the ceiling was their best hope.

Waiting for Dev's 911 call wasn't an option.

Sanders could go ballistic any moment.

Two steps from the bottom, as Sanders jockeyed Kate down ahead of him, Connor made his move. Grabbing Kate with one hand, he jerked her out of Sanders's grasp and pushed up the elbow of the man's gun-toting arm with the other.

The pistol exploded, the silencer only marginally effective in the closed space.

Behind him, Connor heard Kate crash to the floor and moan. But the gun hadn't been aimed her way. He'd attend to her once he dealt with Sanders.

Sanders was strong, though, with powerful arms and a solid midsection—and his strength was amplified by anger or fear . . . or both. His adversary also had a death grip on the weapon in his hand. If he hadn't maintained both the firearm skills and fitness regime of his Secret Service days, he'd be in big trouble.

As they wrestled for control, Connor caught sight of Kate crawling toward them. Aiming for Sanders's legs. Trying to help.

The distraction was only momentary; no more than a blip in his focus—but it was sufficient to give Sanders a very slight opening.

The man swung at him, and the side of the revolver scored a hard direct hit on his left temple.

Pain exploded in his head, and he staggered. Flashes of white obscured his vision. He fought for balance. Stabilized.

Too late.

Sanders had backed away and was holding the gun with both hands, straight out in front of him. He swung it between Kate, who was sitting on the floor near the bottom of the stairs, and him. His eyes were crazed, and his hands were shaking.

One twitch of his trigger finger, and someone would die.

Adrenaline pumping, Connor kept his posture relaxed through sheer force of will and shifted into Secret Service mode. Calm. Cool. In control.

"Greg . . . it's over." He kept his tone placid but firm. "The police are on the way. This will go much easier for you if you just give me the gun."

"No." The man shook his head. "You can't take away my son. Not again. I won't—"

The sound of breaking glass burst from the living room.

Sanders swung toward the noise.

A stumbling figure emerged from the shadows.

Sanders fired.

And as Connor watched in shock and horror, a little blond boy crumpled to the floor.

‖‖‖ 27 ‖‖‖‖

As her son collapsed like a marionette whose strings had been cut, Kate screamed and scrabbled toward him on her hands and knees.

"No!" The thunderous masculine bellow reverberated through the room, and someone tried to rush past her—only to disappear an instant later.

She heard the sounds of a scuffle, accompanied by guttural grunts and the dull thud of flesh hitting flesh. Felt the vibrating crash of her front door, as if someone had slammed it back with superhuman force. Swallowed past the bitter aftertaste of Valium on her tongue.

But her focus was riveted on the pool of blood forming under her son's right thigh.

She moved beside him, desperately trying to coerce her brain to engage, to call up what she knew about first-aid basics. *Apply pressure to stop bleeding.* Yes. That sounded right.

Ignoring the shards of glass cutting into her knee, she managed to balance herself without listing too much to either side, then pressed her palms to the wound and watched the steady rise and fall of his chest.

Please, God, let him keep breathing!

Moments later, a blaze of light erupted in the room, and she blinked against the glare. Voices spoke behind her. Deep. Male. She couldn't make out the words. Didn't try. Didn't care about anything except keeping her son alive until help arrived.

Someone knelt on Kevin's other side. She lifted her gaze, trying to clear her vision. Connor. And he was injured. Blood was seeping out of the corner of his mouth.

"I've got him, Kate." He pried her hands off Kevin's leg and pressed a towel against her son's blood-soaked shorts. "An ambulance is on the way."

Behind her, a man sobbed. She pivoted toward the sound. Sanders sat on the floor in the foyer, hands restrained behind him, head slumped. An armed man with dark red hair stood over him as the distant, faint wail of sirens pierced the night.

She turned back to Connor and cradled Kevin's limp hand in hers. "He's not going to d-die . . . is he?"

"Not if I can help it."

That wasn't the definitive reassurance she'd hoped for.

The sirens grew louder.

"Kate . . . what did he do to you?" Connor's eyes were hard, a simmering rage banked in their depths.

She tried to articulate clearly, even though her mouth felt like mush. "Valium. Kevin too."

"How much?"

"Me, about four 5 mg tabs. Kevin . . . don't know."

Connor shifted toward the red-haired man. "Dev . . . find out how much Valium he gave the boy."

The sirens intensified, drowning out the conversation taking place in the foyer—but in less than thirty seconds, the other man called back. "Two."

After that, Kate had difficulty keeping track of what was happening. The condo was suddenly overrun with people and lights and noise. A paramedic tried to separate her from her son, but she tightened her grip—until Connor dropped down beside her with some wet wipes.

"Why don't you let me clean up your hands? We'll stay close by while the man does his job."

She looked down at her blood-covered fingers—and lost the remains of her dinner.

Connor cleaned that up too.

As he finished, another paramedic knelt beside her and slapped a blood pressure cuff around her arm.

"I'm fine."

"Let's make sure of that." Connor entwined his fingers with hers and gave them a slight squeeze.

"Your knee is bleeding." The paramedic leaned close to examine it.

"Glass." She swept a hand toward the remains of the Waterford vase that had stood on her end table. "Just a cut."

The man put a dressing on it anyway.

Kate fell silent. It was too much effort to speak. Let Connor talk to the man. She was more interested in tuning in to the conversation between the two paramedics treating her son. Nothing ominous jumped out at her—but neither did she understand half their terminology.

When the rumble of male voices beside her stopped, Connor touched her shoulder. "Did Sanders do anything else to you, Kate?"

She shook her head.

The paramedic examined her fingernails and her lips, flashed a light in her eyes. "It wouldn't hurt to pay a quick visit to the ER."

"No. I'll be fine." One of the paramedics treating her son rose, and she looked up at him. "How is he?"

"Bleeding's under control. No evidence of arterial damage. We're getting ready to transport."

378

She attempted to stand, but without Connor's assistance, she'd never have made it to her feet.

"If you're the mother, you can ride with us." The paramedic slung a medical bag over his shoulder. "Might not be a bad idea for him to see a familiar face if he happens to wake up."

Tears welled in her eyes. Spilled out.

She was as much a stranger to her son as the paramedics.

He would see no familiar face.

Apparently recognizing she was on the verge of a meltdown, Connor stepped in. "We'll follow you to the hospital."

She didn't argue. The first time she spoke with her son, she wanted not just her heart but her brain to be functioning at full capacity.

Keeping one arm around her, Connor steered her toward the door. He paused en route to say a few words to the man with auburn hair, who handed over a sweater. Only when Connor guided her arms into the sleeves did she realize her blouse was hanging off. After a short exchange with one of the police officers, Connor continued toward the exit.

As they passed Sanders, he turned red-rimmed eyes her direction. Connor angled his body to block her view of the man who'd killed her husband and stolen her son—but he couldn't shield her from the man's choked, grief-laced words.

"I love him as much as I loved my own son—and I always will. Tell him that . . . please."

She stumbled as they exited, and Connor tightened his grip as he looked down at her. "Would you like me to carry you to the van?"

Yeah, she would. She wanted him to lift her off her feet and sweep her into his arms and make all the problems in her life go away. But no one could do that. So she settled for second choice.

"No, but if you don't mind, I'd like to lean on you."

"For as long as you want to."

How about forever?

He tucked her closer—making her wonder if she'd actually spoken those words.

No matter. They were true.

And once she knew Kevin was out of danger, she was going to focus on creating a forever that included *both* of the special men in her life.

Giving in to a yawn as the first faint streaks of dawn lit the sky outside the windows of the deserted surgical waiting room, Connor studied Kate as she slept on the couch across from him. She'd hardly stirred since she'd let herself fold after the doctor relayed the good news about Kevin—no major veins or arteries had been damaged, nor had Sanders's bullet nicked a bone. They ought to be getting a summons to the recovery room any time.

He could use a few minutes in a recovery room himself—an emotional recovery room. His adrenaline was still pinging from their close brush with death. Any of them could have been killed last night.

Ruthlessly he shut off that line of thought. Better not to dwell on that while it was fresh enough to spike his blood pressure and twist his gut.

But if he'd had any doubts about whether Kate was the one, they'd evaporated when Sanders had pressed the barrel of his gun against her head. Because all at once he'd realized he couldn't imagine a future without her. He'd tell her that too—after he gave her some space with Kevin. The two of them needed time to reconnect; that had to be the first priority.

But while they were doing that, he intended to stick close.

"Connor."

380

At the soft summons from the doorway, he glanced over. Dev motioned him into the hall.

Stopping beside Kate to adjust the blanket he'd finagled from a nurse—and to caress her cheek—he took a long, slow breath, then joined Dev.

Cal was there too.

"Nice souvenir." The senior partner nodded to the purple bump on his temple.

He touched it gingerly and winced. "Could have been a lot worse."

"So I heard. Secondhand."

Connor looked at Dev.

"I rang him an hour ago, when I was wrapping up with the police."

"Why didn't you call me?" Cal fixed him with the narrow-eyed look that had probably served him well in police interrogations.

"It wasn't a three-man job."

"I live closer to your client's condo than Dev."

Connor shifted his weight from one foot to the other. "I didn't want to wake Moira. And I didn't expect Dev to show up—just to call 911 if things got dicey."

Cal planted his fists on his hips. "Let's get one thing straight. Both of you." He included Dev with a flick of his eyes. "We're a team. Marriage doesn't change that. You need me, you call. Got it?"

Pressure built in Connor's throat. Moments like this re-affirmed his decision to join forces with his college buddies at Phoenix. Partners didn't come any finer than the two men standing in this hospital hallway with him at the break of dawn. "Got it."

"Good. What's the latest?"

He filled them in on Kevin's prognosis, then addressed Dev. "How did you get there so fast last night?"

"I didn't take time to dress for the occasion."

Connor inspected his wrinkled T-shirt and gym shorts. "I can see that. Nice look. Early Goodwill, right?"

"Very funny." He shot him a disgruntled look before lifting one shoulder. "You rarely send out an SOS—and I've learned to trust your gut. If you smelled trouble, I figured there was trouble—and I didn't see any reason to sit around waiting when I could be lending a hand. But you had it under control when I got there."

"Barely. Did Sanders confess?"

"Nope. He clammed up tight." Dev smothered a yawn. "But based on what we uncovered during our investigation and the DNA results we should soon have in hand, he's history."

"Plus, he spilled the story to Kate while he was waiting for the Valium to kick in so she could accidentally drown too." He fisted his hands, and a muscle beside his eye twitched.

"Didn't the police show up here yet?" Dev glanced around the deserted waiting room. "I figured they'd be hot on your heels."

"They were. But Kate was too groggy to give a coherent statement. They said they'd be back later."

"Speaking of your client . . . are you staying awhile?" Cal glanced toward her.

"Yeah."

"Let us know if you need anything."

"I will. And listen . . . I appreciate the above-and-beyond effort on this case. From both of you."

Dev waved his thanks aside. "Goes with the territory."

He'd used that line on Kate once too. It had been a lie then. It was a lie now. What Cal and Dev had done went way beyond the requirements of business partners. It spoke of friendship and caring and commitment. He'd tell them that too—except embarrassing his friends wasn't on his agenda for today. "I'll check in later."

"We'll hold down the fort." Cal started toward the exit, Dev falling in beside him.

"Do you think Nikki'll make coffee today if I show up like this and tell her I've been working all night? Use the sympathy ploy? Or should I stop at Starbucks?" Dev's voice drifted back toward him.

"Stop at Starbucks."

"Even after I got that teddy bear for her kid?"

They disappeared around a corner, and Connor shook his head.

It was nice to know some things never changed.

As he prepared to rejoin Kate, his phone began to vibrate and he pulled it off his belt. Might as well take it out here rather than risk waking her.

But as he noted the name in caller ID, he changed his mind about the waking part. If this was what he thought it was, rousing Kate was going to be his top priority.

Someone was calling her name.

A man.

"Kate? Sweetheart? Can you wake up?"

Connor.

From the depths of a dark, cavernous place, Kate struggled toward the light.

Toward Connor.

When she at last opened her eyes, he was sitting beside her—in a place she didn't recognize.

It looked like a doctor's waiting room.

No . . . it was a hospital!

As her brain kicked into gear and memories of last night's events crashed over her, she shot up from her horizontal position. "Kevin! Is he—"

"He's still in recovery." Connor held on to her shoulders, his grip firm and comforting as he scrutinized her. "But I have other news. Are you with me?"

"Yes." She struggled to throw off the drug-induced haze that was fuzzing her mind, then amended her reply. "Not quite—but better than earlier."

"I just had a call from the lab. Not that this will come as any surprise after Sanders's revelations to you last night, but the DNA is a match. The boy he called Todd is indisputably your son."

She'd already known that, but having the empirical proof . . . she choked back a sob as tears blurred her vision.

A second later she found herself in Connor's arms, held close against the steady beat of his heart.

It felt like home.

A throat was cleared behind them. "Excuse me . . ."

Connor released her—with obvious reluctance. But he kept one arm around her as he swiveled around.

An aide stood in the doorway. "Ms. Marshall?"

"Yes."

"Your son is waking up. Would you like to go back?"

"Yes."

Connor stood first and drew her to her feet. "Are you steady enough to manage on your own?"

Was she? The floor seemed solid—but her emotions didn't.

"I don't need the physical support, but I wouldn't turn down a hand to hold."

He twined his fingers with hers. "At your service."

As they followed the aide down the hall, Kate tried to rein in her galloping pulse. She wasn't ready for this . . . but would she ever be? She couldn't take away Kevin's trauma, no matter how long their meeting was deferred. And all she had to offer him in return for upending his world was love. The deep, abiding love of a mother who'd never stopped cherishing the son she thought she'd lost.

She hoped that was enough.

The aide paused on the threshold of a door and motioned them in.

"He's still drifting in and out." A nurse looked over as she adjusted one of the many monitors attached to Kevin. "But the anesthesia will wear off quickly now. I'll be close by if you need me."

Once she exited, Kate moved beside the bed. Kevin's eyes fluttered open as she approached, and she summoned up a smile. "Hi there."

His mouth worked for a moment. "Are you . . . the lady from the escalator?"

"Yes."

He squinted up at her. "Is this . . . a dream?"

"No. I'm really here."

"Dad said it was a dream, but I knew it wasn't because you looked so real—and so nice." He lifted his arm. Examined the IV. "Am I in a hospital?"

"Yes. You had an accident and hurt your leg."

He scrunched up his face. "I don't remember."

That, at least, was a blessing.

Kevin gave Connor a once-over. "Who are you?"

"A friend."

"Do you know my dad?"

Connor hesitated. "Yes."

Leaning his head sideways, Kevin searched the room. "We're supposed to go camping. Is he here?"

"I think camping will have to wait until your leg gets better. And I came to see you instead of . . ." She couldn't bring herself to use the term that belonged to John. Shifting gears, she tucked her hair behind her ear. "I've been searching for you since that day on the escalator."

"How come?"

"It's kind of a long story."

"I like stories. Dad reads me one every night, except now I'm starting to read them myself. The easy ones. Does your story start once upon a time?"

"It can."

"Does it have a happy ending?"

Her throat tightened. "I hope so."

"Will you tell it to me?"

Connor grabbed one of the chairs against the wall, slid it beside the bed, and urged her down.

She sat.

And as he rested his hand on her shoulder, she folded Kevin's fingers in hers, held on tight, and began.

"Once upon a time . . ."

Epilogue

"So you really did it." Connor swiped a crab cake off a passing waiter's tray and grinned at Dev, who was so focused on his new bride he missed the food. That was a first.

"Yeah." His partner smiled, then dragged his attention away from Laura as she posed for the photographer. "Hey . . . where did you get that?" He sent the half-eaten appetizer a covetous look.

Connor finished it off and gestured to the disappearing waiter. "You were otherwise occupied."

"True." His gaze strayed to Laura again. "Besides, there'll be plenty of food at dinner. Right now I'd rather watch the most beautiful woman in the room."

Connor scanned the reception area for Kate. She was chatting with Moira and Cal, Kevin at her side, one hand resting on his shoulder. Her blonde hair, a perfect match for her son's, shimmered in the soft lighting of the country club, and her knee-skimming black cocktail dress showed off her curves to perfection.

The most beautiful woman in the room?

No contest.

But he'd be magnanimous for the bride's sake. "Laura looks gorgeous today. You're a lucky man."

"Trust me, I know. So when are you going to join the club?"

Connor stuck his hand in the pocket of his tux slacks and fingered the small box. "Soon. I didn't want to rush her, with all the adjustments she and Kevin had to make."

"I hear you." Dev searched the crowd, zeroing in on the Marshall duo. "The kid has had some tough breaks, but he seems to be adjusting."

"Thanks to Kate. There've been some rough times, though." Like the countless nights she'd called him in tears, heart aching for her son after he'd cried himself to sleep or awakened in the throes of a nightmare. But those traumatic incidents were far less frequent these days. "The counselor she found has worked wonders. So has her generous helpings of TLC. She's a wonderful mother."

"Speaking of mothers . . ." Dev inclined his head toward Nikki.

Connor inspected their office manager as she approached. She might be eight months pregnant, but her broadening girth hadn't stifled her eclectic fashion choices. Tonight's knee-length outfit appeared to be made of dozens of vibrant-colored floaty scarves that billowed as she walked. It was eye-catching, to say the least.

"You look ready to burst."

Nikki arched an eyebrow at Dev's greeting. "I see marriage hasn't mellowed you. Yet." She turned her back on her auburn-haired boss. "Where's your lovely date?"

Connor gestured toward Kate. "As usual, she's a people magnet. It's hard to get her alone at an event like this."

"I can help with that. Danny learned some new magic tricks, and I persuaded him to give Kevin a private show so the two of you could steal away for a few minutes. Can't let all this romantic ambiance go to waste." She signaled to her teenage brother across the room, who responded with a high sign.

"I owe you one."

"Lattes cover a multitude of favors—and sins. Just ask Dev." She smirked at his partner.

"I think I'll join my bride." Dev adjusted his bow tie and strolled off.

"Stay put. I'll send her over." Nikki picked a piece of lint off his lapel, then moseyed over to the small group that included Kate. She bent down to talk to Kevin, and he gave an enthusiastic nod. Then she leaned close and spoke to Kate.

His date looked his way, and her slow, intimate smile had him reaching up to run a finger under his collar.

Fifteen seconds later, she joined him, still smiling.

He took her hand. "What did Nikki say to you?"

"Why?"

"That look you gave me—it should be rated adult audiences only."

A soft blush tinted her cheeks. "She said I better get over here quick before the electricity zipping from you to me electrocuted anyone who walked between us."

"She does have a colorful way with words—and clothes. But I'm not arguing with her conclusions." He took her hand and tugged her toward one of the sets of French doors that led to the terrace. "Let's go see the moon."

"In February?"

"It's not too cold tonight—and I promise to keep you warm." He waggled his eyebrows.

She laughed. "I'm game."

He led her through the crowd, out the door, and onto the flagstones. It was unseasonably mild for midwinter, but still the air was crisp. Once clear of the door, he slipped off his tux jacket and draped it around her shoulders.

"I can't take this. You'll get cold."

"Trust me. I'm plenty warm." Reclaiming her hand, he strolled over to the stone wall that separated the terrace from the gardens and golf course beyond.

"I missed you while you were gone this week." She gave his fingers a squeeze.

"Yeah?" He stopped and faced her. The sky was clear, and the alabaster moon cast a luminous, almost ethereal light on her face.

"Mmm-hmm. It's been so hectic since you got back yesterday you never told me how it went."

"No problems, but in between his meetings my client dragged me to every modern art museum in New York City. I should have expected some unusual extracurricular activities. This is the same guy who decided to go diving in Bermuda a couple of years ago on another protection gig."

"That doesn't sound too bad."

"It is when he's five-seven and you're six-three and the diving is in submerged caves with narrow passageways. I felt like a contortionist."

She laughed—a musical sound that never failed to delight him. Best of all, he was hearing it more and more often these days. "You don't seem any the worse for wear."

"Tell that to my chiropractor." He rotated his neck for effect. "Did I miss anything while I was gone?"

"I heard from Diane."

"So she followed through on her promise to let you know how she was doing."

"Yes. She's still going to counseling but embracing her new life in Denver. She likes her job, and she's starting to date again. I'm happy for her."

"So am I, after her previous experiences in the relationship department." His pulse ticked up a notch, and he took a steadying breath. "Speaking of relationships . . . there's something I'd like to ask you."

When she lifted her chin, he wasn't sure if the sudden sparkle in her eyes was real—or just a reflection of the lights shining through the bank of French doors behind them.

The band struck up "Unforgettable," and he smiled as the melodic tune wafted their way. "Now that's what I call perfect timing—because you're exactly what that song is all about." He reached into his pocket, pulled out the small, square jewelry box, and held it out to her in his palm. "That's why I've had this on hand for three months, waiting for the right moment."

Her eyes widened. "Wow." The hushed sound was more breath than word.

"Is that a good wow or an I'm-not-ready-for-this wow? Because I can wait if the time's not right." He started to withdraw his hand.

She grabbed his wrist and held tight. "It's a good wow. Don't you dare put that away!"

Grinning, he flipped the lid open.

Once again her eyes widened. It wasn't a traditional engagement ring, like the diamond solitaire on the thin gold band she'd worn from her first husband. Connor had wanted an entirely different style. One that was unique to their relationship and wouldn't remind her of her first marriage.

Based on her expression of delight, the marquis-cut emerald, flanked by diamonds in a platinum setting, had done the trick.

"Oh, Connor. That's stunning!"

He handed it to her. "Check inside."

Her fingers were trembling as she took the ring. His were too as he fished a tiny penlight out of his other pocket and flashed it on the band.

She angled it to examine the engraved inscription. "His heart was yours from the moment you met." As she read the words, her voice choked. "From the fortune cookie."

"And very true. There's a question to go with that ring, but I expect you know what it is."

She looked up at him through shimmering eyes. "I'd like to hear it anyway."

"I thought you might." He took her hands, cocooning them in his, the ring folded inside. "I've made some mistakes in my life, as you know. But I've learned from them. I know what true love means now. It's caring more about the other person than about yourself. It's putting her first, ahead of career or job or ambition or life itself. It's counting the minutes until you can see her again, and knowing the best place in the world to be is in her arms."

A tremor ran through their clasped hands as he paused, but he couldn't be certain whether it came from her or from him.

When he continued, his voice was less steady. "It's loving everything about her—her warmth and caring and generosity and devotion and sense of humor and even the way she fumbles chopsticks. It's realizing the life you thought was fine just as it was doesn't even come close to what it could be with her. It's learning to love her little boy as much as she does—and wanting to be there for both of them in good times and bad."

Taking the ring from her fingers, he positioned it at the tip of the fourth finger of her left hand. "I know we're a few hours short of Valentine's Day—but every day is Valentine's Day when I'm with you. So to paraphrase Robert Browning, will you grow old along with me, knowing—as I do—that the best is yet to be?"

"Yes." The word was a shaky whisper, but the joy on her face as he slid the ring over her finger told him everything he needed to know.

The time was right.

The woman was right.

Life was right.

Framing her face in his hands, he stroked his thumb over her sweet mouth. "Your lips are cold. Shall I warm them up for you?"

"Please do."

He pulled her close, slipping his arms inside the jacket he'd draped over her shoulders, and bent to seal their engagement as the last few muted bars of "Unforgettable" played on the other side of the French doors.

And for the rest of his life, he knew that whenever he heard that song, he would remember this frosty February moment when love—the most precious of all gifts—had graced his life.

"Hey, you guys! They're cutting the cake!"

Pulling back, Connor looked toward the French doors. Kevin was standing on the threshold, gesturing for them to come in.

Nikki huffed up behind him and gave them an apologetic look. "Sorry. Danny ran out of tricks before you finished your treat."

Connor draped an arm around Kate's shoulder and leaned close to whisper in her ear. "To be continued."

She snuggled close. "Is that a promise?"

"Count on it."

As they walked toward the door where Kevin waited, her son cocked his head. "Were you guys kissing?"

He glanced at Kate, letting her take the lead. He'd become a fixture in their lives over the past few months, but while Kevin had seen plenty of exchanges of affection between them and Connor had established a strong bond with her son, was the youngster ready to share the mother he was just beginning to know and love?

"Yes, we were." She placed her free arm around her son and tugged him close. "In fact, Connor asked me to marry him. Is that okay with you?"

Kevin considered him. "Does that mean you'd live at our house?"

"I don't know where we'd live, but wherever it is, we'll all be together."

He thought about that for a few beats. "Epic. Can we go see the cake now?"

The knot in his stomach unwound. "Sure. You go ahead. We'll be there in a minute."

As Kevin scampered inside, Connor regarded Kate. "How come that was so easy?"

She shrugged and dipped her head to fiddle with a button on the tux jacket draped over her shoulders. "I asked his counselor to help me begin laying the groundwork for this."

Placing his finger under her chin, he tipped her face up. "How long ago?"

A flush rose on her cheeks. "Almost from the beginning."

"You were that sure of me?"

"No. I was that sure of *me*—and I was pretty certain you felt the same. I'm glad my instincts weren't wrong."

Giving her a slow smile, he pulled her close. "What do your instincts say now?"

She put her arms around his neck and snuggled close. "That you're going to kiss me again—right in front of the Phoenix staff." She nodded toward the reception room.

He turned. On the other side of the glass, a few feet away, Cal and Dev flanked Nikki. As if on cue, they grinned, raised their champagne glasses—and waited.

"I guess I'm on."

"I guess you are."

"Do you mind the audience?"

"I prefer to think of them as future business-in-laws—and witnesses." She waggled her ring finger their direction, though she kept her gaze fixed on him. "There's no getting out of this now."

He chuckled. "That works both ways. Shall I officially welcome you to the team?"

"By all means."

And with no further delay, he sealed the deal.

394

Read an excerpt from *Buried Secrets*

First in the brand-new MEN OF VALOR series
from Irene Hannon

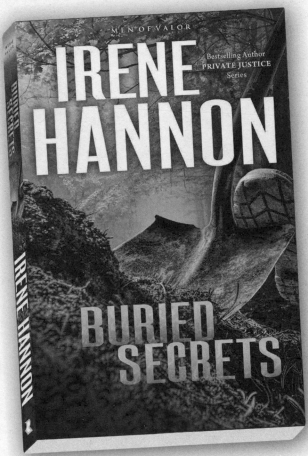

Coming Spring 2015

Revell
a division of Baker Publishing Group
www.RevellBooks.com

Prologue

It was meant to be a joyride.

No one was supposed to die.

"She's not breathing!" Erika's shrill, hysteria-laced whisper pierced the humidity-laden air.

Heart pounding, I fisted my hands. "I can see that."

The clammy smell of panic overpowered the scent of fresh-cut hay in the adjacent field as we huddled on our knees over the motionless figure in the ditch.

"What should we do?" Joe's voice cracked on the last word.

They both looked at me like I had the answer. Like I knew how to make this nightmare go away.

I didn't.

Not yet, anyway.

I was still trying to wrap my mind around what had happened. To figure out how my well-planned life could careen out of control in the space of a few heartbeats.

The answer eluded me. But I did know one thing. Any whiff of scandal could deep-six the coveted job I was a breath away from getting after acing the final interview.

I couldn't let that happen.

When I didn't respond, Joe leaned across the crumpled body and grasped my shoulders, his fingers digging into my flesh like talons. "What should we do?"

I shook him off. "I heard you the first time! Give me a minute!"

I straightened up and checked out the rural Missouri road, with its undulating dips that provided high-speed thrills.

Empty.

But headlights could appear over the rise at any moment, illuminating us like spotlights.

If they did, we were hosed.

My fingers began to prickle.

We had to make a decision.

Fast.

"Should we try CPR?" Joe's voice was shaking now.

I surveyed the broken body. Every twisted angle said it was too late for life-saving measures, but I pressed my fingers to her carotid artery anyway. Just in case.

Nothing.

"She's dead."

Erika began to hyperventilate, her breath coming in ragged, shallow gasps.

I gave her a hard shake. "Stop it! If you keep that up, you're going to pass out!"

"But w-what are we going to do?" Her question came out in a whimpering blubber.

Disgust soured my mouth.

I hate weak women.

If Erika's father hadn't had the kind of connections I needed, I would never have hooked up with her—and I wouldn't be in the middle of this mess.

Anger began to churn in my gut.

"We need to do *something*. Now!" Joe gave the deserted rural highway a spastic sweep.

"I know that! Shut up and let me think."

I glared down at the contorted figure at my knees. I should never have let Erika invite her tonight. So what if they were roommates? So what if the girl didn't have a lot of friends? So what if she was feeling depressed?

Those were her problems.

Except now she was *my* problem.

Despite the fury nipping at my composure, the left side of my brain began to click into gear. Logic under duress had been my father's strong suit too—on his few good days.

But I wasn't like my old man. There were better things in store for me. I had plans. And nothing—nothing—was going to disrupt them.

Including a dead girl.

I held the keys out to Joe. "Open the trunk."

"What?" He stared at me, the whites of his eyes glimmering in the darkness.

"Just do it."

"But . . . shouldn't we call 911 or something?"

"Yeah, that's a good idea," Erika seconded.

What idiots.

Speaking slowly to give my words a chance to sink into their thick skulls, I explained the problem. "We're all high as kites. Don't think the cops won't notice that." I locked on to Joe. "You were driving. What do you think a charge of vehicular manslaughter would do to your Rhodes Scholarship?"

I let him mull that over while I turned to Erika. "And a squeaky-clean state senator who's built his political career on an anti-drug platform might very well disown a daughter who generates bad press that could cost him the US Senate nomination. So much for that grand graduation tour of Europe you had planned for this summer, and that fancy car." I gestured to the Mercedes convertible on the shoulder above us, the hot engine still pinging.

Only the sound of harsh, erratic breathing and the distant wail of a train whistle broke the silence as they digested my rationale.

I gave them ten seconds to think through the ramifications.

Then I held out the keys again.

This time Joe took them.

Since Erika had collapsed into a useless, quivering lump, I waited for Joe to return to deal with the body. "I'll take her arms. You get her feet."

We moved into position.

"On three. One, two, three."

We lifted together. Erika scrabbled backward as the dead girl's head lolled forward.

I paid no attention—to either of them. I was too angry . . . at myself now as much as them.

What had possessed me to go along with their stupid joyriding scheme, anyway? I didn't do foolish and reckless. I didn't do *anything* that could interfere with my plans, with the future I'd mapped out for myself.

Tonight was the biggest mistake of my life.

And I never intended to make another one.

Joe and I hefted the girl into the trunk. The liner would have to be replaced—but we could deal with that tomorrow.

After closing the lid, I retrieved a flashlight from the glove compartment and gestured to the pavement. "We need to make sure nothing incriminating is left behind. Help me look around. And hurry."

As I swept the light back and forth in a wide arc, they hovered at my shoulders like overzealous prison guards.

Talk about a distasteful image.

I shoved it from my mind.

Three minutes later, once I was confident that mashed-down grass was the only evidence of our unplanned stop, we piled back into Erika's convertible.

This time, I took the wheel.

"Now what?" Joe spoke from the backseat as I pulled onto the pavement, gravel crunching beneath the tires.

I'd been thinking about that, my mind working through various scenarios as we'd silently searched the roadside.

"Yeah. Now what?" Erika cowered into the corner of the seat beside me, her voice small. Scared. Tear-laced.

What a loser.

"If someone finds out . . ." Joe's words trailed off.

I clenched the wheel.

Not going to happen.

Ever.

"No one will. I'm working on a plan."

As the minutes ticked by, a strategy began to coalesce in my brain, the pieces clicking into place one by one.

It wasn't bad.

Not bad at all.

And we were lucky in one regard.

Making the girl in the trunk disappear would be far easier than disposing of anyone else we knew.

"Do you still have that state map in your glove compartment?" I checked the rearview mirror as I directed the question to Erika. The road stretched dark and deserted behind us. Perfect.

"Y-yes." Her response came out in a choked whisper.

"Get it out."

I heard her fumbling with the latch.

"Do you have an idea?" Joe leaned forward and spoke behind my ear.

Of course I did. I always had ideas. I was the only one in

this bunch who ever did. Erika was a twit, and while Joe might be smart with numbers, he didn't have one imaginative bone in his body.

"Yeah, I have an idea."

And as the miles rolled by, I laid out my plan.

They listened in silence for the most part, especially when I reemphasized the stakes. None of us wanted to deal with the ramifications of this disaster. On that much, at least, we were in agreement.

When I finished, neither spoke.

I waited them out.

"It might work." This from Joe, though he sounded uncertain.

"It *will* work—as long as we stick together. And there's no going back once we start down this road. Understood?"

Not that we had much choice at this point. We'd already started down the road by moving the body. But I wanted their verbal buy-in.

"Yeah. I'm in." Resignation flattened Joe's words.

"Me, too . . . I guess." Erika sniffled.

"There's no guessing, Erika." I used my harshest tone. These two needed to get with the program. "We're either all in or it's a no-go—and we face the not-so-pleasant consequences."

"Okay, okay. I'm in."

"Good." A gust of wind whipped past, and a splatter of rain stung my cheek. For once the weather people had been right. A storm was brewing. "We need to put up the top." The road in front and behind remained dark and empty, so I pulled to the side. "Don't dawdle."

They didn't—but by the time the three of us got back in the car, my clothes were damp and sticking to me uncomfortably.

Before this night was over, though, they'd be in far worse shape.

Still, if things went according to plan, both the clothes and the incident would soon be history.

And things *would* go according to plan.

I'd make sure of that.

Whatever it took.

PRESENT DAY

Mac McGregor had no trouble finding the site, even if St. Louis was new turf for him. You didn't have to be a detective to figure out that a police cruiser, yellow crime-scene tape, and a media van marked the spot.

Pulling up beside the squad car, he scanned the construction site for the police chief of the small municipality who'd put in the call to County for assistance.

An officer stood in the distance, talking to a woman and a guy in a hard hat. He seemed on the young side, based on a quick glimpse of his profile, but he was the only uniformed presence on the scene. Since Carson was more village than town, maybe they'd had to take what they could get for the chief job when they established the department last year.

Mac set the brake, grabbed the notebook and sport coat in the passenger seat, and slid out from behind the wheel. Once he'd slipped the jacket on, he ducked under the yellow tape and wove through the idle construction equipment.

The trio was facing away from him now, toward a slight depression in the ground, and he stopped about four feet away. "Chief Grant?"

All three of them turned.

He stuck out his hand toward the officer in the middle.

"I'm Chief Grant." The woman to the man's right spoke, her voice brisk, businesslike—and a touch irritated.

He checked out the nameplate above the guy's left pocket.

Officer Craig Shelton.

Whoops.

So much for making a good first impression.

He shifted his attention to the woman—and gave silent thanks for the sunglasses that hid the slight widening of his eyes.

Chief Grant was drop-dead, centerfold-worthy gorgeous.

But he had a feeling she would *not* appreciate his appreciative perusal.

Too bad his so-called buddy Mitch hadn't warned him she was smoking hot when they'd run into each other earlier in the headquarters parking lot. SEALs—or ex-SEALs—didn't set each other up.

Or did they?

Maybe.

He *had* ducked out on his teammate during that dud double date a couple of years ago, leaving his friend to extricate himself from two stunning but intense women who'd dragged them to a lecture by some famous historian. What a load of laughs that had been.

Not.

"May I help you?" Chief Grant's chilly prompt neutralized his amusement.

Clearing his throat, he moved his hand to the left. "Detective Mac McGregor. Your reinforcement from County."

She waited just long enough to make him squirm before she grasped his fingers with a surprisingly strong grip. "Lisa Grant."

"Nice to meet you." He shook hands with the officer too. Like his chief's, the man's eyes were masked by dark glasses. "Sorry about the mistake. I assumed you'd be in uniform."

"Or maybe you assumed I'd be a man." Her tone was conversational, but he heard the steel underneath.

A spurt of irritation spiked his blood pressure—but he tamped it down. No doubt she'd faced her share of bias in a field long dominated by men. And he'd added to it . . . in her mind, anyway.

All at once it felt a lot hotter than it should for a first-week-of-June morning, and the temptation to loosen his tie was strong.

He resisted.

"It's dangerous to make assumptions in this business."

"Yeah." She let a beat pass. "It is."

The air temperature seemed to edge up another degree or two.

Best to get down to business.

"I understand you have some bones that may be human?"

"We have some bones that *are* human." She gestured toward the ground behind her.

He stepped closer and looked down.

The empty eye sockets of a partially unearthed skull stared back at him.

She was right.

The bones were human.

Acknowledgments

Writing suspense books always requires a tremendous amount of research. I spend hours online; visit locations that will be used in the story; and do old-fashioned book research when necessary. By the time I finish a suspense novel, I typically have 75–100 single-spaced pages of notes and research citations.

But personal contact with real-life experts is the only way to add the final touch of authenticity—and several people were instrumental in giving *Deceived* its technical polish.

Tim Flora, president of Mid-West Protective Service, Inc., has been my PI source for the entire Private Justice series. In addition to twenty-eight years of experience in both federal and local law enforcement, private investigation and security, last year he was appointed by the governor of Missouri to the Missouri Board of Private Investigator & Private Fire Investigator Examiners—the state licensing and regulatory body for these fields. Talk about a top-notch PI source! Thank you, Tim, for helping make my Private Justice series the best it could be.

My gratitude also goes to pharmacist Tim Dolan. Medication

dosages were extremely important in this book—especially in the climax—and his input was invaluable as I worked through some of the key timing sequences.

Captain Ed Nestor from the Chesterfield, Missouri, Police Department, continues to be my go-to person for amazing sources. Thank you, Ed!

I also give thanks every day for the professional, conscientious, and talented team at Revell. I'd name names, but I'm afraid I'd leave someone out! Please know that I feel blessed to work with each of you.

I am deeply grateful as well to every single person who chooses to read my books. You make it possible for me to give life to the characters who ask me to tell their stories, and I never, ever take you for granted.

As always, my love to the very best parents in the world, James and Dorothy Hannon. Thank you for giving me both roots and wings.

Last—but definitely not least!—hugs and kisses to my wonderful husband, who's survived 25 years of marriage to a writer. (Trust me, that's an accomplishment!) Thank you, Tom, for understanding when dinner is late because the characters in my head won't stop talking; for repeating things that I don't hear because my mind is far away, busy plotting the next scene; for listening to my angst before every book, when I'm convinced I'll never come up with another good story idea; for hanging in when "just five more minutes" turns into an hour; and for all the other challenges you face every day because you picked a writer for wife. All I can say is, I got the gold ring—literally and figuratively! So happy anniversary, my love . . . and may our next twenty-five years be even more glorious!

Irene Hannon is a bestselling, award-winning author who took the publishing world by storm at the tender age of ten with a sparkling piece of fiction that received national attention.

Okay . . . maybe that's a slight exaggeration. But she *was* one of the honorees in a complete-the-story contest conducted by a national children's magazine. And she likes to think of that as her "official" fiction-writing debut!

Since then, she has written more than forty-five contemporary romance and romantic suspense novels. Irene has twice won the RITA award—the "Oscar" of romantic fiction—from Romance Writers of America, and her books have also been honored with a National Readers' Choice award, two HOLT medallions, a Daphne du Maurier award, a Retailers Choice award, and two Reviewers' Choice awards from *RT Book Reviews* magazine. In 2011, *Booklist* included one of her novels in its Top 10 Inspirational Fiction list for the year. She is also a Christy award finalist.

Irene, who holds a BA in psychology and an MA in journalism, juggled two careers for many years until she gave up her executive corporate communications position with a Fortune 500 company to write full-time. She is happy to say she has no regrets! As she points out, leaving behind the rush-hour commute, corporate politics, and a relentless BlackBerry that never slept was no sacrifice.

A trained vocalist, Irene has sung the leading role in numerous community theater productions and is also a soloist at her church.

When not otherwise occupied, she and her husband enjoy traveling, Saturday mornings at their favorite coffee shop, and spending time with family. They make their home in Missouri.

To learn more about Irene and her books, visit www.irene hannon.com.

Be sure to catch the first two books in the Private Justice series!

"An excellent suggestion for readers who enjoy Mary Higgins Clark's subtly chilling brand of suspense."
—*Booklist*

"Whether it's a fast-paced suspense or a contemporary [romance], fans can't get enough of Hannon's uplifting stories."
—*RT Book Reviews*